# RESPECT

## AN INFIDELITY NOVEL

*"The making of a man"*

D1453288

# ALEATHA ROMIG

NEW YORK TIMES, WALL STREET JOURNAL, AND USA TODAY
BESTSELLING AUTHOR OF THE CONSEQUENCES SERIES

***RESPECT***
An Infidelity Novel
Copyright © 2017 Romig Works, LLC
Published by Romig Works, LLC
2018 Edition

ISBN-13: 978-1-947189-01-0
ISBN-10: 1-947189-01-8

Cover art: Kellie Dennis at Book Cover by Design (www.bookcoverbydesign.co.uk)
Editing: Lisa Aurello
Formatting: Angela McLaurin at Fictional Formats

# RESPECT

——●○●——

## AN INFIDELITY NOVEL

*"The making of a man"*

# DISCLAIMER

———•○•———

The Infidelity series, as well as this novel, contains adult content and is intended for mature audiences. While the use of overly descriptive language is infrequent, the subject matter is targeted at readers over the age of eighteen.

Respect is a stand-alone novel, a spin-off of the five-book Infidelity romantic suspense saga.

The Infidelity series does not advocate or glorify cheating. Respect, as well as the series, is about the inner struggle of compromising beliefs for heart. It is about cheating on yourself, not someone else.

I hope you enjoy the epic tale of RESPECT, the making of a man!

# RESPECT

———●○●———

*"The making of a man"*

Standing at what I believe is the precipice of my life, I, Oren Demetri, was too young to understand that it wasn't and too old to imagine that it couldn't be.

The already hefty accumulation of my successes and failures, bravery and fears, and rewards and suffering, had brought me to this point. It was hard to contemplate the things I'd done, and yet in reality, I'd only begun to learn the possibilities.

I suppose that's how it was for me at twenty-nine years of age on the brink of all I'd ever wanted without fully realizing the price I would pay. Yet in that moment, I knew there would be no cost too great or sacrifice I wouldn't make. I had no idea how far-reaching that moment of self-discovery would be because as the congregation's murmurs quieted, bleeding into silence and allowing the thump of my heart to be the only sound I heard, I was a man filled with love and adoration, emotions in stark contrast to those I needed in the world I'd built or the one I was about to enter.

Angelina Costello was my dream and now my reality. I'd worked diligently to move beyond the actuality of being a dockworker's son to becoming a self-made, successful entrepreneur, all in an effort to earn the right to call her my own. I'd overcome servitude to others, collecting their paychecks and lowly praises, to become the one who signed the paychecks and offered the accolades when they were rightfully earned.

The world was my oyster and walking toward me on the arm of her uncle was my pearl. I'd found her amongst the empty shells life had offered. There was no need to pry open another possibility. Angelina was all I wanted. Yet my path was uncharted. There was more for me to earn, lose, and willingly give.

**The top of that list was respect.**

**This stand-alone novel may be read without reading the Infidelity series.**

From *New York Times*, *Wall Street Journal*, and *USA Today* bestselling author Aleatha Romig comes a stand-alone novel, a spin-off from her beloved Infidelity series. With classic Aleatha Romig twists, turns, deceptions, and devotions, this new epic romantic thriller will delve into a world where family takes on new meaning, and even the inhabitants are suspicious of the next chapter.

**Have you been Aleatha'd?**

# A GLANCE INTO THE FUTURE AND THE PAST

I HELD TIGHTLY to Angelina's hand as the salty breeze cooled our skin. The gray sky didn't detract from the stunning view of the New York Harbor and the Statue of Liberty. My wife's red wind-kissed cheeks rose as she looked from the view back to me. Her blue eyes shone as she took in the possibilities I'd explained in some detail—the plans for shops, apartments, and parks.

Like a sharp stab to my chest, I realized the rarity of the sight before me. I stared at her radiant smile, knowing it was no longer a daily sight.

"This," she said, "Oren Demetri, this is the man I married."

"It'll take time."

"Time to do what's right. Time to make more from less."

"And money." My head once again filled with the figures I'd spent days, weeks, and months crunching. There would be contracts and commitments. I'd make promises and secure debts, but if it made Angelina's face light up on a dreary day, it would all be worth it.

It wasn't a new idea. The renovation of the waterfront began when I was still a student at NYU. In 1972, the city approved the urban renewal plan: over two hundred acres for a new port, hundreds of housing units, and even a waterfront park. However, the timing hadn't been right. The hold on the shipyards and docks at that time was still too strong. It would take more than a document submitted by a community board.

"There was a time," I began, no longer seeing the view before us but recalling a time when youth was my enemy. "...when this was all I knew."

Angelina squeezed my hand. "Use that. Keep it in your heart. This is part of you. Make this place great again for Salvatore and Paola. Make it a place where children and parents can make memories."

My neck stiffened at the sound of my parents' names. My memories of this shore weren't of picnics and kayaks. This was where my father worked, where I worked, where my mother died.

Angelina's tone saved me from the dark turn my thoughts had taken.

"They would be as proud of you as I am," she went on, "if they were standing here today."

Is it wrong for a man in his forties with more life lived than others experience in ten decades to feel a twinge of joy at the thought of making his parents proud?

"And your parents too," I said. "They'd be proud of you. You're why we're here."

My wife's ambition to pay it forward, to do good with the bounty life had granted us, was why we were standing on a cold shore with the briny air that unsuccessfully masked the reek of fish and the smell of decayed iron and steel. The odor still hung thick in the air just as it had when I was a boy. The only missing elements were the cigarette and cigar smoke and the soundtrack of manual labor: supervisors barking orders over the cranks hoisting shipments in nets in the days before cargo containers and hydraulic lifts. Nevertheless, the stench alone served as a reminder that while things changed, they stayed the same.

Angelina shrugged. "I can hope. My family was different. My parents believed in Cosa Nostra. It's what killed..." She didn't finish.

"They believed in family, in honor and respect," I interrupted, keeping her from her darkness too. "My parents taught me to work hard. Your family's lessons have been more specific."

"Oren..."

I shook my head and forced a smile to my lips. "Your family is another reason we're here."

"Change takes time. Now, with Uncle Carmine grooming Vincent..."

My wife was usually right. This was no exception. Change took time. It also needed prompting. Vincent's mindset was the future of the Costello family. Like the shipping industry, times have changed since I was a boy. The wool overcoat draped over my designer suit and my leather loafers that were currently spotted with the dusting of snow and ice, if sold, could have significantly supplemented Salvatore Demetri's annual salary.

My father taught me the meaning of hard work and earning a paycheck. The Costellos taught me different lessons. I could blame them or thank them. I was the man I was because of both influences together: the Demetris and Costellos. The combined DNA made our son.

The end justifies the means... It has all been worth it. If only I could appreciate the spoils.

This outing on the Brooklyn shore was the exception, not the rule. Angelina approved of this Oren Demetri, the one who made legitimate deals and helped others, the husband who took time to be with her, held her hand, and listened to her thoughts. Yet as in the gray skies and darkened skyline, within me—between us—there were layers, dimensions, and sacrifices.

Time was the greatest loser. Or perhaps it was the victor.

It never stopped.

There was only so much and so many ways it could be divided.

I tugged Angelina's hand and led her back to the waiting car. "Thank you for coming to see it."

"You asked."

"Testa will drive you back to Rye."

Her steps stuttered. "I thought maybe we could go to the city for dinner or visit... we're so close."

Close to Brooklyn. Close to her family and where we used to live.

"Another night. It's Thursday. Carmine..."

Angelina's neck stiffened as we both slid into the warm waiting car.

"Franco," I began. "Drop me off at the office and take Mrs. Demetri back to the house."

Angelina appeared to concentrate on the outside scenery as we rode in silence, the chill in the heated car icier than the outside wind. Finally, I tried for a thaw. "How about a Broadway show on Saturday?"

She didn't turn as she spoke, the emotion from before gone. "Don't make promises you won't keep."

I wanted to keep them. I did. I tried. There were only so many balls one person could keep in the air. We hadn't reached our final destination: a life together with unlimited time. That was my goal. Yet there were miles to travel. Though the journey had already been long, it wasn't over.

In many ways, it was like the Todd Shipyard where we'd been. It had been the sight of successes and failures, and there would be more. The road that trailed behind us and the same one that stretched before us couldn't be considered easy or safe. Someday, I prayed we'd look back and see that even though it had taken decades and bloodshed, it was worth the cost.

Success and dreams took time. The images from my childhood resurfaced. Sometimes it was difficult to fathom. A young boy. A small apartment—devoid of amenities and filled with love. My life now was not merely different, but previously unimaginable to that young boy.

In many ways… my justification always went back to one scene that replayed in my mind. Time affects memories. It changes the old reel, making it newer, crisper. The colors become less vibrant. The words morph and their meanings change.

I'm not sure how accurate the version I now see remains. When I close my eyes, I see with the eyes of a little boy, and it still affects me to this day.

The world to a child was epic—huge. Sounds were louder and people were bigger. Yet none of that mattered when your father was at your side: protector, hero, and everything in between.

My father had taken me with him to the pier. And while I understood that we wouldn't stay long, that I couldn't be with him when he had to work, to my young mind it didn't matter. I was special simply because I was walking beside my father. *Just the men,* he'd said to my mother before we left our home. She smiled and nodded as I hurriedly donned my coat.

The wind was brisk, but I didn't notice. Instead, I watched how others addressed my father as *Mr. Demetri* with respect. Each salutation added a degree of warmth to my soul, my pride providing more protection from the cold than the thin layers of clothing I wore.

We approached a man. He was well dressed for the docks. I recalled his shoes—shinier than ones I was used to seeing. They weren't dusty or covered with mud.

"Salvatore," the man said as my father handed him a plain envelope.

"Thank you," my father replied with a nod of his head.

Even as a youth, I found it odd that my father thanked the man. After all, he'd been the one to give whatever he gave. Shouldn't the man have thanked him? It was then I noticed the giants of my father's world—the other supervisors, the men who most of the workers addressed with deference—shrank in this well-dressed man's presence.

After the envelope was given, we quickly moved on. We were beyond the crowd, and yet I continued to peer backward—I couldn't stop watching.

"Oren, it isn't your business," my father chastised.

"Who is he?"

"He's the boss of the pier."

"Is he your boss? I thought you were the boss."

"Every man has someone he answers to."

I glanced back once more as the well-dressed man continued to accept what others handed him. I recognized the supervisors, the ones like my father. I was used to hearing them bark orders. Their quiet murmuring affected me more than I knew. "What are the others doing?"

"Taxes, boy. That's enough questions."

"That boss man, is he with the government?" I'd learned about taxes in school. People paid money to the government so that cities could build roads and schools.

My father stifled a laugh as he tugged my hand, pulling me farther away.

"*Papà*, did you pay him taxes?" I hadn't seen money, only an envelope.

"Some things, *figlio*, are not to be questioned. It is the way it is—the way of my father and his father before him. In Sicily. For generations. It works. We're here in America with a roof, a job, food on our plates, and shoes on our feet. I don't have to fight the cattle call. I'm above that."

"Because you're a boss, too," I said with pride.

"Not the same, but I've worked hard. You will too. It's what Demetri men do. We are determined. It's a good thing."

As we walked along the street toward our apartment, the vision of the pier boss continued to play in my head. "*Papà?* Will I pay taxes?"

"We all pay, Oren."

"What if I want to be the one who people pay? What do I need to do to become a tax man?"

He scoffed, shaking his head. "One doesn't become a boss, *figlio*. One earns it. Some things are not for all."

"Earn it… through hard work?" Though I'd said it as a question, I had confidence in my young mind that I was right.

"Respect," my father replied. "Give it, appropriately. And earn it. You do not need to be paid if you have that. Respect is what defines a true man."

# CHAPTER 1

THERE ARE MOMENTS etched forever in our mind that can neither be enhanced nor diminished. To do either would be an injustice. Such as the hieroglyphs carved within ancient stone, these pinnacles remained stationary throughout time. Winds could rage and rains could flood, yet nothing could alter the magnitude of the instant. As I stood in front of the congregation with the priest by my side, I experienced that revelation. Nothing in my past or future could reduce the overwhelming emotion within me.

Total and utter admiration radiated from my presence, shimmering in my gaze as I lost sight of the periphery. The pews were no longer occupied. Her family wasn't murmuring at her beauty. Even the organ music faded away. I saw only her. In that place, at that moment in 1984, with the blessings of men and God, my life's aspiration was about to come to fruition. It wasn't riches or fame. It's true I wanted the first and loathed the latter. Yet my reasoning for the first wasn't for self-worth. No, it was to provide for her, to be worthy of her. My aspiration since the first time our eyes met was to be the man who could make Angelina Costello mine.

What price had I agreed to pay?

Selling one's soul couldn't bring absolution.

That wasn't the way it worked. The angel walking up the aisle before me was a gift from the heavens; my rational mind reasoned that she couldn't be related to Lucifer. There were laws governing rapture and torment. I'd been lovingly raised by believing parents. Though I'd lost them too young—for me and for them—they'd set my foundation. We were all here within the cathedral, its stained-glass windows creating a heavenly glow as the setting sun brought pictured scenes to life.

Surely, the devil himself couldn't survive in this place.

As Angelina came closer with her hand perched upon her uncle's arm, I reasoned that I couldn't possibly have been casting my eyes upon both my heart's desire as well as the architect of my downfall.

They say that love blinds. My thought was that it didn't blind as much as it changed the hue—rose-colored glasses.

With my pulse racing as I gripped my own hands, I couldn't comprehend the magnitude of my decisions, past or future. It was easier to concentrate on the simplicity of the moment.

Angelina Costello was about to become my wife—Mrs. Oren Demetri, Mrs. Angelina Demetri. I wasn't a narcissistic man. I wanted her to bear my name but not at the expense of her own. She was a strong, opinionated woman who voiced her mind while bringing sunshine to a tired, darkened soul.

I couldn't have been prouder that she would share my name. As a Demetri, I envisioned that together we would face life's hurdles and return breath to my family whom had all but disappeared. Together we would accomplish miracles because that was what someone like Angelina did. She made the world a better place by simply existing in it.

In that split second, I remembered it all: from the moment I first laid eyes upon her up until the moment our lives were ready to become one.

We'd first met nearly a decade earlier at NYU. Prior to that moment, I didn't believe in love at first sight. We were in a sophomore English class the day my life changed. My attraction was visceral, arising from deep within. It hit like a locomotive, knocking me off balance with simply the melody of her laughter. I'd been rereading the assignment when the infectious ring of her amusement woke my tired soul.

I admit that even I was surprised by my attraction and curiosity. This girl—this woman—whose laugh caught my attention was nothing like the women whom I normally noticed. Much to my mother's chagrin, I had an affinity for tight sweaters fitting snuggly over large breasts, trim waists, and shapely legs made sexier by tall stilt-like heels. Too-red lipstick and thickly made-up lashes batting seductively made me smile. I saw each of those attributes as unspoken invitations of a woman's interest and willingness to take my mind off other things.

I knew where to find those women. They were in all the diners and bars; some of them cost money, while others simply a dinner or a drink. Perhaps it was their availability that made them attractive to me and at the same time, forgettable.

The angel in my English course was a contradiction in every way. Her beauty wasn't manufactured. It was sincere and genuine. Unlike the women I'd known, she was unique and completely unforgettable.

That fateful morning, after only a few hours of sleep, my tired mind was trying to wake when feminine giggles filled the classroom. There were three of them, all huddled around one desk, looking at a magazine, the kind of rag they sold at the drugstore with pages filled with celebrities. I didn't have time for useless things like that and probably wouldn't have even recognized the object of their focus. It wasn't the magazine that caught my attention: it was the laugh. Like a strike of lightning to my exhausted soul, it electrified me. My eyes were drawn to the beauty in jeans and a heavy-metal concert T-shirt.

I wasn't the type of man who stared. I'd later blame it on my lack of sleep. Whatever the cause, when the professor walked into the classroom and the angel turned from her friends to move to her seat, her eyes met mine.

My breathing stopped as my heart beat to a new rhythm.

Blue as a clear sapphire sky.

I'd never before been awestruck.

Until that moment.

Before I could turn away, she smiled. A simple upturn of her lips, lifting her cheeks that now glowed with a faint red blush. Mine may have looked the same as warmth filled my skin.

For the next few weeks only our eyes met. Not a word was said between us.

None of this was my style.

A second-generation Italian-American, I was blessed with my father's tall height, an uncommon trait among many of my fellow Italians. My hair was jet black like my mother's, and my skin held the perfect olive hue. Like the girl whose name I'd yet to learn, my eyes were blue, a lighter shade than hers. My muscles were toned from physical labor. I was what my mother called *bello*. She would tell me not to misuse God's gift.

Like any other young man, I didn't always listen.

I used my looks to meet girls... women. Yet with this blue-eyed beauty, I was tongue-tied, awkward, and unsure.

I heard her friends call her Angel and wondered if it were true. Was she simply an apparition? Was that why I couldn't bring myself to talk to her?

And then, halfway through the semester, our professor called out her name: Angelina Costello.

As she rose to retrieve her paper, the air was sucked from my lungs.

"Dude?" my friend sitting beside me asked. "You sick?"

"What?" I asked, turning from my angel to him.

"You look like you saw a ghost. You're pale."

His name was Franco Testa. We had a few classes together. He wasn't one of the stuck-up elitists who were thick at NYU. He'd grown up more like me. We'd gotten in the habit of meeting up for our classes and eating lunch together. We were both working to put ourselves through college. I guess you could say we'd become friends.

"Did you hear her last name?" I whispered.

His smile grew. "I can't believe you didn't know."

"Tell me she's not... not of *those* Costellos."

Franco laughed as others were called to the front to reclaim their papers.

"Oren Demetri."

I rose, pushing myself up from the desk at my side. It was the first time I avoided her gaze. During the walk back to my desk, I pretended to be enthralled by the comments in my paper's margin, but the truth was that I was scared shitless.

And suddenly hollow.

Sometime during the last six to eight weeks, I'd come to anticipate this class. Not because I loved the English language. On the contrary, the language as a whole was plain and unimaginative compared to Italian. No, the appeal was seeing my angel's blue eyes, hearing her glee of life, and watching her cheeks fill with pink as our gazes met.

How had I been so stupid?

If she were really part of the Costello family, not only was Angelina out of my league, but flirting with her could be dangerous to my health.

When I was a boy, I hadn't understood the pier boss whom my father and I would visit. And then I grew older. I saw the capos. I knew them by name and sight. They were revered throughout the neighborhoods... respected. There were always tables waiting for them at the best restaurants. The bills for their food never came, or when they did, they were paid by young, willing soldiers doing their best to move up the ranks.

The family protected those who gave them what they deserved. Quid pro quo. They kept the Irish and Russian crime out of our streets. They were our first line of law enforcement, our community's men of honor and respect. The men who frequented the docks were small potatoes compared to the don, underboss, or consigliere. Though their names may be different, they were all connected. Everyone belonged. Where I was raised, everyone knew who they were. When I was very young, there had been a war. Not one they describe in the history books. Jersey and Brooklyn. The boundaries were set. The end result was the agreement between the Bonettis and the Costellos. Those were names everyone knew.

Of course, there were others that ruled other areas of the city. Together they made up the commission.

As a child, I'd asked my father if the well-dressed man was part of the government. Now, as a young adult, I knew the truth. He and all of those over him were higher than the government—above the government—FAMILY.

Upon learning Angelina's name, I gave up our stolen glances. Knowing I wasn't worthy of her, I concentrated on school and work. I watched and learned.

On more than a few occasions, she spoke to me, knowing my name. I was polite and respectful, as any good life-loving Italian would be. "Miss Costello."

And then tragedy struck. My parents passed away.

The grief of their loss couldn't be soothed by life insurance money, but it helped. It gave me a small nest egg to begin my plans. My father paid into his union for most of his life. They came through when my mother died, though if you asked me, it was the least they could do. Their hands were red with her blood. I could take it a step further, but it wouldn't do me any good.

My mother was first. A year after her body was recovered, my father took his last breath. The loss of his soul mate was more than he could take. My hero wilted away under the cloud of mourning and alcohol.

Again, the union paid.

I sold what was left of their belongings and moved closer to NYU. Finishing my degree was my mother's dream. I wouldn't—couldn't—fail her.

The nest egg helped. I bought the clothes I could afford. I used what I'd learned to achieve the white-collar career my parents never could. But even there, in the glass buildings, I saw the influence. I watched as money changed hands, as contracts were given to contractors—not with the best bids or skill, but with connections.

I had connections. I'd been raised in the mix. Even my friend Franco was connected. Giving up on NYU, he pursued a lucrative career within the family. A small-time numbers runner, he knew who was who.

Though I'd never forgotten Angelina Costello, I gave up the fantasy that she would ever be mine and concentrated on making a name for myself, on making the name Demetri mean something.

The capos from the docks and the ones from the restaurants—I knew all of their names. I had an inside track working in real estate. I revived old acquaintances. I paid for meals, for drinks, and for meetings. I helped orchestrate deals until the deals weren't for another contractor, but for Demetri. The infrastructure of Manhattan was in constant need of upgrade. I invested in raw materials, those brought to the island via the shipyard. I arranged to pay taxes—not the ones that went to Uncle Sam, but the ones my father had paid.

Money begot money. It's power only exemplified in the eyes of those who wanted more.

I moved up quickly. My businesses paid their dues and were noticed.

Five and a half years after my graduation from NYU, while in Manhattan for a dinner meeting, I was once again derailed by the most beautiful blue eyes. It was an unplanned encounter, a soft laugh drawing my gaze across the restaurant. No longer wearing jeans and a rock band T-shirt, Angelina was the epitome of an angel. With her dark hair pulled up and a white dress that revealed nothing except the promise of her curves beneath, I was once again awestruck.

Far from bashful, after our eyes met, she approached me. "Oren Demetri."

Though my mind had been on my impending meeting, I forgot it instantly as my smile blossomed. With a nod, I replied, "Angelina Costello, I believe. Or has someone changed your last name?"

"You have it right."

I was no longer tongue-tied though my concentration wasn't on words but on searching the depths of her eyes, wondering if there was any chance I could again make her blush. Though I knew I would never deserve her, I'd made a name for myself. Would it be enough?

Angelina Costello was the only woman to ever take my breath away. I couldn't not speak to her. "I haven't seen you since NYU."

"I've been living overseas, studying history and architecture in Italy."

"Italy! *Molto bene*. And now you're back?" I asked.

"I am."

"To stay?"

"I believe so."

"Perhaps we could see one another," I proposed, all the while hoping that she would say yes and saying a prayer that she would say no.

Her lips curved upward. "I see you now."

"*Sì*, and I would like to see more."

With a glint to her gaze, she said, "I never forgot you. I thought at one time…" Her head tilted innocently as her lip momentarily hid behind her teeth. "Are you sure you aren't still scared of me?"

"Angelina, I'm quite certain that I'm terrified of you."

Her smile grew. "*Bene.* Then let me give you my number."

# CHAPTER 2

Nearly a year later, I found myself standing in Carmine Costello's inner sanctum, perched and ready to ask the question that I wasn't confident in how he'd answer.

My successes were plentiful. My name had clout. Demetri Enterprises was growing with a bottom line that only years before would have seemed outside my realm of imagination. And none of that mattered. Beneath the expensive suit—custom-made, unlike the first ones I purchased after my father's death—I felt again like the nineteen-year-old schmuck who'd just heard Angelina's last name, rather than the mildly successful entrepreneur. With my heart on my sleeve, I contemplated again how I'd planned to speak to one of the most powerful men I've ever encountered. CEOs and CFOs fifty stories in the air weren't as intimidating as the man before me.

With graying hair and a dark penetrating stare, Carmine Costello wasn't Angelina's father; he was her uncle.

One of the most powerful men in Cosa Nostra was the uncle of the woman I loved. Until her eighteenth birthday, he'd been her guardian. However, from the expression on his face, I wasn't confident that he was aware that the title held an expiration date.

The war between the families that I'd heard about as a child held more meaning for Angelina. Her parents were taken when she was young. Overpowering the family's guards, the killers slaughtered her mother and father in their own bed. For reasons unbeknownst to anyone, she'd survived. Carmine's oath as he held his dead brother was that he would raise Angelina, watch over her, and keep her safe. He and his wife Rose, sometimes known as Rosa, would raise her as their own.

And they did. Angelina never lacked for anything, including love.

My neck stiffened as Carmine's dark eyes met mine. The old saying came to mind—if looks could kill. The difference with sayings and reality was that the right look from Carmine Costello could be deadly.

"Talk to me, Oren," Carmine's deep, gravelly voice bid me.

I'd been inside his office a few times and knew it held all the necessary amenities to exhibit his power: the heavy ornate wooden desk, large chair, walls of bookcases, fireplace, and absence of windows.

On more than a few occasions, Angelina pulled me into the depths of her aunt and uncle's home to introduce me and attempt easy conversation. I'd sat in their dining room at their table and eaten Sunday dinner. However, for a man who'd learned the art of sales where conversing was my forte, I was too easily rendered inarticulate in the presence of Carmine Costello.

First, he was rarely alone. Talking to him meant talking in front of others. Second, though I'd thought I had a grasp of the art of conversation, Carmine was a master where I was merely an apprentice. His arsenal was well-stocked, but words were reserved for the right occasion. Silence was his greatest weapon; he'd insert it into the most unlikely of places. When his lips didn't speak, his eyes took over, speaking volumes.

"He's just testing you," Angelina would say. "He wants to be intimidating."

He didn't need to try.

"He's really a big softy," she'd assure me.

In the span of time that we'd dated, I'd yet to truly witness his softer side.

In the newspapers and reports about him, the reporters had also failed to mention his softer side.

Untimely disappearances. Interesting financial dealings. The speculations ran rampant, yet the reality of the offenses never made their way to Carmine. There was always someone else to blame, someone else to take the heat, or someone else who when discovered was no longer able to dispute the evidence found on or near their remains. I thought of them as the Redshirts on Star Trek—the one person wearing the wrong color. He or she never made it back to the ship. Sometimes that was voluntary, other times not. Throughout the history of the American Cosa Nostra many people received the *Teflon* moniker, but not many were as deserving of it as Carmine Costello.

The large young man who'd followed me into Carmine's office closed the door, leaving the three of us alone.

"Sir." My tone brimmed with confidence that I didn't feel.

"Sit." He gestured toward the chair opposite his desk.

I took a breath as I worked to walk and not stumble. Sit and not tremble.

I fought the urge to clear my throat. "Thank you, Mr. Costello, for seeing me. I know you're busy."

In his signature move, he leaned into his large chair, tipping it backward as he searched my gaze. The silence filled the regal room as his hands came together, his fingers steepling until they intertwined. If it were a movie, perhaps there'd be a soundtrack of a ticking clock. The camera would pan as the second hand moved slowly forward. In reality, it was only my own heartbeat thumping in my ears that provided the score.

I'd checked the carpet for plastic. I wasn't sure if that was real. Maybe that was only in movies. Yet regardless of his decision, I believed I'd live to see another day.

As seconds turned to a minute and the hands of the clock continued to move, Carmine Costello's lips quirked upward. I'd seen his smile and heard his laughter at more than one of the family meals I'd attended. I wouldn't classify it as his softer side, but in the presence of Mrs. Costello and Angelina, his adoration for his family was never hidden. He would move Heaven and Hell for them, if need be.

"My Angelina said you wanted to speak to me. Yet you're not speaking."

The large man behind me joined Carmine in laughing softly in amusement of his joke.

I sat forward and forgetting all my preparation, blurted out my intentions. "Sir, I'd like to ask you for Angelina's hand in marriage."

He nodded slowly as my intent hung in the air. Finally, he leaned forward and said, "Then do it, son. Ask."

It's a strange sensation as the blood that is necessary for life suddenly drains from your face, shooting to your feet. Perhaps that's why they call it lightheaded. How much does blood weigh?

"Mr. Costello, may I have your permission to marry Angelina?"

"Have you spoken to my niece about this?"

I'd anticipated this question. It's one that someday I plan to ask when a young man asks for our daughter's hand—assuming we have a daughter. The question was double-edged. If I didn't talk to Angelina, I wasn't showing her the respect she deserved in taking part in this marriage. After all, we weren't back in the old country. Marriages weren't arranged by families to unite land. Angelina was a strong, independent woman.

However, if I had discussed it with Angelina, and we'd already decided that marriage was in our future, why was I bothering her uncle? Would I not be disrespecting him?

I hoped my answer was adequate. "Angelina knows that I love her. I do. She's said she feels the same. We have talked about spending our lives together; however, I have not asked her to marry me, not without your permission."

"You know my Angelina?"

"Yes," I answered his odd question skeptically.

"She's a Costello."

"Yes, sir."

"Tell me why you love her."

If this were a numbers game, he was asking me to double down. "Have you *met* Angelina?" I replied with a grin.

Carmine's smile grew. "Go on."

"I met your niece nearly ten years ago. A day hasn't passed that I haven't thought of her. I knew without a doubt that I didn't deserve her. Though I never questioned that fact, I never forgot her. When we ran into one another for the first time since college, she asked me if I was still afraid of her."

"And you said...?" he prompted.

"Without a doubt—terrified."

The grin I'd welcomed on Carmine Costello's face exploded as the room filled with his laughter. "Tell me, Oren Demetri, what else scares you."

"Nothing."

"Nothing?"

"Nothing else matters without Angelina. I make deals and alliances. I make money and lose it. My life is insignificant without

Angelina beside me forever."

"And if I say yes, if I give you my blessing... then what will scare you?"

"In all honesty, sir, everything."

Carmine nodded again. "You will love her?"

"With my whole heart."

"Protect her?"

"With my life."

"Give her all her heart's desires?"

"To the best of my ability."

His tone sobered. "Make sacrifices for her?"

"I'll do whatever is within my means. As you know, I have no family—"

"You marry my niece and you do. You don't marry only her. You marry all of us."

As much as that should have petrified me, it didn't. I missed my parents. I missed the sense of belonging. It never happened in business. I was the employee or the employer. It wasn't the same.

"If you'll give me your blessing, I'd be honored to be family."

That night, as Carmine Costello and I left his office, my future was set.

The long paneled hallway echoed with our footsteps against the polished wood floor. As we entered the sitting room, Mrs. Costello and Angelina stood, their expressions questioning.

Finally, Angelina spoke, "*Zio?*"

"Go," he said, "go with Oren." He looked my way. "I know her age. I was at the hospital when she was born. I still want her home before midnight."

"*Zio!*"

Mrs. Costello hugged Angelina and kissed her cheek. "Have fun."

As I took her hand in mine and we descended the steps of their brownstone, I decided where we were going. "How about dinner?" I asked once we were in my car.

"Oren! Tell me what he said."

"No, *mio angelo*, patience. First, dinner."

As a rule, I'm not a gambling man. Purchasing an engagement ring before I had Carmine's blessing was wrong. A part of me worried he'd know. I wasn't sure how, but I suspected it was possible. However, now that I had his permission, being without a ring also seemed wrong.

I parked behind the small Italian restaurant, in a parking lot off an alley. Not everyone knew the lot was even there. It was for Giovanni's honored guests. As the escort of Angelina Costello, I qualified.

The aroma of garlic hung in the air, waking hunger I'd forgotten while with Carmine. I hadn't called ahead, but the hostess recognized us immediately, taking us beyond the main dining room to a secluded table near a corner. We both could sit facing not only one another, but the rest of the room. I'd learned years ago that I didn't want to be the one with my back toward the rest of the room. It was essentially the same as the red shirt, a sign of weakness, willingly accepting the unknown danger. For Angelina, I'd face any danger, but for her protection, knowing my surroundings was more important.

After we were seated, I stood, kissing Angelina's cheek. "Excuse me, *mio angelo*, my pager. I have a call to make."

The twinkle from moments ago disappeared. "Please hurry."

"*Sì.*"

My pager hadn't alerted me. Instead, I'd slipped away to make an important phone call. The recipient was the owner of a well-known jewelry store within the Costello limits. Excusing myself, I called from the payphone in the back of the restaurant.

A little while later, I once again sat opposite her, two glasses of red wine and a flickering candle between us. I reached across the table and took her hand. Warm and petite, it fit perfectly within mine.

"Are you ever going to tell me what Uncle Carmine said?" she quipped, her lips quirking in expectation.

"He told me that he loves you."

Her smirky grin softened. "I know he does."

"He offered to kill me if I hurt you."

"I think it might be Vincent who'd actually do it."

I shook my head, wishing that her words were said in jest. "That's good to know." I kissed her hand once more and swallowed. "I've loved you since the first time I saw you at NYU."

"Oren."

"Please, let me say this?"

Angelina's eyes glistened as she nodded.

"And yes, you frightened me—you still do. Not because of your name. Not because of your uncle or your cousin. You scare me because I don't want to ever disappoint you. I want to be the man who's worthy of your love. I want to wake each morning knowing that you're safe beside me and go to sleep every night the same way. I want to give you everything you deserve, everything we've both lost."

Her head tilted.

"*Mio angelo*, I know that you have a family, but I want to make a new family with you and me. Together. I want us to have what was stolen from both of us. This time we'll be the parents. This time we'll make the safe, loving home. If we need a fortress, I'll build it. Please, Angelina Costello, will you be my wife?"

# CHAPTER 3

WE WERE VIRTUALLY alone. Even those who were near disappeared. A tear trickled from her eye as she nodded, her smile growing by the second. In nearly a year—make that almost *ten* years—I'd never known Angelina to be speechless, and her current inability to respond had me on edge.

Had I gone about this wrong? Should I have asked her before Carmine?

Finally, she spoke, "I-I knew that was what you were talking to Uncle Carmine about, but that's not the same as hearing you propose."

My cheeks rose at the sound of her voice. One hand still holding hers, I wiped the tear from her cheek with the pad of my thumb on my other hand. "And that's not the same as an answer."

Her grip tightened. "You weren't on your knee."

I tilted my head as I digested her words. "You're right. Not because you don't deserve it." I started to move from my chair, but her grasp of my hand stopped me.

"I love you," she said. "I'll be honored to marry you. I don't need a proposal on one knee."

"I'll bend a knee to you every day or night for the rest of our lives." Pulling her hand toward me until it was against my chest, our lips united.

"Thank you for saying yes."

The fingers of her other hand splayed over the buttons of my shirt. It was unbuttoned at the collar, my tie from earlier removed. My suit coat hung from my shoulders, also unbuttoned.

Slowly her gaze went from her hand upward until it reached my eyes. "Your heart's beating so fast."

"It's better than not beating."

"Don't ever say that, Oren. I know what it means to marry me. You can say you aren't afraid of my name, but you'd be a fool not to be. I've lived with it all my life. Women are supposed to be sheltered and protected. We aren't supposed to know what's really happening. There was a time when I was like that, I suppose."

I lifted her hand until all our fingers intertwined. "Until…"

"Until I wasn't. It's difficult for others to hide the reality that your parents are gone."

"I want you to be like that again—sheltered."

She shook her head. "I don't think that's possible. Once you know, you can never not know."

"I'm sorry about your parents."

"And I'm sorry about yours. Life is full of tragedies. That's not what I want to think about. It's just that I'm so thankful that you're willing to enter this world for me. I love you. I really do. I think I have since NYU."

"You think?"

Pink fills her cheek. "You were so handsome."

"Was? Come now, Angelina, you're wounding me."

"Oren, you are still the handsomest man I've ever seen. Back then, all the girls noticed you. We'd watch you."

"I never noticed any other girls, no one other than you."

As we leaned in for another kiss, Giovanni, the owner of the restaurant, approached with a bottle of champagne. "On the house," he said. The cork popped with a mini explosion of bubbly combined with our laughter. "May I be the first to congratulate...?" He leaned toward Angelina. "...the future Mrs. Demetri." And then to me. "You're a very lucky man."

Or stupid.

I saw the alternative in his eyes. Nevertheless, I'd stick with lucky.

"Yes, I am."

Once both of our glasses were filled, Giovanni produced another and poured himself a small amount. Lifting his glass toward us, he proposed, "*Tanti auguri!* To a long life of love and happiness."

It is unlucky to propose a toast and not drink. It was why he had the third glass. I could contemplate how he knew. Perhaps he saw me propose. Then again, I hadn't fallen to my knee. Maybe Carmine had alerted him. Of course, that would mean he was watching us, knowing where we were. Instead, I simply accepted the man's gift and well-wishes.

Once our food arrived and we were alone, Angelina asked, "Uncle Carmine didn't really threaten you, did he?"

"Not in so many words."

"My uncle doesn't beat around the bush. If he threatens you, you would have heard the words."

"According to you, I should be more concerned with Vincent?"

She laughed. "Vinny is like my brother. I love him. I worry about him. He's already too experienced with the law."

Her cousin had been arrested more than once. Like his father, who tended to avoid the back of police cars, in Vinny's many arrests, he'd yet to be convicted.

After we finished a delicious dinner and were shooed from the premises without a check to pay, I laid a hundred dollar bill on the table and led Angelina to the car. Once inside, I told her that I had a surprise.

Her eyebrows danced. "At your place?"

I had a respectable brownstone in Brooklyn. It was all part of the *making me worthy* plan.

"That wouldn't be a surprise."

With a smile, I drove us out of Little Italy. As we progressed, the number of people on the sidewalks decreased. Now we were venturing into an area of the city that bustled during the day, and became a ghost town after nightfall. It was late and the shops were closed. The inhabitants were elsewhere, in restaurants, bars, or locked away safe in their homes. Where I was taking Angelina wasn't one of the biggest and brightest jewelry stores in Manhattan, but I knew the owner. He knew me. I would be treated right. More importantly, Angelina would be treated well. Parking on the street, we walked hand in hand to the front of the dark store. The brisk wind howled between the buildings, whistling through the now-dark sky. One knock on the front door covered with an iron gate and the lights within came to life.

"Oren?" Angelina said as the excitement showed in her eyes. "Did you call ahead?"

"My only business tonight is you."

"That phone call before?"

I nodded.

"But you hadn't asked me yet."

"Not you, but I had permission and hope." I kissed her cool cheek. "I didn't bend a knee. And I didn't have a ring. And yet you said yes."

"I'll always say yes."

As the mechanisms in the door clicked, I explained, "I wanted you to have a choice in your ring. After all, it's something you'll wear every day from tonight until forever."

Her hand within mine trembled with excitement as the door opened, and the gate was moved to the side.

"Mr. Demetri! Welcome," Anthony said as he gestured for us to come inside. Once within, he reached for Angelina's hand and brought her knuckles to his lips. "Congratulations, Miss Costello. I'm honored to have you here at my store."

"Thank you, Anthony. I had no idea Oren had this planned."

Our community may appear large from the outside, but Angelina had been a part of it for her entire life. There were few people she didn't know or who didn't know her.

Letting go of my fiancée's hand, Anthony closed the gate and locked the front door. The cases shimmered, some of the displays empty while others still held their merchandise. Once we were secured within, he led us toward the back of the store, past displays, and beyond what other customers saw. "Come to my office. I have a nice selection. The best of my best. I hope there will be one you will like—one that is perfect for Angelina Demetri."

I liked hearing her future name said aloud.

When I'd called earlier in the night, I'd asked Anthony for his best: his highest quality rings. I told him no price tags. I didn't want Angelina to consider cost. If he had one that she liked and it fit her, we'd leave tonight with the ring on her finger. If her choice didn't fit, he'd size it, and I would pick it up the next morning. No money would exchange hands in front of my Angelina.

Willingly and without question, Anthony agreed.

In reality, he was probably missing dinner with his wife or drinks with his mistress due to my call. I didn't care. It wasn't my concern. The stunning, blue-eyed beauty holding my hand was.

Once we were seated, Anthony laid a black velvet covering over his desk under the bright illumination and then brought out the most gorgeous diamond rings I'd ever seen. Truly, jewelry wasn't my forte, but quality was. Each stone shimmered, sending prisms like rainbows reflecting in Angelina's eyes.

Anthony explained the different cuts, sharing his eyepiece to allow Angelina to see inside the stones. One by one, she inspected each diamond and each ring. Each time she held one between her fingers, she'd look from it to me.

"It's your decision," I said reassuringly.

"But, Oren, they're too much."

"Nothing is too much for you."

Her head shook, her dark hair flowing over her shoulders as she continued her assessment. The bands were primarily yellow gold, with a few in white gold and others in platinum.

"If you prefer one stone on another band," Anthony said, "I can do what you want."

"What *you* want," I repeated.

Over an hour later, we left with Anthony's promise to have the 4.01-carat European-cut diamond ring sized for my fiancée's finger by tomorrow. The platinum band was exactly what she wanted, but it was currently a bit too large.

On the nearly empty street Angelina huddled near my shoulder as we walked hand in hand to my car.

"To your place?" Angelina whispered suggestively.

I removed my suit jacket and placed it over her shivering shoulders. "It's after eleven."

"Uncle Carmine didn't mean what he said. I'm a grown woman."

If there was one thing I could be certain of, it was that I would take Carmine Costello at his word. I kissed Angelina's forehead as she faced me, and our gazes met. "You are definitely a grown woman, and I'm a damn lucky man."

"Yes, Oren Demetri, you are. That's what Giovanni said."

"He was right. Why do you think I'm lucky?"

"Besides my being grown, you're lucky because I'm yours. And I'm lucky too. I was afraid that while I was in Italy, some woman would snatch you up. I may have even asked Vinny to check once or twice for me."

I shook my head. "*Mio angelo*, there has never been another woman."

On the nearly empty sidewalk, our lips met. Sensual and warm, her petite body melted against mine as her arms encircled my waist. We'd been dating for nearly a year; we'd made love. Each time was like our first but better with the knowledge that we were accumulating about one another.

With everything in me, I wanted to make love to her again and consummate our engagement. I longed to see her skin, removing the dress with the neckline that had been teasing me all night. My hand splayed over the small of her back—between my jacket and her dress—as I pulled her waist toward me and her breasts against my chest. My heart rate once again raced as our kiss deepened, and I imagined her warmth beneath me as we joined as one. Behind my now-closed eyes, I recalled the heavenly way she boldly took me inside her, her body holding tight until the friction and desire overwhelmed us, and we both gave in to the inevitable pleasure.

"Oren?"

I took a deep breath and ignoring my growing erection, took one step backward. "If I take you home later than midnight, my luck may run out."

"He's not..."

I kissed her again as I opened the passenger door to my black sedan.

Once we were both inside, she reached across the console and spread her fingers over my thigh. So close. Obviously, seeing my trousers, she knew what she did to me.

"Then let me show you…"

I sighed and leaned against the seat, considering how amazing her mouth would feel, when out of the corner of my eye, I saw movement in the shadows. The reflection of something. It was quick, yet I didn't doubt it was there.

I wasn't a man prone to hallucinations.

I lifted her hand as I turned the key and started the car. Kissing her fourth finger of her left hand, I said, "Tomorrow, *mio angelo*, you will be wearing my ring. Tomorrow…" My gaze met hers. "I'll pick you up earlier than I did tonight, and there will be no long meeting in Carmine's office. And then I'll cook you dinner at my place—soon to be *our* place—and we will celebrate."

Her smile dimmed.

"Oh, baby, you deserve more than giving me a blow job in the front seat."

I wouldn't tell her what I saw—that whomever I saw was the true reason for our departure. I wouldn't say that there could be a man watching us who may want to do us harm. Or maybe it was Carmine's man, keeping her safe. I wasn't going to stick around to find out.

Her safety was my concern. I accepted it wholeheartedly.

There was no guarantee that she was the target. It could have been me.

I didn't always associate with the men and women in the glass buildings in the Financial District. My businesses knew no bounds. A nail salon that fronted for a gambling parlor had the potential to be more profitable than a Fortune 500 corporation. There was danger in my line of business. I had friends and enemies, but having Carmine's niece beside me, kissing on a dark sidewalk, was stupid. I'd taken a risk, and I knew that the outcome could have been different. Risks were for amateurs. My game had just been moved to the professional league.

Putting Angelina even in the vicinity of harm's way was something that I'd never allow to happen again.

# CHAPTER 4

———————•O•———————

I COULDN'T HAVE been more wrong about my not having to meet with Carmine again the following night. With Angelina's ring in my pocket, I approached the Costello home and knocked on the front door.

One didn't simply approach their brownstone. There was always someone to ensure unwanted guests were escorted away. That evening, it was the same young man who'd joined us in Carmine's office the day before. I supposed I should learn his name. However, when I offered mine, he simply nodded, silently confirming that he already knew my identity.

As Angelina opened the door, I was reminded of why she held my heart. With her dark, flowing hair pulled back on the sides and lying long in the back, she wore a light-blue blouse hanging over a tight pair of leggings—or whatever it was the women wore—and I was hit with the mixture of her sweet perfume and an overwhelming desire to grant her the romantic gesture I'd neglected to give her. On the front stoop of her family's home, in front of anyone who could see, I did what I hadn't done the night before. I fell to one knee and pulled the small velvet box from the pocket of my jacket.

Anthony from the jewelry store may have worked all night to fulfill my request. I didn't know if that were true. I only knew that when I arrived at his store an hour before opening, he was there with Angelina's ring in hand. After handing him the amount of cash it would take to buy a small house in the Midwest, I had the ring Angelina would wear for the rest of her life.

"Oh, Oren," she cried, her gaze falling with me to the step. "You don't need to do that. I've already said yes."

When I opened the box, her hands flew up, her fingertips covering her pink lips. The gesture did little to stifle her scream as she bounced on her bare toes. "It's more beautiful than I remember."

"Angel," Mrs. Costello called as she rushed toward the door, wiping her hands on a dark apron hanging from her waist. Coming to a stop with her hands on her niece's waist, she peered around Angelina's shoulder. "Oh, Oren, it's beautiful."

"Thank you, Mrs. Costello."

I rose slowly as Angelina plucked the diamond ring from the box with trembling fingers.

Mrs. Costello smiled approvingly my direction as I stepped inside her home. "Son, put it on her finger."

*Damn.* One knee. Place the ring on her finger.

I never knew there were so many steps to an engagement. One day it'll be my job to inform my sons of the things my father never told me.

I supposed I should be happy that I got the *asking permission* and *asking Angelina* parts close to right. With a nod I did as Mrs. Costello directed, reaching for Angelina's trembling hand and slipping the band over her knuckle into place.

My fiancée's eyes again filled with tears as her gaze went from the diamond upon her outspread finger to me, to her finger, and to her aunt.

"*Bambina, sbalorditivo!* It's lovelier than you described."

"I-I," Angelina stuttered. "Even seeing it, having it right here, I can't find words to describe it."

We all turned to the echoing footsteps. Carmine Costello's expression bore toward me, his eyes set and unrevealing as he came forward. I expected a form of commendation—of the ring that cost the annual salary of the median income, of the fact that we were officially engaged, of congratulations to me or Angelina.

Something.

Looking down at his niece's hand, he simply nodded.

"Carmine?" Mrs. Costello questioned.

He seemed not to notice his wife as his jaw set, and his dark eyes went back to me. "Oren. Come to my office. Now."

"*Zio*, not tonight," Angelina pleaded. "We have plans."

I wanted to turn toward the blue eyes of the woman speaking. I'd been thinking about our *plans* all day. It had been difficult to work and conduct business as our plans made their way into my thoughts, even at the most mundane of times. Nevertheless, with the way Carmine Costello was looking at me and the tone of his voice, my daylong semi-erection shriveled.

There was the possibility that I'd never get it back.

Carmine leaned in, glancing at the ring, and kissed Angelina's cheek. "It's *bellissimo*. Go with your aunt. Oren will be done with me when I say he's done."

I did my best to appear unaffected, yet that fear I'd told Carmine I'd have after Angelina became mine was coursing through my bloodstream and racing at immeasurable speeds. I nodded toward Carmine. "Yes, sir." And then I turned to Angelina. With a quick peck of her cheek, I reassured her, "Our plans will keep."

Carmine didn't speak as we traveled the hallway back to his office. He remained silent as he closed the door, this time with only the two of us present. He continued not speaking as he moved to the other side of his desk and sat. He didn't gesture for me to sit. He simply leaned forward, bringing his elbows to the top of the desk and became fascinated with his hands as the tips of his right fingers met the tips of his left. If he were praying, I was the one in need of salvation.

I stood taller, awaiting his decision and my fate.

Finally, he looked up. "Stefano, I told him not to disarm you. I told him that the first time you came to my home."

*Stefano?* I could assume the young man at the door.

"Sir, I would not disgrace your house with a gun."

His hands slapped the top of his desk. "What about last night?"

I shook my head once. "No. I didn't carry a gun in here last night. I don't have one on me now."

Slowly he stood, becoming omnipotent as he leaned his weight over the desk, his eyes never leaving me. "Last night." His words came slower. "When you had my niece on a deserted street. Last night when you stood and kissed her. Last night when you were within Stefano's sights."

My neck straightened as the small hairs on the back of my neck stood taller with each word. I knew I'd seen someone. "Yes, sir."

"Were you carrying then?"

I nodded and turned, slowly lifting my jacket and revealing the empty holster attached to my belt, near the center of my back.

"Sit down, Oren Demetri."

Taking a deep breath and exhaling, I did as I was told, planting my feet solidly before me, shoulder-width apart, my arms on the armrests and my back straight.

"From now on," he began a command I'd never forget, "you *will* disgrace my house and my niece any time you are not prepared. You will carry a weapon at every moment of every day. My home is safe, but so was my brother's. Never go without. Never." His demanding tone reverberated off the regal walls and bookcases. "I want to trust that you will take care of her."

I nodded as the knots within my gut twisted, creating ancillary knots. He was right. I knew last night that I'd been careless. I could tell him that I'd seen Stefano, though I didn't know it was him. However, I didn't think Carmine Costello was interested in my side of the story. He knew his side. No other opinion mattered. "You can trust her with me, sir. I would lay down my life—"

"She doesn't want you to lay down your life," he interrupted. "She's in love with you. She has been for years. Vincent told me after she moved to Florence for her studies. He said that she would ask about you. Before then, I'd never heard of you. I did my research. You're an impressive man, Oren. You've made a name for yourself. Now she wants that name. My Angelina gets what she wants but not at the price of her life."

"I'd never—"

His hand came up, silencing my reply.

"When is the wedding?"

I breathed a silent sigh of relief at the change in his tone and line of questioning. At least he wasn't saying he rescinded his permission. "We haven't talked dates."

"The women." He nodded toward the door. "If I were a betting man, which I've been known to be—only on sure things—I would say they're talking about it right now."

"I have no preference."

"Of course you don't. It's all up to her. Something else that is now beyond your choice..." His voice faded away as he sat back, his eyes still scanning me.

"If I ever thought that you would be a detriment to her, I wouldn't have given you my permission."

"I was careless. We were caught up in the emotion of the engagement."

"There is always emotion. Let the women have it. They love it. They live for it. They relish being happy and being sad. They can't enjoy one without the other. But it's your job to never let that emotion cloud your judgment. From now until the wedding, Vincent is going to spend time with you."

I searched for words, but they were hiding, such as I probably should have been.

Carmine stood and walked toward me, stopping near my chair, his dark eyes peering down. "What do you have to say about that?"

"I'll be happy to get to know Vincent better."

"I'm not talking about walks in the park."

Swallowing the bile churning in my gut, I nodded. "I'm not without knowledge, but I know I have more to learn."

Carmine nodded as his hand landed on my shoulder. "We all have more to learn. Every day. For the rest of our lives. That's what makes us smarter, stronger, and better prepared. Never lose that." He stepped back and leaned against the massive desk. "I'm not Angelina's father. She lost him too young. You, too, lost your father. I reminded myself of that last night when Stefano told me what he saw.

"That research—that knowledge—is why we're talking now and not last night after you brought her home.

"You've done impressive things on your own. I'll never replace my brother, and I'll never replace your father..."

"Salvatore," I said.

He nodded. "Good name. But with that ring on my niece's hand, you're now my nephew-to-be. We are family. When family has needs, family offers help. Right now, Vincent will help you and show you the ways of keeping my Angelina safe.

"And you will show Vincent the holdings of Demetri Enterprises. Let him learn, as you do. I believe we can help one another. Do you agree?"

My mind was going in too many directions to disagree. "Yes, sir."

"Now, what are these plans Angelina mentioned?"

*Plans… to strip your niece and lose myself inside her.*

I swallowed that response. "Dinner. I have steaks marinating and potatoes in the oven."

His smile grew, the rise of his cheeks eclipsing his dark eyes. "Eleven o'clock."

I didn't speak.

"She will argue," he said.

As she should. She was nearly thirty years old, as was I. Yet I understood that the earlier curfew was more about my recklessness last night than about Angelina. My carelessness lost us an hour. "I'll have her home by eleven."

Carmine was right about the women. When we reached the kitchen where the delicious aroma of something wafted through the air and filled my senses, Angelina and her aunt were looking at a calendar and discussing dates. Mrs. Costello was taking notes, speaking fast, saying names I'd only heard in passing. She fluctuated between English and Italian as if it were one language. By her excitement, it appeared that speaking to the priest was our first priority.

As I came nearer, Angelina's aunt reached for my hand. Looking up from her seat at the kitchen table, her eyes widened as she said, "Oren, tell me the church will bless this marriage."

"Yes, Mrs. Costello, I'm Catholic, and I've never been married." I looked to Angelina. "There's never been another woman, ever, who's held my heart."

"Rose..." she said squeezing my hand. "From now on, please call me Rose. We're to be family. Now we'll speak with Father Mario. Once we know the dates that the church is available..."

"Rose," Carmine said, "You and Angelina decide on a date. I'm sure the church will be available."

I looked to Angelina as she shook her head. The sight of her stole my breath away. There never had been another woman. I'd shared my body with others, but never my heart. It was tucked away until I saw her. From that day on, it's been hers. "I'm open this Saturday," I said with a grin.

"Oh no!" Rose said. "Angelina will have a big wedding. The biggest. The reception will need planning. Food. We need a menu. And music. Carmine, call Francesco. He'll provide the music. Oh, and his daughter. She plays the harp."

I stood dumbfounded, wondering if there was anyone else on the planet who told Carmine who to call.

"This takes time," she said, her fingers feverishly scribbling as she continued speaking.

With a grin, I offered Angelina my hand. "*Mio angelo,* do you want to keep working on the wedding, or can I convince you to join me for dinner?"

She placed her hand in mine, her new diamond glittering as I closed my fingers around hers. We fit together perfectly. "Mr. Demetri, I'm glad you asked. As it turns out, I'm simply famished."

"As am I."

"We have plenty," Rose said, listening to our words as she continued her mental planning. "You may eat with us. Right, Carmine?"

We all turned his way.

"I think I heard something about steaks marinating. No one wants a drowned steak."

"I'll be home by midnight," Angelina said.

Carmine's eyes met mine. "Or sooner."

I simply nodded.

"Take care of our girl."

"She's also mine, and I will." It was a bold statement, but at some point, I needed to stand up for what was mine. I'd been chastised for being careless when I knew better. Instead of making me less, I decided to be thankful it was Stefano and not someone more nefarious in those shadows. That was done. It was time to move on.

This time, Carmine nodded.

Once Angelina and I were outside and walking down the steps and sidewalk toward the tree-lined street, Angelina asked, "What did he want to talk to you about?"

"You."

As I opened the passenger door I noticed Stefano standing in the shade of a large maple. Acknowledging his presence, I nodded his direction. The spring weather was unpredictable. Where last night it had been cool, today the temperature had risen. I stilled a moment with my hand on the door handle of the driver's side. I was in this relationship now with both feet.

I'd take Carmine's advice and learn from Vincent. Keeping my feet on the street and out of a grave was second only to doing the same for the woman in my car. Once seated inside, I reached for the glove compartment, opened it, and removed my gun. Sliding the revolver into the holster at my back, I adjusted my coat and winked. "Are you really famished?"

Without acknowledging the gun, she leaned toward me and splayed her fingers over my upper thigh. "Yes, but I hope the steaks can wait."

They could.

# CHAPTER 5

———————●○●———————

THE NEXT MONTHS passed in a blur. Between the wedding planning, my real work—overseeing Demetri Enterprises—and Vincent Costello, my new best friend, sleep became my jealous mistress. It was like working nights at the docks and going to class during the day all over again. Slumber and I rarely spent time together, and when we did, it was erratic at best. Three to four hours a night was a luxury. Sometimes it was at night. Other times not. Despite the commitment I'd made to my bed, the couch in my office was difficult to ignore on those afternoons when my eyes wouldn't stay open.

Spending time with my future wife wasn't much better. Considering the lectures I'd received from her uncle about keeping her happy, I prayed that this orientation stage would be short-lived. Angelina and I were lucky to get one night a week of alone date time.

It would be different once we were married.

We told each other that.

Sometimes our time with one another was merely in passing as I came and went from her uncle's home. Other times I was there to eat with the family, but with the understanding there would be other responsibilities following. Angelina and I would steal a touch or a kiss when we could.

Her blue eyes would look to me longingly, and I'd do my best to spend a few minutes in her presence.

Slipping up the stairs to her room was a new kind of torture. I couldn't stay, but my body and heart didn't want to leave.

I had a new mindset, a repetitive reel that played in my head. The promise of more. The dangling carrot kept me in the race. Once we were married—I surmised—we'd live together, fall asleep in each other's arms, and wake that way the next morning.

As I drove to whatever location Vincent wanted me to meet him or wherever Carmine had arranged for a gathering, my thoughts often slipped to my parents.

Are our memories accurate? I wasn't sure.

Perhaps the scenes weren't as loving as I recalled, yet it was difficult to think of one parent without the other. Dinner scenes came back. My father was almost always present. I neither appreciated nor disapproved of our nightly gathering. During my teenage years, I wasn't as open to sharing my daily accomplishments or failures, yet my mother always asked. Even when I started working nights at the dockyards, my mother made an effort to spend a few minutes with me—assuring herself that I was well fed and always listening.

I'd never realized that I missed my father during those times, until I looked back at them from a distance. His shift and mine ran one after the other. Sometimes I'd see him in passing. Most of the time I didn't. I was too preoccupied with my own life.

As I strived to be the man Carmine expected me to be for Angelina, I came to the realization that along with my new goals, I wanted what my parents shared. The kicker was that I also wanted more. What I was doing would provide the *more*. Demetri Enterprises would provide more. Connections would provide more.

The end justified the means.

This was just an adjustment period. Everything would be different once we were married.

The structure of Demetri Enterprises was simple and yet complex. It was an umbrella, growing in size as it covered multiple entities, large and small. No one business was more important than another. Together they created the umbrella —my protection from the storms. When one was having financial difficulty, another would flourish.

As I'd mentioned, a gambling parlor fronting as a nail salon was as lucrative as some Fortune 500 companies. The difference now was that I was suddenly on both sides of the aisle. I owned the building. I accepted the rent. Now, with Vincent by my side, I learned to oversee the collection of funds from the activities within.

Gambling was an addicting pastime. Carmine had told me that he bet only on sure things. The knowledge that good men would lay down a week's wages—always with the hope of making it more—was a sure thing. I hadn't given gambling a lot of thought until I saw the dividends for myself. One thousand to twenty or even fifty thousand a night. When people talk of dirty money, they rarely mean literally, and yet it was. Oftentimes, the activities wouldn't end until early in the morning. By the time the profits were counted, my hands were black with smudge and grime from the bills.

Vincent had worked his way above the collection of taxes a long time ago, but I hadn't. My 'spending time' with Vincent was designed as an orientation that became a crash course in Costello family businesses. Above all, it made me known and recognizable to the others in the family as well as to those outside.

I was about to marry Angelina Costello.

Oren Demetri's presence with Vincent Costello gave not only my name, but also my reputation credence.

The Demetri umbrella was not relegated to illegal activity. That wasn't my goal. I incorporated legitimate businesses. I was Salvatore Demetri's son. I was an NYU graduate. Legitimate business was my ambition. Those also came in varying sizes.

There were the mom-and-pop laundromats where I owned fifty-one percent, liquor stores and resale shops where my ownership percentage was the same—greater than fifty but not too high. Allowing the individuals their percentage created their incentive for success. Like pebbles on a beach, the sizes of businesses varied. While one- or two-person establishments had their use, the larger and more dependable profits were found in businesses such as real estate and construction.

That was the task Vincent and I set into motion as we oversaw the Demetri holdings. We pinpointed the business that could be of the most help to the Costellos. Since I was the owner with the most shares or highest percentage of holdings, the decision to help family was solely mine.

Family helped family.

My late nights or early mornings collecting taxes from the most recent gambling establishment earned me a percentage.

That was Carmine's help to me. Most of the money that came to me was reinvested in the building-supply and construction companies. Contracts were awarded to those connected with the family.

Business was my forte. I'd made a name. And in the many months since I proposed to Angelina, my profits had increased at a steady yet reasonable rate. Nothing too much to set off alarms, but consistent increases nonetheless.

"Soon," I whispered as I leaned in for a kiss. It was a rare night with Angelina at my home, soon to be hers. She'd been making changes to the interior. Admittedly, prior to the proposal, my furniture was sparse. The kitchen and bedroom were the only rooms where I spent my time. The living room had a couch and a television, not that I had much time to watch it.

Now as I looked around, everything was changing. There were curtains over the blinds. The couch was no longer alone, but accompanied by chairs and accent tables. There were lamps and rugs. It was the same space, yet it felt different—in a good way.

"I miss you," Angelina said.

"*Mio angelo,* you'll be tired of me once we're married."

"Never."

The date of our wedding was approaching. Once we said 'I do' and the blowout of a party that Rose, Angelina, and Bella, Vincent's recent bride, had planned was over, I had a two-week honeymoon booked in a remote location of Aruba. Guaranteed seclusion. That's what the travel agent said. Hell, at the rate I'd been burning my candle at both ends, I was concerned that I might sleep the entire two weeks. Assuming I didn't, there was more than a secluded suite. The resort had swimming pools, waterfalls, and chef-prepared meals.

My recent increase in income production was wearing me down, but at least there was a light at the end of the tunnel, and more importantly, I had the extra cash to guarantee Angelina the honeymoon of her dreams.

"I'm ready to move into your house."

"*Our* house," I corrected as we sat on the steps of our back porch overlooking the courtyard. It wasn't as nice as the Costellos', but it was comfortable, especially on an unusually warm late-autumn evening. Without air conditioning, the porch was preferable to the heat inside.

Of course, Angelina needed to be home—at least tonight's curfew was midnight. And that was convenient because I had a pickup at two-thirty. Counting the money would probably take me until daybreak.

Angelina laid her head on my shoulder and sighed as she held tightly to my arm. "I'd hoped…"

I kissed the top of her head. "What, *mio angelo*, what did you hope?"

"When I was younger, my uncle would introduce me to 'nice men' as he called them—from the family."

My chest tightened thinking of him trying to pair her off with anyone but me.

"Good Italian boys, Aunt Rose would say. Boys who'd make your papa proud."

I reached for her hand. "I hope that he would be—"

She didn't let me finish. "He would, Oren. Never doubt that. It's just that I never wanted that. I-I've never felt unsafe in Uncle Carmine's home or even when I was at NYU or in Florence, but still… my parents… I thought maybe with architecture I could move beyond it."

*It—family.*

Her voice was low with a faraway tone.

"It won't be like this once we're married," I said again. "Imagine going to sleep with you beside me every night."

She nodded.

"Your uncle, he's home at night with Rose."

"Yes, but Vinny… Bella said he's been gone a lot."

I knew he had. I'd been with him when I wasn't doing what I did. "An adjustment period. I'm learning. Vincent is learning some things about Demetri. He's especially interested in the technology ventures. There are so many possibilities. We haven't even seen half of the advances.

"Just think. They have telephones that go in cars now. In cars. They have prototypes of ones that you can carry with you. And computers in homes. My father and mother would be overwhelmed."

She sat back and brought her palm to my cheek, cupping my face and pulling it toward her. "*Tesoro*, that makes me happy."

"If you want a phone in your car or a computer for home, I'll buy it tomorrow."

Her head moved back and forth as her smile grew. "No, your excitement. It makes me happy. I can hear it in your tone. Lately, you've sounded... tired."

"I'm sorry. I'm just... it's almost over. We'll be married and I have Demetri Enterprises. It needs more of me than I've been giving."

Her smile fell. "I hope you're right. I worry. Uncle Carmine, he approves of you and speaks highly of you. If you're helping Vincent, if Vincent is helping you, then why would he want it to end?"

I wouldn't admit that I had the same fears. I couldn't. "Not end, change. Become more manageable."

"I trust you."

"With your life, *mio angelo*. With your life. Because you're my life. I love you."

"I love you."

Spearmint. I savored the flavor of her kiss.

Wrapping my hand behind her neck, my fingers tangled in her long hair as I pulled her lips closer. As our kiss deepened, Angelina moaned and moved onto my lap. Her blue-jean-clad legs straddled mine. My hold dropped until I had her small waist surrounded.

"I don't deserve you," I said, my tone deep and gravelly, wanting nothing more than to pick her up and carry her to our recently redecorated bedroom.

"No, Oren Demetri, I don't deserve you." Her kisses peppered my cheek. "You work too hard."

"Baby, I'm hard, but it has nothing to do with work."

Her recently kissed lips curled upward. "If I spent the night, we could take care of that."

"If you spent the night, I suspect that I probably wouldn't see you again until our wedding day. My workday would go from fifteen to twenty-four hours."

"I'm a grown woman."

My hands moved under her long, flowing top over her soft, warm skin and up to her bra. "Yes, *mio angelo*, you are." As I unsnapped her bra, her head dropped, her forehead landing on my shoulder with a sigh.

I continued to caress and knead. With each ministration, the night air filled with her whimpers as she fidgeted, our bodies wanting what couldn't happen with the material of our jeans between us.

"Take me upstairs." Her command was thick, doused in desire.

The watch on my wrist showed me that the impending curfew was near.

"Soon, and then we'll be just the two of us for two weeks."

"We may starve."

"Why? There's a chef."

Angelina's smile broadened. "As long as they deliver it to our bed."

*Soon.*

# CHAPTER 6

THE MEMORIES OF the last months faded away as the periphery haze within the sanctuary thickened. There was no one else besides her. Only my angel.

In the past week, we'd never been left alone. A chaste kiss was the best we could do. I hadn't laid eyes upon her since our rehearsal and dinner the night before. It was difficult to believe that she could be more spectacular than she was in this same cathedral last night, wearing a sapphire blue dress, but now... she was. I feared I would be rendered speechless, a babbling imbecile when asked if I would take her as my wife.

*I do.*

I practiced the words in my head.

Angelina's gaze met mine through the lace veil. Her splendor was beyond my comprehension. Her beauty went beyond the surface. Yes, the surface was utterly stunning, yet it paled in comparison to her heart and soul. Deep within, she was perfection.

Venus and Aphrodite were but mythical goddesses in lore. Angelina was my goddess of love and beauty. Standing in front of her family, friends, and associates, I willingly surrendered my all to her. Without a doubt, I'd been lost to her since the day we met, her existence affecting me like no other had or would.

*Star-crossed lovers?*

I didn't believe it could be possible. Our destiny was together. It had taken too long to make it to this pinnacle. We were meant to be—forever. I knew that with every molecule within my body and soul.

The organ's music rang through the large pipes, vibrating through the air and rattling the old altar. I continued to grip my own hands, unable to take my eyes off of her, the white dress, veil, and bouquet in her grasp. She was the epitome of a blushing bride. Even beneath the lace, her gorgeous face with rosy cheeks shone through, not to be outdone but rather complemented by her piercing blue eyes and radiant smile.

Was that a tear glistening upon her cheek?

With each step Angelina and Carmine took toward me, I fought my own ongoing battle. The way Angelina's gaze stared into my own, as if telling me without words that she deemed me worthy of her love and adoration. I wanted it to be. But how does one become worthy of his life's desire?

She and Carmine came to a stop beside me. I cleared my throat as we all turned to the priest.

"Dearly beloved…"

His deep, commanding tone replaced the organ music as he began the ceremony and mass. When it was time to give the bride away, I looked directly into Carmine Costello's dark eyes. I didn't waver. He lifted her veil and kissed her cheek. Though his lips said 'Her aunt and I do,' in answer to the priest's question of who gives the bride away, when he looked up, his stare bore through me as it had months ago on that afternoon in his office when I'd asked for her hand.

I nodded, accepting the responsibility, taking her petite hand to my arm, and turning again to the altar.

Like the unexpected onset of a cool front on a stifling summer afternoon, the air cleared.

With Carmine stepping back to his pew—his place beside Rose—we were finally alone. It was just Angelina and me.

Yes, we were surrounded by family, friends, and others. Vincent was to my right with Bella beside Angelina. There were other people near and far; bridesmaids and groomsmen created a semi-circle. They were cousins of Angelina's who'd desired to play a part. Within the mix was a small blonde flower girl. Apparently still hearing her own music, she spun in circles making the miniature bride's gown, complete with a small tiara similar to the one in Angelina's veil, billow around her feet. The ring bearer stood still as he'd been instructed, consumed with his own mission. The carpet surrounding his shiny shoes was littered with white strings as he pulled them from the small pillow in his grasp. The faux rings dangled from a ribbon.

Beyond the wedding party, the pews were filled to capacity. Ladies in hats and men in their Sunday best—the standard black suit dominated the view. Only the slight rustle of hand fans created the background as the priest continued his prayers.

Technically Angelina and I weren't alone.

And yet the absence of Carmine's stare was a refreshing breeze to my soul.

This day was what I'd worked to achieve, and staring back at me with the most intense blue eyes was everything I'd ever wanted.

Between verses and prayers, the priest spoke about marriage and its role throughout time. "Beginning with Adam and Eve, God intended for man and woman to be together…"

A rather homely young lady strummed a large golden harp. Immediately the cathedral filled with a joyous melody, no doubt second only to the angels singing in heaven. As the music progressed, I regretted my first impression of the girl's outward appearance. Undoubtedly this talented musician was the daughter of the man who would provide the music for the reception. Rose had known what was deceiving on the surface. This girl had been included in Angelina's aunt's plans made on the first night of our engagement.

As the groom, I had more to say than my two-word answer.

The priest turned to us. "Angelina Costello and Oren Demetri, have you come here to enter into marriage without coercion, freely and wholeheartedly?"

With her hands in mine, I answered truthfully. "Yes."

Her answer was the same.

"Are you prepared, as you follow the path of marriage, to love and honor each other for as long as you both shall live?"

It was my desire and perhaps, even longer. The jury was still out on life beyond our earthly bodies, yet at that moment, I didn't want this restrained to a mere fifty or sixty years.

"Yes," we replied in unison.

"Are you prepared to accept children lovingly from God and to bring them up according to the law of Christ and his church?"

"Yes."

And then the time came for the words I'd rehearsed. I remembered my line. After all, the script hadn't been too complex. I'd confidently uttered my two words when Father Mario asked his question.

"Do you, Oren, take this woman to be your lawfully wedded wife, to love and protect, to have and to hold, for richer, for poorer, in sickness and in health, from this day forward, until death do you part?"

Something about the last line unexpectedly hit me hard. I didn't outwardly flinch, but the pistol under my tuxedo jacket, the one that was never far from me even in slumber, was a reminder that death was more of an inevitability than a farfetched unpredictability. Probably every man in the church—save the priest—was armed. It was the way of life and death. Nevertheless, I'd spend my time on this planet assuring that Angelina's and my time together would be long and fruitful.

After our exchange of the rings, when at last my bride and I turned toward the congregation, we basked in the smiles and applause. There was no doubt that this was an occasion of all occasions. The pride and joy of the Costello family—the princess—was now married. Taking in the adoration, I leaned in and gave my wife another kiss, enjoying the way her cheeks grew pink in front of the crowd.

"I love you," I whispered, "and I'm going to make you proud."

Moisture gleamed in her eyes as her smile bloomed. Despite the murmurs of others, I only heard her voice. "You already do, Oren Demetri. I'm proud to be your wife."

Rose spared no expense as the reception continued beyond the fall of night into the early hours of the next morning. The wine flowed as course after course of food came only to be replaced by more. Guests laughed, sang, and danced. There were toasts to our future and ones by closer family with not-so-veiled threats. They were all said in fun, but what is it they say about truth in jest?

The hall in Brooklyn was large. While the family partied inside, Costello soldiers patrolled the exterior. The gathering within contained not only the Costello family but others from the commission. The invitation to attend was an honor. It would be treated as such. The women weren't the only ones to plan the festivities. Much time and debate over the guest list occurred within the walls of Carmine's office.

Inviting the Bonettis was a step in the redemption of past sins as well as a demonstration to the world regarding the strength of the New York commission. The soldiers who'd done the deed nearly a quarter of a century earlier—killing Angelina's parents—were no longer with us, nor was the Bonetti consigliere who'd ordered the act. Her parents weren't the only casualties. The war had resulted in more bloodshed than had been seen in decades.

The Omertà was clear: victims and family had the right to avenge wrongs.

What was committed against her parents was wrong.

Now it was done.

Both families survived. All five families survived. The lines were drawn, and over the last twenty-five years a kind of peace and understanding had ensued. Each festivity that united the families validated a future. Not inviting the Bonetti boss or underboss or any of the others from the other three families and their wives could be construed as an insult. Amazing how something as simple as a wedding invitation had such far-reaching implications.

The families of the New York commission needed a united front. Philadelphia, Chicago, Vegas... the outside world was there, watching. The commission was stronger united.

When Rose had proclaimed that Angelina's wedding would be big—huge—she spoke the truth. This was about her and her family. I was simply the man at her side.

At a little past midnight, hand in hand, my wife and I made our way to the remaining guests to say our goodbyes as they all wished us well.

"*Evviva gli sposi!*"

"Two weeks?" Carmine asked not for the first time.

We'd discussed the plans for our honeymoon at some length. There were deals in the works in need of overseeing in Brooklyn as well as in the city. I'd played a role. I would again but not during the next two weeks.

Before I could respond, Vincent's hand came down heavily on my shoulder. "Pop. It's their honeymoon." He spoke to me, "Enjoy. Just remember when you're home, you'll owe me."

"It's my honeymoon," Angelina repeated playfully, seemingly unaware of how accurate Vincent had been. "He's all mine for two weeks."

"And you should enjoy," Carmine replied with a kiss to his niece's cheek. "Check in. Let me know you arrive safe. The only foreign country you should visit is Italy."

"*Zio*, I've been to Italy. This is the tropics."

His nose scrunched. "Sicily is warm."

"*Zio*." Her head tilted to the side.

Carmine eyed me up and down before turning back to Angelina. "Then it is right that you go to a place you've never been with your new husband."

*Her husband.*

That was me.

Carmine extended his hand. "Keep her safe."

"Always."

# CHAPTER 7

OUR FIRST NIGHT as husband and wife was spent in the airport awaiting our early morning flight. With cups of coffee as fuel, we sat in vinyl chairs as the crowds gathered. Surrounded, we relished our isolation. I watched for threats yet found none. The light at the end of the tunnel was bright and accepting. We'd made it.

As the sun moved higher, casting pink hues over the skyline, our plane ascended into the clouds, skirting the city as it flew south along the coast to our tropical location.

Though I couldn't remember ever being so exhausted, I didn't sleep in the airport or on the plane as Angelina rested with her head upon my shoulder. With her dark hair pulled back to a low ponytail, small wisps of loosened tendrils fell over her peaceful expression. While I fought the urge to clear them away to better see her face, I realized that she too had been under a lot of stress and needed the rest.

It had been too easy to concentrate only on the demands of my schedule, but planning our wedding had been more. And now we were traveling through the sky to have our reward.

I didn't rest as we flew, knowing if anything happened, she was mine to protect. She, on the other hand, rested comfortably. At the same time, I was invigorated by her slumber. Instead of being worried or scared, she was secure knowing I was with her. That was what I wanted forever.

There was a car waiting, the driver holding a sign with our names. This was the life I wanted to give her, people at her disposal as she enjoyed life's bounties.

The exclusive resort was everything the travel agent had promised. Our room was not a room, but a luxurious hut secluded in a grove of palm trees overlooking the ocean. The bedroom was large with a whirling fan attached to the thatched roof that circulated the warm air. The infinity pool on our balcony appeared to never end, blending into the crystal blue waters.

As we explored our temporary home, it was my new wife's reactions that I enjoyed. The surroundings could have been an igloo in the Arctic if it brought the same joy to her expression. Angelina squeezed my hand and whispered her approval as we were given the full tour.

Our days were spent lounging in the sun and shade, and our nights were filled with one another. It was exactly as I'd hoped, falling asleep with her soft, warm body at my side and waking the same way.

We ate fresh fruits that dripped with sweet goodness, as well as other foods that we couldn't pronounce. Seafood was plentiful, as were the refreshments. As the sun beat down, we sipped tropical iced drinks in all colors.

The resort offered jeeps and drivers to take us to other areas of the island. We laughed as water fell from over a hundred feet above in a clear, cool fall. The refreshing mountain runoff cooled our sun-warmed skin. We clung to one another, steadying each other, as our bare feet slipped upon the wet, smooth rocky surface.

Time gave us freedom to go where we'd not been able to go—not only with our lovemaking, but with our words. We talked without the restraint of curfews. Our past was behind us with only the future beyond. As sparse, fluffy clouds floated through the cobalt-blue sky, we shared the depths of our dreams and aspirations.

I was a simple man. I longed for the love and devotion of my childhood with the spoils of success. If my goal had been to obtain more than my parents, I could stop now. I was there. However, that wasn't what I strived to accomplish. I wanted more: for Angelina's every desire to be granted, for our children to be loved by a family that reached beyond the two of us, and for them to be raised to strive for even more. Satisfaction was a poor excuse for lack of incentive. I'd willingly pay my dues to watch those I loved enjoy what was mine to give. I wanted what my father once told me was not mine to demand, but to receive and to give. I wanted to be respected.

Angelina had dreams, too. She wanted children and a family—to have what was stolen from her and what her aunt and uncle supplied. She also wanted more. To my great surprise, she wanted to work, something that Carmine apparently had discouraged. She didn't want the money—nor need it. Her desire was to use her degrees. Though she'd studied architecture, it was history that she loved. Her master's degree was in both. She spoke about dynasties and historical periods. Awe and excitement brought her visions to life in her words. Ancient civilizations and people. She painted colorful, vivid pictures with her descriptions.

Without mentioning it to anyone, before we became engaged, she'd applied for a job at the Met—The Metropolitan Museum of Art—for a part-time position working with recreating historical scenes. The position was to help create and design sets for different displays based on the historical information and the architectural ruins.

Though she'd applied before we were engaged, now that we were married, she knew that she didn't want to do it forever. Children were in our future, and we weren't exactly young. However, this was still a dream. Angelina wanted to prove to herself that her studies were valuable.

With her sunglasses on her head, she looked my way. Her lip disappeared behind her teeth as her eyes widened. "I know I should have told you or Uncle Carmine, but I knew what he'd say. I also hoped that after we were married, his opinion wouldn't matter. Only ours. Things were so hectic before the wedding, and besides, I didn't expect to get the job."

"And why would you doubt that you'd be hired?"

She shrugged. "I've never worked. Not really. It was a long process. I met on multiple occasions with many different people. The position was dependent upon a grant. Into the process, I was asked to help write the proposal. I'd never done that except in theory. It all took time. The money was finally granted very recently. I only found out last week."

She'd known for a week.

At first, I was taken aback that she'd known and hadn't said anything. And just as quickly, I recalled our opportunities for private discussion. There hadn't been many in the last... months. "And what did you tell them?" I asked.

"I said I was getting married. I hoped they'd hold the position until I returned; if they couldn't, I understood."

"So you accepted it? Without talking to me?"

"No. I asked them to hold it. When they said they would—that I'd been instrumental in obtaining the grant—I told them I'd give them my answer when we returned." She took a deep breath and looked into my eyes. "I told them that I hoped when I was back to New York that we could make it work."

"You want it?"

"I do."

"To travel into the city?"

She sighed. "I can't explain it. Even if we decide it won't work, I did something—me. Because of my help, the Met secured a grant that will help to build replicas that will educate and inform. I'd like to be an even bigger part, but knowing that I was a part... even a small part... it makes me happy." With each word, her eyes radiated her desire. Her need to do more for others emanated from her soul.

She was an angel. Of that I was certain.

I shook my head as I cupped her cheek. "*Mio angelo*, if it makes you happy—whatever it is—I'll never say no. You worked hard. You deserve this."

Her squeal of excitement echoed, scaring a flock of birds, sending them scattering from a palm tree. It also dimmed my dread of facing Carmine, telling him that I'd given my okay while suspecting that he wouldn't approve. He'd worry about her safety traveling into the city. He'd insinuate that I was incapable of providing for her—why else would she work? But for her, I'd stand my ground. This wasn't about money, and when it came to her safety, it was time for him to realize that it was no longer his concern. It was mine.

"I love you," she said.

After wrapping me in a hug, we both lay back in the shade of the cabana. Her dark glasses went over her eyes as she relaxed.

I wasn't quite as tranquil. While the crash of waves filled my ears, many thoughts ran through my brain.

"How would you feel about a driver?" I finally asked.

Time had passed and she appeared near slumber. My angel was lying with her tanned bikini-clad body next to mine. Slowly, at the sound of my question, she lifted her sunglasses and looked my way. "Why? I can take the subway. There's a stop not far from the Met. I've done it many times."

"Because you're my wife."

"And your wife can't take the subway?"

"I have a friend, Franco." A smile came to my lips as I tried to lighten the change in mood. "You probably don't remember him, but he sat beside me in our sophomore English class."

Angelina was now sitting, her sensual legs crossed in front of her. "I only remember you from that class."

"He remembers you. He's worked hard but didn't stay in school. I've known him for a long time, as long as you. He's worked for Vincent and for some of the others. He's loyal. I trust him."

"Was he at the wedding?"

"Not inside."

She nodded knowingly. "Oren... I..."

"Think about it, *mio angelo*, for me. Let me have the peace of mind to know that while you're traveling around the city, you're safe. If I can't be with you, then someone I know is."

"Oren, I don't want to be kept. I've never wanted that."

"Does a kept woman have a job?" I leaned toward her, pushing her gently back to the soft terrycloth lounge cover. "Does a kept woman show the world her incredible knowledge, skills, and intelligence by writing grant proposals and designing stages from history?" I didn't let her answer as my lips captured hers and my bare chest pressed against her, flattening her breasts. "This opportunity means so much to you. I can see pictures in your words. I know that your sketches will be magnificent."

"Oren?"

Finding my way between her now outstretched legs, I held myself over her and continued to pepper her with kisses as my hands began to roam. "Now, tell me, *mio angelo*, does a kept woman have her husband's full adoration as she holds his heart in the palm of her hands?"

"I-I… don't…"

I kissed her again, my kisses moving from her soft pink lips to her exposed neck and collarbone. As her neck stretched and her lips parted, I reiterated, "Not kept, cherished."

Her breasts heaved behind the small triangles of material as she fought not only her rebuttal but her notions.

"*Mio angelo*, you are cherished. A driver?"

Our location was secluded, only the two of us surrounded by trees and water. Whenever the waiter came near, he rang a bell. There'd been no bell. I lowered my kisses to her flat stomach and progressed lower until goose bumps sprung to life in my wake. "Angelina?"

"Oren?"

I moved lower, inch by inch, the taste of saltwater from our recent swim combined with my angel's sun lotion and her magnificent scent on my lips. "For me?"

"Y-yes." Her answer was breathy, dripping with desire. "Yes, a driver."

# CHAPTER 8

—————•○•—————

THROUGH THE WINDOW of the plane, the night sky was filled with glittering snowflakes. White blanketed the ground beyond the plowed wet tarmac. We were back in New York.

"It looks cold," Angelina said.

I simply nodded. The warmth of our honeymoon in paradise was gone. My mind was now filled once again with all the things I needed to do. Our time to spend together was back to the exception more than the rule. However, this would be different; now, we were married.

That should make it better, right?

"*Mio angelo*, we'll go back to our home and get warm."

Her lips curled upward. "I like the sound of that, our home."

Once we collected our suitcases, we stood out on the sidewalk, our breath puffing out clouds. Angelina rubbed her gloved hands together as I assessed the line of taxis. Hordes of people were ready to make their way to the city. Before I was able to hail a cab, I noticed the black sedan slowly moving through the arrival lanes. It was like the night by the jewelry store. Something in my gut told me it wasn't my imagination. We were being watched.

My first instinct was to reach for my gun. It was there, where it belonged in my holster. I'd had to keep it in a locker at the airport during our trip. We'd stopped by the locker to retrieve it, before going for our luggage.

I scanned the crowd. The sidewalk was bustling, even this late on a Saturday night. Pulling a gun wasn't a good idea. Instead, I reached for my wife's hand and pulled her behind me.

"Oren?"

The car came to a stop at the curb. I held my breath as the driver's door opened.

"Demetri," Jimmy De Niro said with a nod.

I simply nodded in return, thankful he was one of Carmine's men. "Wait here," I whispered to Angelina as I took the few steps to the car.

"The boss sent me. He wants you now."

"Carmine?" I asked, knowing the answer as I looked at my watch. "It's nearly ten o'clock."

"Yeah, he said right away."

I tilted my head. "Angelina?"

"Her aunt's waiting."

I took a deep breath and turned back to my wife. "Home will need to wait."

Though she looked disappointed, she didn't say a word as we loaded our suitcases into the trunk of the car and eased our way into the backseat. From our view, we could only see the back of Jimmy's head— his large head. I'd become well acquainted with him during my recent Costello crash course. Known as the enforcer, Jimmy had been with the Costello family since he was young. As a teenager, he started his career running numbers, relaying messages, and taking care of cleanup. It wasn't long before he became more.

I'd yet to see his handiwork and prayed I never would. However, the word on the street was that if you got a knock on the door in the middle of the night and it was Jimmy, your life insurance better be paid up.

From a crewman to a capo, he was advancing through the ranks. It seemed that now he was even being entrusted with Carmine's niece, unless this was the equivalent of a middle-of-the-night interruption—in which case, my gun would be useful.

My thoughts went to the car phones I'd told Angelina about. It would have been good to hear Carmine's voice before getting in the car, reassuring us that it was his plan. Everyone knew that Carmine was skeptical of technology. Vincent and I had discussed it numerous times.

The feds were using technology to hurt the families. Carmine's trust rested in people, not electronics.

Jimmy's eyes occasionally peered into the rearview mirror, looking at me, and then back to the road. Each time he looked, our gazes met. Each look added to my renewed concern.

"I guess I'll be able to tell Aunt Rose about the honeymoon sooner rather than later," Angelina whispered with a forced smile.

I squeezed her gloved hand and returned the faux grin as questions swirled through my thoughts.

*What was happening?*

*Why couldn't it wait?*

White lights flickered in the trees lining the Brooklyn street. Christmas was only a few weeks away. It would be easy for a lost soul to mistake the quiet neighborhood for one like any other. The only indication that the Costello home was special was the multiple cars on the street. To the unknowing neighbor, it would appear as though there was a party within. Yet I wasn't getting a celebratory feeling from our driver.

When Jimmy pulled the sedan close to the curb in front of the Costello brownstone, I stepped out first. Barely a silhouette, I caught a glimpse of Stefano in the shadows. Despite the layer of snow, his dark coat and gloves hid him well. It was the faint mist of his breath hanging in the cold winter's air and reflecting the lights from the porch and trees that gave him away. If I hadn't been looking, he'd have been easy to miss.

I held Angelina's hand as we climbed the tall steps. Our shoes crunched over the salt and deicer. Once at the top, the door opened from within.

"Angel," Bella said, her expression gloomier than her tone.

"What is it?" Angelina asked.

Without giving us time to take off our coats, Bella reached for Angelina's hand. "Come to the kitchen." She turned briefly to me. "He wants you in his office."

Angelina's eyes opened wide as she stared questioningly over her shoulder at me as her cousin-in-law pulled her toward the back of the house.

Respectful of Rose's home, I knocked the snow from my coat and did my best to wipe the frozen mix from my shoes before I made my way down the hallway behind the ladies. The echo of the wood floor faded away as I neared the office. I stood unmoving for a moment, taking in the muffled voices coming from behind the closed door. I couldn't make out the words, yet the urgency of the tones rippled through the air.

Taking a deep breath, I rapped upon the hard door. Immediately, it opened. I recognized the soldier though I didn't know his name.

"Oren," Carmine called from within. "Come in."

The scene could have been from a movie: men in dark suits, a haze of smoke lingering in the air, and a muted hum as all the eyes turned to me. I didn't even think to look for the plastic that I'd joked to myself about on the day I'd asked for Angelina's hand. And yet with the way each man was looking my direction, it should have been on my mind.

I took a step closer to the center of the circle. Carmine was holding court behind his desk. He'd stood when I entered, but now he was again seated. I knew most of the men in the room, mostly by association. They were an elite group: made men. The man to Carmine's right was Carl Gioconda, the Costello consigliere. As the chief advisor, he was often with Carmine or near enough to contact. It wasn't unusual to see him in this house.

I scanned the other faces. Sets of eyes nodded or blinked, yet no one else greeted me verbally. It was then that I realized that Vincent wasn't present. However, Bella was in the kitchen with Angelina. Something wasn't right.

"Sit," Carmine said.

Carl nodded toward me and spoke to Carmine. "In or out?"

"Both." Carmine turned to me. "We won't keep you, Oren. I'm sure you're tired after your trip."

"I'm fine."

"Fine?" he snorted. "Perhaps that will change."

I simply swallowed. There weren't words coming to mind.

"I called you here because you need to know what's happened in your absence."

I nodded.

"After the reception there were words concerning you," Carmine went on.

"Me?"

His hand rose. "Words said in passing. And the way people are, things aren't always the way they seem. I received a call the morning after the wedding from a friend. Tony Mancini overhead a conversation that occurred. There was some talk. And then last week Frankie Russo was questioned by Peterson. He didn't spill, but there're rumors of a grand jury."

I was creating a mental checklist. Tony was one of the Costello capos, one also suspiciously absent from this gathering. I recalled that he'd been at the wedding and the reception. I remembered talking to him. If he overheard something, he overheard it at *my* reception.

Peterson wasn't one of the family. He was a prosecutor, always shooting his mouth off on television, known for his work with RICO: the Racketeer Influenced and Corrupt Organizations Act. Little more than an inconvenience, he was known to dig for the sake of digging.

Russo also wasn't one of the Costellos. He was part of the Luchi family, operating mostly in the Bronx. A few members of the Luchi family had recently been indicted on heroin charges. Their shipments came straight from Sicily. There was a lot of money in that, but thankfully, it was one of Carmine's hard rules. There was enough to be made in other activities; the Costellos didn't promote illegal drug sales. It was another line in the sand.

I nodded. "What did Peterson ask?"

"It's more about what Peterson alluded to knowing."

I shook my head, wishing for one of the first times that I could recall that I was alone with Carmine or maybe Vincent. With a roomful of eyes on me, I wasn't feeling open for discussion.

"You said that this concerns me?"

"It has been said that it does. I don't believe it. I said it doesn't," Carmine's voice was final. However, as he spoke, Carl Gioconda shifted in his chair.

"The questions Peterson asked. No one should know," Gioconda said.

"Who did Mancini overhear?"

"Johnny Bonetti."

I was having trouble keeping up. The Bonettis operated in New Jersey primarily and were also involved with drugs. Narcotics. That was the family whose consigliere, years ago, went over the head of the Bonetti boss and called for the hit on Angelina's parents, Angelo and Gina Costello.

"Johnny was talking about you."

"About me?"

"Oren," Carmine said, interrupting my exchange with Gioconda, "you and Vincent, you both have learned. It was helpful. I need you. Angelina needs you. I want you to work with Vincent, but not so much in plain sight anymore. No more pickups. You did what I wanted. Take Angelina home. I'll see you tomorrow."

It was like seeing the head of a pin. There was more stabbing into the depth, yet I couldn't see any of it without prying the pin from its place. I wasn't in a position to pry it out. And though I didn't understand what had just happened, I replied, "Yes, sir."

As I started to stand, Carmine spoke again. "Vincent's at your place."

"Why?"

"I know it wasn't you. Vincent knows it wasn't you. Johnny, he was fishing, throwing bait in the water—chum—looking for sharks. It's better if you lie low. Work on what you do. Vincent is making sure everything is ready for your return."

"Is there a concern at our home?" My heart was now pumping at twice its normal rhythm. "Should Angelina stay here?"

"No. You're one of us. Vincent set up a crew. For a few days they'll make sure everything is safe. No need to worry."

Right.

Easier said than done.

I was worried, but I couldn't argue with Carmine, especially not in front of everyone. "Yes, sir, I'll get Angelina."

"Jimmy's waiting. He'll drive you home."

The rest of the room remained quiet until I shut the door behind me. As soon as I was in the hallway, I heard what I was sure was Gioconda's voice.

I hadn't had that much contact with the Costello consigliere over the last six months, yet it seemed that I was not on his approved list of Costello visitors. I needed to find out what Johnny Bonetti said and how it related to me—after I ensured that Angelina was safe.

# CHAPTER 9

My throat was dry and my palms moist as I made my way from the office toward the women. Though I knew she was tired from traveling, I liked the tone of Angelina's voice as her story of the waterfalls rang through the air. Once I stepped through the doorway, our eyes met. It was the first time I'd felt like smiling since seeing Jimmy.

"Mrs. Demetri," I said with a tired grin, "let's go home."

"You're done… with…?" The unfinished question hung in the air.

"For now."

As I waited for Angelina, lifting her wool coat from the back of the chair where she had it draped, Rose stood and placed her hand on my cheek.

"You're a good man, Oren Demetri. We know that."

"Thank you, Rose."

"You love our Angel."

My gaze went from Rose to Angelina. "I do."

"Go home. We'll see you in the morning at Mass and then dinner here. That's what family does."

"Yes, ma'am," I answered without first checking if Angelina agreed. I wanted to come back in the morning. I wanted to sit in Carmine's office with only him and Vincent. Maybe I'd get answers that I wasn't getting tonight.

"I don't know what's going on," Angelina whispered as we neared the front door.

"I don't either. Hopefully we'll learn something from Vincent."

"Vincent?"

"Apparently, he's at our house."

"Bella only said he was out. I'm surprised he wasn't in that meeting or whatever it was."

"*Whatever* is right. I'm not sure what it was either."

Angelina just shook her head as we stepped into the cold. Jimmy opened his car door on cue and stepped back to open the one to the backseat as we approached.

My wife and I didn't speak during our short ride to our home. I was certain that by what we'd said and her expression she was as confused as I. Discussing any of it in the presence of Jimmy De Niro didn't seem like a good idea.

The ride through the slushy streets wasn't long. Our brownstone was only a few streets over from her family's home. We'd walked it many times. I hadn't bought that house because of the proximity to the Costellos, but it was convenient. However, the more I thought about Vinny being in our home uninvited, the more I reconsidered my assessment. Maybe convenient wasn't the right word.

The Windsor Terrace area was a good neighborhood in Brooklyn, better than where I'd been raised. Definitely a step up. I'd lived in this borough my entire life. So had Angelina. It was home, and it would be for a while.

Currently, most of the money Demetri earned went back into the company, buying more, increasing the reach. That didn't mean that I didn't have dreams of better, of more. One day, I wanted to move Angelina beyond where we'd been and out of the city. She deserved more.

It's a strange almost indescribable sensation, approaching one's home after being gone for two weeks and finding the windows filled with light. Yet that was exactly what caught my attention as Jimmy eased into an open parking space one house down from ours. Stepping from the car, I looked up. Even coming from the second floor of our brownstone was golden illumination leaking from behind the blinds and new drapes.

"Vinny?" Angelina asked.

"Probably. Let me go in first," I said as I opened the small wrought-iron gate leading to our stairs. I turned and nodded to Jimmy. He was standing beside the car ready, in position to protect Angelina from behind if needed. It was right for me to protect her from the front.

Reaching into my coat, I eased my gun from the holster and flipped the safety.

"It's just Vinny," Angelina said, this time with more confidence.

I didn't respond, hoping she was right. Nevertheless, I couldn't shake the odd feeling I'd had since Jimmy found us at the airport. Two weeks wasn't long enough to be away—I'd love to take her back to the security of paradise—and yet at the same time, it was too long. Things could obviously change in an instant.

I turned the knob or tried to. It didn't budge. With my free hand, I slid the key into the lock. Turning it, I pushed and opened the door within.

"Hello?" My voice echoed off the wood as I scanned the foyer.

Footsteps came closer as I lifted my pistol.

"Whoa," Vincent said as he turned the corner, coming face-to-face with the business end of my firearm. "Nice greeting."

I lowered my gun. "You alone?"

"It doesn't matter." *I'm family. You trust me.* He didn't say the last two phrases, but they were there.

It did matter if he were alone in our home or if he'd brought strangers with him. None of this was right.

Angelina came up beside me. Tilting her head toward the street, she said, "Vinny, what a nice surprise." She lifted her hand in a wave. "Thanks for the ride, Jimmy."

Angelina gave Vincent a quick embrace as I turned the safety back on and secured my gun. Pulling our suitcases inside that Jimmy had carried up the steps, I closed and locked the door.

"Are you alone?" I asked again, wanting an answer.

"Yes, inside."

"What's happening?" Angelina asked.

He didn't respond to her; instead, looking at me, he asked, "Pop told you?"

"A riddle. He told me a riddle."

He looked back at Angelina. "Did you see Bella?"

"Yes. She seems tired and overly emotional. You should go back and take her home."

As we hung our coats on the coat tree, Vinny grinned for the first time since our reunion began. Walking back to the kitchen, he said, "She's a bundle of hormones."

"What? She's pregnant!" Angelina exclaimed, wrapping her cousin in a hug. "She didn't tell me."

"Yeah. Just found out. I'm not supposed to say anything. Mom and Pop know and her parents. But…" He nodded at Angelina. "…family. I trust you won't say nothing."

Releasing himself from his cousin's embrace, Vincent sat at the table and leaned the chair back on two legs.

*Sure. Make yourself at home.*

This was ridiculous. I wanted to spend the evening with my wife in our home for the first time. Instead, Vincent Costello was sitting at my kitchen table with an open beer, undoubtedly from my refrigerator.

"What happened?" I asked.

"Angel," Vincent said, "can you give Bella a call? Tell her I'll be there soon."

Her lips flattened into a straight line. "Go ahead, Vinny, just say you don't want to talk in front of me. That you don't want me to hear what you have to say. Tell me I don't need to know."

"It's not your worry."

"If it's my husband's—"

She stopped. Her lips came together and neck straightened as she inhaled.

Angelina hadn't stopped questioning because I said anything, and I doubt it was because of the look Vincent was giving her. I'd suspect Angelina stopped trying for information because it's what she knew, what she'd lived all her life. She understood that it was a losing battle. If whatever I learned was something I could share, I would. But neither of us would learn anything if she didn't leave.

"Fine," she said. "Do you really want me to call her?"

"Yeah, she worries about everything lately. Let her know I won't be long."

"I'll use the phone in the bedroom."

I suddenly recalled the lights I'd noticed coming from the second floor. "Have you walked upstairs?" I asked Vincent.

"I did. Angel's really done a lot. Place looks great."

I nodded, still not thrilled with his invasion, but happy to know the house was clear.

Before Angelina disappeared, Vincent called, "Angel, thanks. Bella does like to get updates—to know that I'm good."

She smiled with a nod as she disappeared down the hall.

Once Angelina's footsteps faded away at the top of the stairs, Vincent leaned forward. All four feet of the chair came to the floor with a thud. "Not that I don't enjoy our time together, but I'd rather be with Bella, and I suspect you'd like to be upstairs." Before I could respond, he went on. "So let me cut to the chase. Mancini claimed he overheard a conversation at the wedding reception. He said he heard Johnny Bonetti mention that you'd helped him out of a jam. Took a balloon and cleaned it using the liquor store on Carroll. Bragging how you helped him in a pinch."

"I haven't."

"Then Peterson referred to that same store when he questioned Russo."

I shook my head. "It's true that I own a chunk of that store. It's in Costello territory. Why the hell would anyone think I'd run Bonetti money through there?"

"Exactly. Luchi started asking questions on the street after Russo was questioned. Wanted to know more about the store. Wanted to know how the feds knew about it—I mean, fuck, there's a store on every damn corner of every fucking block and they ask about one with your name on the deed. He wondered if you were helping or double-crossing Johnny."

My head was spinning as I sat. It was all I could do to keep my lips closed.

"He also wondered if it wasn't a double cross," Vincent went on, "why you, the newest member of the Costello family, why you'd be cleaning dough for Bonetti and how he could get in on the action. Like cackling hens, one starts squawking, and pretty soon it's a damn barnyard. Gioconda took bits and pieces and weaved it together to come up with a conspiracy. He wanted you called on the carpet."

I shook my head. "We're gone for two fucking weeks, and everyone's gone mad."

"It's no secret that Gioconda has had a stick up his ass since you proposed to Angel. He doesn't know you, which means he doesn't trust you. He's looking for a beef."

I was beginning to understand more of Carmine's reasons behind Vincent's and my recent time together. It wasn't just my crash course; it was Carmine's proof to Gioconda. Vincent was my spokesperson, my personal public relations—make that, family relations—representative.

"Thank you." I meant it. This was new to me. Yes, I'd grown up around it—in it—but not as a part of Cosa Nostra. I had the right blood—ancestors from Sicily—and according to Rose Costello, the right religious affiliation, but that didn't make me much different than any other Italian-American in New York. From Carl Gioconda's perspective, there was nothing ensuring my allegiance, nothing other than my marriage that connected me to the Costello family. Apparently, Carmine had named Vincent my other connection—my tether.

Vincent simply nodded at my gratitude.

"Why didn't your father say more tonight, explain any of this?"

"I'm sure he will."

That wasn't encouraging.

"But," Vincent went on, "you were called to the table tonight for one reason. It wasn't to call you on the carpet though I'd bet that balloon that was exactly what Gioconda expected was going to happen. Pop called everyone who's important into his office for the show. You were the main attraction."

A balloon was a thousand dollars. I'd take Vincent's balloon and see him another, except I agreed. Gioconda was obviously unhappy with the way things went down. Taking a deep breath, I stood up and looked around my kitchen. Maybe a beer wasn't a bad idea.

"Listen," Vincent said. "This isn't like the businesses you showed me. It doesn't work like that. There's no board of directors, no negotiation. Right now, the only opinion that matters is Pop's. You were in his office tonight because he wanted everyone in that room to know that he trusts you. He's standing behind you. Church tomorrow and dinner. It's a message. You and Angel will sit with the four of us in the pew. One big happy family."

"Okay. We've sat together before."

"But now it's different. Now she's got your name. It's official."

*Why did it feel more like I had her name?*

I was still trying to process everything I'd heard. Though the queasy feeling hadn't gone away, there was relief in hearing Vincent's words.

Finally, I concentrated on the positive. "Your father believes in me."

"Hasn't had a reason not to. You don't plan on giving him one... do you?"

"I wasn't planning on it."

"You know," Vincent said, "the only other way to make this more official."

"This? My marriage?"

Vincent stood and laid his hand on my shoulder. "Knock her up."

I had to laugh. "Thanks for the advice. I thought the priest and crowd at the church, oh and the license we signed..." I lifted my left hand. "...the rings. I thought all of that shit made it official."

"Hey, it's not like I'm asking you to head to a drop. Besides, putting a bun in the oven's not as tiring as bagman for the late-night action." He wiggled his brows. "The late night is the same. Just more fun."

Concentrating more on what he wasn't asking me to do, I said, "So that's done?" I was asking about being a bagman.

"For now. Mancini's accusation has Pop thinking about the possibilities. Work on Demetri Enterprises. Let us assign someone else to collect taxes. You do the legal shit, doing what you do. You own buildings. If you're not there, how do you know what goes on in the backroom? Stay away from the gambling. Focus on legit. Concentrate on the bigger fish. From what you showed me, the construction and real estate are the fucking whales. Make sure the books are spotless. Keep everything clean while Peterson snoops around. He'll get bored and move on. The feds always do. They want their names in the fucking paper—Giuliani's minions. Don't give Peterson anything to take to that rat.

"Gioconda's issue will help you with Peterson," Vincent went on. "Let the prosecutor see you at church, Sunday dinner, and drinks at Evviva's. It ain't a crime. Then, when the time's right, we'll look into other opportunities."

Fuck, the queasiness was back with a vengeance.

"Okay." I wanted the legit side. I always had. "What about outside?" I tilted my head toward the window.

"Pop wants to make sure everything quiets down. He made his stand tonight with the family. None of them would be stupid enough to go against him. That still leaves the Bonettis and Luchis in this mix. It doesn't seem like this is worth starting another war over, but if one of them assholes thinks it is, you're protected. Your house is being watched."

I recalled the Met. "Do you remember Franco Testa?"

"Yeah."

"I'm thinking about hiring him."

"In what capacity?" Vincent asked.

"Angelina's driver. I don't like her being by herself."

He nodded. "You trust him?"

"Hell, I don't know who I can trust."

"Let me ask around," Vincent said. "Testa's done some jobs for me. He's been on Morelli's crew for years. Longevity is a good thing. If he's as good as I think he is, it sounds like he's getting a promotion."

"Thanks… for everything."

"Don't make me regret it."

"Like I mentioned," I said as I led Vincent toward the front door. "I don't plan on it." I patted his shoulder. "Congratulations on the kid."

"I wasn't lying about the hormones. You'll see soon enough."

As I locked the door, I had too many things on my mind to consider that he might be right.

# CHAPTER 10

SUNDAYS CAME AND went as we sat in the same pew near the front of the cathedral, listening as Father Mario talked about the trappings of this world and extolled the path to heaven. He encouraged confession of sins. I often wondered as I gazed around the congregation at the men seated about me if Father Mario could handle the truth that could be revealed behind the curtain.

*Were the sins forgivable? Could saying a Hail Mary make up for the things that were done?*

One thing was certain: if Father Mario did listen to all of the sins of the members of the congregation, his schedule would be fuller than mine.

Christmas came, and the New Year was upon us.

Each Sunday after Mass, the six of us would head to the Costello brownstone. Vincent and I'd join Carmine in his office as the women prepared our feast. I didn't select that word lightly. Sunday meals were more than a dinner, more than a supper. They consisted of course after course of the most delectable food ever known to man.

Truly, if we were being watched by anyone besides the soldiers patrolling the exterior, on most Sunday afternoons and into evening, our greatest crime was gluttony.

It was a Sunday afternoon in January, with only Vincent as my witness, that I broached the subject of Angelina's new driver and more importantly, the reason.

"I'd like to hire Franco Testa as Angelina's driver."

Carmine's dark eyes lifted from whatever he'd been studying on his desk and peered at me through the smoky haze of his cigar. "You think Angel needs a driver?"

I supposed I should be happy that he didn't mince words.

"Yes. She accepted a part-time position in the city working at the Metropolitan Museum."

"You allowed this?"

Though internally I was running a marathon, externally, I was pleased to see that the glass of whiskey in my hand was ripple free. "Yes. She worked hard to get it. I want her happy."

"She's not happy as a wife?"

I didn't turn his way, but Vincent's deep exhale signaled I was in for a tongue-lashing or at least a difficult road. "She is. Of course, when children come she'll be home, but now I'm gone a lot. She has her degrees and wants to use them."

He leaned back and eyed me up and down. "Is it money?"

"With the addition of Testa to my payroll, her job will cost more than it earns. It's not about money."

"Part-time?"

This was ridiculous. Angelina was my wife. I was simply requesting the hire of one of Carmine's soldiers, advancing him from Morelli's crew to a driver and bodyguard. "Yes, sir."

"You say she worked hard for this? Yet it happened in the last month... since your honeymoon?"

"Sir," I began, unsure how much to tell him and not throw Angelina to the wolves—one wolf. "It began at NYU. It continued in Italy. Angelina is more than beautiful. She's intelligent and talented. This job is designing sets for the Met. The people there see her for what she is."

"A Costello."

"A Demetri," I corrected, "who will help them by utilizing the knowledge she's acquired over the last decade of her life. She's already helped them by securing a grant." I placed my whiskey on the table beside the chair and leaned forward. "I admit to being busy, but her desire to work isn't new."

"She doesn't need to work."

"She doesn't. She wants to." It was a good thing that I wasn't connected to a stress test or EKG. If I were, it would be sparking from the speed my heart was racing.

Vincent nodded and added, "She used to go to the city to the museum a lot."

"She's always liked that stuff," Carmine added.

"Yes, sir." I didn't tell them that the reason of her recent visits was that she was applying or interviewing for the position.

"It sounds like you've already made a decision. Yet you come to me?"

"Out of respect. Angelina and I made the decision together. I think it would be better for her to have someone with her. She's content to take the subway. I'm not. Her safety is my number one concern. I've known Testa since NYU. He's on Morelli's crew. I won't ask for him if you don't approve of him leaving the crew to work for me. Or if you have a better suggestion."

"Than her working? I can think of a few." When I didn't respond, his lips came together as he leaned back, rocking his large chair. Finally, he looked to Vincent. "You knew?"

His head bobbed. "I knew Oren wanted to hire Angelina a driver. It got me thinking about Bella. Now that she's carrying my kid, I don't think having someone there when we can't be is a bad idea."

"Your mother, she's never had a driver."

"Pop, she has you or Jimmy. She has for years. Before Jimmy, there was Rocco."

"They drive me." Carmine seemed to reflect for a moment upon his recent response. "And her." His hand came down upon the desk. "Work! A woman working. I don't understand that. Rosa, she has been satisfied to be a wife and a mother… and an aunt."

There was no more to say. I lifted the glass and took a drink of the amber liquid, the rich bold flavor heating my lips, tongue, and throat.

"Vincent," Carmine finally said, "talk to Morelli. Make sure he can handle the loss. Make sure his crew can fill in." Carmine raised his chin toward me, his jaw tight. "Safety. I'm glad you're thinking of her safety."

"Always."

"I don't like it, but our Angel has always been strong-willed."

"Yes, sir." I slowly let out the breath I'd been holding. I wasn't sure that discussion went any better than I imagined, but it hadn't gone worse.

"It's why you're here," Vincent said to me with a grin.

I nodded, returning his smile.

The subject at hand changed, letting me know that the decision had been made. I'd talk to Vincent later and learn when he would talk to Morelli. In reality, Angelina's job had already started. I'd just rearranged my schedule, taking her to the Met and meeting her once her day was done. I liked having the time together in the morning and evening, but it wasn't always practical. By the time I reached my office, there were usually twenty urgent messages.

Now with the new technology I'd bought, I could make telephone calls from my car. The car phone consisted of a bag on the floorboard of the sedan with a handset attached by a cord and an antenna that clipped to the window. The mornings I didn't have Angelina with me turned my commute into productive work time. That wasn't possible with her at my side.

The nice part of my schedule over the last month had been the return to mostly Demetri Enterprises. Doing as Vincent had said, that was where my energy was focused. If Peterson were looking into my holdings, he was doing it without my knowledge. I was learning the ins and outs of keeping my business secure. It was difficult to be ahead of the feds, but any business needed security. There were firewalls and secure servers.

There'd been a few subpoenas for appearance before a recently convened grand jury. They'd been issued to all members of the Luchi family. The focus was heroin.

If I'd dodged a bullet with the shift in my attention, I was grateful. If I'd simply had my name thrown out there to bring Gioconda's eyes to me, I'd take it. I'd work hard and avoid losing the trust that Carmine had given me.

# CHAPTER 11

—•○•—

Time continued to move, and the weather began to warm. Sprigs of green popped from dead branches, forming leaves on the trees outside our brownstone, a sign that life was renewing. It turned out that new leaves weren't the only sign.

I'd made it home in time for dinner. On the days that my angel didn't work, I tried. She wasn't necessarily alone all day. Besides her aunt living near, Bella and Vincent's home wasn't far away, as well as other cousins who lived close to us. After all, this was where she'd been raised. She had friends and family all around the neighborhood. Each time we saw Bella, Angelina would fawn over her growing midsection. I hadn't really paid attention to all the changes that occurred during pregnancy. But that was all about to change.

I wouldn't say that coming home to dinner cooking on the stove was the best part of marriage. There were many perks. I'd take having Angelina in my bed as number one. However, anyone who knew what it was like to come home to an empty house and has a stomach would agree that opening the door to the savory aroma of something cooking was fucking fantastic. They say that some of the strongest memories were tied to our sense of smell. All I knew, without a doubt, was that opening the door to a cloud of deliciousness was second only to the pleasure of having her beside me in our bed.

In the few months since we'd married, I'd become like Pavlov's dog. My mouth watered in anticipation as I ascended the stairs. As I opened the door, I realized it wasn't only the smell, but the noise too. An empty house was too quiet. Once I entered, I stood and listened. A television played from the back of the house as dishes rattled. I couldn't help the rising of my cheeks as my grin grew. This was what I'd always wanted. I hung my coat on the hall tree and walked softly down the hallway.

There was an old heavy door that swung both directions to close off the kitchen. We never closed it, leaving the room open to the rest of the house. In the summer, having it closed made the kitchen too hot. The rest of the year, the warmth from the stove helped heat the rest of the house. Standing in the doorframe, I stopped and took in my wife, my presence not yet registering to Angelina.

Each day was like the one before; she continually took my breath away. In blue jeans, stocking feet, and a soft pink sweater that hung lower than her ass, with her hair piled on her head, she was stunning. Her attention was on the evening news as she tapped her fingernails on the counter.

It took me a second to realize that she was upset. I saw it in the way her shoulders quaked. Could she be crying?

*Had something happened?*

I was too busy with everyday life to worry about world events, and yet I knew that often news of family doings would first be brought to light by some reporter on the street. I came up behind her. *"Mio angelo."* My hands grasped her shoulders as I leaned closer. Her perfume was light with a hint of jasmine. Its sweet scent replaced whatever she was cooking as I kissed her cheek. "What's happened?"

She shook her head, her muscles going lax as she melted against me, her back to my chest. "Oren…"

My name disappeared as her face fell forward.

I spun her around and lifted her chin. Her blue eyes were red, as if she'd been crying for a while. Wrapping my arms around her, I held her, unsure of what had happened or how to fix it. Finally, her muscles found the ability to support herself as she stood taller.

I tilted my head toward the small television. "Did something happen?"

"There's always something happening."

She was right, but that didn't answer my question. "*Mio angelo*, talk to me."

Her breasts pushed against me as she inhaled and feigned a smile. "I made you lasagna."

"I love your lasagna."

"I know. I was hoping it might help."

I grinned. "Baby, have I ever told you that you have your uncle's ability to talk in riddles?"

She shook her head. As she did, her eyes closed, and more tears trickled out.

Taking her hand, I tugged her toward the kitchen table, encouraging her to sit. With our knees touching, I continued to hold her hand. "Does this have to do with your family or another? Is Bella all right?"

"She's good. Everyone. It has to do with everyone, and I don't know how I never realized it. But it does, Oren. Oh my God, it does, and it scares me so much."

My neck straightened as the small hairs on my neck stood to attention. "What scares you? Tell me. I'll take care of it."

She let go of my hand and stood. "You can't." Her hands slapped the side of her thighs. "I should have realized it with Bella, but I didn't. We haven't… the church said… and now… now it's too late."

She was the love of my life, and she was driving me fucking nuts. "Angelina. Stop talking like Carmine. Tell me what has you upset and scared."

More tears as she turned a small circle. "I'm scared, but I'm also happy."

"What are you talking about?" My question came out louder than I intended.

"Oren, I'm pregnant. We're going to have a baby."

"A-a baby?" Though words were difficult to say through my shock and confusion, I sprung from the chair and again reached for her shoulders. I needed to see her eyes, wanting a visual confirmation of what she'd just said.

Angelina nodded, her cheeks rising as she continued to cry through her brightening smile. "You can't fix it," she said with a giggle. "You're kind of responsible."

"Kind of?"

The smile before me dimmed. "I mean, you didn't do it alone. I was there too."

I continued to stare.

"Say something."

"I'm at a loss," I admitted. "I'm thrilled. But now I'm also worried. Are you all right? Why are you scared? Isn't this what we wanted?"

"Yes, we did… do," Angelina said. "I just didn't expect it to happen so soon. There are so many things. I'm just getting started with my job. I don't want Bella to think we're trying to take anything away from them. I suppose since we weren't trying to *not* get pregnant, I shouldn't be surprised."

I wiped the tears from her cheeks, remembering Vincent's warning about hormones. "*Mio angelo*, I'm happy. As long as you're safe and healthy, I'm thrilled." I turned toward the stove and oven. "I don't need lasagna to lighten the blow. However, I'm not sad you made it." I really looked at her—my gaze zeroing in on every inch of her. "Are you feeling okay? Have you been sick?"

She nodded and then shook her head. "I'm feeling fine. I didn't realize that I was pregnant until I started thinking about my period. It was then I realized I was late. I haven't felt sick at all. I bought the test this afternoon. It said to wait until morning, but I couldn't wait." She shrugged. "It was positive. I've been waiting for you to come home, praying you wouldn't call and say something came up."

"Only you."

As we ate her delicious dinner, we talked. I understood that it was all new, and to be honest, I was fucking scared to death—terrified—but that didn't answer my question about her fears. That answer didn't come right away.

We waited to tell the rest of the family until after she saw her doctor. It wasn't that I didn't believe my wife or the little stick-thing with the positive indicator, but that didn't confirm our growing baby like the sound of swoosh-swoosh from an ultrasound over a week later.

At that first appointment, the doctor said Angelina wasn't far enough along to hear a heartbeat with a regular stethoscope or the thing he could put against her stomach. The ultrasound confirmed what she'd known. Together we watched the screen. Though the image was fuzzy and didn't look like a baby, the doctor said it was. We had a child growing inside her. Near the end of the year, barely past our first anniversary, we'd have a new little Demetri.

It was about two weeks after the appointment that I finally got answers. I'd finished having Thursday night drinks at Evviva's, an out-of-the-way Italian restaurant in Little Italy where the Costello family met weekly like clockwork. It was my recurring command performance. I hadn't missed one Thursday night since we returned from our honeymoon. It was part of what Vincent had said: church, Sunday dinner, *drinks*...

Thursdays, upstairs in the restaurant, was more of a roll call. The important business was handled later in private after some of us left. It always followed. I was there for dinner and drinks, but mostly because Carmine wanted it known that I was welcome. It was my sole appearance at Costello business gatherings. I didn't run errands or pick up bags any longer. I was keeping my books clean, doing what I was told.

Though I'd been following the rules, I hadn't earned the right to continue the meeting in the basement. That was for the made men, the same men who'd stared me down in Carmine's home office. Gioconda was there, as was Vincent, Jimmy, Mancini, Morelli and more.

After I hired Testa, Morelli gave me a hard time about stealing one of his best men. We both knew that as long as Angelina was secure at home or work, Testa would still be running errands and jobs for Morelli. It was just that now Angelina was his primary concern.

I paid him well to keep her his priority.

As I approached our home that night, I became acutely aware of the foul cloud surrounding my clothes. Though I hadn't smoked at Evviva's, I was in the minority. My jacket reeked of cigars and cigarettes. I'd become more aware of it with Angelina's recent sensitivity to certain scents. Removing my jacket, I stood outside on the stoop and shook it before entering the house. I planned to leave it in the foyer, but still it could use a good airing out.

In the short time since we'd learned she was pregnant, I'd come to expect any possible mood when I arrived home or perhaps a combination of a few. There was truly no way to predict. Sometimes she was exhausted and napping. Other times she was sad or happy or both. There were certain commercials on the television that were guaranteed tearjerkers.

I'd never noticed them before. Now that they incited waterworks, I had to wonder why.

Did causing pregnant women to cry truly entice sales?

"How was the meeting?" Angelina asked from the living room as I entered. She was wearing an old sweatshirt with a blanket over her legs as she sat curled up near the end of the sofa.

I couldn't stop my smile. The TV image the old shows used to portray of a wife meeting her husband at the door, a drink in one hand and wearing a dress and heels, oh, and a pearl necklace, was about as far from my reality as day from night. I wouldn't have wanted it any other way. "Drinks," I corrected.

"Yeah, right. How were *drinks*?"

"I had Coke."

She smiled and shook her head. "And you say I talk in riddles?"

I sat heavily beside her with a sigh. This was what I adored: quiet time together.

Angelina had turned down the volume of the television when I entered. Technology was amazing. It was no longer necessary to walk to the television to adjust the volume or change the channel. Though the remote was connected by a long cord, it reached to where Angelina sat. I gave her a kiss. "I missed having dinner with you."

"It was just leftovers," she said. "There's more if you want some."

"No," I said, putting my arm along the top of the sofa and my feet up on the coffee table. "I'm good just sitting here with you."

"Do you want a real drink?" she asked. "I'd love a glass of wine. And even though the doctor said one now and then wouldn't hurt, I think I'll stick with water."

She had a glass sitting beside her.

"I'm good. Let me just drink you in."

Her smile broadened, and then it wilted as her neck stiffened. "Oren, I've been thinking. Do you think it can be broken?"

"What?"

"The chain."

"The chain?" I asked.

"Yes."

*Fucking riddles.*

She turned her piercing blue stare my direction. "I keep thinking about our baby. I keep thinking about my parents, Uncle Carmine and Aunt Rose, Vincent and Bella, and their baby." With each word her eyes glistened, yet her voice was strong and determined. "The news on TV... I want to break the chain." She took a deep breath and reached for my free hand. "I'm sorry. I know you're here getting deeper and deeper involved with Uncle Carmine because of me. But what if our baby is a boy?"

My lips curled upward. "That would be fine. So would a girl." I didn't care.

"No."

"*Mio angelo*, I know I promised you that I'd give you your heart's desire, but I don't think anyone but God can decide our baby's gender. Yes, biologically the burden falls to me, but I didn't exactly make a decision to produce only daughters, nor do I think that's possible."

It was her turn to smile. "I mean, no, I don't want our son to be involved in the family business, and I don't mean Demetri Enterprises. If we have a son, I want him to have the love and support of my family— they're good people—but I want that without the obligation."

While there were those who'd disagree with her assessment of her family's goodness—for good reason—I wasn't one of them. The Costellos had accepted me. They'd done it for Angelina, yet they'd done it. Even tonight's command appearance was part of that ongoing recognition. "I agree, they are good people. But..."

"Tonight, a few minutes ago on the news, they said Donatello Cirelli was arrested. They showed him in handcuffs being led into the police station."

Don was another of the Luchi men. The heroin was their downfall. "You shouldn't worry; the Luchis are—"

"But I do," she interrupted.

"You know your uncle has rules about the drugs. Besides, from what I hear, the Luchis are being too bold. Acting like they're untouchable. If Don was arrested, I'd suspect they have RICO evidence."

"Oren, if this baby is a boy, I don't want him to be part of this. It needs to stop. I want him to have choices that Vincent never had."

"Vincent isn't unhappy."

"No, because he never imagined anything different. He's been in jail. He never went to college. You and I did. Promise me that we can give our son something different than this..." She pointed to the television.

On the screen, there was a blonde woman pointing to a map and talking about a warm air front coming in from the west. Nevertheless, I was certain Angelina wasn't talking about the weather. In her mind, she was still seeing Donatello Cirelli in handcuffs. I'd promised her the world on a platter, but I couldn't promise her this. "I can agree that together we can try."

She sighed as she settled against my side. "You asked me what scares me. This is what scares me."

# CHAPTER 12

———●○●———

THE WARM FRONT came and stayed. Flowers bloomed and leaves grew bigger. A green canopy grew over the street in front of our brownstone. With each day, the heat continued to climb, taking us from spring to sweltering summer. During the day, children opened fire hydrants and played in the cool flowing water in the streets. Adults turned up fans to high and opened windows, attempting to circulate the stifling, sticky air.

Demetri Enterprises was increasing its reach despite the nagging omnipresent concerns within the families. It wasn't only the feds that were causing friction; there was also growing unrest between and within the families. Though at first I'd been put off by Gioconda's distrust of me, in hindsight I realized it had been a blessing. I'd been able to spend the last six months concentrating on what I knew, planting and growing businesses encompassed within my Demetri umbrella.

Money begot money. The more revenue that Demetri made, the more it invested.

As the weather warmed, so did my prospects for ventures. I traveled about the city meeting with clients, and even more came to me in my air-conditioned office.

Our home was different. Seeing Angelina's waist expand as our baby grew within her while her beautiful face glowed with the sheen of perspiration made me even more determined to provide more. She deserved a home with central air conditioning.

She deserved more than I was providing. I tried to do what I could. I offered to help around the house, but often I left for the city early in the morning and didn't return until dinner or many times late at night. Things would happen. Fires needed dousing. Oftentimes, I'd unexpectedly be called to one of my businesses or perhaps a command performance with Vincent or Carmine. I never knew for sure what my plans would include. When they'd change, I'd try to remember to call Angelina; however, admittedly, that wasn't always the case. It would be my intention, a fleeting thought, and then after a meeting ran long or I received an unexpected telephone call, I'd look at the clock and realize I'd missed dinner.

My angel liked bright flowers. Daisies were my go-to apology. I tried to keep it to one bouquet a week. If she received flowers every time I was late or missed a meal, our house would look like a florist or damn funeral home.

"*Mio angelo,*" I said into the phone one evening in late July. Resting my head upon my hands, with my elbows on the desk, I ran my fingers through my dark hair and awaited her response. At first there was nothing. I wondered if the call had disconnected.

Understandably, she was upset. It was the second dinner I'd missed in less than a week. We may have been married for less than a year, but I was experienced enough to know she'd be angry.

Finally, she spoke, "I know what you're going to say." The fact that she didn't say hello didn't go unnoticed. "You're going to tell me that you're going to be late."

My skin chilled at the sound of her voice. Instead of anger, I heard nothing—her tone was devoid of emotion. I would have preferred her Costello temper.

"I figured that out," she went on, "about two hours ago. Don't worry about dinner. It's gone."

"I'm sorry. I received…"

My apology lingered as my ear was met with the steady dial tone.

I'd wanted to tell her about the counteroffer I'd received on the building site. I'd told her about the real estate opportunity. She knew it would mean big things for us and for Demetri Enterprises. I missed dinner because of the last-minute negotiations. And then we agreed, and my latest offer was accepted. There were still contracts to sign and red tape to unravel, but in a gentleman's agreement, it was secure. I'd spent a lot of time on the back and forth. It was truly a coup for Demetri—for us.

Instead of saying any of that, I sighed, shook my head, and hung up the phone.

I could call again, but there was a good chance she wouldn't answer. Even though I was disappointed that I didn't get the chance to share the news, I reminded myself that I'd also disappointed her. I'd do something to make it up.

My first thought was flowers, but there was already a bouquet on the kitchen counter. Maybe I could come up with something else?

I made a mental note to stop somewhere and pick up a gift on my way home. If I hurried, I'd find a street vender open somewhere between here and home. As I contemplated the best possibilities, there was a knock on my office door. Almost simultaneously, it opened. I saw her blonde hair first.

"Mr. Demetri," my secretary, Lisa, said, as she entered, "I'm going to head home, unless you need anything else?"

I looked down at my clock. "Lisa, it's after eight o'clock. You should've left hours ago."

Her shoulders shrugged as her bright red lips pursed. Lisa was exactly the type of woman I noticed before Angelina. She was always dolled up to a T. From eight in the morning to eight at night her hair never moved. It was, for lack of a better description, big. I was certain there was another name for it, but *big* worked. Fluffy? The way women's hair looked on television. Her skirts were tight and blouses flattering. Her high-heeled shoes usually matched her jewelry, often in bright colors. She showed just enough to entice, but not too much to appear unprofessional. It was impossible for my clients not to take a look. Many often turned and gave me 'that' look.

"I don't mind," she said. "Really, I don't. I wanted to wait until Mr. Feinstein left. I'm assuming you finalized the deal?"

I tilted my head.

"I'm sorry," Lisa said. "I'm not being nosy. It's just that… well, I know you've been working on this for a while. I made copies of the papers for him. That's going to be a great investment."

While I considered commenting that it wasn't her place and I wasn't in the habit of taking business advice from secretaries, I realized that if only momentarily, I was happy about the deal, and it was nice to be able to talk about the success to someone. "Of course, you'd know what's happening," I said. "Yes, we did come to an agreement. Those papers were only preliminary. It all has to go through legal, but it's looking good."

Her smile grew. "I'm so happy for you."

"Thank you, Lisa—"

Before I could tell her again to go, she spoke, coming closer. "I finished typing the letters you wanted to go out tomorrow. If you could sign these, I can have them in the mail first thing in the morning." She handed me a small stack of papers, her perfume preceding her as she came nearer, a deeper musky scent than what Angelina used to wear before scents became an issue.

Angelina's had been light and floral. It was almost like it wasn't there, yet it was. I may not have even realized it was perfume were it not that now it was gone.

Inhaling the heavy too-sweet scent, I took the letters from Lisa's grasp and began to sign at the bottom of each page, scanning what she'd written. Each one was the same, exactly as I'd dictated. When I looked up, Lisa was still near, but turned away, looking out the window at the dark night.

This office was better located than the one that previously housed Demetri Enterprises. No longer in Brooklyn, my new corporate office was in the city. That may sound impressive, but New York was big. This wasn't the real estate of a successful company. It was the placement of an up-and-coming business. One day, Demetri would be high in the sky in the financial district.

I believed that.

The view that Lisa was staring out to was nothing spectacular.

"Lisa?"

"Hmm?" she said as she turned. "Oh, I'm sorry. I didn't realize how dark it had gotten."

"That's why you shouldn't stay here this late. Are you parked close by?" I don't know why I hadn't thought of that before. I wouldn't want Angelina in the city this late.

She shook her head, her large earrings bobbing as she moved. Her brightly painted lip disappeared behind her teeth. "I don't have a car. I never learned to drive. It's all right. The subway is close."

"You shouldn't take the subway this late, not by yourself."

She smiled though I could tell it wasn't real. It was her mouth, but her eyes were thinking about something else. "I'll be fine, Mr. Demetri. I'd better go." She turned and took a step before stopping. Looking back my way, she went on, "I hope you celebrate your success tonight. You deserve it. Are you sure you don't need anything?"

"No, I should be going too."

"Do you think…?" She stopped.

"Do I think what?"

"I hate to ask, but it is so dark. Do you think that if you're leaving, you could give me a ride home?"

Her question caught me off guard. Assuring her safety was the right thing to do, but yet it didn't feel right. I stood, reached for my wallet, and pulled out a twenty-dollar bill. "I need to get home. I'm already late. Here, call a cab. Keep the rest and if this happens again, use it."

Her cheeks flushed as she took a step closer, looking at the bill in my hand. "No, I shouldn't."

"Nonsense. You're here after dark because of me."

"I'm more than willing to be here… after dark… for you. You're my boss. I'm here whenever you need me—whatever you tell me to do. You don't have to pay for my taxi."

I may be married, but I wasn't dead. I also couldn't miss her proposition. The way her breasts moved with her shallow breaths—it was practically a flashing neon sign. I'd like to say that I wasn't tempted, but as I mentioned, I wasn't dead. Besides, celebrating the deal I'd accomplished would probably not be happening when I got home. Nevertheless, despite my anticipation of a less-than-warm reception, my home was where I wanted to be. "Go home, Lisa. I'll see you in the morning."

"Yes, Mr. Demetri." She reached for the twenty and flashed a smile. "A taxi will be better. On the subway, I have to transfer and well…" Her long lashes fluttered. "Thank you."

I nodded, unable to turn my gaze back to my desk as she turned, and her hips swayed as she walked away.

Sitting back down, I concentrated on my wife—the woman I loved—and the child growing within her. She was obviously upset despite her cool tone. Maybe if I convinced her to get mad and let it out, we could make up.

That was the celebration I wanted.

Those were my thoughts as I tried again to call Angelina. As I lifted the receiver, from the other room I heard Lisa collecting her things, the file cabinet opening and closing, and speaking softly. I hoped she was calling for a cab.

I wasn't interested in my secretary in a sexual way though I'd be lying if I said my body didn't react to her proposition. Nevertheless, she was a competent employee. She didn't need to be walking in those shoes on the street this late at night.

The outer office door closed, its sound echoing through the now-empty office as I dialed the number to my house. It rang and rang. I hung up and tried again. Perhaps I accidentally dialed the wrong number.

*Ring.*

*Ring.*

Then again, maybe she wasn't home. Maybe Angelina went to Rose's or Bella's?

I had plenty of options, but the only reality was that I wasn't getting an answer.

But what if it wasn't an obvious option? What if it were something more sinister? I couldn't stop my mind from going there.

Both Rose and Carmine's and Vincent and Bella's homes were only a few blocks away. Bella wouldn't go out, not with the baby due soon. Did

Angelina walk? I didn't want Lisa walking, but I sure as hell didn't want Angelina walking alone at night. I didn't care if it was a good neighborhood or not. There was too much going on for Carmine's niece—my wife—to be out walking at night.

I tried to quell my anxiety, telling myself that she wouldn't walk. She'd know better. It wasn't only her safety now but our child's too. Even if she were mad at me, I believed she'd be smarter than that.

I dialed Franco's pager, entering my car phone number with a 5. It was my signal to call me on that number in five minutes.

# CHAPTER 13

As my mind continued to wonder and worry, my body forgot about celebrating. Making sure my gun was in place, I locked the office and rushed to my car. My number one priority was somewhere not talking to me.

I had one pressing need: making sure that Angelina was all right.

Franco's call came as soon as I turned on the car.

"Franco?" I asked, not making sure it was him.

"Yeah, boss. You need me?"

"Did you drive Mrs. Demetri somewhere?"

"Yeah. I took her to the Met this morning. I brought her home about four. She hasn't called."

"Where are you?"

"Jackson's."

*Fuck.*

Jackson's was a storefront owned by Morelli. The upstairs was a small delicatessen—which actually served good sandwiches and was busy during the day. The basement was another thing. Once a week it was filled with tables and chairs. Only the ones who could afford the entry fee were able to sit at those tables. Five thousand dollars to plant your ass on a card table chair.

It didn't sound like much of a deal. Nevertheless, it was always full.

The poker was high stakes, and everyone knew the entry fee was worth it. I hadn't thought about it when I called, but tonight was Wednesday—poker night. I knew without asking that instead of watching over my wife, Franco Testa was working the game for Morelli. It took a crew to watch over the door and the players. The insane amount of cash alone made it dangerous.

Morelli and I had made an agreement regarding Testa, but regardless, his directives came first. Morelli outranked me by a thousand. I may have been Carmine's niece's husband and his nephew-in-law, but Morelli was family from way back, and besides, he was made.

"You sure she hasn't called? She isn't answering the phone," I said.

"I can ask Morelli. If he can spare me for a few, I could go to the house."

The streets were less congested than they'd be if I'd left when I was supposed to. "No, I'm on my way home. Let me know if you hear anything. If I need you, I'll call."

"Sure thing," he said just before the line went dead.

I called my house again.

Nothing.

Lisa's advances were long forgotten as I made my way from the city to our neighborhood. My only thought was Angelina. I imagined what I could find. For some reason, I wasn't seeing her on the couch watching television. Instead, my thoughts were filled with gruesome scenes. My stomach knotted as a cold chill passed through me, leaving my skin damp with perspiration as I floored the gas pedal and wound my way toward our home.

Navigating the dark streets, I came to the conclusion that I needed to talk to Carmine about Testa. After all, he had Stefano watching over his home and Rose. Someone needed to be close by Angelina at all times. The protection Vincent had arranged after our wedding had moved on. And yet the threat seemed more real than ever. If not Testa, I'd ask for someone else. Assuming my imagination was playing tricks on me, I didn't plan to repeat this scenario again.

I whipped my car into a spot near the curb a few houses down. Slamming my car door, I raced toward our house.

"Angelina!" I called. The front door banged against the wall of the entry and bounced back as I rushed inside. Screaming into the dark hallway, I repeated her name. The living room was dark and quiet. The light from the street post was my only illumination as I hurried deeper into our home. Even the kitchen lights were off. Except for the echo of my own shouts, the house was quiet. Too quiet. I stepped into the kitchen and scanned the dim room. Nothing was out of place. The counters were clean and dishes were put away; the bouquet reminded me that I hadn't stopped to get her anything. It was then that I remembered her saying the dinner was gone. I didn't give a damn about the food. I needed her.

*Fuck!*

My mind was too many places. "Angelina!"

My heart rate accelerated as I shut and locked the front door before taking the stairs two at a time. My shoes pounded the wooden stairs as the summer heat and humidity rose with each step. "Angelina!" The door to our bedroom was open and the light was on, but the room was empty. Again, everything was in its place. Even the bed was untouched.

It was then that I noticed the golden line of light spilling from beneath the bathroom door.

I took a step closer, but there was no noise coming from beyond the door. A lump formed in my throat as I reached for the door handle. I'd seen a news report recently about a suspected mob hit in Chicago. The victim was rumored to be an associate who'd snitched. The news tried to sensationalize it, but the fact remained that the victim was found with a gunshot wound to his head, lying in a bathtub of his own blood.

If the rumors were true, it was a warning to others. No doubt with the national news coverage, the warning was heard loud and clear.

With my heart hammering against my chest, I gripped the knob and turned.

A sigh escaped my lips as I took her in. There in all her naked beauty was my wife. Her head had been lying back against a towel and she had headphones over her ears attached to a cassette player on the edge of the tub. The door opening must have startled her because now she was sitting up, her blue eyes opened wide, and the water sloshing near the edge of the tub.

"Oren! What in the world?"

Too many emotions.

Relief.

Annoyance.

Happiness.

Fury.

"Answer the goddamn phone." My demand came out louder than I planned. I'd spent the last however long it took me to get home with terrible images in my head. Now here she was, safe and sound, and I figuratively was ready to kill her.

Not literally.

Literally, I was beside myself with all of it.

Angelina's resolve was strong as she stared my direction, the headphones now in her hand and her gorgeous bare back straight. "I answered the damn phone. I told you your dinner is gone. I hope you ate."

"No, I've been too worried that something happened to you."

"Well, something did," she responded, crossing her arms over her chest, shielding her growing breasts from my view.

It didn't matter. The bubbles were gone, if she'd had any. Though slightly distorted by the water, I had a perfect vision of every inch and every curve of her sexy, soft skin.

She continued, undaunted by my gaze. "My husband stood me up for the second time in a week. That's what happened." The emotion she hadn't shown on the phone was back, not only in her tone, but also in the way her blue eyes shot daggers my direction.

I wasn't the only one who was angry. "You hung up on me."

"And you stood me up. I worked today and still made you dinner. And then I sat here all by myself and ate it."

"I tried to apologize. You hung up."

Her lips came together in a straight line as her eyes blazed, reminding me of the fire inside the woman I loved.

"I've heard it before," she said.

I took a deep breath. *"Mio angelo..."* I softened my tone.

"No. Don't do that."

A smile tugged at my lips. How could I marry a Costello and not expect a temper?

Kicking off my shoes, I threw my suit coat to the floor and pulled the knot from my tie.

"No, Oren," she said watching my every move. "Don't you dare. I'm mad at you."

My lips curled higher. "Baby, I'm mad at you, too."

The fire in her eyes from a moment earlier now simmered with smoldering blue coals as she shook her head. "You can't just think…"

Her words stilled as I lowered my trousers and boxer shorts. This time my body was reacting to the right woman, to the one who infuriated me like no other and whom I loved with all my heart. I pulled off my socks and leaned over the tub. Slowly, I scanned my wife from her painted toenails all the way up to her enchanting eyes, allowing my gaze to linger and enjoy everyplace in between.

With her hair piled up on her head and small damp curls around her face, she was radiant. When our eyes finally met, my tone was thick with desire. "What, Mrs. Demetri? What can't I think? What can't I dare?"

"You can't think that sex will make it better."

I shook my head as I stood up and stepped into the water near her feet. The temperature was cooler than I expected. The tepid liquid was a comforting contrast to the summer's humidity. I winked as I drank her in. "Awfully presumptuous of you, Mrs. Demetri. I never said a word about sex. I simply want to join my wife in a cool bath."

Her brow lengthened and head tilted as she eyed my obvious arousal. The water rose, getting precariously close to the rim as I lowered myself to the bottom of the tub, lifting her feet one by one onto my legs and facing her.

"They say cold water…" she began.

"No, *mio angelo.* Not with you right there. That's not happening. I don't even think it's possible." I scooted forward and reached back to pull the plug and allow some of the water to disappear down the drain. Once it was at a safer level, I replaced the plug and turned my attention back to my wife. With my hands on the edge of the tub, I inched closer until our lips touched.

The concerns from earlier faded, not away, but they mixed with my array of emotions, creating a concoction so overpowering that it bubbled within me, needing an outlet. Momentarily the deals from the day were gone. The anxiety over the growing unrest between the families disappeared. My fears of losing the one person who means everything to me were gone. The only thing that mattered was here and now.

I wanted my wife.

"O-Oren..." My name was elongated as my lips continued their assault. "I'm still mad at you."

"Good. I'm still mad at you. Answer the damn phone."

Hardly foreplay discussion, yet that was exactly what we were doing. Her body was responding in kind as my kisses moved from her sensual lips down her slender neck and to her soft shoulder.

"Don't hang up on me again," I reprimanded as my lips made their way to her breast. I relentlessly taunted her dark pink nipples. Her moans filled the night air as the nub hardened under my touch, and her hips writhed beneath me.

Angelina entwined her fingers in my hair and pulled me closer as she countered, "Don't miss dinner again without calling first, not later."

"I. Told. You. I. Was. Sorry." Each word was punctuated with a kiss or a nip.

Her lips opened, but only whimpers escaped until she found her words. "Oren... did you...?" Her speech was now shaky as her skin peppered with goose bumps. "Did you eat?"

I kissed lower as my touch feathered her soft curves. "Not yet, *mio angelo*. Not yet."

One day we'd have a large tub, one with jets, that fit both of us. That day hadn't arrived. I sat back. With my erection bobbing with my movements, I worked my way out of the tub and pulled the plug. Angelina didn't say another word as I offered her my hand and helped her from the disappearing water. Neither of us worried about the way the liquid dripped from our bodies, trailing across the wood floor as I led her from the bathroom to our bed.

My timbre was ladened with lust. "I'm going to show you how sorry I am."

Her lips curled upward as her gaze softened. "Remember, I'm really mad." She lay back on the pillow. As I climbed over her, kissing her baby bump that was becoming more than a bump, I moved lower.

"Really mad?" I asked, peering upward.

"Uh-huh…" she replied, her voice cracking with desire as her back arched and legs quivered.

Pulling her ankles over my shoulders, I kissed her hips and inner thighs. I continued to move down her soft, wet body as the water from the bath settled into our sheets.

"Not for long, *mio angelo*. Not for long. I promise you'll forgive me."

"R-really mad…"

# CHAPTER 14

IT WAS IMPORTANT to understand history to understand the current state of affairs.

The 1970s had been a disaster for economic growth in the United States in general. The recession was crippling as even energy was conserved.

That said, at the same time, the opposite was true of the LCN—La Cosa Nostra—families' influence. During times when businesses failed and unemployment skyrocketed, people needed money.

Desperate times—desperate measures.

Profits from gambling increased. The lure of getting something from nearly nothing was enticing. It wasn't uncommon for a man to bet a full-week's salary with the hope, dream, and possibility of turning it into a month's income.

Sometimes it paid off; more often it didn't.

Regardless of the risk and usual loss, life had responsibilities. Rent was still required by the landlord. Children needed food. Utilities must be paid for heat and lights to remain working.

It was in times like that when connections paid off.

The same people who reaped the benefits of the common man's

gambling losses fortunately had cash on hand. Markers were made—loans were requested and favors asked. Of course, if money was loaned from a 'friend,' the payback was different than the interest expected by banks. Points on a marker were determined by the person loaning the money. A point was one percent. There was no rhyme or reason to the number of points assigned. Perhaps the first loan would have one point, and payoff was easily accomplished. The next time the need was greater and the points rose. However it was figured, once a borrower agreed and accepted terms and the money, he or she was beholden to that agreement. Not paying could range from expensive, to painful, to deadly. Until the loan was paid in full, the borrower was in the loaner's debt. Even soldiers found themselves indebted with points too high to pay.

That was when the true debts came. In exchange for one week's payment, a favor was requested. A hit. A grab. It didn't matter as long as the shylock was paid.

Time continued moving forward. Loans still worked the same way they did a decade ago, yet the economic scene of the eighties was considerably different than it had been. The entire economy was on an upswing. For Demetri Enterprises that was a good thing. Faltering businesses that had survived the last ten years were ripe for picking. Those that failed could be rebuilt. Supply-side economics was my golden ticket. Lower tax rates allowed more money to flow. The more I invested, the more breaks I received. With the way things were going, Angelina's and my net worth was on an upward climb. Soon, I'd be able to give her all that she deserved.

The opposite was true for the families. The loss of income brought on by the improved economic state was part of the reason for the influx of illegal drugs. If people didn't have a reason to borrow money, drugs gave them one. The plan was simple: give people a motive that didn't go away and a need that continued to grow. Supply them with an addiction that required feeding at any expense.

Drugs were similar to gambling, with the added physiological dependence. It wasn't only the psyche that needed, but the body itself.

Carmine's mindset to stay clear of heroin was keeping the Costellos out of the fray, but the fallout was potentially too big to avoid. The increased stress on the street as well as in meetings was palpable. Thursday nights were growing tenser with each passing week. Though recently the Luchis had shouldered the brunt of the arrests, within each family there was the potential of unrest. The grand jury that Carmine had talked about came to pass. Thankfully, the Costellos were left unscathed. No subpoenas. Nevertheless, there was a sense lingering in the air that the luck wouldn't last forever.

Some of Carmine's capos were talking. Though no one dared go against the boss, there was discontent with the perceived loss of income. It was true that many of the Luchis were paying the price for the drugs, but it was also evident that over the water in New Jersey there was an income stream difficult to miss.

Courtesy of Gioconda's uncertainty, I was on the outside looking in. Even from my view, it didn't take a mind reader to know what was happening. Angelina kept me up to date on the local and national news. And then there were the less obvious signs: the exchanged looks and terse greetings. On Sunday afternoons, I was supplied with just enough information to feed and fuel my concerns.

Soldiers were being watched while others had gone missing. The stakes were too high for insubordination, and as tensions built, everyone was suspect.

There was even talk of defection. It seemed unfathomable that it could happen from one of the made men, but the idea of a soldier breaking ranks to earn more money was a valid possibility. If one man thought he could earn more or advance faster with the Luchis or Bonettis or... the list went on, then what was to stop him?

And yet that defection could also come with secrets, ones that no family wanted shared with another. In my mind, it was the reason for some of the recent MIA.

Dead men didn't talk.

This unease was what propelled me to ask for around-the-clock security for Angelina. I didn't know how Morelli took it, and the deal was costing me a fortune—after all, Testa was losing out on some of Morelli's income. Nevertheless, Franco Testa willingly took the position I offered. Perhaps it had helped that the offer didn't come from me. One doesn't simply tell Carmine no. That went for Testa and Morelli. It was a relief to know that I could assure Angelina's safety at any hour of the day or night, no matter where I was or if I was delayed. The money it cost paled in comparison to the sense of security.

"Pop," Vincent said on Sunday afternoon in Carmine's home office, "the family's strong."

"Yes," Carmine replied, moving his gaze between Vincent and me. "Precautions. I think it's time."

I bided my time, listening more than speaking.

"Precautions?" Vincent asked. "Gioconda says we should keep it steady."

Carmine nodded, taking a puff of his cigar and blowing it out as he leaned back. "I know what he thinks. I think too.

"Talk to us, Oren," Carmine said, turning to me. "It's been nearly nine months since your wedding. Word is that Peterson only gave you a glance. He moved on."

"The Luchis are more exciting to watch than I am," I said, relieved that it was true.

"Good. Luchi may be exciting, but exciting is also stupid. I told Ricardo that." Carmine swatted away the smoke encircling him. "He ignored me. Now look. He said I live in the past, and we need to change with the times. That's where Gioconda was right. It's also where he's wrong." He looked at me. "The times… they're good to you, right?"

I wasn't confident enough to know what Carmine was thinking—or even saying. All I could do was answer honestly. "Yes. I've done as you said. Demetri Enterprises is clean and growing."

Clean was a relative term, and in relative terms, Demetri was clean.

It wasn't spotless, but nothing was.

I still owned property used for illegal activities. I no longer collected the daily or nightly receipts, but I still collected my share of the tax—a considerably smaller share than went to Carmine. The extra money went into the books as rent or filtered in under other possible earning streams. Everything balanced. Even if the feds created a storm, I'd have no red flags waving for their attention.

"But more money is always needed?" he asked.

I shrugged. "Of course. That's the goal."

"Taking care of our Angelina and now your child, that's the goal?"

"Yes."

"Enjoy sleep while you can," Vincent interjected, momentarily derailing the serious tone of the conversation. After all, this was Sunday afternoon, not Thursday night. The three of us were family in the true sense of the word.

Carmine smirked with a quick nod of his chin. "You didn't let your momma or me sleep either. Karma, *sì*, it's true."

Vincent laughed. "It's worth it. He's going to be a little me. Strong. So strong already. A fighter. I know it."

I sat back and listened as Vincent and Carmine extolled the attributes of Vincent's recently born son, Luca. I wasn't sure how at merely a month old, Luca's potential was a certainty to his father and grandfather, but to hear them talk, the two of them already had his résumé and future all figured out. I couldn't help but think about the conversations Angelina and I had. Many nights we stayed up late in our bed talking about her concerns—rightful concerns—over our child's future.

We didn't know the sex, so a daughter was still possible. However, Angelina was proof that a daughter didn't assure a reprieve from the business of the Costello family.

She'd experienced the devastating side as a child. As we looked out into our future, neither of us wanted that for our sons or daughters. Especially with the current sense of another war permeating the air.

My fears regarding Angelina the night I couldn't reach her may be considered by some as nonsense. Women and children were respected. It's the way of the LCN. Yet times were changing, including the respectability and honor. Often the unsuspecting or innocent were used as a warning. That was what had happened with Angelina's mother. What better warning to Carmine than to harm two of his own.

Bella and Angelina, as well as Luca and our child, were vulnerable. It was fact.

The reason we didn't yet know the gender of our unborn child was because when the doctor asked if she wanted to know, Angelina declined. Like many other recent disappointments, that was my fault. I was supposed to have been present at the appointment, but instead, it was Franco who drove her. A meeting I had scheduled for an hour ran longer than expected. The dividend was impressive. It was a proposal to purchase a foundering chain of restaurants, a fast-food chain. The last thing I was interested in was the fast-food business, but the underlying potential was too good to cut the meeting short. The real estate alone was invaluable.

That didn't matter to my wife. To her it was simple. Once again, I'd failed. Though an ultrasound wasn't an entirely reliable procedure to discern gender, the technicians or doctors usually tried their best. However, since I wasn't present at the appointment, Angelina chose to not learn what they might have assessed. She said she'd wait, and we'd find out together when our baby came into this world.

*Into this world.*

There was so much meaning in that simple phrase.

This planet.

This continent.

This country.

This city.

This family.

This *world.*

We'd stayed true to our decision to attempt to break the chain of family expectancy for our child in another way. Instead of following tradition in naming our son or daughter, Angelina scanned books of baby names. She vowed that our child would have his or her own unique name, one that would give choices, not repeat the ways of those who came before.

We'd mentioned our possibilities to Rose and Carmine. Though they didn't know our reasoning, they chose not to argue with their niece, and for that I was elated.

"Oren." Carmine's deep voice brought me back to reality.

"Yes, sorry. I was thinking about our baby."

He smiled and nodded. "More family. It's what a man dreams of. I wish my brother were here to see his daughter and grandchild. Angelina is beautiful. You make her happy. I see it in her eyes."

I knew the answer was 'not recently, I hadn't.'

Among my many failures, I hadn't kept my promise about calling before missing a dinner. I could say I tried, but then she'd ask me how difficult it was to pick up a phone. She was right. If only each fight ended like the one a few months back.

They didn't.

Recently, I'd even found our bedroom door locked when I arrived home after eleven o'clock. It's an old house. I didn't doubt that I could kick it in, but then again, it would need to be repaired. Another purchase in our future was a new couch. The one we owned was fine for sitting, but it didn't work well for sleeping an entire night.

Instead of answering Carmine truthfully, I opted for a Costello enigma—answer in riddles. "She's radiant. She makes me happy, and I do my best."

"It's not easy when you never know what to expect," Vincent said, shaking his head. "Since you took my advice from before, and you remember..." His eyebrows moved up and down. "Here's more. Don't expect those hormones to calm down as soon as the baby's born. I'm not sure Bella will ever be totally happy again."

"You'll figure it out," Carmine said dismissively. "They're women. Buy her something nice. Now, back to what I was saying: Ricardo Luchi is stupid. It starts at the top. He makes mistakes and takes chances. It moves down the line. That's what they've done. They're hurting us all.

"The Costellos, we've been smart. We need to stay smart. Because of their mistakes, the feds... they're watching everyone. Wires and invasion of privacy." His palm slapped the desk. "It's like this isn't America anymore. That's why other than Evviva's, we talk here. No one gets in here to plant bugs—and makes it out. We take no chances of being overheard." He looked to Vincent. "Remember that."

"I worry that Ricardo's carelessness will affect more of us. We've talked—the others and myself. I'm not alone in these concerns. There's unrest all around, like I haven't felt since Angelo, God rest his soul."

I sat taller at the sound of Angelina's father's name.

"I've decided," Carmine went on, "that for our family, it's time to invest in the future."

"Invest?" I asked. "Do you want me to help?"

"You're family. I don't need to ask."

"No," I replied. "I'm offering. How can I help?"

"Invest in Demetri."

"I am. I have been."

"No, *we* will," Carmine said. "Some cash invested here and there. Vincent and I spoke about the different companies you own or have a piece of... so many. It's perfect. Many people have one or two. You have many. The bigger ones, keep completely out of everything at this point. Too easy to alert someone. It's the small ones for now. And we have friends. What Bonetti said you did for him, we know you didn't. But this won't be one balloon. We have a fucking factory full—a goddamn circus.

"The clean ones, they can help our friends. But the books must remain spotless. Those will be the businesses the feds watch. Let them watch. They'll find nothing."

I knew enough about money laundering to understand how Demetri could help. His request didn't surprise me. I'd been warned it was coming. I guess I was just happy it had waited.

That was the past.

Game on. It was my court and Carmine's ball. The only objective was to win.

# CHAPTER 15

TIME CONTINUED TO tick away and before long, snowflakes and cold replaced the green grass and humidity. The one-year anniversary of our wedding was an occasion of celebration. Despite the continued unrest, Carmine insisted that it be a family affair. Along with him, Rose, Vincent, Bella, and Luca, Angelina and I appeared the happy close family as we dined at Giovanni's, the small family Italian restaurant where I'd proposed. It wasn't only appearance. We were family, and it was getting increasingly difficult to know who to trust.

Although I knew Angelina was concerned about the tension, she was absolutely radiant in her emerald green dress with the high waist that did little to hide our nearly nine-months-along, growing beach ball of a baby.

"*Mio angelo,*" I whispered as Carmine raised his glass of wine. "Have I told you today you're gorgeous and I love you?"

Her smile bloomed. "*Tesoro,* you are my only love."

I laid my palm over her stomach. "Not for long."

Our baby pushed against my hand, causing both of us to smile.

"To family," Carmine said, his cheeks glowing in the flickering candlelight as he looked about the table.

We all lifted our glasses.

"I look around, and my heart is full," he said as he toasted. "Two years ago, Bella and Oren weren't part of us. A year ago, we didn't have Luca. And soon…" He smiled toward Angelina and I. "Another baby. Our Angel, I know that your parents are smiling. I know my brother. He's celebrating in heaven with us tonight."

I squeezed my wife's hand as we all drank.

It may have been an outward sign of our family unity, but Carmine had also taken precautions. The usual crowd was missing. We had the entire restaurant to ourselves. Throughout the evening, the wine and food continued to be served as Giovanni made sure everyone was happy, and no one went without.

It was difficult to not feel the surroundings for what they were, a private family celebration. Despite the costs currently being paid in the field—the loss of some recent soldiers and even what Carmine was asking me to do with Costello funds—this, sitting around this table with Angelina by my side, was what I'd wanted. As Luca slept in his mother's and then his grandmother's arms, I knew that despite our concerns, I wanted this sense of belonging for our son or daughter, too.

When the evening finally ended and as I helped Angelina with her coat, Carmine tipped his head to the side hallway.

"Give me a minute," I whispered in Angelina's ear.

She smiled, holding Luca as Bella gathered the array of items they'd brought with them, which by the way, seemed like an extraordinary amount. We'd learn soon enough if all of it was necessary.

"Watch over her," Carmine said in his deep stage whisper.

I nodded.

"No," Carmine said. "I know the baby's coming. Stay with her. I trust Testa, but yet I don't. Right now… we don't know. Stay close. Be ready. I have a meeting next week. Things…" He looked around. "…I can't say, but nothing is as important as my family. Besides Testa, Vincent will find you a few more. He has Dante watching Bella and Luca. We all need to know our backs are being watched."

I knew I couldn't ask for particulars, but that didn't stop the questions from forming. All I knew with some certainty was that the pot of New York families had been simmering and the boil was coming.

Testa pulled the car to the curb as snow fell, melting on the concrete. I scanned the buildings across the street and up and down the block, not knowing if it was better with fewer people on the street in the winter or worse. The glow of the streetlights as the white fluffy flakes fell left me chilled in a way weather never had.

I'd managed to postpone a few meetings. Christmas was approaching and everyone's schedules were affected. It wasn't until a little over a week later when I woke early one morning to Angelina's distant cries that my world went out of kilter.

I patted the empty bed beside me, sitting up and looking about our dark bedroom. "Angelina!"

"I-in here…"

I jumped from the warm blankets and hurried toward the bathroom. With the door partially opened, I found Angelina kneeling on the floor, a dampened towel in her hand.

"What?"

Her eyes opened wide just before her face scrunched in pain.

I fell to my knees. The floor was slippery yet sticky. "What is it?"

"I think it was my water."

"Your water?"

"Oren, my water broke. Our baby's coming."

I couldn't imagine what it was like to give birth. All I knew with some certainty was that watching the woman you love, the person who means the most to you in this world, in pain was possibly one of the worst experiences of my adult life—and it had a lot of competition.

I'd go without sleep. I'd drive Vincent to a location, knowing that I didn't want to see what happened within. I'd sit under the dark stare of Carmine Costello. Hell, I'd do anything, sell anything, or buy anything, to take away her pain.

"*Mio angelo*," I said, hours after we'd arrived at the hospital, holding her hand and standing beside the hospital bed in her delivery room. "Take the epidural. Please, I don't want you to hurt."

Perspiration covered her face as I used a cool cloth to wipe her forehead.

She shook her head. "I can't. It's too late now. They say I'm too far."

I'd taken the classes, well most of them. I understood the biology, but if there was medicine to help her, one that didn't hurt the baby, why couldn't she have it? They'd offered it to her earlier, but now it was obvious her pain was worse. "What do you mean, too far?"

Her grip of my hand intensified.

There was a wide belt around her midsection, its purpose to measure things within. The baby's heart rate was on a television screen as well as a Richter kind of chart, similar to one that measured seismic activity. Currently, the little line was going up and up.

"That's it, Mrs. Demetri," the nurse said. "You're doing great. This is a big contraction."

Angelina didn't answer as her face turned red, and she continued her vise grip of my hand.

"Why can't she have the epidural? They said in those classes it would help?" I'd been to enough of the classes to pick up a few things.

"Mr. Demetri, your wife is already eight centimeters dilated. If things progress as we expect, an epidural won't have time to work. Besides, when it's time, she needs to be able to push."

"Then give her something else, something that can work."

Angelina's grip loosened as she took deep breaths. "No. I don't want anything that will pass through the placenta."

I should have paid better attention in those classes. Hell, I should have attended all of them. She and the nurse were speaking a different language, using words I'd heard, but was without complete knowledge of their meanings.

"I'm ready to push," Angelina said.

"Not yet."

Another nurse came in the room with a bowl of ice chips. Handing it to me, she said, "Here. These will help."

"Ice?" I truly was a college- and street-educated man, but at that moment, synapses weren't firing. "Why ice?"

"Give them to me," Angelina said, the tips of her lips trying to smile.

"Okay." I handed her the bowl.

She shook her head. "No, one at a time."

If I'd been a cartoon, a small light bulb would have illuminated over my head. "Oh." I pulled the chair closer to her side and lifted one small chip, more like a half moon, to her lips. I hadn't noticed how dry and parched they'd become.

Angelina moaned as she sucked the ice between her lips.

I'm not sure how they expected things to progress. Because despite the nurse claiming we didn't have time, we went on with ice chips and contractions for what seemed like hours, or maybe it was days. I lost track of time as her pains grew increasingly stronger, only to fade away for a while, allowing her a few minutes of sleep. And then they'd come back even stronger. Finally, the nurse said what we'd been waiting to hear.

"It's time. We'll call the doctor."

If the beginning of Angelina's labor felt like time stood still, the next hour happened in record time. If I could have changed places with her at any moment, I believe I would have, and yet I don't know if I could do what I watched her do.

The weaker sex.

That's what they call women. I'm most certain that whoever has said that has not watched as a small human entered this world by leaving a supposed 'weaker' person's body. I knew men who could handle almost anything, yet I'd bet not one of them could do what she did.

In that moment, I understood why the church called children gifts from God.

The whole thing was a miracle and amazing.

I held Angelina's hand, wiped her brow, and said anything I could think to say as the doctor said the words we both wanted and dreaded.

"Congratulations, Mr. and Mrs. Demetri, you have a son."

"A son," my wife said as tears descended her cheeks.

"A healthy son," the doctor confirmed. "Look at him."

Our son announced his arrival to everyone within an eight-mile radius, his cry ringing loud and strong.

"A son with healthy lungs," one of the nurses said with a smile.

Barely cleaned, wrapped in a thin blanket, our son was laid in my wife's arms by another nurse.

It was a moment in time that I'll never forget. Never in all my life had I been prouder and at the same time more terrified.

All I could think about was the conversation between Vincent and Carmine, the plans they had for Luca. The prospect was stifling while at the same time my heart was bursting.

I reached out as a tiny hand came up and grabbed my finger.

Angelina laughed as tears continued to flow. "Lennox, that's your dad, and I'm your mom.'"

His light eyes stared up at her. I'd read somewhere that babies can't focus too far away, yet as soon as she spoke, he seemed to zero in on his mother. It made sense. He'd been hearing her voice for nine months.

"Hello, Lennox," I said. "Welcome to the world."

"We're going to keep you safe," Angelina professed as he continued to stare upward.

"Or die trying." My response was only whispered, but my wife heard it. My son heard it.

Like the movie about Moses.

*So let it be said, so let it be done.* That may not be a direct quote. I may have paraphrased, but the meaning was sincere.

"Lennox Demetri," I said, thinking how I wished my parents could meet the next generation of Demetris. "We vow to give you more."

"We love you," Angelina said.

A while later, they moved Angelina to her own room. I stood back and watched as the nurses helped her move to the new bed. She'd told them that we wanted Lennox in the room with us. He was there, all bathed and sleeping in a clear tiny box of a bed on wheels. All we could see was his little face. He was mostly covered by a blanket. They had a small blue cap over his dark hair and little white mittens without thumbs on his hands.

As I stared, I longed to remove the mittens. I was fascinated by his hands. His fingers were long and strong with perfect small fingernails. I'd felt his strength in the way he gripped my finger, and at that moment, I knew what Vincent meant about Luca being strong. Lennox would also be strong.

With her long hair flowing over her shoulders, I was once again enthralled with my wife. She'd recently given birth to a nearly eight-pound baby boy, and she was radiant. Her smile was everything as she looked from Lennox up to me.

The nurse pulled the covers up to Angelina's waist. "You have guests, Mrs. Demetri. However, it's late. I'd recommend only two at a time."

The sky outside the window was black. It was true that at this time of year, the number of daylight hours were fewer; however, as Lennox came into the world, we'd essentially missed the entire day: December 16th, our son's birthday.

"I can go get them," I volunteered.

Angelina smiled and shooed me out.

At first, I didn't pay attention to my surroundings; my mind was too consumed with the day's events. I supposed in some way I rationalized that this was a hospital, not a deserted street. Admittedly, as I left Angelina, my guard was down.

That all changed as I turned the corner and found a private waiting area with Stefano and Franco stationed outside the door. Nodding at them, I opened the door. Inside, Carmine, Vincent, Bella, Luca, and Rose were all gathered.

"Oren!" Bella and Rose called in unison as they both rose from their seats.

Though my gut told me something had happened—something big—I kept my smile in place for them. "We have a son."

Everyone's smiles grew as congratulations came from all around the room. Bella and Rose hugged me while Carmine and Vincent shook my hand and patted my back.

"Take the women to Angelina first. They want to see and cackle," Carmine said. "And then, Oren, return to us."

I did as Carmine instructed, gesturing to Rose and Bella to follow me beyond the visiting area to the restricted-access ward. All the way through the hallways, Rose asked me questions about the birth. As we approached Angelina's door, I noticed a man I recognized standing just beyond her room. He was another of the Costello soldiers, yet I couldn't comprehend why he was here.

"What...?" I said, more to myself than to anyone.

Rose patted my hand. "Go. She's safe. So is your son. Carmine will explain."

My gut churned as I nodded at the man and left the women alone. The hallway back to the small waiting room grew with each step; trepidation overwhelmed me as I forced my body forward. Maybe it was the adrenaline from the birth. Perhaps I'd used it all, yet a part of me knew that whatever I learned would be life altering.

As I opened the door and stepped in, both Vincent and Carmine turned my way.

"There was a meeting tonight, a dinner," Carmine began without any preamble. "The one I mentioned. We were talking. All of the bosses were invited—even Ricardo. Just the five of us and our seconds." Carmine tilted his head toward Vincent, who was not only his son but also the Costello underboss. "At Sparks Steak House on East 46th Street..."

I knew the place. It was pricey and nice. It was where people went to impress. I'd taken prospective clients there for business and also taken Angelina there before we were married. In the world we were treading, it was a bold move, perhaps meant as a statement to the feds or the underlings. It was a sign of unity. Sparks was in the heart of the city, not an out-of-the-way place for the five heads of the families to meet. And then... my knees weakened, and I fell into a vinyl chair as I listened to the rest of the story.

As Carmine spoke, my blood raced, dimming his tone. The internal struggle was real. This was the world my son had been born into. This was our reality, and at that moment, I knew that our future couldn't be more unclear.

I listened as Carmine's deep voice spoke steadily.

Gioconda had driven him and Vincent to the dinner. They arrived at the steak house by five-thirty. The meeting slash dinner wasn't scheduled until six o'clock, yet most of the bosses were present. Although the meeting itself was to cover the heroin mess of the Luchis, the atmosphere was joyous. After all, it was nearly Christmas… and Carmine admitted he was in good spirits, knowing that Angelina was in labor. He was anxious to get the gathering done and come to the hospital.

With the other four bosses already inside, a bodyguard drove Paulie Castellano, the head of one of the biggest families, to the meeting. His underboss had recently died of cancer. Carmine said that some of those in attendance at the steak house were theorizing about who Paulie would name to that recently vacated position. It needed to be someone he trusted. After all, Castellano had just recently had his own brush with the law and been released from jail on an astronomical bond. He needed someone who could take the helm if he were sentenced for a stay in the big house that could last longer than a while.

At 5:45 pm, Paulie's bodyguard pulled his Lincoln up to the front door of the restaurant. It was a no-parking zone, but that didn't stop Big Paulie. He dined at Sparks often and was accustomed to the royal treatment.

This would be different.

Without any prelude, three assassins dressed like Russians with long off-white coats and fur hats opened fire on Castellano and his bodyguard as they exited their car. It wasn't an ambush in a back alley. This was a blatant assassination in the heart of New York City, on East 46th Street.

Carmine was now seated, his head moving from side to side. "They say he was hit over six times. In the goddamn street." His volume fluctuated. "Hit in his body and head. There are already pictures.

"The cops, they covered up Big Paulie, but not his guard. The pigs just left him lying there." Carmine's head continued to shake. "Nine years that Paulie's been in charge of his family, and nobody challenged him. And now…"

"Oh my God." It was all I could say. It was a good thing that Angelina and I had been busy all day and not eaten. If I had, I feared I'd have gotten ill right there in the waiting room.

"It was a shock to everyone," Carmine said.

There were probably no two men in the world whom I respected more than the two before me. In the last year, I'd watched and learned. I'd seen both of them face adversaries with a cool, calm demeanor—that manner, in reality, was more frightening than anger. Yet tonight, on the day of my son's birth, they were both visibly shaken and with ample reason.

My mind continually went to Lennox. A Demetri, but also a Costello.

"I need to tell Angelina," I said.

"Bella and Rose know. But they won't say anything. You're her husband. The timing is up to you." Carmine nodded. "She needs to know, to understand the increased security and need for safety."

The knots in my stomach twisted. Closing my eyes, I saw her smile as she looked from Lennox to me. I didn't want to sully her joy. "I agree. However, if you agree, I'd like it to wait for a little while. Let her enjoy today. Let her enjoy Lennox."

Carmine nodded. "A good name, a strong name, a fighter… Lennox Cost—" He stopped. "No, Lennox Demetri."

"Yes."

"A powerful name for a powerful man. That's what we need."

I said a silent prayer that my son would be a strong and powerful man but not for the wrong reasons.

# CHAPTER 16

———•○•———

I MANAGED TO keep the recent turn of events from Angelina while we were secluded in her hospital room. Since the childbirth, she'd been worn out, allowing us to avoid the television and concentrating instead on Lennox when she was awake. Along with the biggest bouquet of brightly colored daisies I could find, I brought her favorite cassettes and Walkman from home, hoping to avoid the radio as well. All it would've taken was her turning on either one—the TV or radio—for only a moment or two to learn what I knew was better for her to hear from me.

That didn't mean I was anxious to tell her and burst her bubble of happiness.

Yet with each passing moment, my time was running out. The news of Big Paulie's assassination was everywhere.

When I was outside her room, I saw the pictures Carmine had mentioned, the ones of the car, the covered body of the don, and the uncovered one of Bilotti. There were televisions in the waiting rooms, near the nurses' stations, and even in the hallways. Every time I left her room, it seemed as if there was another special bulletin.

I wasn't sure what strings Carmine pulled to have around-the-clock protection for Angelina's room, but I was glad he did. She wanted Lennox with her, and I concurred. They were both under the watchful eye of not only me, but also Costello soldiers.

While the reprieve from life that we found within the pale walls of her hospital room was nice, unfortunately, it was short-lived. My recent conversation with Carmine ran loops through my head.

Angelina and Lennox had been cleared as healthy and ready for release, which meant one thing: we needed to leave.

As we gathered all of Lennox's things—gifts and flowers had arrived nonstop—instead of facing the reality awaiting us, I bided my time by focusing on everything else. "How does one baby have so much stuff?" I asked, as we combined multiple small outfits into fewer bags, trying to consolidate the bounty.

"The family is big."

Maybe not our blood family; however, for anyone within the Costello family at-large to not acknowledge Carmine Costello's new grandnephew would be considered disrespectful. For all intents and purposes, Lennox's birth was equivalent to the boss having another grandson. While that filled me with a mixture of emotion, it was the truth. It was also why Angelina needed to know what had happened.

I listened as the nurse discussed Lennox's feeding schedule and the need for another appointment with his pediatrician in a week. The doctor had been in to check on Lennox multiple times. While I knew I should be the one to accompany Angelina to see him again, in my heart I assumed it would be Franco driving them.

My attention went to the window. Beyond the glass the view was filled with a mix of rain and snow. With the temperature dropping, snow would prevail. Within, the windowsill was overrun with multiple vases of flowers and plants. On the floor, was a collection of light-blue gift bags. As I assessed it all, I contemplated asking the soldier in the hallway to help carry some of it to the car. As I debated, Angelina began securing Lennox in his car seat, all dressed for his ride home in a brand new blue outfit with a small white bow tie. I shook my head at the outfit as she swaddled him in blankets, no doubt preparing for the cooler air outside.

When the nurse left to go fetch a wheelchair—Angelina was doing well but it was something she'd said about hospital policy—I decided it was time to explain what my wife had missed. I was running out of time.

Instead of a backdrop of peacefulness, the private hospital room filled with Lennox's complaints as Angelina continued to buckle and strap him inside the seat, tucking the blankets around his moving legs. Her tired smile turned my way. "I don't think he likes the car seat."

"I'd guess it's the bow tie."

She shook her head. "It's cute, and it came from Vinny and Bella."

"I've never seen Luca in a bow tie. I think this is some master plan to make Lennox look weaker."

Angelina leaned forward and kissed our son's small head. "You look very handsome and strong. Don't listen to your father. He's just jealous. I'll buy him a bow tie and then you can match."

I grimaced at the idea. Matching one another was silly enough without a bow tie. "*Mio angelo,*" I began as our son's discontentment quieted. "Franco is picking us up."

She nodded, but her attention was back to Lennox.

Taking a deep breath, I went to her, needing her to listen. "We need to talk about something first."

"What?"

"You haven't been out of this room much since Lennox was born, but there're a few things that happened. I'm sorry that I haven't told you sooner, but I wanted to shield you for as long as we could. I was going to wait until we got home, but I just spoke to Carmine. He thinks we should go straight to his house from here."

She shook her head as she rocked the seat back and forth. "No, Oren. I'm tired, and I want to go to *our* home with *our* family."

"We will. It just may be in a few days."

Tears filled her blue eyes, and my thoughts momentarily went to Vincent's warning. He'd been right about the out-of-whack emotions. They hadn't disappeared as soon as Lennox was born; if anything, they'd intensified. Then again, it had only been a few days. Maybe I needed to give her some more time.

This was all new—to both of us.

"His nursery is waiting," she said. "Whatever Uncle Carmine wants can wait. Let me call him. I'll talk to him. He'll listen to me."

Holding her shoulders, I kissed her forehead. "Let me talk first."

She nodded again.

"Something happened. I've been waiting to tell you. But the truth is you'll notice as soon as we leave the room. We have more protection here than just Franco. Your uncle's people have been here since Monday. Assigning them to you and Lennox was his doing, but I approved."

The sadness in her blue eyes morphed to fear. "Why? What happened? Was there a threat?" She gasped. "To our son?"

"No, not to him. Not to us, either. We're just being safe—taking precautions."

Apparently, our small son had grown tired of his cries going unresolved. His little eyes were now closed as if there weren't a care in the world besides his next feeding or diaper change. I turned Angelina toward the bed and encouraged her to sit beside the car seat. Even though Lennox had quieted, she was still rocking the large handle.

"Monday night," I began, "there was a planned meeting of all the bosses at Sparks Steak House on 46th. Carmine and Vincent were there, but inside. When Paulie Castellano arrived, he was shot and killed outside on the street. Obviously, he was there because of the meeting. It wasn't secret. People from all around knew it was going to happen. The rumor is that the hit came from within his family. The problem right now is that there are a lot of different speculations—an inside job isn't the only rumor.

"All of the other bosses were already inside the restaurant. Some of Castellano's people are saying that it was a conspiracy, that the other bosses knew it was coming, and that's why they were all inside the restaurant early and not out on the street."

Angelina's eyes grew wider with each word.

There was another good reason for the suspicion. There's a rule in the LCN—a rule whose violation is punishable by death. It states that a boss can't be marked without the approval of the rest of the commission. The commission was made up of all of the five family dons. If Big Paulie's murder was approved, all the other bosses in attendance knew it was about to take place.

It was a bitter pill to swallow. It would mean that Carmine was part of the plan or at the very least, privy to it. However, Carmine stated unequivocally that he didn't know anything about it.

He said it once in my presence. It was in the waiting room. I saw how visibly shaken he and Vincent were.

He didn't need to say it again.

"It makes them all suspects," I went on. "Not for the police. Their personal alibis are solid. They couldn't have been on the street when they were inside. That doesn't mean they didn't approve or order it. Though from your uncle's mouth, they didn't, or at least he had no knowledge.

"Our increased security is over the concern that anyone in Paulie's family believes the rumors about the other bosses…"

With each sentence, more of the color drained from my wife's face.

"Is that why Uncle Carmine wants us at his house? Wouldn't we be safer away from him?"

I shrugged my shoulders. "He's well protected."

"So was Big Paulie."

"Not as much as you'd think. He was stupid and arrogant. He thought he was untouchable. According to the news reports, neither he nor his bodyguard was even carrying. Carmine doesn't think that way. He believes we're all touchable."

Another concern I didn't bring up to Angelina was that like Carmine, Big Paulie had been anti-illegal drugs. It was the same unrest we were feeling within the Costello family, and now with the possibility that it was an inside job, that concern was amplified.

"For now," I said as reassuringly as possible, "your uncle wants us and Vincent's family all together." I reached for her hand. "One day, *mio angelo*, I'll build you a fortress." I looked down at our sleeping son. "A place where you and Lennox are safe. For now, I think we should listen to your uncle. Besides, you'll have Rose and Bella to help you."

"I thought I'd have you to help me."

Her words tore through me like a jagged knife. "I will. I promise. Right now, there are things to secure and alliances to reconfirm. Once it calms down, you'll have me. I promise."

Angelina nodded quickly as her chin fell forward.

Letting go of her hand, I placed the palms of my hands on either side of her face and lifted her eyes to mine. "Your and Lennox's safety is the most important thing. Never doubt that."

"I don't. I'm just... scared." Her eyes went to Lennox. "He's three days old and this is what his world is about?"

I wrapped my arms around her, pulling her close to me. "I'm scared too. We'll get through this together. Once it's clear that the bosses didn't know, the heat will be off the other families." I feigned a smile. "I never thought I'd hope for an inside job, but that's what I'm hoping it was." I shrugged. "Or maybe the feds. Paulie was their star witness in their upcoming case."

"Why would the feds off their star witness?"

I shrugged. "Maybe because their case is crap. Now they have an excuse when it fizzles."

Angelina looked up, smiling through her tears. "Hey. You're going to spend the night in my room in Uncle Carmine's house."

We'd been married for a year, yet the thought of the scene she described sent a chill down my spine colder than when I'd been told of Paulie's death. In all the time of our dating, her room had been the place of only stolen touches and kisses. I placed too much value on my life to get caught in Carmine's home with my pants down—literally. This was different. This was a command presence. Assuming Rose didn't create a bed for me on the couch in the living room, I would be sleeping with my wife under Carmine Costello's roof... if I actually slept.

I hadn't done much of that since Monday.

It wasn't because of our son's schedule; however, I presumed that wouldn't help with my slumber once we were settled.

Instead of saying all of that, I went with the answer that would keep the smile on my wife's lips. "Yes, *mio angelo*. Yes, I will."

She leaned forward and brushed my lips with hers. "Okay. As long as you're there, I'll be there. We'll be our family within the bigger family."

We didn't have any choice.

We both turned toward the opening door. "Mrs. Demetri, it's time..." the nurse said, arriving with the wheelchair.

# CHAPTER 17

—●○●—

THE WINDS OF winter blustered beyond the windows of the Costello brownstone. Large flakes of white snow whipped in waves, creating drifts as the temperature plummeted. Slush turned to ice, changing bridges and roads within the city into rinks unfit for navigation. And yet commuting outside would have been easier than the conversations occurring in Carmine's office.

Despite the storms at hand—metaphoric as well as meteorological—the mood within the home outside of Carmine's office was festive. The multicolored lights on the tall tree by the front window reflected onto the hardwood floor and beyond into the hallway. Stockings were hung on the mantel with *Luca* and *Lennox* scrawled in shimmering glitter. Bells jingled each time the front door was opened or closed. Christmas was near, and Rose Costello had her family close. She had no intention of allowing the worries from outside to dampen the spirit within.

Angelina and I were welcomed within the Costello home with open arms. That invitation did not extend to Carmine's office, not when others were present. And as hours and days passed, others were constantly present; however, even the 'others' were limited. Only the truly trusted made it into the Costello home. Gioconda and Vincent spent hours at

Carmine's side. Other capos came and went, but always with Stefano or Jimmy present who were always visibly armed. The constant presence of at least one of Carmine's bodyguards wasn't a threat but a steadfast warning. No one was above suspicion as the fallout from Paulie's death began to settle and accumulate like the snowflakes upon the ground.

Through it all, my job was to maintain life as normal—as normal as it could be living in the boss's home with a newborn baby.

Understandably, as time passed, my concept of normal skewed. It was already so far from what I imagined as a young teenager living near the docks that in many ways I couldn't comprehend it.

My world was now made up of babies crying, women chatting, cash making its way onto my books, and soldiers in dark suits with guns at the ready. It wasn't quite what Hollywood tried to portray, yet it wasn't anything I could have ever conjured on my own. The little boy who accompanied his father to the dock to pay taxes was now living with that tax collector's bosses. Day in and day out, they knew me by name and by sight. Though Carmine kept me out of the discussions, my presence within his home was a clear message.

I didn't question my reality, nor did Angelina.

It was what it was.

I worked to comprehend all of its elements. Books and movies made the higher-ups in LCN look like crazed killers. And yet I knew the men behind the office door. I'd met them and their wives. I knew they were good men with families whom they'd vowed to protect. They were determined men who knew a way of life that had served them and most of their fathers before them. We were in the middle of the world within the world that many stated was only make-believe.

While Giuliani was planning his big 'Commission' RICO case, the world was questioning the true existence of organized crime. Perhaps it was a way to save his state, to make it a less scary place, I could only speculate, but following Big Paulie's death, the governor of New York, Mario Cuomo, came out publicly to denounce the existence of the Mafia or Cosa Nostra. He called the reports an ugly stereotype. When asked if the Mafia existed, Cuomo replied, "You're telling me that the Mafia is an organization, and I'm telling you that's a lot of baloney."

It felt at times like I was living in reality and make-believe at the same time—a fine line separating the two worlds. My office and Demetri Enterprises was the world I'd wanted to build. Maybe not completely, but it was growing. Within most of that umbrella, Oren Demetri was an entrepreneur who now received the elevator pitches, instead of giving them. Men called me *Mr.* Demetri and women offered me solace from the stress of my life and home.

And then there was the imaginary world that wasn't—the one that existed within the Costello brownstone. In this alternate reality, the dichotomy separated by the wooden door at the end of the hallway was astounding.

As I drove the snowy streets from Manhattan to Brooklyn, I sometimes wondered what my father would say. Could I explain or justify my decisions? I wasn't sure. What I knew with some certainty was that I'd do anything to place my son in my father's or mother's arms. Since that wasn't possible, I'd do all I could to keep Angelina and Lennox safe and move beyond this line between make-believe and reality.

Despite all that occurred beyond that door, the home as a whole was safety personified. I found comfort in leaving Angelina surrounded by so much love. She and Bella were like two peas in a pod, their little sons asleep in their arms or lying side by side in a playpen while the three women baked and cooked like there was no tomorrow.

Amazing scents wafted continually from the kitchen as did the ring of female laughter and babies' coos. If one spent time in the kitchen, dining room, or living room, it would be easy to forget that the fates of families and the Cosa Nostra way of life was literally hanging in the balance.

The office was empty after a day of intense discussion. The six of us—Carmine, Rose, Vincent, Bella, Angelina, and I—sat around Rose's dining room table late one night. It seemed that something was bothering Rose, yet she wasn't saying. Finally, Carmine asked the question I too had been wondering.

"What is troubling you?"

I inwardly laughed at his words, certain her list was as long as mine.

"I don't want to talk about it. Not at dinner. This is our time."

She had all of our attention.

"Fine." She sat straighter. "I'm heartbroken by the church."

Of all the issues happening, her response caught me off guard.

It was Angelina who explained, shaking her head. "Aunt Rose got a call today. The mass for Paulie has been canceled. Well, it has to be private. Very private. No one outside the immediate family."

"What?" Carmine asked, his face contorted in obvious confusion. "Who said? It's not right. Let me—"

Again, it was Angelina. "*Zio*, I know you don't want us to talk about it… especially at the table, but I saw the news. It wasn't the priest's decision. It came from the Roman Catholic Archdiocese of New York. They sent a ruling banning a public mass. They claimed it was due to Paulie's notoriety in his background."

I stared at my wife, not questioning her information. She was a news junkie. If there'd been a report, she'd seen it. However, it was as I looked back at Carmine that I understood Rose's angst. What would happen when his time came? What if it'd been Carmine on the street? Would the church that they'd supported their entire lives turn its back?

"That's ridiculous," Carmine said, his tone lighter for one reason, and she was seated beside him. He covered her hand with his. "*Tesoro*, you heard our governor; it doesn't exist."

"But…"

"But we eat. Christmas is soon, and we have all our family here. Enough."

And of course it was. Carmine had spoken.

Conversation moved from Paulie Castellano's ultimate shaming, not from the goons who murdered him on the street, but from the church that accepted his offerings and reserved a pew for his family near the front, to the way Luca was starting to pull himself to his knees.

The snow waxed and waned as the days turned to weeks, and the temperature fluctuated. During it all, my information regarding the doings of the family came in bits and pieces and mostly through Vincent.

Sometime in the last two years, I'd been deemed worthy—at least in Angelina's cousin's eyes. As Christmas passed and we skirted closer to the New Year, the talk within the office and on the street grew louder: the family formally run by Big Paulie was meeting to determine their new boss. It would have to be one of their made men, and all eyes were on the capo John Gotti.

The word finally came about two weeks after Paulie's death. As per the commission, the other four families would have a voice in approving the family's decision. Not approving would potentially single out a family, unless the entirety of the commission chose to disapprove. The information had been leaked. Tomorrow each boss would need to send an answer. It made sense that they would meet in secret before and determine how to proceed.

Tensions were high as the meeting—the one that no one knew about—occurred. I didn't know where it was happening, only that while it did, it made each boss's home a target. Within the Costello brownstone, I was stationed as the last line of defense. While in the city at the office, I'd received a call from Vincent telling me to come home immediately. It didn't matter that I had appointments. I hurried back to Brooklyn.

By the time I arrived, Vincent and Carmine were gone, and Testa was inside the front door. The outside was well protected with soldiers watching the front and back entrances. From what I understood, the goal of the 'non-occurring' meeting was for the other four families of the commission to stand as one.

I couldn't imagine the pressure of being in the room with those eight men, the bosses and their underbosses. It was a different world than it had been merely a month before. Momentarily, Luchi's heroin was tabled. Each man had the weight of many on his shoulders. And yet as I looked about the living room, seeing Rose, Angelina and Lennox, and Bella and Luca, I hoped that whatever decision was made, that the Costellos were on the right side. I'd heard the voices through the door, the angry arguments for and against Gotti. Gioconda, Vincent, Morelli, and more. None of it would matter. When it came time for Carmine to voice the family's decision, only one answer mattered.

His.

Would the rest of the family unite or revolt? What would happen between families? My mind had difficulty keeping the questions from multiplying.

Helplessness enveloped me as we all congregated together; no one said a word about what was or wasn't happening. If Paulie's family got wind of the meeting and any of them still thought the hit had been approved by the commission, then all eight men were sitting ducks. If Castellano's death had made national news, the extinction of four New York bosses would be on the cover of every newspaper all over the world.

I didn't want to think about it or look into Angelina's eyes clouded with worry.

The clock continued to tick.

With a rerun of Dynasty playing softly on the television, we all turned as Testa rose to open the front door. I sat forward, reaching for my gun as the door opened. There was a collective sigh of relief as first Carmine entered, followed by Vincent and Stefano.

We all stared in silence. It was then I realized that someone must have turned down the volume on the television. It was dead silent. In a miracle from heaven above, even the boys were quiet.

Carmine's deep voice rumbled through the room. "We all stay together through the New Year. Then, you will all go to your own homes."

Angelina exhaled and reached for my hand.

"Carmine? It's safe?" Rose asked.

"*Sì.* I wouldn't say it if it wasn't."

"A few more days," Rose said, looking around the room with glistening eyes. "I love having you all here."

"They live but minutes away," Carmine said, dismissively waving his hand as he turned and walked up the stairs. "They'll be back."

It was the first time I could recall seeing him go to his bedroom in the two weeks we'd been there. It was the first time that he didn't go straight to his office. I wasn't sure why it struck me as significant, but it did. It meant he was satisfied. It meant that whatever happened, it was in the best interest of his family, his beliefs, and his way of life. It meant he'd made the right decision. I was certain.

After kissing Angelina's cheek, I said, "I'm getting some water. Would you like any?"

"A glass of wine."

"You're nursing."

She tilted her head toward the stairs. "One glass. This deserves celebrating."

"I'll help you," Vincent volunteered.

We walked in silence until we reached the kitchen and closed the door. I didn't think I could ask what had happened, but I hoped he'd volunteer.

Instead, Vincent went to the cabinet that held the wine glasses and opened the cupboard. As he gathered the stemmed glasses, I couldn't take it any longer. "So… is a celebration in order?"

"I suppose that depends."

*Fucking Costello riddles.*

"Do *you* think it's in order?" I tried again.

"I think Pop did what he had to do. There was one holdout. But he'll accept Gotti—we all will. The one, it was a statement. He's still upset about the rule being broken. Tomorrow, each family will give its approval. It'll be official."

For some reason, I was happy that there was one holdout. It wasn't that it would stop Gotti's appointment. It was the confirmation that I hadn't realized I'd needed. The evidence that Carmine had been honest that night in the hospital when he'd said he hadn't known about the hit—that all of the family bosses were shocked. Over time there'd be more speculation, but the man I respected had been vulnerable and shaken in my presence, and yet through it all he'd been honest. There were many things that could be said about the men and families of LCN, but despite their activities, there was honor and respect.

I suspected it would take some time for Gotti to earn what Carmine had. Time would tell if he would. The potential demise was averted. Life could go back to the issues at hand: the heroin and the feds and RICO.

It would take time to see how the latter changed their tactics. Their case had been showcased around Castellano. And now even the governor was denying the existence of LCN. Now what would the feds do? To what lengths would they go to win their case and substantiate their claims?

I wasn't sure what would happen, but on that night, those were too big of questions to ponder. I wanted to believe that Angelina was correct, and a celebration was in order.

"Let me carry the wine," I volunteered.

Right now, we'd concentrate on the positive. We'd celebrate because soon I'd be able to take Angelina and Lennox back to our home. Soon, we'd be the family Angelina wanted.

That was my plan.

# CHAPTER 18

—————•O•—————

OUR PLAN WORKED. Within the walls of our Brooklyn brownstone, our family resided as temperatures warmed, cooled, and warmed again. The cycle continued as time moved forward: things changed as well as stayed the same. We visited the Costellos every Sunday after our mandatory pew-sharing at church. Lennox grew bigger, his energy abounding. Angelina and I made a decision that while contrary to our religious belief was one that satisfied our moral one.

We decided that we'd protect and support Lennox as a Demetri and a Costello, and when the time came, we'd do our best to keep him on the sidelines of the world in which his mother was born. However, despite the directive to go forth and multiply, we wouldn't have more children. It was a mutual decision made within the bonds of our marriage. The events surrounding Lennox's birth had affected not only us but also the world we knew.

Even now, years later, the far-reaching effects could be felt.

The feds were making cases. Indictments and subpoenas were commonplace. The Costellos had deep pockets when it came to some of the best legal advice as well as other resources. Miraculously, sometimes evidence disappeared and witnesses had a change of heart. That wasn't

ALEATHA ROMIG

only with the Costellos but with all the families. Influence continued to abound on both sides of the judicial bench.

With my assistance and the help of others, the Costello family continued to move beyond having its center in the world of illegal dealings. The family as a whole—and many of the individuals within— was venturing into lucrative and legit operations. The surface was becoming shinier; however, even that knowledge wasn't enough to satisfy Angelina or me regarding the future and Lennox.

We needed to make a logistical move.

I'd found land outside the city in Westchester County, on the shores of the Long Island Sound. It was an absolutely stunning lot with a sparkling view. I hadn't been as excited about anything in a long time as I was the day I took Angelina to see it. As we stood in the open expanse with the water glittering before us, I explained the home I wanted to build for her and Lennox—a fortress away from the mix, a place where our son could play in a yard with a pool for her.

"It's so far away from everyone," Angelina said as she reached for my hand and turned to the right and the left. A few homes in the area were built while others were in various stages of construction. "And they look so big. We don't need that much room. There're only three of us. We only need two bedrooms."

We had three bedrooms in Brooklyn. I agreed we didn't *need* more. I wanted more.

"Just think about the yard," I prompted. "Imagine the two of us sharing a bottle of wine on a balcony outside our bedroom. *Mio angelo*, I'll build you a bedroom so large you can read on a sofa near the windows and watch as the sun rises over the water." When she didn't respond, I continued, "Remember how much you enjoyed the swimming pool on our honeymoon?"

"Yes."

I motioned, pointing this way and that. "Your very own pool. Lennox can take swimming lessons. There's a country club down the way. Think of the friends he'll make, that you'll make. Lennox will be with a new set of friends. He can do what boys do. And then when you're at home, we can activate a state-of-the-art security system and close the gate. You'll be safe."

She squeezed my hand. "I see how happy this makes you, but you're rarely home now, and your office is just over the bridge. Will I ever see you here? Will *we* make friends or just me?"

It was our never-ending argument. I wasn't home enough. I'd gotten better at calling and since Lennox was born, Angelina was busier and more occupied, but no matter how many nights I tried to come home at a respectable time, it was never enough. If I made it home three nights a week for dinner, it should have been four. Four should have been five and five, six. After nearly five years of marriage, I doubted I'd ever succeed. "I'll say what I always say: I'll try. I am excited about this home—our home. I brought you here hoping you'd be also."

She let go of my hand and turned a complete circle. With a sigh, she walked toward the shore, a thin strip of sand that went on in both directions, accented with clusters of large rocks here and there. For what seemed like an eternity, I watched as her dark hair and the skirt of her dress blew in the saltwater breeze. I studied her gorgeous figure and watched as she bent down and scooped a handful of pebbles and then stood again, and one by one, tossed them into the water. Slowly, I came up behind her, wrapping my arms around her waist. Without a word, she laid her head against my shoulder, still facing away from me, and sighed.

"*Mio angelo*, talk to me."

"It is best."

Her body melted toward me as she exhaled. From the slight quiver in her breath, I suspected she was crying. Not at all the reaction I wanted or planned.

"Best...?" I encouraged.

"Lennox will be starting school soon. It's in his blood. The way he and Luca play. One day the cops and robbers will be real. One day, he'll learn he's the robber and yet believe that it's the right side—because it is, in our minds. I used to play the same thing with Vinny." She spun in my arms until our gazes met. Her eyes were moist, but there were no tears. "Sometimes I feel so isolated." Her hand came to my chest, her fingers splaying over my heart. "Don't be upset. I'm not saying that to hurt you. I'm being honest. You're always busy with something other than Lennox and me."

I nodded, swallowing the lump in my throat that her words created.

"I'm afraid that being here in Rye, it will be worse, and yet it's best for him."

"So you approve of us buying this land, building a house?" I realized there was probably more against than in favor of in her statement, but I was grasping at straws.

"Oren, if I know you, you've already bought it."

My eyes closed as I confessed. "I had to move fast. This is a fantastic location. It wouldn't have lasted..."

The hand on my chest moved to my cheek, urging my eyes to open. Instead of anger, I saw her radiant smile. "I know you, Oren Demetri. I love you. I know you think this is best, and I trust you."

"You're right, I did buy the land, but I haven't hired an architect. But I do know the one I want... well, the one I want to make the first draft."

"You do?"

"Yes," I said. "I want you."

"Me?"

"You're so talented. You never went back to the Met after Lennox was born. He's four and a half. How about you use your education and talent to design our perfect home?"

Her eyes sparkled in a way I rarely saw, only when she was looking at our son, but in this moment, those glistening blue orbs were directed at me. "Oh, Oren! It's been so long."

"Tell me what you need. I can get you the elevations, the lot size, the codes and covenants... whatever you need."

Angelina took a step away and turned from the beach to the property. This time, her expression beamed with a new enthusiasm. It was what I'd longed to see. "I think I can."

I went to her. "*Mio angelo*, I *know* you can. Once you're done with your vision and sketches, we'll have the official blueprints made."

"Thank you," she said with her gaze full of wonder. "I promise a balcony from our room overlooking the sound."

"And a pool."

"Oh! I saw this magazine with a pool house made mostly of glass."

My heart twinged. Glass. Could it be made safe?

I wouldn't take away from her newfound excitement. "Scour magazines and books. Come up with whatever you want. This is your home, *ours*. Make it a place where we can grow old, a place that is unique and says Angelina Demetri designed me. And then let me consult some engineers and make it safe."

She exhaled. "Oh, this is more than I ever imagined. But does it need to be as large as the other homes?"

"I know it will only be the three of us, but what if we have company? What if one day we need rooms for grandchildren?"

The earlier worry and discontentment was gone as her cheeks rose.

"Filled with family. Lennox's family. Our family. I like that."

"Then you draw it."

"I will."

And she did. Our dining room table in our Brooklyn brownstone became her workroom. The table was consumed with the clutter of stacks of magazines and all kinds of home designs. Each periodical and book was littered with small colored papers bookmarking the designs she liked. When I'd come home, instead of the cold reception for being late, she'd chat on and on about ideas she'd seen, thoughts she had. After dinner, we'd spend time looking through pictures and designs together.

Even Lennox joined the excitement, showing me pictures he'd drawn of our new house.

The news of our imminent move wasn't as well received by her family. Carmine and Rose liked having their niece and grandnephew nearby. However, Vincent's response was different. Though he and Bella now had a second child, a daughter, Luisa, for his parents to fuss over, he was increasingly curious. I had the impression that he may be thinking about making a similar move.

The initial planning and design of our home took months. If the blueprints were being made by a firm, I would have expected a shorter timeline—I had for much larger projects—but I couldn't rush Angelina's creative instinct. She decided that each bedroom should have its own bathroom. We'd go from one and a half bathrooms to seven. There would be two rooms with balconies that would be ours and Lennox's. The kitchen was modern and open. Over the garage was a full guest suite, like an apartment within our home.

When I first saw her sketches of the back of the house—the side overlooking the sound—my gut twisted. I'd done my own research. Windows could be constructed with bulletproof glass. Of course, the cost was astronomical as compared to regular windows. Nevertheless, it could be done. She had windows everywhere.

"If I'm going to live on the water, I want to see it."

I couldn't argue.

She found the picture of the pool house she'd mentioned the first day I showed her the property. In her plans it was attached to the kitchen with—of course—a window-lined corridor. Minus a large fireplace and beams, it was primarily constructed of glass.

"Just think," she said as she explained, "with air conditioning, it can be kept cool in the summer, or if it's not that hot outside, the windows can be opened to a beautiful breeze, and in the winter, the sun will warm it with the help of the fireplace and heat, but oh, Oren, it will be perfect in any season."

We weren't able to move before Lennox began school.

He started kindergarten in Brooklyn. Though it hadn't been our plan, it was a familiar start for him. Angelina told me about his teacher and classmates. We knew the majority of the parents, and he'd known most of the children. They were part of this life, this neighborhood, our current world. Along with designing the new home, my wife's days became filled with transporting him to and from school and helping Bella. It was more difficult for Bella with Luca now that they had Luisa.

Finally, nearly a year after I bought the property, construction began. Contracts were awarded to contractors I knew and trusted. Unlike any other construction that I'd financed, this was our home. Detail to security was essential. Materials were checked and double checked. Angelina said I was paranoid, but if one panel of glass was thought to be bulletproof and it wasn't, someone would know. That someone, no doubt, had nefarious plans. I wasn't willing to take the chance.

"Look over here," Angelina said one evening before the sun set when

I met her at the construction site.

Lennox was occupied running up and down a mound of dirt, busy in some make-believe world.

I followed her through the skeleton of our home. The steps to the second floor were only boards.

"Stay out there," I yelled to our son. I turned to Angelina's scowl at my tone. "Don't look at me like that. I don't want him climbing these stairs."

Angelina laughed and shook her head as she tugged me upward. "He's not a baby. He's more grown up than you realize. Besides, he's already been up here. I showed him his new room.

"Come here." She tugged me toward a large opening. "There will be two doors." She walked into the framed room. "And this is our room."

It was difficult to judge the size with the transparency of the framing, but it seemed like it was exactly what I'd promised. "The balcony?" I asked.

"Over here." She led me forward. "From up here, we'll be able to see the yard, the pool, and the beach."

As she was chatting on about the bathroom, I pulled her close, silencing her words with a kiss. Her body lost tension as she melded against me. I missed this side of my wife. I wanted this, more than anything. I made a silent vow that once we were in this home, she'd be the only woman I wanted. I would never again step outside our marriage.

I wasn't proud that it had occurred, and I justified it with the fact that it had never been with the same woman twice. I could make every excuse in the world and maybe even assign blame, but none of that mattered. I knew what I'd done was wrong. I knew the vows I'd spoken. I knew the vow I'd broken. I also knew how incredibly frustrating it was to continually fail the woman I loved and see the disappointment in her eyes.

I could say that on occasion I chose to see a different gaze. None of those excuses or reasoning mattered. No one mattered more than my angel.

"Oren?"

Somehow with her in my arms and thoughts of how it should be, my body had reacted. She pushed her hips toward me as my erection grew beneath my expensive suit.

"*Mio angelo*, I want walls and a bed."

She giggled. "I can tell."

"I love you."

Her hand again came to my cheek. "And I love you. Maybe we can find walls and a bed in our house, the one where we now live."

It had been too long. "I'd like that. I also love seeing you happy."

"I want to be," she said. "I really do."

High above within the skeleton of our home, our lips found each other's. She tasted sweet, a spearmint indication of the gum she'd been chewing. For a moment, we were rulers of our new world, and I believed in the strength of our foundation. Just like the house being constructed below us, our love was strong. It would prevail.

# CHAPTER 19

———•O•———

WATCHING OUR HOME come to life was nearly as rewarding as watching Angelina give it the essential elements. Many times, with Lennox by her side and Testa at the wheel, she would travel from store to store with strips of different paint colors, tile squares, and carpet samples. When I'd return home, she'd excitedly show me what she'd found and the beautiful combinations.

Each room and color scheme made her eyes sparkle as she'd describe what would be. If it was her wish, I agreed. There was no expense I spared. Finally, the day came, and the movers arrived to Windsor Terrace.

Though I was at the office, Angelina called to let me know they'd arrived. With Lennox at school, she was devoted to assuring the safe passage of our belongings.

When my first meeting of the afternoon cancelled, instead of asking Julie, my secretary, to fill the timeslot, I decided to have her clear the rest of the day. It was out of character and felt exhilarating. After all, this move was monumental for our small family.

There was something about what we were doing that created an overwhelming sense of hope. It was as if there was once again optimism for our future. Not that the expectancy had ever died; it had simply waned. The pressures of everyday life can do that.

As this rare emotion sprinted through my veins, tingling my skin, I reached a conclusion. Instead of spending my day as I usually did—reading reports, checking expenditures, visiting construction sites, and meeting with people to discuss the same things we always discussed—I wanted to experience our move firsthand.

My secretary's head tilted. "Are you sure, Mr. Demetri? You're going to leave early?"

"Yes, I am. I am sure, and I am leaving." The words felt right.

Besides, I didn't need to explain myself to her or even to the people she would need to reschedule. They were coming to me, not the other way around. I'd worked long and hard to be in this position, and for once, I was going to take advantage of it.

"Okay," Julie mumbled as she scribbled notes on a pad of paper in her hand. "I'll reschedule. But just so you know, Mr. Salado has been on the schedule for nearly a month. He's confident you'll want to hear his proposal."

Julie was the most competent secretary I'd had in forever. She'd also been around longer than most. A few years older than me, she was happily married with two children. I'd told myself I mostly hired unmarried women because they were less likely to have family issues. That wasn't sexist: it was simply fact. However, if I'd been concerned about that with Julie, I'd been wrong.

Over the time she's been my executive secretary, I was confident that if the need arose, she could run the entire company. She was quick on her feet and intelligent. She was an excellent problem solver and excelled at time management. The woman could multitask with the best of them. Since she accepted the position, I was rarely faced with a meaningless appointment. She prescreened everyone. If Julie said Mr. Salado's proposal was worth my time, undoubtedly, it was. However, as far as this afternoon was concerned, my mind was made up.

"I'm sure I'll want to hear it, another time." I looked down at my calendar. "I can stay late on Wednesday or Friday. If early works better, schedule that. Let's get him in soon."

Her concern lessened. "Thank you. I'll call his assistant right away. May I ask? Is there a problem?"

My smile grew. "No, there's no problem. I want to spend the afternoon with my family."

Her forehead lifted as surprise filled her eyes. "I see. Well, I'm certain Mrs. Demetri will be happy to hear that."

"I hope so. But please don't call her. We have movers coming today, and I want to surprise her."

Julie nodded with a grin. "Your secret is safe with me. I'll reschedule the afternoon."

"Thank you, Julie. Please divert my calls and only contact me if it's truly an emergency."

"Yes, sir. Unless the building is on fire, your afternoon is free."

Julie and I had come to a comfortable understanding. My plans for the afternoon weren't the only secret of mine she possessed. It seemed that many female employees came to my office with expectations. While I was no saint, I'd never slept with any of the women working directly under me. Technically, since I was the CEO of Demetri Enterprises, they all worked under me. Nevertheless, I shied away from women I'd be forced to see the next day and the day after. That didn't mean that the ones in the past who had made it to my executive office didn't make their availability known.

I wasn't quite sure how it worked in the secretarial pool, but I guessed that like men, women talked. I probably had a reputation. Prior to working for me, Julie had been working in another department. I'd seen her reports and heard positive things about her. I was in need of a new executive secretary, and tired of turnover, I wanted someone competent.

When she was approached by human resources, she apparently wasn't sure about applying for the position despite the increase in pay. Reluctantly, she agreed to an interview. During our first meeting, she unequivocally made her marital status known. I assured her that I too was married. With a proud posture and serious expression, she replied, "Yes, Mr. Demetri, but I intend to stay that way."

I did too, but nonetheless, her declaration was impressive. At that moment I knew I wanted her to work for me. If this feisty five-foot-three-inch woman could look me—the owner of the company—in the eye and state her case, she could handle anyone. I was right. Julie's been with me for the last three years. She runs a tight ship, and from a managerial point of view, I couldn't be happier.

All of that didn't mean that since her presence, I hadn't accepted the attention of other female employees. Julie not only handled Demetri Enterprise business well, but she was outstanding at keeping my indiscretions from crossing the threshold to my office—literally and figuratively. She also took the liberty to remind me of appointments with my wife, send Angelina random gifts, and circle my anniversary with a large red marker on my calendar. Technically, she was only old enough to be my older sister, yet she'd taken on a kind of mother role that for some reason I didn't mind.

As a side bonus, Angelina and I had gotten to know her husband, Albert. He was a good man, hard worker, and cared immensely for his family. I was lucky to have Julie working for me, and I knew it. And if I ever forgot, she was capable of reminding me.

As I gathered my things and was about to leave, I relished the overpowering hopefulness that I felt. When had I been this optimistic for my and Angelina's future?

Was it the first time I saw her after college? When I proposed? On our wedding day? Maybe our honeymoon?

I couldn't say. Instead, I wanted to revel in it as long as it lasted.

"Mr. Demetri?" Julie said as I was leaving.

"Yes?"

"Don't forget, she likes colorful daisies."

I nodded.

Hustling through midday traffic, I pulled up near our home, the one where we would no longer live. For a few minutes, I stayed in the car, watching from afar.

Under the canopy of trees, shaded from the summer sun, a cavernous moving truck had slowly begun to be filled. I grimaced as two big burly men carried furniture down the steps. With a footed loveseat in their grips and sweat dripping from their faces and staining their shirts, they moved in sync until the furniture piece was inside the truck. When I opened the car door, even from a few houses down, my wife's voice came into range. Her tone brought a smile to my face.

"Be careful with that... That's fragile... That belonged to my parents..."

A chuckle escaped my throat as I continued to watch. Only a few steps behind the movers, she followed, giving orders. Her voice was strong and authoritarian despite the discrepancy in her size and theirs. Her dynamic spirit continued to amaze me. It radiated from her. She was a star, and yet there was nothing flashy about her appearance: her hair was in a ponytail and she was wearing a well-fitted T-shirt and a pair of those pants, the ones that weren't shorts, but weren't pants. They came to her calves. She'd told me what they were called, but I didn't remember nor had I cared. Not until now.

As Angelina continued to bark orders, the woman in my vision was so much more than the sophisticated lady who wowed everyone at Carmine's parties and more than Lennox's mother, dressed to meet the teacher. She was my angel. In that instant, my memory flashed back to the nineteen-year-old at NYU, the one who first caught my eye and still owned my heart.

If sworn under oath, I'd be tempted to testify that somehow my wife had found the secret to eternal youth. She was simply perfect, and I was enamored.

I chuckled as her voice came in and out of range. Never once did I hear from the men carrying our belongings. Instead, I only saw their heads nod in agreement. She may have been half their size or less, but if I were a gambling man, I'd put my money on my angel.

Slamming the car's door, I started down the sidewalk toward our home, a bouquet of multicolored daisies in my hand. Angelina turned my way. For only a moment her head tilted, as if she were seeing a mirage, and then her entire expression blossomed. Hurrying my way, she called, "Oren. What are you doing here?"

"I live here. Well, technically I still do, but not for long."

Her eyes sparkled as she reached for my shoulders. "It's so exciting. I thought I'd be sad. After all, this was our first home, but I'm more excited than sad."

With the bouquet now behind her back, I surrounded her waist and pulled her close. Under the shade of a big tree we kissed, her sweet pink lips pushing against mine as she lifted herself to her toes. When we pulled away, I looked down into her natural beauty. Smiling, I lifted my thumb. With the pad, I rubbed a smudge of dirt from her cheek. "You're stunning."

Her hands flew to her hair and then her cheeks. "I'm a mess. But I swear... those movers have to be watched every second." Her body twisted. "Did I see flowers?"

I presented her with the bouquet. "I know the vases are packed, but I wanted to get you something."

"Oren, you got me a house."

"*We* did that. It wouldn't be what it is today without you."

She kissed my cheek.

Our attention was diverted back to our brownstone as two other men exited the front door with chairs, each carrying two piled on top of the other.

"Oh no." She handed me back the flowers. "That's our good dining room..."

I shook my head, ready to follow yet certain she could handle it, when out of the corner of my eye, I caught a familiar dark stare. Across the street in the shadows was her cousin with his arms folded over his chest, leaning casually against another brownstone.

I nodded his direction.

Tossing a toothpick from his lips, Vincent checked both directions on our quiet street and crossed, coming my way.

"Nice flowers," he said.

"In the neighborhood?" I asked, ignoring the flowers.

"Always... at least usually. Pop wanted to be sure everything was good with the movers."

I scoffed. "Everything's good with Angelina. The movers may have another story."

He laughed. "She's been busting their balls for the last hour. It's been too good of a show to walk away."

"Does she know you're here?"

"No. She's got it handled. I was just checking. You know? Didn't know you'd be here. She's family."

"Thanks." I could be offended that he doubted my presence. Then again, I hadn't decided to be here until recently; therefore, he was justified. I suddenly wondered how many other times he'd checked on Angelina and Lennox when it should have been me.

"Well, you did it."

Vincent's tone, neither congratulatory nor derogatory, caused my question to disappear. I took a deep breath. We *had* done it—Angelina and me. Everything was set for our move. The new house was perfect. Using Angelina's design and talent for the details, together we'd constructed a fortress hidden in plain sight: a safe house concealed inconspicuously in a good neighborhood behind a gate. From the street, it appeared as any other house. Yet the electric fencing, cameras, thicker-than-standard walls, and bulletproof glass made it unique. They made it exactly what I'd wanted for my family.

And still, in some ways, it seemed too good to be true.

So close and yet not there.

Perhaps that was why I chose to come home instead of stay at the office.

My only response, "I'll be happy when we're settled."

"You may have started a trend. I've been looking too."

I turned his way. "At property? Where?"

"Here and there. Pop doesn't want us to move... *either*," he added. "But he's watching. He won't say it, but he admires your drive and ambition. Despite obstacles big and small, you don't give up."

"He said that?"

"Nah, you know Pop?"

I did.

"He talks in pieces," Vincent said.

*Fucking Costello riddles.*

"He knows," Vincent went on, "that I'm thinking about moving Bella and the kids. He's watching you. I'm watching." He patted my shoulder. "Don't screw up."

"Thanks. No pressure." I snorted.

"Ah, we all have pressure. The pot's boiling. Everything is swirling inside a fucking pressure cooker, and it's about to blow. It's been bubbling since Paulie and even before. Now with Sammy talking..."

Vincent didn't need to say more. Gotti's underboss, Sammy Gravano, had spilled his guts to the feds and was scheduled to testify under oath. If the reports of what he'd said were true—and we had reliable inside sources—his testimony confirmed the earlier suspicions: Gotti had called for the assassination of Castellano. Not only called for it, but he'd been in a car with Sammy a few blocks away when it happened. He'd planned the killing of a family boss—broken a steadfast rule—and now Sammy was breaking another by talking.

He was breaking our *Omertà*.

"I guess there's some reassurance in knowing Paulie was the only target," I said.

Vincent shrugged. "He was the only target for the bullets. Seems to me if the bosses had handled it differently, if they'd fought amongst themselves, it could have ignited a full-out war."

"Thank God they didn't."

"The feds think they—the bosses—are all stupid criminals. They're not. *We're* not. We only want what's best for those we care about."

I nodded. "The Costello family's moving in the right direction." Though I believed that, I also knew things were turbulent.

My mind slipped back a few years. They say that hindsight is 20/20.

I hadn't realized at the time how beneficial Gioconda's suspicion of me would be. He was right to be cautious. I was new and relatively untested. I'd like to take more credit for helping Angelina's family through the last few years, but as in most things, the decisions all came down to Carmine. Maybe with the feds' wiretaps and the rumors of discontent, Carmine didn't see me as a target of suspicion, but as a safer alternative.

I doubted I'd ever have a heart-to-heart talk with him to find out exactly what he'd been thinking. No matter the why, Carmine's instructions for me to keep Demetri Enterprises as clean as possible and use my connections primarily for cleaning family money and spreading the wealth—reinvesting it in many different places—allowed the Costellos to survive the storm that many families were struggling to navigate.

I'd heard a story that years back the family was struggling financially. If that were ever the case, it wasn't any longer. Much of their underworld money was now out in the world, growing and even being assessed for taxes. If and when the feds looked, the Costellos had financial records that could withstand scrutiny.

Admittedly, Carmine's insistence to keep the family steadfast in old-time racketeering and away from the heroin and cocaine mess also aided in keeping the Costellos further off the radar. The topic of illegal drugs ignited the masses. Giuliani could get on the television and preach that the mobsters were ruining the youth with drugs.

I agreed with Carmine that as a revenue source, drugs were risky. I also questioned the claim that *the families* were responsible for the ruination of our city's youth. From what I'd seen, they were doing a good job of that all by themselves.

Currently, the city—and beyond—was riveted to their TVs and newspapers for updates of a long ongoing drug trial. To give the feds more ammunition, it revolved around a Queens pizzeria with an alleged connection to Sicilian drugs. Each night, Angelina gave me updates from the prognosticators on the evening news. It was time for everyone to lose interest. The trial had already been going on for a year.

With the threats from outside and concerns within, it was difficult to stay out of the fray.

Vincent simply nodded at my earlier reassurance. Finally, he said, "Pop got a subpoena a few days ago. He's got his guys working on it. With Sammy squealing, they're hoping for more."

"Doesn't seem like they need more."

"Rumor has it that they're going for the angle that all the bosses knew what was going on—they approved it. Conspiracy or some bullshit allegation."

I turned and stared into Vincent's dark eyes. "He didn't know."

"I know that. If you're asked, remember that."

As two men carried a large chest of drawers wrapped in blankets out our front door and maneuvered down the steps, my stomach twisted. The night of Lennox's birth came back to me. "I don't think I'll ever forget."

"You know," Vincent said, "you think you know people. You think you can trust them… and then they turn, like Sammy. I'm not condoning what Gotti did. Hell no. It was wrong. I'm just saying that if Sammy was with him, then Gotti trusted him. There's a lot of things I hate. Fucking rats top that list."

"Is there anyone who isn't trusted? Is your father concerned?"

Vincent shrugged. "I'm not sure he trusts anyone right now, me included. And he knows he can—trust me. It's just a rough patch. We'll get through it. We always do. That's the thing with you moving away… I get it. Pop does too. But to the outside, it looks like you're abandoning family."

Keeping my expression in check, I met him eye to eye. "If Carmine is worried about my loyalty, he can ask me himself."

"He just did. It just sounded like me."

"Our moving to Rye," I went on, "hasn't been a sudden decision. The damn house took nearly a year to construct. We're having a housewarming party next Saturday. We're not hiding. Every fucking person will know where we are. If I wanted to hide, I'd take Angelina and Lennox and flee the country."

"Doubt the feds would let you."

"Well, that's comforting."

Vincent's demeanor lightened as Angelina came into view, following closely behind a man with a box. While her lips moved, his head simply nodded.

"Just keep up drinks each Thursday," Vincent said to me. "Even if church here is only once a month…"

I started to respond, to tell him there was a nice parish in Rye, but a slight shake of his head stopped me.

"Keep Demetri clean and come when called. Make appearances with the family now and then. Pop knows where your heart is. He knows mine too. The fucker whispering in his ear is my concern at the moment. Gioconda is a snake—fucking anaconda. Pop won't talk about it. Everyone is under a microscope."

"Vinny!" Angelina called our way. "How long have you been here?"

Suddenly nothing but smiles, Angelina's cousin leaned in and kissed my wife's cheek. "I was just seeing if this was really happening." He laughed. "And enjoying watching you take charge of the show."

She nodded as a small smile came to her lips. "I always do. It's best you remember that."

Vincent looked my way, and my lips came together in a smart decision not to respond.

"I mean," Vincent said with a grin, "look at Oren. He's the flower girl."

I shook my head. I'd completely forgotten I was holding Angelina's daisies.

She took them from me. "He's holding them for me. And yes, the move is really happening. We're going to Westchester County. It's not like it's the other side of the country." She bounced with her excitement. "I can't wait for the housewarming party next week. Bella and the kids have been up there. Luca and Lennox love the pool. You should see them. They're like fish. I can't wait for you and the rest of the family to see it, too. You know, Bella has a great eye for decorating. She's been a marvelous help."

"Yeah," Vincent said, "you've got her talking about how outdated our house is. Sooner or later we'll be moving too."

"Not too far," I said. "You don't want to raise suspicion."

His eyes narrowed.

"What's going on?" Angelina asked.

"Nothing," Vincent and I both said in unison.

Angelina shook her head and turned to me. "Will you go tell the movers to be careful with the boxes from the dining room? I swear they've become immune to me. They'll listen to you. That's my mother's china."

"Anything else?" I asked Vincent.

"See you Thursday—drinks."

"Of course."

As Angelina and I walked into the house, leaving Vincent on the street, Angelina sighed. "I thought maybe us moving away might bring you home on Thursdays."

"Me too."

# CHAPTER 20

———●○●———

FROM THE OUTSIDE, the windows glowed with golden light. Cars lined the driveway to capacity as other cars parked along the street. Inside our new home, a variety of melodies rang out from the grand piano, infiltrating the air and combining with the din of conversation to add to the festive atmosphere. Most of the rooms on the main level overflowed with family and friends, all clustered in small groups, talking and laughing, each adding their own spice to the mix. People even spilled outside onto the patio around the pool.

I'd never been much on parties. My forte was one-on-one. If given ten minutes of a person's time, I could assess everything about them and determine my best plan of action. If I was in need of their assistance, I capitalized upon their strength. If instead, it was my favor the person wanted, I sought out their weakness. I'd found it beneficial to assess both.

Truthfully, as I scanned the faces, I assessed that I'd been alone for ten minutes or more with most of the people in our home. I knew their strengths and their weaknesses.

Standing near the periphery of the party, I swirled the melting ice in my Balvenie whiskey—an expensive single barrel scotch whiskey and one I knew Carmine enjoyed. He'd scoff at the melting ice detracting from the strong taste, but I admittedly wasn't the drinker he could be. I found keeping my wits, especially in such company, was a good plan. Alcohol could be considered a weakness to many of those inside my home and outside of it too.

As faces came in and out of view, I nodded to Albert and Julie. There were other people from the corporate offices. It was as I scanned that I realized that along with the normal crowd, there were a few I didn't know. They were new neighbors and people who lived nearby, people who Angelina had come in contact with during the construction.

My wife had that knack, the gift to make friends with simply a word or a smile. Allowing the small amount of whiskey I'd consumed to lighten my mood, I wondered how many of her new friends had any idea of the dark pasts and presents of their fellow guests. She no longer carried the name Costello. The neon sign of her connection was gone.

Could these 'nice' people have any idea of the life-and-death deals the debonair men in tailored dark suits standing merely feet away made on a regular basis? Did they recognize any of their faces from the six o'clock news or perhaps from mug shots they'd seen in the newspaper?

Inwardly, smirking at the diversity before me, I conceded that as a rule of thumb, no one looked their best in a mug shot. It wasn't like the police photographer was trying to create a family heirloom. More likely, the opposite: a terrorizing image to influence jurors.

Tonight, the men I'd come to know, both Costellos and associates, were dressed in their finest with their wives or girlfriends on their arms. The women whose high-pitched laughter infiltrated the drone, sparkled from their heads to their toes with shimmering dresses of all lengths and colors, high heels that tapped upon the tiled floor, and dainty clutch purses that they tightly held to their bodies. Their hair was styled and makeup done to perfection. It was as if, unlike the new neighbors, each woman on a Costello associate's arm understood the significance of her hostess—the honor it was to be in Angelina's new magnificent home.

If an observer didn't know the history of some of those in attendance as I did, perhaps it would be possible to see their fellow guests as simply friends gathered for a housewarming party. Even those guests who didn't understand and were clueless about the power emanating from the rooms seemed to enjoy themselves, talking, drinking, eating, and laughing.

About a half an hour ago, I'd left Carmine, Vincent, and Gioconda, along with a few other gentlemen, in my private office. There seemed to be a sense of proprietorship that accompanied Carmine. My office was his office. I'd stayed in the smoke-filled room long enough for niceties—cigars and the drink still in my hand—and then I'd politely excused myself when the conversation exceeded my rank. Being the owner of the home and office apparently didn't influence what could be said in my presence.

I'd learned over the years that the lack of knowledge of some of the more intimate workings of the Costello family had its advantage. I had no desire to exercise my right as the homeowner in an attempt to cause a shift in the relationship that to this point was working.

"Very nice, Oren."

I turned to the deep voice, my expression stoic, purposely not revealing my surprise that Gioconda was talking to me. "Thank you, Carl. I'm glad you could make it."

"I needed to see what would move you to take Angelina away from her home."

The tightness in my chest increased. "This is her home now. *Ours*," I added with emphasis.

"Yes, and very nice. Perhaps you could give me a tour of the outside?"

I took a deep breath and placed the glass of watered-down whiskey on a nearby table. For the party, I'd convinced Angelina to hire a catering service to allow her to enjoy the guests. It took a little encouragement, but finally she gave in. Someone would remove the unattended glass, saving me from finishing the weakened concoction.

As Gioconda and I walked toward the open glass doors at the back of the house, I turned in time to see my wife's blue eyes meet mine. Without a word, she asked if everything was all right. In the same silent language, I replied that I didn't know.

With each step, the weight of my revolver reminded me of its presence under my suit coat, in a holster in the waistband of my trousers. I'd taken Carmine's advice from years ago to heart. The holster was as commonplace in my attire as my shirt, jacket, or tie. Rarely did it make its presence known, yet undoubtedly, it reassured me.

I wasn't without practice. I went to the shooting range. I was proficient. Yet in a shoot-out with Gioconda, I'd probably never have the chance to remove it from the holster, and if I did, I doubted I'd have time to hit the safety. And if by some miracle I succeeded, I would ultimately fail.

Gioconda was made. Without a threat to Carmine, Angelina, or Lennox, I couldn't kill a made man. I wasn't looking to kill anyone. The concern lurked in the back of my thoughts. Yet so far, I'd made my mark in the Costello world as an earner. An earner could be made if the books were opened.

While it was an honor, it wasn't my goal. I was content where I was, as long as Carmine found my services worthwhile

As we walked beyond the guests gathered about the deck and lighted pool, the piano music coming from within faded. With each step out into the large yard, the atmosphere cooled. I wasn't sure if it was brought on by the actual temperature as we neared the water, or if it was that since

Gioconda's request for a tour, not another word had been uttered.

The night air filled with noises of Long Island Sound. Soft waves splashed upon large stones on shore and echoed as distant foghorns reminded water vessels of potential obstacles in their path. Above us the sky was dark and peppered with stars, so much more vivid than in the city, yet not nearly as bright as they could be. The moon was a crescent sliver accenting the water's waves with a silver hue. Across the sound, the lights of Long Island illuminated the horizon.

When we came to a stop with our shoes on the pebbles and sand, I finally decided that as host, it was my right to question. "Did you want to talk or simply see the water?"

He turned toward the Long Island Sound. "It's dark and deep."

"Yes, it can be."

"Do you ever wonder what's hidden under the depths?"

"It hasn't crossed my mind."

"More important things to think about?" Gioconda asked as he removed a cigar from the inside of his jacket, flicked the paper ring to the ground, and produced a silver lighter from his pocket. The lighter ignited with a spark as he lit the thick stogie. With the smoke quickly dissipating into the breeze, the orange glow bounced with each word, bobbing up and down. Before I could respond, he asked another question. "Why did you do it?"

I wasn't sure what he was asking. "You need to be a little more specific."

"Make the move. You had a good thing living close to the boss. Your hands are relatively clean, and he's gone out on more than one limb for you. You repay him by taking his niece to fucking Connecticut."

We were still in New York, but I doubted Gioconda needed a geography lesson. "She'll always be a Costello. It's in her blood."

"Lennox's too."

"True," I replied through clenched teeth. I turned back to the house. It truly was spectacular all lit up and filled with people. "Don't you think that my wife, the boss's niece, deserves this? Do you think I should have denied her?"

"There's talk that it's more. Lots of rats these days. The way to fight them is with solidarity. You moving, that's the opposite."

"I'm loyal to my wife's uncle. If he doubts that, he can ask me."

"Maybe he just did."

I didn't have a response. It was the same thing Vincent had said only a few days ago. But Gioconda wasn't Angelina's cousin. He had no personal stake in my success or longevity for that matter.

"We can go back up to the house and get you another drink," I suggested.

Gioconda blew smoke into the breeze. "He's not worried about the subpoena. I think it can be taken care of. He's solid. But the feds are going after everyone. I'm not confident that you can take the pressure."

I wasn't about to plead my case. I'd stated my loyalty. We stood surrounded by the foghorns and waves for what seemed like minutes. Finally, he asked, "I give you time, yet you don't take it?"

I turned to face him. "I'm not sure what you thought I'd take." That ability to assess people, the skill I possessed, was working overtime. Something told me that Gioconda was fishing and doing his own assessing. A man who babbles on to prove his point accomplishes the opposite. "I told you and I told Vincent that the Costello family is my family. I'm loyal. If taking care of Angelina and lending assistance when asked isn't enough, then your decision is made. Nothing I say will dissuade you or him."

The orange glow bobbed up and down in what I hoped was

Gioconda's understanding of my position. "I'll take that drink. If we know you're solid, the boss may have some new requests."

"He knows where I live," I said as we turned and walked back up the lawn toward the house.

If I became a stool pigeon and one day was asked to explain the meaning of our conversation, I wasn't completely sure I could do it. Over the years I'd come to the conclusion that it wasn't only Costellos who spoke in riddles.

As we stepped up the stairs to the patio, the music grew louder, and couples emerged onto the concrete, their bodies coming together as the dancing began.

I looked up to see Angelina and Carmine watching our approach. My wife's expression grew too joyous, her mask for hiding her fears. One more step and her voice came into range.

"Forgive me, *Zio*. It's time to dance." She turned my way. "*Tesoro*."

I reached out until her hand was in mine. Nodding to the two men, I allowed Angelina to lead me onto the concrete dance floor. My hand surrounded her petite waist as the fingers of our other hand intertwined. Her cheek moved close to mine as her sweet perfume filled my senses. Our feet moved to the music, waltzing about the patio with others.

From a distance we appeared the happy host and hostess, yet her grip upon my hand told me there was something more. As the music grew louder, I leaned toward her ear and whispered, "What's happening?"

"I'm not sure," she replied, her tone also soft. "Uncle Carmine was looking for Carl. He seemed agitated that the two of you would be alone."

It was then I remembered Vincent's comment about the snake whispering in Carmine's ear. "Gioconda asked me for a tour."

Angelina leaned back, our feet never missing a beat. Her blue eyes met mine. "He asked you?"

"*Sì*, why would I ask him?"

"I don't know, Oren. Something doesn't feel right."

A lady's hand landed upon Angelina's shoulder. "Wonderful party, Angelina."

My wife's demeanor instantly returned to the perfect hostess. "Thank you, Melanie. Melanie, this is my husband, Oren Demetri. Oren, Melanie Thomas. She and her husband, Jim, live three doors down..."

The next day we made the trip to Brooklyn, sitting in our assigned pew. It wouldn't happen every weekend, but Rose had asked. Once we got back to the Costello home, I approached Carmine with the subject that had been eating at me.

The ability to do so was the honor of being real family, having the boss's attention on a Sunday afternoon. I wasn't much for volunteering information, yet I didn't like the idea of suspicion directed my way.

Carmine, Vincent, and I were in the office when I spoke. "It was a nice party last night."

"Your house is lovely," Carmine said. "Of course, I didn't see it from the water."

I sat taller. "Gioconda asked for a tour."

"He asked you?"

Vincent shifted slightly in his chair as Carmine's question hung in the air of his office like the smoke from his cigar.

"Yes, sir. He asked for a tour of the outside. Once we were at the water's edge, he spoke about loyalty and our move to Rye."

"And you told him, what?"

My eyes darted to Vincent. "I told him that if you questioned my loyalty simply because I provided your niece with a new home, then you should ask me."

Carmine's chin lifted. "Are you now telling me what I should do?"

"No, sir. I was assuring Gioconda that I would never lie to you. If you ask me, I'll always tell you the truth."

He leaned back against his leather chair as his fingertips came together. The silence created a hum. Finally, he looked at Vincent. "Did you see Luca and Lennox swimming?"

The knot in my stomach unwound. His response was my kernel of hope. By not asking me about my loyalty, Carmine Costello had told me without words that he trusted me.

# CHAPTER 21

———— •○• ————

As DAYS TURNED to weeks and weeks into months and months to another year, the pieces of the figurative puzzle slid about the board. Pictures of conspiracies began to materialize, yet were always incomplete. Like riddles, the puzzles often refused to give up the entirety of their story. It was up to the eye of the beholder to understand.

Life as we all knew it continued for most. The casualties were no more than normal. Our three-person family adjusted to life in Rye. My commute was longer, but the peace of mind at knowing Angelina and Lennox were in a safe zone made it worthwhile. Of course, a longer commute meant that once again I wasn't present as often as Angelina would like or expect.

Our marriage was a never-ending sea with waves of highs and lows. Our highs were earth shattering. They blossomed with the promise of more. Wine on our balcony. The resonance of Long Island Sound the background melody for our lovemaking. Yet as with any wave, there were crashes—lows. We were both hot-blooded Italians, and at times we said and did things we later regretted. After the crash, the wave would again begin to build, upward to more.

Life took on its own avenues. Seasons passed.

Long gone was the excitement over designing our home. However, new excitements took its place. For the most part, Angelina busied herself with many things Lennox. Getting to know the other mothers and our neighbors kept her occupied while I was engaged in business. The local parish had a school for Lennox to attend, which pleased her family in knowing our son was still enrolled in private school. No longer in kindergarten, he was advancing within the second grade.

Demetri Enterprises was continuing an upward momentum. The structure had moved beyond New York. We were nationwide. It was more than I would have ever dreamt. However, it was also time consuming. Each offer or proposal took weeks or months of research. By expanding beyond our local borders, Demetri Enterprises had begun to look like more than a local entity. The expansion gave my company the clout that it wouldn't have had only years ago. Each move took Demetri another degree off the radar of the local prosecutors as well as the feds.

While our personal lives ebbed and flowed, life within Cosa Nostra grew tumultuous at best. As Vincent had said, we were all in a pressure cooker, and someone kept turning up the heat.

Carmine's attorneys earned their pay by keeping him out of the limelight. He made a few appearances for grand jury testimony, but somehow he never seemed to have the answers they found helpful.

Nevertheless, between the everyday disagreements that arose within and between families and the added stress of the subpoenas and grand jury command appearances, nerves were stretched taut. It didn't take much for people to snap. Arguments could erupt in the least likely of places.

On an otherwise seemingly average late-autumn Thursday night during drinks, one particular discussion grew louder than necessary. The point of the weekly assembly at Evviva's was a display of solidarity to those within and outside of the family. It was a coming together. It was where Carmine had welcomed me into the fold. The scene caused by two soldiers raising their voices and shoving one another accomplished the opposite.

I'd been talking to Testa when the disagreement erupted. He had come to my office to drive me to the informal gathering. While he still drove Angelina in and out of the city, she'd made her case for driving herself and Lennox around Rye. Perhaps it was a false sense of security brought on by the distance to Brooklyn, but I agreed.

I wasn't a fan of being driven. I liked the freedom to drive myself, the knowledge that my car was near. Yet over the year or more since we'd moved to Rye, Testa and I had developed a Thursday night routine. I'd drive to the office in the morning, and then he'd take the train into the city. Maybe after all the questions of my loyalty, I appreciated having someone who trusted me by my side. I couldn't pinpoint the reason I liked arriving and leaving with him. I just did.

He and I had been discussing Angelina's car, of all things. Minivans were the current rage for families with children. I liked the idea of the larger vehicle. Angelina, on the other hand, was not interested. She was happy with her Lincoln and was eyeing the new smaller BMW sedans.

The raised voices came out of the blue, angry and accusing. A table tipped and drinks spilled as one of the soldiers was shoved. I couldn't make out what they were saying. If I'd been on alert, I may have paid more attention; however, there was usually a calm to Thursday nights, a fellowship of sorts.

My first thoughts were one, shock that anyone would disrespect the Costello 'drinks' in such a manner, and two, curiosity at who would be so bold.

The entire room stilled as every eye went from the two soldiers to

Carmine. Without so much as a look of agitation, the boss motioned to Stefano and Jimmy. Almost immediately the two young agitated soldiers were taken out back.

I recognized one of them; he'd been around for a while. The other I wasn't sure about. "Who's the young one?" I whispered to Testa.

"Nicholai. They call him Nick. He's got a hot temper, but the word is that's he's good at collecting."

A hot temper wasn't an asset as far as I was concerned. I was pretty good at keeping mine in check most of the time. It seemed like the only person who was capable of eliciting that emotion from me was the same one who induced my others. Whether it was love or anger, Angelina could draw it out. We were evenly matched. I did the same to her. Perhaps that was what love was about.

Nicholai looked rather scrawny to me, not like Stefano or Jimmy. I scoffed, thinking how they'd show him a thing or two, reminding both of them to mind their manners, especially in front of the boss.

There was something to be said for diversion as a strategic tactic. It worked best when the victims were unaware. Once it became known, it was too late.

The noisy display by the soldiers had been just that—a diversion. As the room began to regain its low din of conversation, everything changed.

Forever.

We'd been on the cusp of change for years, but we hadn't realized the possibilities. That night would forever be etched in my memory, stained with crimson, its copper scent a stench I would never forget.

Vincent was standing near Carmine, yet his two main bodyguards were absent, taking care of business in the alleyway. Gioconda was talking to Mancini near the window. If it were a movie, the camera would pan the room, forever memorializing each person's place for posterity.

It happened fast, a commotion. Attention diverted.

There were times in life that moved quicker than light and others that seemed painstakingly slow. As a pawn in a game much bigger than I realized, I couldn't be sure which passage of time occurred that night. It was too rapid to account for everything and yet too deliberate to not feel each second as it burrowed into my being.

Our weekly gathering had continued to occur at an out-of-the-way restaurant in Little Italy, Evviva's, a hole-in-the-wall, its entrance on a downtrodden street that guaranteed the keeping of tourists at bay. Despite the appearance, the food was outstanding and the drinks even better. The menu wasn't why we congregated in the same place week after week, or year after year though. It was because the location was protected.

With the feds hot on the trails of all the bosses, each don had to be careful. This restaurant was owned by Scopo, one of the trusted Costello capos. Not only did Scopo pay his employees well, but Carmine also paid Scopo generously for the honor of housing the weekly meeting. The entire building was constantly swept for bugs. No one would be listening in on the gathering and especially not in on the later meeting downstairs in the basement.

Electronic surveillance was an ongoing issue for all the families. The feds were using audio tapes of private conversations. Catching a prominent member on a tape was ammunition to make him squeal. Rats were surfacing from every hole in the city, ready to turn state's evidence to avoid jail time. While no family was immune, I hadn't been privy to any ousted rats in the Costello regime. Then again, it seemed unlikely that we were without.

As the conversations began to resume, with no warning the front door swung open. The action could have gone unnoticed except for the gush of cool autumn air that momentarily dispersed the smoky haze.

It's funny the assumptions a reasoning mind can make. For a split second, I assumed that someone had arrived late. That was all the time it took—a microsecond.

The shooter had one target.

Without a word or preamble, the single shot rang out.

Had he entered with a drawn gun?

Who let him in?

Questions came and went as fast as the cool air from the doorway.

A second gun blast echoed from the walls.

It would have taken out the shooter had he not fallen at the right moment to his knees.

Gioconda's unsuccessful shot didn't stop the rest of the men. Every gun in the restaurant was leveled at the first shooter, poised and ready, including mine. The kid—no more than nineteen or twenty—had tossed his revolver on the ground as if it were too hot to handle at the same time he'd landed on his knees. With tears on his cheeks, he placed his hands on his head.

In the time it took his elbows to quake, I assessed his age—too young; his ethnicity—he was Italian, but not true. He probably was not full-blooded, yet he had the look; and his culpability—guilty without a trial.

More questions: to what family did he belong? Did he belong? Who sent him?

We wouldn't have time to learn.

The boy's body trembled to the point of convulsions.

Shooting him now would be killing an unarmed man. Yet I doubted there was a man within the restaurant not willing to do it.

It was then that I saw the boy's target, the man lying upon the ground.

All air left my lungs as Vincent cradled Carmine Costello upon the gritty, worn carpet.

I was no longer concerned about the kid—he was fully surrounded; it was Vincent's bellowing that dominated the chaos.

"Get the car! Fucking get the goddamn car!" His head whipped from side to side. "Stefano? Jimmy?"

I turned to Testa. "Go, get my car, now."

As Testa followed my orders, I took a step closer to Carmine. His head lay in his son's lap. Gioconda moved closer, blocking my way. If I'd been thinking of my own life, the consigliere's stare would have been enough for me to back away. I wasn't.

"Vincent," I said, hoping my calm would help Angelina's cousin hear me. Through the fog of the turmoil, our gazes met. "My car's coming. Testa's getting it."

His nod was my ticket to get closer. I met Gioconda's gaze once again and walked past him. Vincent was the underboss. While Gioconda may not approve, Vincent outranked him. In private, in a non-life-or-death situation, there may have been discussion. This wasn't the place. Gioconda stepped aside with a scowl.

Kneeling beside Carmine's body, I reached for his thick wrist. There was a pulse. I wasn't a doctor, and I couldn't assess if it were weak or strong. I was only certain that beneath my own fingertips, there was a thumping. Blocking out the room, I said a prayer that it wasn't my own rushing blood that I felt. Briefly, I noticed the floor where I knelt was devoid of blood.

It didn't make sense, yet I didn't have time to comprehend.

*Costello riddles.*

One plus one weren't equaling two.

My gaze went to the boss's body. Carmine's jacket was torn, a hole dead center of his chest.

I pushed away the thought that I'd have to tell Angelina: first her parents and now Carmine. The news would break her. I didn't doubt it would. And while the anguish could suffocate me, I filed it all away for later. This wasn't the time. This was survivor mode.

There was a season for grief. Father Mario had told us that.

It wasn't now.

"Testa," I repeated to Vinny. "He's getting my car."

Vincent's face searched mine, a million questions passing through his stare, and yet the loudest was the one he'd asked me before—that Gioconda had asked too. The one Carmine hadn't: could he trust me?

It wasn't the place to plead my case. I'd decided not to do that over a year ago with Gioconda. My allegiance up until this moment should speak for itself, yet I knew Vincent was reeling from the reality of his father's unmoving body. I wanted to give him reassurance.

In the room full of confusion, I simply nodded.

Vincent's eyes momentarily closed, and then as if he'd literally been lit by a flame, he moved his attention beyond me. Heat radiated from his presence. His complexion reddened as his gaze moved from me to the room of watchful eyes. He looked to Morelli and then to the shooter, each passing second the tendons of his neck becoming more prominent. The veins in his face bulged. He had energy to expel, and yet he tenderly held his father.

His voice reverberated through the room. "Take him," Vincent said, his voice commanding and strong—the tone of a leader. When Morelli nodded, Vincent continued, "You know where I mean. Hurt him. Break him. Find out who the hell sent him. I don't give a fuck what you do to him. Except don't you fucking kill him. Leave that to me."

"Vincent, you concentrate on Carmine. Let me..." Gioconda's words faded into the murmurs as Vincent's stare dismissed the consigliere.

As I followed Vincent's line of vision, the blood that had been coursing through my veins, fueled by adrenaline, came to a screeching halt. Like a flowing stream turning to ice, my blood stopped, pooling in place. It was the vision of the boy. The panic in his eyes as his gaze moved from Gioconda to Vincent stopped my circulation.

What had the boy done and why?

Did he regret his move? Did that matter?

The boy's fear was palpable as he stared the grim reaper in the eyes. His face fell forward, undoubtedly knowing that before the night was over he'd be roasting in the pits of Hell.

Whatever deal this child had made was signed with blood, binding and unbreakable.

A life for a life.

I wondered what he was promised.

Had he saved a woman—his mother or maybe his sister? Did he satisfy a family debt? What deal would possibly make a young man commit such a heinous and unforgiveable act in front of a room of made men?

No matter what it had been, the payoff would never be enough.

While I couldn't begin to comprehend what would happen to the boy over the next few hours, I could be certain—in the marrow of my bones—that whatever the future held, it didn't include an easy death. By the time his heart quit beating, that boy would welcome Hell and Satan himself with open arms.

Pits of fire and gnashing of teeth would be a reprieve from what Vincent and Morelli had in mind.

Another epiphany struck. Though I'd been brought into this life, into LCN, and willingly accepted each assignment, up to this point I'd been spared. For nearly nine years since my proposal to Angelina, my view of

Cosa Nostra had been veiled with a rose-colored hue, courtesy of Carmine and Vincent's protection. Everything that I'd witnessed, heard, and been privy to was a walk in the park on a sunny day compared to what I'd been spared.

My heart ached for the unmoving man.

I wasn't naive. I knew Vincent and even Carmine had blood on their hands. I knew why Jimmy was called an enforcer. I knew why Stefano was trusted with the boss and his family. I even knew that Testa had earned his right to protect Angelina and Lennox. However, as my gut knotted, I finally understood that knowing and witnessing were two different things.

The room turned back to Carmine as his breathing labored and body flinched.

The boy's sobs added to the bedlam. A hush fell over the restaurant as heavy footsteps came rushing toward us. Gioconda grunted as Jimmy charged forward. Pushing the consigliere and me out of the way, the hulk of a man fell to the floor and reached for Carmine's shoulders.

"Testa is coming," I managed to say as I teetered, shoved aside like a feather by the force of his hand.

Vincent nodded at Jimmy.

It was then I saw Jimmy's hands. My first instinct was to look down at my shoulder, where he'd just touched me. The blood hadn't made a handprint, yet it was visible against the gray of my wool jacket. I whipped my head right and then left, assessing those who'd entered with him.

There wasn't anyone else. He'd entered the restaurant alone.

"Where's Stefano?" I asked.

"We need to get the boss in the car." Jimmy's response didn't answer my question, but it reminded me of what was most important.

Jimmy's girth was legendary; however, watching as he lifted Carmine—who was also large—to his feet was impressive. I stepped closer and willingly accepted a portion of Carmine's weight as Vincent held his father from behind and Jimmy and I walked on both sides of him outside the front door. Though Carmine's face fell forward to his chest, miraculously his feet supported him, enough for the four of us to make it to the curb.

Testa pulled forward, my black Town Car moving just outside the circle of illumination from the streetlight. In the distance the city filled with sounds. There were sirens and horns.

"Go," Vincent said after we got Carmine in the backseat. "I have business."

I moved to one side of Carmine, and Jimmy went around to the other. As the car pulled away, leaving the scene of what I'd never forget, we drove the direction of the alleyway behind the restaurant. I turned to the window just in time to see the carnage. Partially hidden by a dumpster, Stefano and the two men who'd caused the disturbance were lying in clumps, red pools shimmering in the moonlight around their collapsed bodies. Were there more? I didn't have time to count.

"They were shot?" I asked, but couldn't be sure that it was audible. My tongue was thick and dry as my stomach continued its twists and turns.

Jimmy didn't have the same problem. With Testa behind the wheel, Jimmy barked orders—directions to turn and places to avoid.

It was at that point of the night that my memory turned fuzzy. With each pass under a light, I was mesmerized by the blood on Jimmy's hands, on my jacket, and on Carmine's suit coat. There hadn't been blood before, and now that it was there, panic or maybe shock began to set in.

The scenes beyond the windows blurred until I realized we were headed for Windsor Terrace, not the hospital. "He needs a hospital," I pleaded, my dry mouth sticking with each word. "We need to get him medical attention."

It was as if I were speaking into a tunnel. My words echoed in the interior of the car. Only Jimmy's voice and the tires squealing were audible as we took turns at unsafe speeds.

As Jimmy unbuttoned Carmine's white shirt, leaving his red fingerprints on each button, I tried to help. It was then that I saw what I'd not seen before. Below Carmine's tailored suit and under the white starched shirt was a Kevlar vest.

"Oh thank God Almighty," I sighed, unsure if this time the words were said aloud.

The car came to a halt in front of Carmine's brownstone.

Carmine's dark eyes opened as the car jolted. "J-Jimmy?"

"I'm here, boss. You all right?"

Carmine coughed, shallow at first and then deeper. His hand tried to move upward. "Chest hurts a little." His eyes turned toward me. "Where's Vincent? Stefano?"

"He's... They're..." I stuttered with my answer.

Jimmy's dark eyes met mine. "Taking care of business, boss," the large man said in my stead. "We need to get you inside. The doc's coming. You're going to be bruised."

Carmine's body flinched as he tried to adjust his weight.

"Let me help," I said.

"No." Carmine's usual strong voice was gone, yet his command held the same power. "Go. Get the car far away. Don't go back to the restaurant. Don't go to Angelina, not yet. Go to your office. Fuck a secretary. I don't care. When the cops come looking for this car, it needs to be gone. Make it disappear. You left the meeting early. You had work."

I stared, unsure how to respond.

"Did you hear me?"

"Yes, sir." I nodded as Jimmy helped Carmine out of the car, supporting most of the boss's weight as together they went up the stairs of the brownstone. For only a moment before Testa took off again, I saw Rose at the top of the steps, her hands clenched over her heart as Carmine's head shook dismissively at his wife's concerns.

We were silent for a few blocks until finally Testa spoke. "Boss, where to?"

"Pull over." I'd barely gotten the words from my lips before I opened the door and vomited.

# CHAPTER 22

—————●○●—————

No longer dry, my mouth filled with spit and bile. As I spat the disgusting combination from my lips, I was consumed with shame at my physical reaction. That was until I saw the red on my own fingers, undoubtedly, from Jimmy's hands. Scanning myself, I noticed that my jacket and trousers were also marked. Without warning, my hands began to shake with involuntary tremors.

Closing my eyes, I inhaled—the combination of blood and vomit a putrid stench that would forever be in my memory. Another breath and another. Finally, I consciously willed the trembling to stop. Once it did, I stood and stepped over the mess I'd deposited in the gutter, closed the back door and opened the front passenger. Sitting inside my own car, I sat beside Testa, for once content to be driven.

I turned his direction. "There's blood in the backseat." I wasn't sure why I felt the need to tell him that, but I did.

He looked my way and lifted one side of his lips in a lopsided grin. "I never liked how this car pulled to the left."

My eyes narrowed. "What?"

My fried brain couldn't decipher another riddle.

Testa put the car in gear and moved us along the street. As if in a dream, we were advancing through the city. The sky was black, but with the streetlights, it was as if day had re-dawned.

Testa's voice brought me back. "When I brake, this car pulls. Damn roads are slippery. Could get in an accident."

"The blood?" I said again, not certain what he was saying.

"It won't clean. Blood don't clean from fabric or carpet. There's always a trace."

I looked down at my hands, still tasting the rancid remains of my regurgitated dinner. I tried to make a plan. "Take me to the office. I need a shower. I also have a spare suit there."

"Yes, boss, and then?"

"Then... I'm not sure." It was difficult to think too far into the future, but I tried. "Tomorrow I buy Angelina another car. I'll take her Continental. You take her shopping and get her something safer, whatever she wants."

A surreal conversation as if we hadn't just seen a man shot—four men or more shot.

Testa nodded.

I followed most of Carmine's advice. After I'd showered, brushed my teeth two or three times, and changed clothes, I stayed at the office. It wasn't where I wanted to be, but I knew why I was there. The clock continued to tick as I made phone calls to prospective clients and wannabe business partners. Each discussion was traceable. The telephone company would have records. Oren Demetri had been working late on Thursday night, as he did many other nights.

I didn't fuck a secretary as Carmine suggested. Julie had long gone home, and that wasn't an option. Even though there were women still in the building who were probably willing, I wasn't looking. The only woman I wanted to see was my wife. I doubted that my return home would end the same way as an invitation to my office presented to one of the secretaries from the evening call center would. Nevertheless, I wanted who I *knew*, who I *needed*, and who I hoped *needed me*.

I longed to be with Angelina, to hold her, and to explain what I'd witnessed. Mostly, I wanted to reassure her that Carmine was safe.

Following the boss's instructions kept me away from home until after ten o'clock. I figured that was late enough. On any normal Thursday— one without an assassination attempt—I'd get home about the same time.

On our drive to Rye, Testa and I discussed the blood-splattered car a little more. I'd given it some thought between phone calls. If a person wanted to get insurance money for a wrecked vehicle, they'd report the accident. If on the other hand, the goal wasn't a payout but to destroy the vehicle, a junkyard was the answer.

As it turned out, junk was a profitable business, a business in which I'd already invested. A few years back I'd been made an offer to utilize land upon which nothing could be built. On the outskirts of Jersey was a three-acre plot of land, heavily guarded by a few good old boys and mean-ass dogs. Over the years it had proven a good Demetri Enterprise investment.

That investment was about to reap me another more beneficial profit.

"Tomorrow," I said, "before daybreak, take the Town Car to the junkyard in Jersey. Frankie's expecting you. They know what to do. It'll be wrecked and torched with my suit inside. It's in the trunk. Once the metal is cool enough, they'll crush it." I'd called him earlier in the night from an empty office.

If and when the dots were connected and anyone came looking for the car that drove Carmine Costello away from the scene of his attempted murder, there'd be no picture left to make; the dots would be erased.

"I'll take care of it."

Before we could say more, my beeper vibrated, and a moment later my car phone began to ring.

I looked at the car phone. Unlike home phones, car phones had a display showing the telephone number of the incoming caller. Though my nerves had calmed as we entered Rye, I was terrified of the number being Vincent or Carmine.

I wanted to go home. What if they wanted something else?

Relief settled in as I saw my own home phone number. "*Mio angelo,* I'm almost home."

"O-Oren." My wife's voice was almost unintelligible. "Oren! Talk!"

"I'm here, *mio angelo*. What is it?" Her panic rejuvenated my own, bringing the twisting back to my gut and a sheen of perspiration to my freshly showered skin. What could be happening now?

"Uncle Carmine." Her phrases were separated by cries. "The news said...he was shot. Is he..? Is he... dead? Why didn't you call?"

It had never occurred to me that by delaying my arrival home someone else would deliver the news to Angelina about Carmine—that the television news station would tell her what should have come from her husband. Her panic shouldn't bring me relief, yet it did. "It's all going to be okay," I tried to reassure. "I'm almost home. Don't watch the news. They don't know what they're saying. Keep the doors locked and the alarms on. I'm almost there and can disarm them myself."

"Is he dead?" she asked again.

"Baby, five minutes."

I hung up without answering, allowing her question to hang in the air like the ring of the foghorns over the water. Could car phones be bugged? Why hadn't I thought of that before? Was the news reporting him dead? Did Carmine want people to think that? Did Vincent?

Once again, I had more questions than answers, and I was present when he was shot.

"Boss," Testa said, pulling me from my inner dialogue. "I'll take the car and park it out of the way for tonight. Tomorrow, I'll take it to the junkyard."

My thoughts were all over the place. Thank God he was keeping things straight. "Good. I don't want it at the house. Tomorrow, I'll take Angelina's car into the city. Use yours to pick her up, take Lennox to school, and then go car shopping."

Testa agreed as he steered the winding streets of our neighborhood toward our home. A button within the car opened the gate to our property. Another button on my keyring disarmed the alarms. He brought the car up to the front door. After I got out of the car, I stopped with my hand on the car door and leaned back inside. "I'm not proud of what I did."

"What you did? You helped save the boss's life."

My head moved slowly from side to side, unwilling to say what I meant. "I don't know what happened. It all hit me."

Testa's chin snapped up and then down in understanding. "You get used to it. Don't think twice. Anybody who isn't affected, especially the first time he sees it, ain't a soldier—he's a psychopath."

I thought of soldiers, of tried-and-true warriors for the family. "Stefano? He didn't come in with Jimmy. I thought I saw..." I purposely let my words fade into the evening breeze.

Testa shook his head. "Stefano went out fighting for the family. A man can't ask for a more honorable way to go. He went fighting, taking a rat with him. You shouldn't have seen them. If we'd had more time, they would have been hidden. It all happened too fast. The cleaning crew will get the bodies moved. I'm sure they already have."

"What will they do?"

"Like I said, the cleaning crew will take care of it."

"You said blood doesn't clean."

"Ain't nothing clean in that alley. Once it's hosed down, it'll be hard to separate the people blood from rat blood, piss, and all-around trash."

I took a deep breath. "You're saying that I'm not a psychopath."

"Yeah, boss, I'm saying you wouldn't be going in that house to *his* niece if you were."

I stood taller, expanded my chest as I inhaled. Deep into my lungs...the night air was cool and life-giving, so unlike the coppery scent of blood. I let my gaze fall upon the driveway, our home, the quietness of the neighborhood. The sky was black above the house's lights. And then I turned back to Testa one last time. "Do you... get used to it?"

"The last few years, working for you, I've had it easy. But it never goes away."

"Like riding a bike."

He nodded with a sad grin.

I thought about how Vincent and Gioconda questioned my allegiance, yet Jimmy didn't. He didn't question Testa's either. He didn't question Testa driving Carmine. It had to mean he trusted him. "So when you went for the car, Stefano was dead?"

He nodded again.

"The other two?"

"Like I said, Stefano went out fighting. Boss, you don't want to know more. I'll tell you... if you order me to tell you. If you don't... you can sleep tonight knowing that sending me out there helped Jimmy and Stefano save the family. This thing..." His hands move around. "Whatever's happening now—tonight—is an onion."

"An onion? It stinks?"

"That but mostly it has layers. Nicholai was scrappy. He didn't say who sent him to make a scene. We didn't have time to make him talk. He had backup waiting. Anyways, I got the feeling they was supposed to go back inside once they finished off Jimmy and Stefano and take care of things in there." Testa's hands left the steering wheel and slapped back down. "I don't know. I really don't. I just believe that if even one of them had made it back inside past Jimmy, things could've been different."

The adrenaline was gone. Exhaustion washed through me in a wave, weakening my knees. My knuckles blanched as I gripped the top of the door tighter. If what he was saying were true, this was a planned assassination, not only of Carmine but of the Costello family. "Stefano? He wasn't part of it?"

Testa's head moved back and forth. "He was going, practically gone, by the time I got out there. I don't know. I don't think so." He shrugged. "I sure as hell hope not."

"Jimmy?"

"He'd take a bullet before letting one hit the boss...he'd take one for Vincent too. He'd protect them both with his life. It's the commitment. We all make it. Only some of us mean it."

"It's hard to know who to trust."

"The boss is safe," Testa said. He tilted his chin toward the front door.

I turned to see my wife who'd opened the door. No longer safe behind alarms, she was standing in the doorway, her eyes red and puffy. A white satin robe wrapped around her body blew in the breeze, showcasing her petite frame as her arms wrapped around her own waist. No doubt, she'd been watching as we pulled up.

"Good night," I said.

"I'll be here for Mrs. Demetri and Lennox in the morning."

"I trust you," I said.

I did. Just like I wouldn't be going into the house to my wife—Angelina Costello—if I weren't trusted, he wouldn't be allowed with my wife and son if I didn't trust him. For some reason, I respected the fact that Testa hadn't proclaimed his loyalty. It almost made it better.

"Thanks, boss. I won't let you down."

Nodding, I shut the car door and turned back to Angelina.

# CHAPTER 23

―●○●―

WITHIN THE ARCHWAY to our home, Angelina's body became liquid in my hands. Her dark hair was tousled from the wind and worry. I wrapped her trembling form in my embrace and breath by breath, accepted her fear and sorrow, wanting to take it away and make everything better. "He's—"

Before I could complete my sentence, she stiffened in my grasp. Her head snapped up and tear-swollen eyes narrowed. "Where the hell have you been? You smell... clean." She took a step backward.

I reached for her hand and tugged her toward me. "I had to shower at the office. My suit... was dirty."

Her tone and expression said it all. The pain she inflicted was as debilitating as the idea of losing Carmine. Daggers shot from her tear-filled eyes as she weighed my words. "Dirty?"

I'd never come home to her with the scent of another woman on me. I wouldn't do that to her. However, over the course of our marriage, my clean and showered arrival was met with as much discontent as my entering with the aroma of another woman's perfume.

Angelina's head continued shaking back and forth as she attempted to push me away. "I don't believe you. Where have you been? Were you even with Uncle Carmine when he was shot?" Anger gave way to grief as her face fell forward. "Is he…? Tell me."

I wouldn't release her, no matter how hard she pulled. Instead, I moved us inside our home, in the foyer. Once I had the door shut, when I should have been comforting my wife, I instead defended my actions.

"*Mio angelo*, stop. You're not thinking straight. First, no, he's not dead. Let me tell you what happened."

"Oren, goddamn you."

I scoffed as I pulled her close to me once again, holding her tightly to my chest. With my chin over her head, I said, "Oh, don't worry. He will. But not for what happened tonight."

Her fists pounded my chest, each strike losing strength. "Tell me you were there! Tell me you weren't with some whore."

I took a step back, my heart racing. Our gazes met, each second of her accusations fueled my rebuttal. "There was one goddamn woman I wanted to be with tonight, and I'm here. I came home as soon as I could because I wanted to be with you. I came home because I wanted to be the one to tell you what happened." My voice grew louder. "I came home to find and give some goddamn comfort because what happened tonight shook me in a way I've never been shook." Letting go of her, I turned a circle, still in the entryway, trying to calm myself as the night's emotions bubbled to the surface. No longer was it bile but rage.

With anyone else, I meet their emotions with indifference. Not Angelina. I wanted her. I needed her. I loved her, and sometimes I hated her. "That's why I came home. Fuck, maybe I should have looked elsewhere for comfort."

Her anger disappeared in a wave as sadness fought for supremacy.

I've never hated myself as much as I did at that moment. "*Mio angelo*. No. I'm sorry."

"Go! Just go! I'll call Aunt Rose. I'll call Vincent or Bella. Go wherever you can find whatever in the hell you don't get here!"

"Do you think for one fucking second you could listen to me and not fucking yell at me? I took a damn shower to get the blood off me. Nothing else!"

"Mom?"

We both turned toward the staircase.

*Fuck.*

"Lennox," I said more sternly than necessary, "go to bed."

His blue-eyed stare didn't even register my voice. He was looking at his mother. "Mom, what's wrong. Why are you yelling?"

Angelina's stance softened as she turned to the stairs. "Honey, sometimes grown-ups yell when they're scared. You need to go back to bed."

"You and Dad are scared?"

I walked behind Angelina and wrapped my arms around her waist, talking over her shoulder. "Uncle Carmine was almost hurt tonight."

Angelina's face turned to me, warning me not to say too much.

"Is he okay?" our son asked.

I nodded and softened my tone. "He is. We'll see him soon, I'm sure. Now listen to your mom and go to bed."

Angelina went up a few stairs and palming our son's cheeks, kissed his forehead. "Good night, little man. There's nothing to worry about. We'll be quieter."

He lifted his hand to her cheek. "You're crying."

"Not anymore."

"Good. I don't want you to cry."

She kissed his head. "I love you, Lennox."

"'Night, Mom."

"Good night."

Lennox nodded as he disappeared to the second floor.

"I'm sorry," Angelina and I said in unison as she turned my way.

She was a few steps higher than me, her lips above mine. I reached again for her waist and pulled her toward me. Her chin lowered allowing our lips to unite, bringing me the comfort I'd been seeking since before I came home.

Angelina's arms surrounded my neck. "I love you, Oren Demetri. I also hate you."

I knew exactly what she meant. Instead of saying that, I said, "Tonight, could you maybe just love me?"

"Tonight." She nodded as she took a step down and then another. Once we were both on the landing, we reached for one another's hand and our fingers intertwined. Hand in hand, we walked into the sitting room. "Can you tell me what happened?" she asked.

Sitting knee-to-knee on the long sofa, I looked down at our hands and then to my own lap. "This wasn't the suit I wore to the office today. The suit I wore and my hands..." I lifted the one not holding hers and splayed my fingers, inspecting them. "...had blood on them. Testa said it wouldn't clean. I needed to get out of the suit and do whatever I could to clean my hands. My car was seen driving away from the scene. The blood can't be traced back to me."

Her once-narrowed eyes opened wide. "Uncle Carmine's blood?"

"No. I'm not sure how much I can say. Your uncle is going to be all right. Testa drove him home with Jimmy and me."

"Home! Why not a hospital?"

"Because your uncle is a smart old fucker. He told me once to never be unprepared. He told me to always carry my gun." I laughed at the memory. "Fuck. That seems like a lifetime ago. Anyway, I have. I've listened."

Angelina nodded.

"Your uncle was prepared. He was wearing a bulletproof vest. Jimmy said Carmine would be bruised, but that's a hell of a lot better than dead."

Angelina's head fell forward, her dark hair veiling her face. Yet by the way her shoulders shuddered, I didn't need to hear the tears. Letting go of her hand, I wrapped my arms around her and held her tighter. Kissing her head, I waited for her to speak.

Finally, she did. "So the news was right? He was shot?"

"Yes."

"He's going to be okay?" she asked again for confirmation.

"Yes, *mio angelo*. He's safe at home."

Angelina let out a long sigh as she wiped her cheek. "I was so scared. I'm sorry I assumed… It's just that my emotions…"

I kissed her again. I didn't want to hear her apology. Not tonight. She deserved one more than I did. I was the one who gave her cause for those suspicions.

When our kiss ended, her blue eyes met mine. "I want to go to him. I could call Mrs. McCoy down the street. She adores Lennox. She can stay with him. Take me to Brooklyn."

"No."

Angelina leaned back, her neck straightening as she searched my expression. "Did you say no?"

"I did. What's the news saying?"

"They said 'suspected mob kingpin Carmine Costello was shot.'"

"They're not reporting his life or death?"

"No."

"We're safer here. He told me to leave, to get rid of the car. There's blood in it. He also told me not to come to you right away. To make an alibi."

"Blood? But you just said it wasn't his blood?"

"No. It wasn't."

Her hands flew to her lips. "Oh my God. Vinny?"

"No. Vincent is fine. He's… taking care of things."

"Do I want to know what that means?" she asked.

"Baby, I don't even want to know what that means. The blood was Stefano's and that of two soldiers." Or more. "I don't know them. You wouldn't know them."

"Stefano? Is he…?"

I nodded.

Her eyes closed as a new tear escaped onto her cheek. "Oh, poor Theresa."

I hadn't even thought of Stefano's wife. Maybe I was getting used to all of it after all. There was something impersonal about keeping everything business. Maybe that was why it was so upsetting to see Carmine on the ground. To me, he's more than a mob boss. He's more than my boss. He's Angelina and Lennox's uncle. He's Rose's husband and Vincent's pop. "I'm not sure we can trust the phones," I said. "I don't know what Carmine wants. If he wants to lie low, we need to let him. Vincent is taking control right now. I'd say the next move is up to him until Carmine makes his survival known."

Her eyes closed and opened. "Okay."

As Angelina agreed, a buzz sounded from the entryway, alerting us that someone wanted to enter our front gate. The hairs on the back of my neck stood to attention. "Wait here." I walked back to the entry to the small box in the wall and pushing a button, spoke. "Hello."

"Sir, it's Scopo."

My eyes narrowed suspiciously. "What?"

"Mr. Costello sent me to get Mrs. Costello and the children. He said to bring them here."

Angelina rushed to my side. "Children?" she whispered. And then without waiting for me, she pushed the button and spoke into the speaker. "Bella?"

"Angel." The voice was farther away, but it was definitely Vincent's wife.

Angelina's eyes opened wide as we released the button. "We're letting them in." She wasn't asking.

I nodded. "Bella and the kids. Not Scopo."

"Fine. I don't care. This is my house too. I'm not turning away family."

I would never turn away family. However, it was the escort who worried me. I pushed another button, the one that opened the gate. Turning to Angelina, I said, "Wait in here."

"Oren."

I reached for her hand. "Please, *mio angelo*. Tonight has been..." I shook my head and lifted her knuckles to my lips. "Just...please? Please stay inside. Let me be sure that Bella and the kids are safe... and alone."

Her lips came together, stopping any rebuttal she may have had. "Okay."

I reached for my gun and stepped outside the front door, closing Angelina inside. As I did, Scopo's black sedan made the turn in our driveway, coming to a stop in front of me. From where I stood, I could see that he was alone in the front seat. Before I could speak, his door opened. With my nerves shot, I clicked the safety off, keeping my gun near my leg.

Without a word or any acknowledgment of my weapon, Scopo nodded my direction and then opened the back door of the sedan.

Bella stepped out. "Oren, thank you." Her eyes were puffy like Angelina's.

"Anytime, Bella." Placing my gun in the holster, I opened the other back door. Within the car, I was met with Luca's questioning eyes. "Luca, come on in, your cousin's waiting." After helping him out, I reached inside and scooped up a sleeping Luisa. Shifting her small body in my arms, I propped her on my shoulder, remembering what it was like when Lennox was three years old and so trusting.

As Bella came closer, her voice cracked. "We didn't bring much. Just Luisa's diaper bag and my purse. There wasn't time…"

I put my arm around her shoulder and motioned toward the front door. "Go on in. Angelina's waiting." When the door opened, I passed Luisa to my wife. All of her earlier anger disappeared as she cradled the sleeping princess.

"Luisa," she whispered with a smile.

Closing the family inside, I reached back to my holster and turned back to Scopo. "Thank you."

He nodded. "The boss said to bring them here. I know when to follow orders. It's not my place to question who's giving them."

"They'll be well protected. Will you see him?" I meant Vincent. That was the boss he was referencing.

"Eventually."

I didn't want more details. "Tell him they're safe and welcome as long as he needs." I tilted my head toward the driveway. "The gate will close behind you. The alarms are on."

I waited until he drove away. And then with my gun secured, for the second time in less than an hour, I entered our home and locked our door. Once the sensor alerted me that Scopo had left the property, I hit the perimeter alarm.

Luca ran past me, bounding up the stairs to Lennox's room.

"Don't wake Lennox…" My words went unheard as Luca disappeared on the second floor.

Angelina's voice from the sitting room came into range. "Let's get Luisa settled, and then we can have some tea."

The two women came my way, Luisa now in her mother's arms. "Make it wine," Bella replied.

"I'll pour three glasses," I volunteered.

It seemed like that kid who'd shot Carmine wouldn't be the only one to have a long night.

# CHAPTER 24

————•○•————

WE WERE SURROUNDED with radio silence with the exception of slivered messages from Testa, being as he was the only one to come and go from our home. Telephones couldn't be trusted. In reality, trust was a commodity that was in short supply.

Though Testa had disposed of my car as we'd discussed, he hadn't taken Angelina shopping for a new one or Lennox to school. Bella and the children continued their stay as we all found shelter within our walls. That was why Vincent had sent to me those he held most dear. They were secure without relying upon human loyalties. Electronic alarms, reinforced walls, and bulletproof glass didn't break their allegiance.

Despite our well-being, we were blind to what was happening outside our perimeter. In some ways, I presumed it was similar to those people hunkered down during a catastrophic storm. Together they were safe, yet their thoughts never went far from what would be left of their world once the doors were opened.

Would it be left standing? Or would they find that it had been demolished by winds so devastating that nothing was left in the wake?

With each passing hour, the lines of concern grew deeper in Vincent's wife's brow. She spent hours staring through the kitchen windows into the blue autumn sky. Normally a beautiful woman, within a few days she'd aged, the change brought on by sleep deprivation and sheer worry. For the children's sake, we all tried to act as if our get-together was innocent, but even the boys acted differently, as if they could sense the overwhelming tension. Only Luisa behaved as a typical three-year-old.

I had tried to resume life as normal on Friday morning, going into the office and leaving Testa to defend our home, but I didn't stay long. For the first time that I could remember, my mind refused to concentrate on Demetri Enterprises. The tension was palpable, thick in the air, like dense fog covering our lives. I decided it was better to be absent than to be present and make a wrong decision.

On Saturday I decided to attempt work again, this time from my home office. In reality I was fearful of what news would come and determined that unlike the news of Carmine's shooting, when it came I'd be with Angelina.

The call from Julie came before noon. We both regularly worked Saturday mornings. It was usually a time to catch up on the week's deadlines. "Mr. Demetri, a Detective Jennings is here to speak to you."

"Does he have a warrant?"

"No, sir. He isn't asking for anything other than a moment of your time."

I hadn't heard from Vincent or Carmine since Thursday night. Testa had informed me that Carmine was doing well, just sore, and was not seeing visitors. When I asked about Vincent, I was told he was handling matters for the family. At least that was a confirmation for Bella that he was still alive. Nevertheless, I was navigating without a chart over murk-covered choppy seas. Even the foghorns over the sound couldn't help me find our way.

I contemplated my options. Inviting the police into my home didn't seem like the best option. For that matter, neither did seeing him in public. There were too many eyes dissecting every move. "Julie, inform the detective that I'm out of the office today."

"Yes, sir, I told him that."

Carmine's words, *you left early*, came to mind. Early? What did that mean?

"He said he can meet you and what he'd like to discuss is very important."

The sound of Lennox and Luca running somewhere in the house confirmed that I couldn't allow him here. "Tell him I can be at the office in an hour. Ask him if he can come back."

Julie's end of the phone line was silent for a moment, and then she was back. "Sir, he said he'll wait."

*Fuck.*

"I'm on my way."

A few minutes later as I put on my suit coat, Angelina asked, "What does this mean?"

"I don't know."

Her voice was low. "Bella hasn't heard a word from Vincent. Our only confirmation on Carmine is Testa. Something is wrong." She wrung her hands. "There are a lot of things wrong. I don't like any of this."

I reached for her hands, tugging them apart and holding each one in mine. "I feel the same way, but what can I do? I can't have the police coming here and seeing Bella and the kids. Carmine told me to say I left drinks early. I'm not even sure what that means. Did I see him shot?"

Angelina shook her head. "I think it means you didn't." She squeezed my hands as she leaned into my chest. "Oren, please come home."

Letting go of her hand, I lifted her chin until her worried blue stare met mine. "I will, *mio angelo*. You aren't getting rid of me that easily."

Her tired lips turned upward. "Today, I don't want to get rid of you."

I nodded. "I'm glad to hear that." After kissing her lips, I continued, "I've called Testa. He'll be here soon. He has the ability to open the gate and momentarily disengage the alarms. Don't let anyone else in. I don't care who it is. Let Testa decide once he's here." My head shook back and forth. "I think he knows more than he's saying. We have to trust someone, and I'm choosing him. I don't want you and Bella here unprotected."

"You said this house is a fortress."

"It is. But I want someone here who can add a human element."

"If you trust him, I do too."

"Don't use the telephone to try to reach anyone besides me. And if you call me, make it generic. I'm not sure our phones are safe. I think that's why we haven't heard from anyone."

Luisa's whines came from the other room.

"We need whole milk," Angelina said, "and diapers. Bella wasn't planning on staying this long. We have food, and she can wear my clothes and Luca Lennox's, but diapers and whole milk and… fresh fruit would be good."

Now that Lennox was older, we were not well prepared on the baby front.

"I don't mind shopping," she added.

I shook my head. "Right now, I think it's better if you all stay here. I'll call you after the meeting with the cop," I said. "Make a list. I'll stop on my way home."

My wife's eyes opened wide. "Do you even know where a grocery store is located?"

I kissed her forehead. "I've told you before that I'm a man of immense knowledge."

She shook her head. "Okay, but know this, I may get used to it."

"Don't."

"Please stay safe."

Fifty-six minutes later, the doors of the elevator opened to the lobby of Demetri Enterprises. Scanning the entry, I took a deep breath. The reception room was normally bustling on a weekday, but this was Saturday. Only the weekend receptionist was present to answer phones and take messages.

I wasn't sure what I'd expected, perhaps a firing squad, but instead, in plainclothes sat the only other person in the room. A man staring straight ahead who turned toward me as the elevator doors opened. I instantly assumed he was Detective Jennings.

I took a step closer as he stood. He was at least six inches shorter than me with a waistline probably twice as big. His rumpled jacket either meant that he'd been wearing it for a while or that he didn't have many options. His tie was loosened and as I drew closer, the reeking odor of stale coffee and cigarettes assaulted my senses.

"Mr. Demetri," he said, his teeth yellowed by probably both of the substances that caused the aromas.

"Detective Jennings, I presume." I didn't offer him my hand.

"Yes, sir. I have a few questions."

Looking around the virtually empty room, I offered, "Please follow me to my office."

As we passed Julie's office outside of mine and my gaze met that of my secretary, I shook my head. There was no need for her to offer this policeman coffee or any of the usual niceties that occurred when I was alone with clients. After all, Detective Jennings wasn't a business meeting, and besides, I wanted this session completed before coffee could cool enough to drink.

"Thank you, Mr. Demetri, for agreeing to meet with me."

Hanging my jacket in the closet, I made my way to my desk and sat. Despite my recent lack of sleep, I was a fashion model wearing expensive office attire compared to my visitor. First and foremost, I was showered and shaved, unlike his scruff that had surpassed a five o'clock shadow by at least twelve hours. My shirt was crisp and white, my gray silk tie straight, and my wool slacks probably cost a week of his salary. I wouldn't even begin to venture the expense of my Italian leather loafers on his income—perhaps a month's rent? "Detective Jennings, please..." I motioned to the chair opposite my desk. "...have a seat."

As he did, he reached for a small notebook from the inside pocket of his jacket. "Mr. Demetri, I'm going to jump right to the point."

"Please do, I have business."

"Where were you Thursday night at approximately seven o'clock?"

I leaned back, contemplating my response, my hands upon the arms of my chair, neither gripping nor clenching. The epitome of relaxed, I tilted my head, giving his question due thought. Finally, I spoke, "Thursday? I'm not certain of the time. I had an early dinner in town and came back here to finish working. I'm often here late."

"So you were here?"

"I was. Again, I'm not sure of time. Is there a problem?"

He let out a long breath. "Perhaps you haven't seen the news?"

"I'm not much for TV."

"Newspapers?"

"Again, when I have time. Often my wife keeps me informed of current events."

He stared my direction. "How's your father-in-law?"

"Dead."

"Excuse me?"

"My wife's father died when she was young. I never met Angelo Costello, but I've heard good things about him."

Detective Jennings shook his head. "Carmine Costello."

"He's my wife's uncle, not her father."

"I apologize." His neck straightened, small rings of white becoming visible as his skin unfolded. "How is Carmine Costello?"

"I haven't seen him. We often get together on Sundays. I'll be sure to let him know you're concerned."

"You said dinner—on Thursday night. Where did you eat... in town?"

"Evviva's." I didn't want to be caught in a lie, insinuating other lies. Carmine told me to say I'd left early, not that I never attended.

"Do you eat there regularly?"

"The pesto is worth the trip. I suggest you give it a try, homemade and second only to my wife's."

"And who were you dining with?"

I shrugged. "Friends."

"There are reports of your car leaving Evviva's on Thursday night."

I nodded. "As I said, I ate and then left. That would be in my car. It's too far to walk."

"Sir, we'd like to take a look at your car."

"And why is that?" I asked, sitting forward.

"Have you seen Carmine Costello in the last forty-eight hours?"

"He was at dinner on Thursday."

"What can you tell me about Lorenzo Greco?"

I shook my head. "Doesn't ring a bell."

The cop lifted the paper on his spiral tablet and pulled out a picture. He stared at it for a moment before placing it on my desk. "Not much to recognize. Just wondering if any bells are ringing yet?"

I looked down and pursed my lips. The grainy black and white photo did nothing for the boy. His face, what could be seen of it, was badly bruised. The photo was only of the torso up, but it was obvious that part of his head was missing. I pushed the picture back. "I'm not sure I could identify that person even if I did know him."

"His name is Lorenzo Greco. He is—make that *was*—nineteen years old. His father died six months ago, a nasty accident on a construction site in Midtown. His father worked for C&G Contractors who had the winning bid to construct the new skyscraper where an old warehouse had stood. Interestingly, Demetri Enterprises is the second largest stockholder in the concrete company used by C&G Contractors."

I shook my head. "I didn't know we weren't first. I'll have to get my staff on that."

"Mr. Demetri, are you going to tell me that you're unaware of the death of Buono Greco?"

I wasn't completely unaware. However, sharing my knowledge at this point wouldn't shorten this conversation. My real information came from a discussion I'd overheard months ago during drinks. The word was that Buono was late making points and over his head at twenty thousand G's. Someone had saved him last time, earning him a pass. No one in the discussion seemed to know who'd been his savior. This time he wasn't as lucky. Apparently, his pass had been revoked.

Buono Greco slipped from a suspension beam one rainy afternoon. His safety harness hadn't been properly buckled. Most of the talk on that Thursday was about a lawsuit his wife filed regarding safety. Some money-hungry ambulance chaser took on more than he bargained for.

The filing never saw the light of day, dismissed by a circuit court judge upon preliminary review. The fact that it landed on the desk of

Judge Wicketts was more than likely prompted by Bonetti money. Everyone knew Judge Wicketts was easily influenced by union money.

I may have a stake in the concrete company, but the Bonetti family was neck deep with the construction unions. One hand washed the other.

The case had claimed unsafe working conditions, which wouldn't bode well for the union. Instead, if I remembered correctly, the case was dismissed with counterclaims that Greco drank on the job and refused many direct orders to comply with the posted instructions. Magically, a history of recorded grievances against Greco appeared. According to the documentation, prior to the accident, he'd been placed on probation. The word from the court was that his probationary status rendered the claim null and void. The case was dropped, and the union and C&G Contractors were found in compliance on all charges. The minimum death benefit was awarded, which was a drop in the bucket to the amount Greco owed.

It was a big win for the union, dodging the bullet on another payout. On the other hand, it left Buono Greco's debt unpaid.

# CHAPTER 25

———•○•———

"Buono Greco?" Again I shook my head. "No bells."

Jennings continued his expectant stare. I knew the routine. I did the routine. I leaned back and waited, my face expressionless as I recalled the story I'd heard. It seemed highly possible, and I speculated that Buono's debt could have precipitated Lorenzo's participation in the attempted assassination.

As I continued pondering, the detective spoke again. "So you're saying that you're not kept apprised of accidents on your worksites?"

"Detective, it would bore you to know the number of companies Demetri Enterprises has a stake in. As you said, Demetri isn't the primary stockholder... and even if we were, are you saying that this was a concrete accident?"

"No, but it was connected."

I shook my head. "I assure you that I'm kept apprised of many things, but the daily workings of every company associated with companies under my umbrella would require more time than I could possibly devote. Now, if you could get to the point. I have appointments regarding other aspects of Demetri Enterprises as well as a wife waiting for my return. I'm sure you're familiar with the push and pull. Hard to keep everyone satisfied."

"It's a tightrope, Mr. Demetri. I'm here to help you."

"Then get to the point because wasting my time with this conversation isn't helping Demetri Enterprises or my wife."

"Interesting the order you listed your concerns."

"Are we done?" I asked.

"A man was killed in an accident at a company connected to you, and now it appears that his son, Lorenzo, decided to swallow a bullet after he was seen outside the same restaurant where you dined on Thursday night."

"That is sad. It's curious how lives intersect without knowledge of one another." I pushed the picture closer to the far edge. "Suicide. While I can't in good faith condone that action as I believe it's a sin, I understand the difficulty dealing with the loss of a parent at a young age."

"Remarkable that you have a moral compass."

I didn't respond.

Detective Jennings nodded. "Losing a parent... your wife?"

"No, me. You have homework to do. I'll save you the time. I'm familiar with what it's like to lose people you care about."

"Mr. Demetri, why would a nineteen-year-old commit suicide? And how did his face end up like this?" He lifted the picture toward me. "This isn't showing his body. The boy went through hell before deciding to end it all. As you can imagine, his mother is distraught. First her husband, now her oldest child."

With neither one of them qualifying for large sums of life insurance. That was my assumption, not the detective's.

"I assure you, I have no idea of this boy's motivation. Other than his father's employer's connection to Demetri Enterprises and apparently, my fortuitous choice in dining establishments, can you explain what this matter has to do with me?"

The detective sat forward, his legs spread and belly hanging over his belt as he stared my direction. "The last few days have been less than a *fortuitous* period of time for people you know."

"I didn't know this Lorenzo."

"How about Nicholai Lombardi, Daniel Bruno, or Carl Gioconda?"

I wasn't fast enough to stop my face from twitching at the last name on his list. "Carl Gioconda?"

"Yes, he seems to be missing. His wife called in a missing-persons report earlier today. He hasn't been home since Thursday morning."

I shook my head. "Poor Maria." I had to wonder why in the hell Maria would choose to involve the police. Why hadn't she called Carmine or Vincent? I couldn't think about that right now. Instead, I went on, "I'm afraid that I'm of little help. I am not even sure of the other names." My hands came up in the air. "...I'm sorry."

"You're sorry?"

"I'm afraid I'm not of much help."

"Nicholai Lombardi was found in a dumpster with an apparent fatal gunshot wound. The gun was found on the body of Daniel Bruno with Bruno's fingerprints. Bruno, too, appeared to have a fatal gunshot wound as well as multiple lacerations."

"That is upsetting." I turned toward the window and back, wondering where Stefano was and if he'd been found.

"Now, you said your car is in the parking garage?" Detective Jennings asked.

"I don't recall offering you that information, but yes, I have a car in the garage."

"Mr. Demetri, your association with the Costellos up to this point has been deemed familial, based on your marriage. Perhaps..." He looked around the office. "…it seems as though you have a successful business—an umbrella? That was the term you used." I didn't respond. "I would hate to see your reputation tarnished. It seems that people associated with the Costellos are falling upon ill fortune. I'd hate for it to affect you or your business. Perhaps you could search your memory and maybe some more bells will ring? Otherwise, we may need to investigate your dealings closer."

Furrowing my brow, I smiled. "Please, Detective, feel free to look into anything you'd like. Feel free to speak to Father Marco about our family connection, Sunday service, or birthday parties. I'm sure you'll find it very enlightening. I doubt anyone would turn down Mrs. Costello's home cooking every Sunday. As for Demetri Enterprises, I stand behind my company and all of its investments. I assure you that it's survived more than its share of audits. However, before you ask to see anything—my records, my car… anything—or speak to anyone, I suggest you come armed with a warrant. I have nothing more to say. You see, this has already taken too much of my day."

He nodded. "We know Mrs. Costello is staying at your home."

"I haven't seen Rose Costello since the last Sunday we dined together."

"Bella Costello."

I scoffed. "My, it seems that you've been spending an undue amount of time on me and my wife's family."

"I thought you might be curious about Bella Costello's husband."

"Why would I be?"

"That's what we're trying to determine. Some believe that he's in danger."

Danger was better than dead. "I hadn't heard."

"So you're okay with supporting another family for an indefinite amount of time?"

"Detective, I'm okay with supporting my family. My wife's family became mine the day we married. Perhaps if more families took care of one another we could avoid tragedies like that misguided boy. Is there anything else, or will you be going?"

He started to stand, but stalled on the edge of his chair. "There's hearsay that a shooting occurred inside Evviva's on Thursday."

I didn't respond.

"Mr. Demetri, you could make this a lot easier on yourself and your company if you'd just tell me what you know."

"If you're referring to Lorenzo Greco—"

"No, I'm not. His remains were found across town. I'm referring to your wife's uncle."

"Again, I'll be sure to let him know that you're concerned about his well-being." I stood and walked to my office door. Opening it, I said, "It has been a pleasure."

Jennings stood. "We'll have to do it again." He stopped. "Now, to your car."

"Did you forget to show me that warrant?"

"I simply want to take a look."

"I can't stop you from entering the garage. I have a reserved parking space. However, to take a look inside will require a judge's signature."

"I'll be back."

"I'm looking forward to it. However, next time please contact my attorney, not my secretary. I believe he should be present before we have any more chats."

Once he was outside of Julie's office, I sighed and leaned against the wall. Looking her way, I asked, "Did he ask you anything?"

"He asked how late I worked on Thursday. I told him I left after six, that my son had a football game I didn't want to miss. He then asked if I knew if you were here. I told him you weren't in the office when I left, but on Friday morning I found you had left a stack of notes on my desk, so I knew you'd been back in the office." She bit her lip. "Did I say anything wrong?"

"No, Julie. You were honest. However, in the future, I'd like a warrant before either of us answers questions."

"I wasn't sure…"

I lifted my hand. "Don't worry about it. Why don't we both go home until Monday?"

She scanned her desk. "I only have a few more appointments to confirm—"

"They can wait," I interrupted. "Go home to your husband and kids. That's what I'm going to do."

It was what I wanted to do, but not what I did, not right away.

I couldn't go home to Angelina and Bella with the questions running through my head. Why had Detective Jennings asked about Vincent and Carl? What was happening that I didn't know?

Instead of following the advice I gave Julie, I messaged Testa on his beeper. Each minute as I waited for his return call, my nerves stretched, growing tauter; they were on the verge of snapping when a call came from my home phone.

"Boss."

"Everything okay?"

"Quiet, except for the kids."

I scoffed, appreciating his candor. The boys could be loud. Somehow with all the questions swirling through my head, I'd forgotten that he was at my house with my family. He probably wouldn't know any more than I did. Yet I had to ask. "Meet me for lunch?"

"Sure."

I didn't need to say where.

The diner was off the highway, about halfway into Westchester County. A mom-and-pop establishment that only served breakfast and lunch. Since it was past the lunch hour, we'd barely made it before closing time, yet we were greeted with smiles. It was a cute place where the windows were always clean and brightly painted with smiling sunshine faces that advertised the daily special. I wasn't feeling much like eating, but since I hadn't eaten since breakfast, I went ahead and ordered a sandwich.

"Any signs of trouble at the house?" I asked as I brought the steaming cup of coffee to my lips.

"Not at the house."

"I was questioned by a Detective Jennings. What do you know about Vincent?"

"I know he's running the show. I know he's getting to the bottom of a few things."

"Carmine?"

"He's good. He still wants time, according to Vincent."

"Jennings asked me about the boy. If I remember correctly, his father had some miraculous savior when he was in debt, but then his time ran out."

Testa nodded.

"Nothing more?"

"Boss?"

"Fine, what about Gioconda?"

Testa's eyes shot my direction, no longer concerned with the sugar packets he'd been moving about the table. "Remember what I said the other night?"

I leaned forward, lowering my voice as my jaw clenched. "You might be more specific because a lot was said the other night."

"If you tell me to tell you, I ain't got no choice. But if you don't, it might be better."

I shook my head. "How can it be better?"

"Because of today."

I sighed with my voice low. "Fucking say a whole damn sentence. I'm so sick of riddles I could scream."

"Today, boss, you was questioned. You can't tell nothing you don't know. I'm sure it's a shitty position, but it's the one the boss—the bosses—want you in. It's not my doing."

"So you're trusted and I'm not?"

"That ain't what I said." He leaned across the table. "If you think Mrs. Costello would be at your house and the boss don't trust you, you're wrong." He leaned back. "I don't think they're doing it for the wrong reasons."

My words came forward, and my teeth ached from the pressure. "It's not your fucking place to decide if the reasons are right or wrong."

He nodded. "You're right. You say it, I'll spill. I work for you. Just know, I don't want to go against the other bosses' orders."

I sat back against the vinyl booth. I wouldn't ask him to go against Vincent or Carmine, and Testa knew it. Turning, I stared out into the nearly empty parking lot. There was my car—actually Angelina's—and Testa's. It was then I noticed the beat-up Fairmont, light blue and covered in road grime. It might not have caught my attention except I could tell the driver was still inside. My chest tightened as I turned back to Testa.

"Fuck. See that blue car?"

"Yeah."

"That's my friend, Detective Jennings. We didn't say where we were meeting on the phone."

"He must have followed you." Testa shook his head. "He thinks you're a weak link. You're not. But he's going to hound you."

"I told him I wouldn't show him anything unless he gets a warrant."

"Need a judge to sign for a warrant," Testa said with a flicker of a grin.

"I don't have a fucking idea if my phones are clean."

"Boss is assuming no one's is. That's why no one is talking right now."

"Can you let him know about the possible warrant?"

Testa nodded. "Yeah. I'm pretty sure no judge will sign. Besides, your car became a torch yesterday. It's going to be the size of a box by tonight."

I sighed. "We've been talking about Angelina getting a new car for a while now."

"Yeah, sorry about the accident. Fucking roads."

I nodded and propitiated our story. "Glad you weren't hurt." It was then I noticed the bruises and cuts on his knuckles.

"A little banged up," Testa said, flexing his fingers, "but no worse for wear."

"I'm headed home. I fucking hope something breaks soon."

"It broke. We just have to wait for the floodwaters to recede."

"Are you going to tell me what that means?"

"That's up to you."

I looked him in the eye. "Is my family safe?"

He nodded. "All of them. Vincent is doing what needs to be done. Sometimes it's hard when you look at a face day after day, year after year. You hear it talk. You get used to the way it sounds. You never suspect it's out to get you. Vincent saw it. He tried to say something before, but he wasn't in the position. Now he is. The boss's letting him. As long as he stays low—Vincent's in charge. He needs that right now to get everyone on board. Once the news floods the channels and the water recedes, then Vincent will step back. It's not his time yet." Testa nodded. "But he's sure as hell showing that when it is, he's ready."

"I saw a picture of that kid."

Testa's lips came together before he said, "Damn shame. Too young to take his own life, but sometimes it's the easier option."

I laid a ten-dollar bill on the table to pay for my and Testa's eighty-cent coffees and my four-dollar sandwich. I couldn't eat even with it in front of me. "Fuck, I need to buy diapers."

With a smile, Testa reached into his pocket and pulled out a list. I recognized Angelina's writing. "The missus said to give this to you. I offered to do it, but I think she likes the idea of you doing it."

Reaching for the paper, I shook my head.

Fucking life-and-death things were happening, and I was buying diapers, baby wipes, and whole milk. My blood pressure climbed as I read. There were more items. I'd volunteered for the job, yet I felt like a sap when the real men were fighting a fight I wasn't privy to. It wasn't that real men didn't shop. It was that I knew there were bigger things happening.

A little while later, as I turned my shopping cart at the end of an aisle in the grocery store near my home, I came face-to-face with Detective Jennings. I shook my head. "I hope you're enjoying your babysitting mission."

"You didn't finish your sandwich."

"You need a more exciting life."

"You're driving a different car."

I looked from side to side. "Apparently, my lawyer missed the memo of this meeting. We'll need to postpone."

"The car you're driving…?"

My eyes opened wide, more in annoyance than question.

"I know it's yours. I pulled up the registration. Where's the one you drove the other night?" When I didn't answer, he looked down into my cart. "Looks like you have more than three to feed."

"You're welcome to discuss my family's diet with my attorney."

"It could be so easy, Mr. Demetri. Talk to me."

I winked. "It already is easy. Good day, Detective."

# CHAPTER 26

———————•O•———————

SUNDAY CAME WITH word to miss church. The unusual message was secondhand, but it was the only way any news came. While the children made do, Angelina and Bella were visibly shaken. Their concern extended beyond Carmine to everyone connected to the Costellos: cousins and friends who were like family.

Blood relatives and those made by blood.

We all knew in the depths of our hearts that what had occurred at Evviva's wasn't strictly the case of a rogue kid. There was an ambush planned. What we didn't know was how deep it went.

"What would've happened if things had turned out differently in the alley?" Angelina asked late Sunday night as we both lay awake staring at the ceiling of our bedroom. It had been over three full days since the shooting. Bella and Luisa were asleep in one of the guest rooms and Luca was with Lennox. Our home was filled with family as Angelina had wanted, but the circumstances were nothing like we could have predicted.

I reached across the cool expanse of our king-sized bed for her hand. Under the covers, our fingers intertwined as we each rolled toward one another. Outside our home, rain pelted the windows and doors, the dropping temperature adding ice to the wintry mixture. With the wind howling off the water, the pinging precipitation echoed like gunfire against the glass.

Answering Angelina's question wasn't a conversation I relished having; nevertheless, I'd never sleep with the rapid-fire assault from Mother Nature. Now, with a rare reprieve from listening ears, was as good a time as any to finally tell my wife everything that I could.

With Angelina turned my way and me hers and our hands clenched, she waited for my answer. I searched for her blue eyes; however, in the darkness everything was shadowed in shades of gray.

After letting out a long breath, I began. "I don't know what I can say."

"I won't say anything to Bella. I just feel so helpless here. The lack of information is killing me."

"No, baby, you're not helpless. You're helping Vincent by keeping Bella and the kids busy. He knows they're safe. He wouldn't have had them brought here if he doubted that."

"I know that. But the fact that he did worries me too. I'm scared about Uncle Carmine. Vincent didn't send Bella there. She and I both wonder if it's because Uncle Carmine is more injured than we've been told, and Aunt Rose needs to concentrate on him."

I shrugged, pulling her hands as I moved. "I don't think that's it. I saw him walk up the stairs. I heard him talk. He told me what to do: not to come home yet, to go to the office and work. He didn't explain, but I think that it was because my phone calls are traceable. He was getting me away from the scene and having me establish an alibi."

"Did he tell you to shower?" There were so many layers to her simple question.

I lifted her hand to my lips, leaving a soft, lingering kiss on her knuckles. "I did something else that night that I didn't tell you about, something I'm not proud of."

"Oren, don't. I don't want to hear…" She tried to pull her hands away from mine as she began to turn, and her words faded into the roar of the outside winds.

"No, listen…" My eyes were more adjusted to the darkness, allowing me to see her clearer; her face was illuminated with slivers of the night's light shining through our blinds. Against the white of the pillows, I could make out the curves of her face, her cheekbones, and the pout of her lips. Letting go of her hand, I secured a loose strand of silky brown hair behind her ear. "…please."

Her fight lessened and body relaxed as she nodded.

"Everything happened so fast," I began. "I told you that I was there at Evviva's when it happened. I don't think I saw Carmine struck by the bullet or him fall, but I saw the kid." I rolled to my back, no longer willing to watch her emotions play out in her expressions. Yet instead of seeing the ceiling high above me, I was recalling the scene from seventy-five hours ago. "*Mio angelo*, he was so young."

"The one who shot Uncle Carmine?"

"Yes. The policeman who questioned me said he was nineteen." I fought the emotion that I shouldn't have, that I couldn't show to my wife—that real men didn't display. "I couldn't help but think about Lennox. Fuck, the last seven years have flown by. We're going to blink, and he and Luca will be that old."

Angelina scooted closer until her head was on my shoulder, her soft hair flowing over my pillow. "It scares me too," she whispered. "What did you do?" One of her arms went over my torso, her warmth giving me the comfort that I didn't deserve as her petite frame spooned against mine.

"I pulled my gun, ready to take the kid down." The reality ate at my soul. Shaking my head, I went on. "I've been places before… places where I knew what was happening. A long time ago, before we were married, Vincent had me drive him to this house in a run-down area. I can still see it in my mind. The house was falling apart, the gutters hung down, and the building was in need of paint." I shook my head. "But you know what I always see when I remember that?"

"No..." Her voice was soft, an answer to my question without pulling me from the memory.

"There was a kid's bike in the yard. I don't know why I remember that, but I do.

"Vincent told me to stay in the car. That night, we'd been collecting family money. I hated doing it, mostly because it seemed to happen in the middle of the night when I wanted to be sleeping. I guess it was all part of letting me see more of the life. Anyway, I did as he said and stayed in the car. He never specifically said why we were there—I'd assumed collection, until I saw a flash through the window. I told myself later that it had been a TV or something." My pulse increased as the memory became more vivid. "When Vincent came out, he looked exactly as he had when he went in. He was calm, like he'd just gone into a store and bought a pack of gum.

"His gun was concealed, but there was an odor. I smell it every time I go to the shooting range. It's not strong, but it's there, right after a gun fires." They say sense of smell was the paramount one in the replaying of memories. I ran my fingers through Angelina's hair. The aroma of hairspray, shampoo, and the faint sweetness of perfume reminded me that I was in bed with her, not sitting in my car in a driveway nearly ten years ago. "When I'm at the shooting range and I inhale that scent, my mind always goes back to that driveway, that flash, and Vincent getting back in the car."

"You've never told me any of this."

I shrugged, causing her head to bob. There were many things I'd never shared. "Anyway, I'm not unaware of what goes on, but seeing it all unfold and knowing that I could have pulled that trigger hit me hard."

Angelina lifted her head, her gaze meeting mine. "Oren, did you shoot the kid?"

"No. The last time I saw him he was alive. He'd pissed himself because he was so scared, but he was alive. My thoughts weren't really on the kid. I was too worried about Carmine—he's the boss, but he's more than that. I thought of you."

"Me?"

"I didn't want to tell you that your uncle was dead." I took a deep breath. "Stefano and Jimmy were outside with those soldiers—fucking traitors. Vincent yelled for a car. That's when I told Testa to go get mine. Carmine needed to get out of there. I think Vincent was also calling for Stefano or Jimmy. Like I told you, it was all happening at once.

"The alley. I don't even know what happened except if those traitors had made it through Jimmy and Stefano, well, I'm not sure who would still be standing. Jimmy came back inside. He didn't say a word about the ambush. He was only worried about Carmine. And then Testa came back with the car. We got Carmine out." I shook my head recalling the scene. "Jimmy's an ox. He lifted your uncle like he was Luisa."

I rolled toward my wife. "After I learned about the bulletproof vest and after Carmine and Jimmy got out of the car..." I closed my eyes.

Angelina's warm hand came to my cheek. "What happened?"

When my eyes opened, her face was blurry. I tried to blink her into focus, ignoring the moisture leaking from my eyes. "I told Testa to pull over... because... I lost it. I reacted like a fucking baby. I vomited in the damn gutter."

Her lips came to mine. This time I pulled away. "Don't you see? I'm not who they think. I'm not who you think I am."

"You are who I think you are. You're better than that."

Turning away again, I faced the ceiling and lifted my free arm to cover my eyes. "My suit had blood on it. Jimmy touched my shoulder, and then I helped undo Carmine's buttons, Jimmy's and my hands working together. Blood from his hands got on my hands. I'm probably the reason there was more on my clothes. And then there was the fucking throw-up. Shit splattered against the cement. I brushed my teeth until my gums bled. I couldn't get the damn taste out of my mouth."

My wife sat over me, her hair a veil shielding us from the wintry storm. She lifted my arm away, forcing me to look at her, to show her my shame.

"Oren Demetri, if I'd wanted to marry a man who could walk out of a building without a care in the world after shooting someone, believe me, I had my choice. I wanted to marry you."

"Why?" I asked in earnest.

"Because I loved you. I do. I have since you were a tongue-tied boy in my English class." Kisses peppered my cheeks. "I still love you," she said.

"Boy?" I thought of Lorenzo. "Here I thought I was a man."

Her head shook. "Now you're a man. And no longer tongue-tied."

This time I framed her face, my palms on each side until our eyes met. "No other woman has ever caused me to be tongue-tied."

"And no other man has had my heart."

As she continued to kiss me, her hands on my shoulders, her body against mine, a wave washed through me, giving my soul purpose. Whatever this flood was, it filled my bloodstream with a need to move beyond what had happened and a desire to show my wife that she'd married the right man. Reaching for her waist, I rolled until she was the one on her back, her blue eyes staring at me, her beautiful face surrounded by a halo of hair. My body covered hers. "You love me?"

She nodded.

"More than you hate me?" My body hardened as she wiggled beneath me.

"Right now."

"I'll take that."

With the wind and ice roaring beyond our windows, Angelina and I came together in a way such as we hadn't in a while. It wasn't that our marriage was without sex. It was that sometimes it became mechanical. This was different. The tension of the last few days fueled our desire— our need—to connect. The heat of our union reignited a flame that life, snow, and death somehow hadn't completely extinguished. Momentarily, the world beyond our bedroom was gone. I wasn't the man who'd gotten ill at the sight of blood and bodies. She wasn't the woman who reacted with constant suspicion and discontent. Together we were one fire, one flame, burning out of control, each of us finding release and pleasure in the one person we loved, needed, and trusted with our secrets and shame.

We both gave what we could, each accepting what was given.

Without the other, our fire would extinguish, but together we could keep it alive.

# CHAPTER 27

—————●O●—————

THE PIECES MADE sense: the debt the kid Lorenzo had tried to pay was his father's. However, I still wasn't seeing the whole picture—or perhaps I didn't want to see it. The story finally became clear a week later, after seven days of family togetherness. We'd feigned a nasty stomach bug with Lennox's school. Angelina had gone to pick up his schoolwork. I wasn't sure what important study a second grader needed to accomplish, nevertheless, she brought home books and notebooks. No matter what the nuns deemed crucial to his education, neither Angelina nor I wanted him out of the house even in Rye.

I didn't know what excuse Bella had given the parish school in Brooklyn. It didn't matter. According to Vincent—through Testa—his family was not to be seen outside of our home. That was, until Testa arrived Thursday evening with a nice new minivan. In all the uproar, I'd forgotten about his assignment to purchase Angelina a new car. My old one was now reduced to rubble, hopefully buried and at the bottom of a trash heap.

However Angelina had not forgotten that she had a new car coming. Upon seeing the minivan in the driveway, she unequivocally stated her disapproval. "I will not drive that. You need at least three children to drive one of those ugly things."

When Testa entered the house, I tried to break the news in a gentler way. "I thought we talked about sedans?"

Angelina's stare relayed her discontent even though she'd only verbally shared it with me.

Testa grinned. "It's just a test drive, ma'am."

"A test drive?" I asked.

He nodded. "It seats seven. Room for all of us."

Bella jumped up from the sitting room where she'd been pretending to read one of Angelina's magazines. "All of us? Does that mean me too?"

"Yes, Mrs. Costello. Your husband and father-in-law are waiting."

Her wide eyes met Angelina's as they filled with tears, and the two women came together. "I'm going home."

Angelina nodded as she hugged Bella.

Contemplating the idea of all seven of us in the same vehicle, I said, "I'm driving."

My declaration was met with multiple sets of suspiciously narrowed eyes. I'd been responsible for Angelina for nearly nine years and Lennox since he was born. Vincent had entrusted Bella, Luca, and Luisa to me for a week. I trusted Testa, but nothing since the shooting felt right.

After all, Sunday we'd missed Mass. Today was Thursday and I'd just eaten dinner at home, something that never happened. For the first time in my memory, drinks with the family had been postponed. There were too many variables, too many things out of the norm and out of my control. If I'd been wrong about Testa and we were driving into some sort of ambush, it would be me behind the wheel.

I nodded to Testa. "You ride shotgun. You're a better shot anyway." My reasoning seemed to satisfy the masses as Bella rushed around, rounding up Luca and Luisa.

Angelina helped as they gathered the few things the Costellos had brought and the things we'd acquired. Diapers wouldn't be any use to us. Angelina wasn't having more children. The minivan wasn't really a test drive. It was simply Testa's way of providing transportation for us all in one vehicle.

The wintry mix we'd had a few nights ago was gone, and the air had warmed. It was autumn in New York, and anything was possible. I watched the roads and my rearview mirror as we drove from Westchester to Brooklyn. Just as I drove close to the Costello brownstone, a car pulled away from the curb.

"Your parking space," Testa said.

I exhaled as Jimmy stepped from the shadows onto the sidewalk. Gentler than I'd ever seen him, he helped Bella, Angelina, and the children out of the van and quickly inside. As Testa and I reached the top of the steps, something caught my attention. Tilting my head, I alerted Testa to the light-blue Fairmont parked a few houses down.

Detective Jennings.

"He wasn't following, boss," Testa said, and I knew he was right. "I was watching. He must've gotten tired babysitting you and is now watching this house."

"Simply a family gathering."

Walking through the door onto the wood floor, I was overwhelmed by memories. The magic aroma of Rose's cooking lingered in the air. The familiar scent that accompanied the home filled me with relief I never would have imagined feeling the first time that Angelina brought me here. I looked up to see Vincent and Bella. Their family gathered in a group hug farther inside and down the hallway.

For a week, Bella had been remarkably strong, and now in her husband's arms, her sobs echoed against the paneled walls. Her arms were around his neck with Luisa in her father's arms and Luca standing at their waists, his arms holding everyone.

"Shh," Vincent soothed as Bella cried, and Luisa asked what was wrong. I envied the little girl's innocence, yet from the expression on Luca's face, he didn't share it. He'd sensed the danger despite our best intent. He was part of the world. It was part of him, inbred in a way that even at barely eight years old, he understood beyond his years.

I couldn't venture to guess what Vincent Costello had done in the last seven days. I wasn't supposed to give it much thought. Yet as I stood there seeing him with his family, I fought the moisture again pooling in my eyes. Whatever he'd done and decisions he'd made had been for family. He'd survived the storm, and now he was getting his reward.

Taking a deep breath, I turned to the sitting room. There seated beside her uncle was my wife. He appeared healthy, his cheeks full with color as her hand rested upon his knee and Lennox leaned over him in an embrace. At first, I couldn't speak, not until a hand landed on my shoulder.

"Oren," Rose said. "*Mille grazie.*" She palmed one of my cheeks and kissed the other.

"Thank you? I've felt a little helpless. I don't think I deserve thanks."

She shook her head. "You're a good man. In a family, every job is important. You helped save my Carmine, my family. I'll never forget what you did, and nothing means more to me than my *famiglia—niente.*" She nodded toward Carmine and Angelina across the room. "You're a good husband and father. How hard would it be for you to let someone else watch over them if you knew there was danger?"

I nodded, knowing where she was going. "The only one I've trusted is Testa."

"My boy, he trusted you. You weren't helpless. You did what he couldn't as he dealt with other things."

My lungs filled as my chest expanded. "Thank you, Rose."

I turned as Carmine stood. The vision was like a miracle. Step by step he came toward me until he offered his hand. I stared for only a millimeter of a second before shaking his. I couldn't recall the last time he'd shaken my hand, maybe before our wedding or after Lennox's birth. Maybe never. His strong grasp was solid as if he hadn't recently cheated death.

"Angel, Bella, children..." Rose called. "Come to the kitchen. *Dolci.*"

I smiled, knowing she wouldn't need to call Lennox twice for desserts as he, Luca, and Luisa hurried toward their prize.

"Come," Carmine said, "Vincent and I will share. For you only." He looked to Jimmy and Testa. "Go have *dolci*, then watch over us. We're fine in the office."

Jimmy nodded.

I followed Carmine and his son into Carmine's office.

Vincent broke the rhythm of our shoes upon the hard floor as we stepped beyond the threshold; slapping my shoulder, he said, "Thank you. I missed them."

"They missed you."

His smile was weary. "I couldn't worry about them. I had to do what needed to be done. That house of yours... I thought it was overkill when you built it. Not anymore."

"We didn't have any threats. They were safe."

"You did," Carmine said.

"What?" I asked, turning to Carmine.

The boss shook his head as he sat behind his desk and leaned forward. "They didn't make it to your property. I'm sure you would have handled it if they had. You couldn't have known, but twice our men stopped predators before your fortress was tested. We had a few men we trusted watching."

"I don't think they could have made it in."

"The important thing is that we never found out."

"Yes," I agreed.

"Sit down, Oren," Vincent said. "I know you think you were left out, but it was for a reason. That cop was watching you—the one outside. He's not good at hiding. We needed you with the women and children. Not a demotion but an important role. This…" His hands moved about. "…what happened…" His eyes closed in reflection as his head shook. When the dark stare met mine, he continued, "It was a bloodbath, and that hasn't been who you are."

"We're not ready to ask that of you. Not yet," Carmine said.

The addition to his sentence gave me pause, yet I did as he'd earlier instructed and sat. Between Vincent and Carmine, I was able to fill in the blanks to the story I thought I knew.

"I'm telling you something that very few will hear," Carmine said. "I made a mistake that I don't want you or Vincent to ever make. I put blind trust where it didn't belong. We're all family, but we still need to keep our eyes open. I'm alive because Vinny didn't stop. He warned me. I didn't listen, not completely. I didn't want to believe that someone I trusted with my secrets and my life, in my home, someone I've known since before either of you were born… I refused to see that he would betray that trust."

"Gioconda," Vincent said.

I nodded, this confirmation a staggering punch to my gut. What Carmine was saying was true. I knew how much faith had been put in Carl Gioconda. I sometimes wondered why Carl's distrust of me wasn't taken more seriously by Carmine, though I would never have questioned that aloud.

Vincent and Carmine went on to tell a magnificent and haunting tale of betrayal and deception. They couldn't be sure, as Gioconda never fully confessed, but the night of our housewarming party, Vincent believed that Gioconda was already laying the groundwork for the takeover. Our talk on the shore of the sound was simply to feel me out. Since Gioconda had always proclaimed to not trust me, he threw me a line to see if I'd bite. When I didn't, he moved on. Apparently, his distrust of me ran deep. He neither trusted me to support the Costellos nor to turn against them.

Gioconda relied not only on greed, but on debt. Over the years, he'd helped soldiers and their families in times of financial need. Many of the loans were known to Carmine, but not all. That in itself was a violation of family policy. The boss was entitled to a kickback on all points collected. If Gioconda had been collecting taxes and not paying his due, he was in the wrong. That was the rumor Vincent had heard in passing, the reason his defenses were up and ears were open long before this eruption.

As Carmine and Vincent spoke, I got the picture of a man wanting more than he had. Gioconda claimed to side with Carmine against the sale of illegal drugs, yet in dark alleys and backrooms, he spoke to capos and soldiers, enticing them with the potential income that they were currently denied because of Carmine's convictions. Morelli had been the one who went to Vincent and told him what some of his crew had been saying.

Morelli, Stefano, and Jimmy were all eyes and ears, collecting intel. They were aware that things were happening, but not the depth, or that it was about to come to blows.

Gioconda had been the one who saved Buono Greco from his initial debt. It was a win-win until Greco couldn't pay. The points continued to multiply. The amount became insurmountable. Buono paid with his life, believing that the payout from insurance and a lawsuit would relieve his financial obligation. It didn't happen, leaving his family still in debt. Gioconda made Lorenzo a deal. If the boy had succeeded in killing Carmine, the debt would have been cleared. Not only that, but once the coup was complete, Lorenzo would have been set for life as one of Gioconda's trusted soldiers.

It wasn't Gioconda who shared his plans but Lorenzo—before he ate his own bullet. I'd heard that Vincent could be very persuasive.

Buono's wife liked the money her husband made gambling. Since he'd died, she'd found a little salvation in a bottle. The rest of her time was reportedly spent in search of a new breadwinner. Lorenzo claimed that the only reason he'd agreed to the plan was to save his sister. He went to his death without giving up her location. The Costellos have been looking for her for the last week, but so far, she's the missing piece.

Everyone else involved in the coup had been dealt with. The final death toll of Costello soldiers would take some time to rebuild. Besides the four lost in the alleyway, there were over a dozen more. Vincent didn't ask for loyalty. It was or it wasn't. Anyone with evidence that Vincent felt placed them on the side of Gioconda, on the side of changing the Costello legacy forever, was no longer a problem. Many of the bodies had yet to be discovered. Vincent was certain that some never would be.

"Not enough left," he said.

"Four?" I questioned when their story stilled.

"Four?" Vincent repeated.

"You said there were four in the alley. Stefano, Bruno, and Nicholai. Who was the fourth?"

"You shouldn't know him. According to Jimmy, he was waiting, knew they'd get thrown out."

"I wasn't sure of the number I saw." My earlier question spurred another. "Stefano?"

"A true, trusted soldier," Carmine said. "The coroner's report said he died in his sleep."

Vincent scoffed. "Apparently, with a little incentive, they missed the fact he had a hole in his chest. The most important thing is, Theresa will be taken care of."

"Things could have gone so differently," I said.

Vincent nodded. "You sending Testa out... they didn't expect that."

Testa hadn't shared the entire story, yet I recalled him telling me he would if I ordered him to. I hadn't. I'd taken the information he'd given me. He hadn't lied, only shielded me. One day I may ask, but for now, he had been right. I would sleep with the knowledge that sending him for the car helped save the Costello family.

THE NEXT THURSDAY, in front of family during drinks at Evviva's, Carmine called on family for retribution for his friend. Gioconda's body had surfaced, inside his car, found at the bottom of a pond. Carmine claimed that he would find the snake who'd murdered Gioconda and tried to take over his family. He would find justice.

The capos and soldiers clamored with agreement. Their boss was alive and strong, proclaiming not only his strength, but the strength of the family. Gioconda was identified as being involved with the Grecos but not in his true role.

The elaborate charade cast a shadow of suspicion on Gioconda while saving the Costellos from admitting that over a dozen people were no longer breathing because of them. Carmine was alive, strong, and in control. Those in the know understood that when the day came for Vincent to take over the Costello family, his advancement would not be simply nepotism but because he'd earned it. He'd saved the family.

As I listened during drinks, I became acutely aware that somehow even when it hadn't felt as though I was inside, I was. A week earlier I'd been in his office: I was inside Carmine Costello's inner sanctum. I'd also done my job. Caring for the women and children whom he and Vincent loved was my inside job.

I'd been dead wrong when I'd assumed I wasn't helping the family. I'd be dead if I hadn't.

As drinks continued, glasses were raised in memory of Gioconda and the fallen soldiers as low murmurs of agreement and question lingered in the smoky air.

"His killer will be dealt with," Carmine said. "I will always remember Carl as a friend and ally. Any other talk will not be permitted. We are family, and we take care of those who take care of us. Blood in. Blood out."

"Blood in. Blood out," everyone repeated as my eyes met Testa's, and we lifted our glasses in agreement with the boss.

"Now another toast," Carmine said. "To Stefano De Luca, one of the truest men I've ever known."

Each person Carmine deemed worthy received a salute. Finally, Carmine announced that with the passing of Gioconda, Pipi Morelli was the newly appointed Costello consigliere.

I grinned, realizing that I never knew Morelli's first name. My inside status was in a forever ebb and flow.

# CHAPTER 28

—————●O●—————

LENNOX BUSIED HIMSELF with one of those computer games that kids held in their hands while their eyes stayed glued to the small screen and the world passed them by; Angelina, meanwhile, literally watched the world passing by outside our car as we drove home from a gathering at the Costello brownstone.

Time had done what it continued to do… the clock ticked second by second as days and weeks caused the turning of another page on our calendar. More winters passed and seasons changed. It had been three years since Carmine's shooting. While the event would be paramount in all our memories, the subject was no longer discussed as we all moved forward with our lives.

And yet the deception and betrayal that Carmine and the Costello family had endured lingered omnipresent, often visible as a shadow of concern sprinkled with uncertainty in the darkness of the boss's eyes. He'd faced death and overcome. The battle wasn't his alone. He'd lost more than one friend to his own orders. He'd been hurt, not only physically but also his soul had taken a hit. The experience marked him, leaving him darker than the man he had been. It wasn't that he had been open and friendly before, but now he was even less so. His true and seemingly only joy came with his family. Today marked a special occasion. It was Luisa's First Communion. We hadn't been able to attend the church service, but we arrived in time for the party.

The little girl I'd lifted from Scopo's backseat was now six years old and extremely bright. The nuns had prompted Vincent and Bella to allow her to advance a year ahead in school. Despite her intelligence, or maybe because of it, she was filled with as much energy as her brother. Luca was now nearly eleven and Lennox ten. Each year the boys grew another year closer to the age of Lorenzo Greco at the time of his death. Knowing that their adulthood was around the corner filled me with concern.

After riding for what seemed like hours in silence, I asked Angelina a question. In reality we were barely out of the city on our way home to Westchester County. Nevertheless, the silence had begun at the Costello brownstone, and I hoped by initiating conversation, I could get her to talk. "Are you sorry?"

With her elbow against the bottom of the car's window, Angelina turned my way, her expression furrowed as if she either hadn't heard or understood me. Finally, she replied, "I think you are going to need to be a little more specific about what I may or may not be sorry about. *I'm sorry* we missed church today with the family. *I'm sorry* that a phone call of yours couldn't be done at a more appropriate time than Sunday morning. Luisa has only one First Communion, and we missed it. Do you want me to go on about other things I may be sorry for?"

Damn. Silence was my better option. Maybe someday I'd learn.

Momentarily I closed my eyes while still maintaining my bearing of the road. I didn't want to argue, yet now I at least had a better idea of what I'd done. The call had come at an inopportune time, but that didn't lessen its importance. It was a conversation I couldn't miss. It was with the boss of the Bonetti family. Vincent had coordinated the call. He didn't know when Benny Bonetti would call. The timing hadn't been planned. One didn't simply say to a don, *sorry, I have plans.*

I looked at my wife. "I guess that answers my question. I think I wondered if you were sorry we moved out here. Every time we go back, I feel like you hate me more."

"I don't hate you, Oren, for making us a home. For that... I'm not sorry." She turned her head to the backseat. In the rearview mirror, I could see the headphones over Lennox's ears. Her voice took on a more natural tone. "I look at him and I'm not sorry. I know it was right. There's something about Luca—a look. I can't really place it. It's his father's, my uncle's, and it was my father's. I see it in my cousins and in family friends and associates. Our son doesn't have that." Her chest rose and fell as she took a deep breath. "His biggest concern is if he'll get to pitch this year in Little League. He's in the major league."

I opened my eyes wide. I didn't follow sports, but everyone knew the pitcher was a big deal. There were times I was relegated to the discussion with other men in our neighborhood at backyard gatherings. I remembered when I was a kid, my father was up in arms about the Dodgers leaving Brooklyn. It was something he never got over, refusing to support the Yankees. That did little for my love of the sport. Nevertheless, I was a talker, a negotiator. I brushed up on stats and could talk Yankees or Red Sox if necessary. Personally, I'd prefer a nice debate about distribution versus manufacturing, but I played the role of suburban husband when I had to for Angelina. And while there was appeal in rooting for the underdog, since the Red Sox hadn't seen a series win in going on eighty years, the Yankees were usually the topic of conversation.

Was my son really that inclined to pitch? "Will he?" I asked.

"Quite possibly. He was drafted from the minors. At ten years old, that's a big deal. Maybe sometime you should see him play. He's good."

"I will. Just let me know when his games are."

"Right. I hope you don't mind that I wait to tell him until I see the whites of your eyes. I've watched too many times as he's looked up at the stands and been disappointed."

My knuckles blanched as I gripped the steering wheel tighter. "Just say whatever you want to say. You've been pissed off at me over something since the party."

"I'm not pissed at you! It's not always about you."

My head nodded, her tone confirming my original observation.

"I'm not," she went on. "I'm sad. And it's upsetting when you disappoint Lennox."

My gaze shot back to the rearview mirror. If he were listening to what we were saying, he wasn't showing it. "What is he playing in the backseat?"

"It's a Game Boy." She laughed. "But don't call it a game. It's a system. He'll correct you in a second."

"He'll correct me?"

"Yes." Angelina laughed. "In a heartbeat. I'm pretty sure he takes after his father."

I was thinking his mother but whatever. "So... a Game Boy is what?" I was up on a lot of technology, but kids' toys aren't really my thing. Cellular telephones, however, were amazing. No longer a bag plugged into the car, my latest cellular phone was the size of a pack of cigarettes, fit into a pocket, and flipped open like a prop from Star Trek. "It looks like a fancy calculator."

"Oren, really? He's ten. Why would he be staring at a calculator? We got it for him for Christmas almost a year ago and it's been practically attached to his hand ever since. It's a small console that plays games. He can control what happens. Right now he's obsessed with baseball. I would bet he's playing the newest MVP baseball game."

I thought about her description of our son. "So he's always right, and he likes to control things?" I was most certain he was more like his mother.

"Yes. Sound familiar?"

"Very." Before I got myself in more trouble I asked, "Whatever happened to reading?"

She grinned. "It's 1996. The turn of the millennium is coming. You know, Y2K? It's time to get with the program."

"You know, I don't try to disappoint him. It's—"

Her hand came up, not allowing me to finish, not that I could blame her. I wasn't saying anything new: Work. Family. Commitments. Same excuses I'd been giving forever.

I reached over and splaying my fingers, covered her knee with my hand. "I'm sorry if I'm the reason you're sad."

"You're not. Remember, it's not always about you."

That was a relief, but why was she sad? Instead of asking, I turned her way and squeezed the knee under my grasp. "Do you want to talk about it?"

"I almost can't say it. I'm having trouble comprehending that it's true."

She definitely had my curiosity. "Try," I encouraged.

"That girl who was serving drinks at Aunt Rose's..."

I nodded. I'd seen the girl. Angelina had even chastised me for not thanking her when she brought me a beer. The next time she brought one, I did. I didn't consider myself ungrateful; it was that the girl was doing her job. People aren't thanked for their jobs. Granted, she seemed young, but it was her job nonetheless.

"She's fifteen years old."

I grimaced. "Yeah, she looked young."

Again Angelina looked over her shoulder as she lowered her voice. "Just turned fifteen." She shook her head. "Bella had told me a little about her, but Aunt Rose filled me in today on all the details. The whole thing makes me sick."

"Baby, you've lost me completely."

Her voice became even softer. "Uncle Carmine doesn't want anyone to know who she is. Vincent found her."

"Vincent found her...? He found her on the street? In a crack house? A foster home? What?"

"He found her in Chicago. He's been looking for her for three years."

My eyes opened wide and stared at my wife as if for a moment I forgot I was driving. "No." It was the only word that came to me.

Angelina nodded. "Yes. The information is still fuzzy. What Vincent did find out was that after the husband died, the mother was drinking and in need of cash. She sent Silvia to Chicago to live and work under the radar. After the shooting, she followed. Apparently, she didn't feel safe in New York. From what Aunt Rose has learned, the mother lived with a friend for a while before making her way back into the life she knew—a goomah—sleeping with anyone for a roof over her head. The reason Silvia was hard to locate was because the mother basically sold her for domestic help. According to Aunt Rose, Vincent said he found her because eventually she had been moved to another home. She began working for some distant cousins. That was about to end because her mother's current boyfriend found out about her and decided she could make them more money doing *other* things. He decided it would be a good idea to auction the girl."

My gut twisted. "I've heard that shit like that happens, but seriously?"

"It happens," she said. "I've heard stories that I'll never forget."

"Was she?" I almost didn't want to know. "Was she auctioned?"

"Uncle Carmine called in a few favors. Her mother's boyfriend works a crew for a capo under a boss that Uncle Carmine knows. The mother's name isn't Greco any longer—she's been married a few times between boyfriends."

"It's only been three years and she's married *a few times*?"

"I know, right? I'm just sick. I can't imagine what that poor girl has seen and heard... and now this."

"What happened?"

"The boss Uncle Carmine spoke to knew about the history. He knew Silvia's brother was the one who shot Uncle Carmine. He apologized for not bringing the girl to Uncle Carmine's attention earlier. He told him that if Uncle Carmine wanted her, he'd tell the mother she was gone. No questions asked. No money exchanged. A life for a debt."

"He bought her?"

"Somehow." Angelina's hands went in the air. "I don't know if he paid. I don't think I want to know. According to Aunt Rose, Silvia doesn't fully understand what was about to happen to her. Her mother told her some story years ago about how she was old enough to earn more money and help pay their debt. She told Silvia they'd never see one another again, but that was okay. She's an adult now and whatever she does is for the good of her family."

Again my knuckles whitened from my grip on the innocent steering wheel. "An adult? She's fifteen."

"Barely. What do we expect? The woman sent her son to pay a man's debt at nineteen."

I shook my head. "Can you imagine what could have happened to the girl?"

"God yes, Oren. I've been sick about it all afternoon. I tried to talk to her a little. She's shy and so sweet and innocent. She thinks she's Aunt Rose's maid. She should be worried about school and boys, not cleaning and cooking and not whatever else her mother had in mind."

"What about the bitch of a mom and that boyfriend? Did Vincent just let them get by with this?"

Angelina shook her head. "I didn't ask. I don't think I want to know. I mean, I would hope they're no longer around. Then again, if they're living in some godforsaken shithole, that's what they deserve.

"I'm sickened with myself. It upsets me that I want them to find harm—to burn in Hell for what they did to an innocent girl—but I do. I really do. People like that don't deserve children."

I swallowed my thoughts as we exited the interstate. All afternoon, I'd been worried about bringing up a business opportunity to Carmine. That was why we didn't make church. I was ironing out some of the particulars on a chain of three jewelry stores located in different family areas. That was why I was speaking to the Bonettis. The deal was about sealed, but no other don would agree until I had Carmine's approval. Now my concerns and even the jewelry stores seemed to lose their glitter in comparison to my wife's worries. "Don't beat yourself up. You didn't just try to sell your child."

"Well, thank God Silvia has lasted this long. The thing is that Uncle Carmine and Aunt Rose are worried that if people in the family find out who she is... that her brother... who he was... what he did... they're worried about what could happen to her. I mean there were people at Uncle Carmine's today who would say that the girl owes a debt to our family." Angelina's hands went in the air. "She's a child."

Loosening my grip of the wheel, I reached over to Angelina. She turned her hand over on her leg, palm up so our fingers could come together and intertwine. "She's in good hands. Your aunt and uncle will keep her safe."

It was true. Where the world saw criminals and killers in Carmine and Vincent, we were privy to two men who'd made it their mission to find this child and save her from her family's poor decisions.

As I pulled our car through the gate to our house, Angelina sighed and laid her head against the seat. "I wish we could help."

I recalled something Carmine had said at the gathering. He'd asked me if Angelina was happy and then said she wanted a daughter. I'd been taken aback, knowing we'd both agreed to only one child. A daughter could be safe, but there were no guarantees we wouldn't have another boy. I pushed away the idea that there was any possibility that his comment had something to do with this girl.

That would be ludicrous.

Securing the car inside the garage, the thought was forgotten, replaced by Angelina's question.

"We could watch a movie? All three of us?"

I tried not to grimace. It was Sunday night, but if I went to my home office, I could get a few hours of work accomplished.

When I didn't respond fast enough and Lennox opened the car door, his headphones still in place, Angelina answered for me. "Never mind, I'll read."

I forced a smile. "You like to read."

# CHAPTER 29

———●○●———

"YOU'RE GOING TO California?" Angelina asked, her voice a higher pitch than normal. "Oren, we have plans this weekend. You said you'd try to make Lennox's game. He's started as pitcher the last three games and his father hasn't been to one. And then, Saturday night, Melanie and her husband invited us to a barbeque at their house. You like Jim. They're the ones who had the Super Bowl party. I asked you, and you said yes. Now, I'll have to go alone."

I shook my head as I added another shirt to the suitcase. "I didn't plan this trip."

Her hands slapped the sides of her jean-covered legs. "Of course not. You never do. You also didn't say no."

"I can't say no to your uncle."

"I don't understand. What business does Uncle Carmine and Vinny have in California, and why do you need to go?"

"He wasn't very specific, something about negotiating. He said I could help and learn in the process."

"And it has to be this weekend?" she asked again.

Standing, I reached for her shoulders. "*Mio angelo*, I asked the boss to approve a multifamily-territory deal that I have in the works. If it goes

258

through, the potential for us and for the families is limitless. It's a great investment for this improving economy. Your uncle said he would give his okay if I'd do this. He also said something about a gift for you."

She sighed and turned toward the bouquet of daisies I'd brought home to tell her the news of my impending trip. "I don't want a damn gift. I want my husband home. I want a family weekend."

My brows arched. "I guess that's what I'm getting with Vinny. And if you don't want gifts, throw the damn flowers away."

"That's not the family weekend that I had in mind. And I don't think the flowers should be sacrificed just because they were bought by the wrong person, for the wrong reason."

"I bought them to tell you that I love you."

"No, you bought them to soften the blow of your leaving." Her neck straightened. "I could call Uncle Carmine and talk to him."

"You could, but then it makes me look weak."

"You're not weak, Oren. You're over-obligated."

*Didn't I fucking know that?*

"You need to learn to say no," she went on. "I mean, to someone besides me."

I leaned forward and kissed her forehead. "But, baby, I'll say yes when I get back."

"Don't make promises you can't keep."

"I will keep it. I'll have Julie clear next weekend. How about we go somewhere? It's nearly summer, we could go to the coast? A weekend drive along the shore?"

"Lennox has a game next Saturday, and he can't miss it."

Letting go of her shoulders, I turned toward the bed and closed my suitcase. "Sounds like you're the one telling me no." Which wasn't an unusual scenario either.

As I turned to kiss her goodbye, Angelina turned away. "Just go, Oren. We'll be here if you ever have time, or maybe we won't."

"That's just wonderful. This is your family."

"Really, Oren? I thought you said they were *ours?*"

Her parting words added more acid to my already-bubbling stomach. This trip was different. I felt it in my bones. Even though I'd discussed the jewelry stores with Vincent, I'd agitated Carmine by not talking to him first. Another time, I would have been told to work out the details with Vincent and then confirm with him.

It seemed like as time passed since the shooting, talking to Carmine had become more difficult. Angelina and I still had Sunday dinner at least once a month in Windsor Terrace, yet Carmine was more and more reserved. It was as if he'd built a wall slowly, brick by brick, around himself.

This trip was to prove to him that I still had the family's best interests in mind and that I wasn't stepping over him to other dons. It was a show of family allegiance. All he'd told me was that I was to watch, help, and learn from Vincent.

One favor for a friend.

I didn't know his friend, nor did I owe his friend a favor. But I knew Carmine, and if this favor was what I thought it would be, I dreaded it with the better part of my being. If this trip was what I anticipated, I wasn't sure there'd be a better part of my being left.

Sunday evening in a hotel suite in Los Angeles, I heard the instructions I'd been dreading.

"Come on, Oren. How many years have you been a part of us?"

Sitting back in the soft chair, I lifted my feet to the coffee table. "Maybe part of me thought the millions of dollars I've secured for the Costello family would be enough."

Vincent nodded. "You're a damn good earner. You're also fucking great at keeping your books crystal clean. Pop wants collateral."

"I've never taken a life."

He lifted his chin. "What about William Ashley?"

"What about William Ashley?" I asked.

William Ashley owned an electrical-materials distribution center in Pennsylvania. We were about to embark on a deal when the feds decided I needed another audit. I had some revenue I couldn't account for, so since we were in negotiations, I had access to Ashley's books and cooked them. Instead of Demetri, his company had the revenue. He didn't know it was even there until the feds looked at our impending deal. Suddenly, I wasn't the target of their racketeering case—he was. Of course, he couldn't justify the extra four hundred G's.

I lost money on the deal, but when the charges were made public, Ashley took his own life. His wife had left him, ashamed of his illegal doings. It was more than he could handle.

"You don't think you're responsible?" Vincent asked, his opinion clear in his tone.

I swirled the cheap whiskey from the room's liquor cabinet around the bottom of my glass. Fucking small bottle cost more than a large one would at a real store—if I actually liked this shit enough to buy a bottle. "I didn't tell him to swallow the pills."

"No, but he did that because of what happened... because of what you did."

"I saved Demetri, and it didn't hurt the Costellos either."

Vinny shrugged. "We lost a few hundred G's."

"I've more than made that up over the years."

"The point is that we do what we do for honor and respect. This man, Pop calls him *old man Montague*. He helped Pop out of a jam years ago. The other day, he called in a favor. Pop feels that the man's entitled. Honoring debts is what keeps us respected. You help us. We'll help you.

"This man that we're about to off—Collins—he's the old man's son-in-law."

It was the old dilapidated house all over again. Vincent was talking about murder as if it were a trip to the supermarket. The difference between the two of us was that I hated chewing gum.

"The old man spilled his guts to Pop," Vinny went on. "Something about this dick threatening to divorce the old man's snooty daughter and taking their kid. The old man won't have it. He has his share of dealings and doesn't want anything public. He wants Collins out of the picture before he has a chance to cause any problems for his business or his family.

"Think about that," he said. "Think how Pop would feel if you or Bella wanted to skip town with one of his grandchildren."

I fought the urge to say that Lennox wasn't Carmine's grandchild, but I refrained. In reality, the generalization was a compliment, coming from Vincent. "He wouldn't have it," I said.

"He told Pop that he tried another route. He offered this guy another option. The old man has money to burn. Pop said his house is a fucking castle." Vincent shrugged. "Anyway, the guy refused. He said he didn't want money, only his daughter and freedom. I'm here for only one reason."

I closed my eyes and opened them, hoping that maybe I'd be back in the cool car in front of the dilapidated house. When I opened them, I was staring at the same man who'd walked out of that house, but instead of just being the driver, this time I was the assailant. "You're here for me. It's like Costello life 101 all over again."

"I'm here to help you. We're here to help this man find his freedom.

He's just going to do it alone. And give yourself some credit," Vinny said with a too-casual grin. "I'm not a college guy, but don't the numbers go up? You're past the 100 level. I'd say if you do well on this trip, you're ready to graduate."

Costello training 400 level. Vincent taught me in my final class that it wasn't enough to see the intended victim. Not if the cause of death was to be an accident. If this had been a simple hit, no real contact was necessary—simply say goodbye and pull the trigger. This was different. My negotiating skills were needed to learn Russell Collins's habits, his likes and dislikes. It was like a fucking blind date.

Just before I walked up to the man I knew wouldn't be alive in twenty-four hours, I turned to Vincent who was sitting at a table near the back of the hotel bar. "I don't want this for Lennox."

"You've got balls. I'll give you that."

I looked to the man who was my wife's cousin, my boss's son... to the man who had been my teacher and friend, the man who would one day be in charge. He'd trusted me with his family when times were rough. I wanted to trust him with mine.

"One day it'll be you in the big house with the goons. We all know that. It could be you now if you wanted, if the boss was ready to step down."

"Ain't anyone who steps down."

"I made my decisions and agreed to all of this the day I married your cousin. One day it'll be you who makes the decisions. I don't want this for Lennox."

"This life's an honor. One day I'll take after my father, who took after his father. It's what Luca will do, what he should do. The honorable thing. The respected thing. You don't want Lennox to be honorable?"

"I want Lennox to have choices."

"Family isn't a choice."

"It can be. It can be your choice."

"Don't disappoint me or Pop. The future isn't written."

It wasn't a promise, but it was the best I'd get. I'd have to hold tight to what Vincent said, knowing that my future actions weren't for some old man in Georgia to benefit from a debt an old man in Brooklyn owed. What I was about to do was for my son, for the future of Demetri—my family's future, not the company. What I was about to do was pay a debt so my son wouldn't.

For over an hour I talked with Russell Collins. For an Irishman, he was friendly enough and a little too honest. The mess with his wife weighed heavily on his mind. His golden eyes dulled as he spoke about his loveless marriage to an ice princess. He mentioned that her family had money. He didn't make it sound like it was excessive, yet from what Vincent had told me it was.

He simply wanted out. And yet when he spoke about their daughter, his demeanor changed. His cheeks glowed with love and pride to match his red hair, and the gold of his eyes glittered. Only three years old, she was obviously the joy of his life.

"I don't think I could take my son away from his mother," I confessed as I sipped my second beer.

Collins scoffed. "Then I bet your wife is a mother in more ways than just giving birth. You know, like she takes care of your son?"

"She does it all," I confessed. "I'm... busy a lot."

"My wife isn't busy. She's home. She wouldn't know work if it bit her on her skinny ass. That doesn't mean she takes care of our girl. No, there's a nanny." He lifted his glass. "Damn good one too. I'm hoping she'll leave with us."

My eyebrows rose. "You interested in her?"

His laughter filled the bar. "No. Not like that. But she loves Alex. She's more of a mother than my wife could ever be." He took another drink of his sweet tea. Damn Southerner couldn't even be a drinker. "Honestly, my wife didn't have a great example. Her parents are wacked, too. That's why I have to get Alexandria out of there. I don't want her to fall in the same mold. I wouldn't be surprised if my father-in-law doesn't think he has her whole future mapped out. Not my girl. She'll be what her mother isn't, a fighter. I'll see to that or I'll die trying.

"Shit!" he said, looking up at the television above the bar.

My eyes followed. Across the top of the screen was a ticker declaring Jeff Gordon the winner of whatever race we were watching.

Recalling my backyard barbeque experiences, I zeroed in on this man's interests. We'd talked too much about his wife and daughter. His unhappiness may be a cause of heartache, but it wouldn't work for a tragic accident.

"You don't like Gordon?"

"I'm from Georgia. Bill Elliott is my man. And this win will help Gordon in the points race, not that Bill has a chance. Mostly, I'm pissed the damn race ended on caution. That's not how any race should end. If they'd lifted it—even with a few laps to go—we could've had a sprint to the end."

"You said you like racing?" I asked.

"The faster the better."

"Ever think of driving one of those cars?"

His lips curled upward. "One year, when we were first married, my wife gave me a..." He lifted his hands and made air quotes. "'...race-car fantasy weekend.' Let me say, other than having our daughter, it was by far the best damn thing the woman has ever done for me—ever." He lifted his glass. "She's not much in the giving department...

if you know what I mean."

I grinned as I flagged down the bartender for one more beer. While I wasn't interested in his wife's inabilities in the bedroom—because we both know that was where this conversation was headed—the information on fast driving was my ticket. This give-and-take between us wasn't so much a negotiation as it was an interrogation. The trick was not letting him know that. To do that, I needed to share too.

"I don't have any complaints about my wife in that department as long as she's talking to me."

He slapped the bar. "Don't you love that silent bullshit?"

"No, not really."

"It's like I wish mine would raise her voice or get angry. Instead, she's dead inside—nothing there, always the perfect aristocrat. It's bullshit and I'm over it. Telling her our marriage was done was liberating."

"I'm not sure I want to admit that to myself or my wife." I confessed. "I know we aren't where we once were..." It was the first time I'd said aloud that my marriage was in trouble. I figured it was safe. Vincent couldn't hear me, and this man wouldn't be sharing anyone's secrets after tomorrow. "Oh, but let me say, my wife is good at raising her voice. She can also do the silent thing. I think you're right: I prefer the fight. It gets the blood pumping.

"So," I asked, switching gears. "...the race-car thing does that for you? Gets your blood pumping?"

"Oh, let me tell you, in 1987, Bill Elliott set a record, not there..." He pointed to the screen of the television again. "...at Talladega. He clocked a lap at 212.8 miles per hour. That would be fantastic! I've never come close to that speed. Even the race-car-weekend thing was monitored for safety bullshit. But near Savannah, where I live, there are some open roads. My speedometer tops out on my car at 160. I've had it sitting there for miles. The hills and curves… it's a high I can't even describe…"

A few days later I was sitting in Carmine's home office, and he handed me a newspaper clipping. It was the proof of my allegiance. The edges were smooth, the color black and white. The date at the top told me it was from a recent publication, the *Savannah Morning News*:

*Russell T. Collins, of Savannah, Georgia, passed away unexpectedly early Monday, May 27, 1996, at the age of 31. Russell is predeceased by his parents, Marshall and Joyce Collins. He is survived by his loving wife of nearly seven years, Adelaide Montague Collins. Russell and Adelaide married June 10, 1989. He is also survived by their daughter, Alexandria Charles Montague Collins. Russell is lovingly remembered by his wife, daughter, and all who knew him and his love and devotion for his family and Montague Corporation. Services will be private. The family requests no flowers; however, contributions may be made in Russell's name to Emory University.*

My stomach twisted as I read… *loving wife*. It was a nicer spin than the stories he'd told me. Was that how my obituary would read?

Though my gut continued to churn, my expression remained stoic. I'd done what had been asked of me. Once again.

But at what cost?

A part of me died with the red-haired, golden-eyed man, a part I'd never be able to revive. Even so, even with the loss of a part of my own soul, the incident hadn't been as upsetting to me as Carmine's shooting. I decided that made it worse. Like Vincent all those years ago at the dilapidated house, I'd accepted my actions.

The humanity seeped from my soul as I made a small hole in the rental car's brake cylinder. A few stops would have been doable, but then as the car made its way onto the open highway early Monday morning as Russell Collins drove himself to the airport, the fluid would be gone.

Undoubtedly, the pedal when depressed had made its way to the floor. That small defect could have been discovered at the scene were it not for the cocktail containing gasoline within a flammable container in the trunk of the car. Highly combustible, the concoction ignited upon impact. With nothing in the cocktail or the container foreign to the products within any automobile, the mixture was virtually untraceable.

Perhaps a factory defect?

The final result was not printed in the obituary. The small clipping hadn't said that Russell Collins had been driving at an excessive speed, that he had been unable to slow his vehicle despite coming upon a congested area of traffic. It didn't say that he opted to hit a steel side rail instead of killing another person with his out-of-control rental car. It didn't say that as an experienced driver familiar with the safety features, he probably assumed he'd walk away with scratches and maybe a broken bone or two. The obituary didn't say that the car was immediately engulfed in flames. It didn't say that the fire was so intense that Russell's realization—the one where he realized that his time on this earth was about to end—probably never fully filled his consciousness. It didn't say that based on the conversation he'd had the night before with a complete stranger, the stranger assumed Russell Collins's last thought wasn't about saving himself, but about his red-haired three-year-old daughter.

Straight-faced, I handed the clipping back to Carmine and asked, "Sir, have you given the jewelry stores more thought?"

# CHAPTER 30

——————•O•——————

ALONG WITH CARMINE'S promise to support the jewelry stores in all the territories, Angelina's uncle made good on his other promise: a gift for Angelina. Though I'd given the idea a fleeting thought, my mind had understandably been elsewhere since Luisa's First Communion. I had enough difficulty comprehending that a parent would virtually sell her child, the idea that the said child could then be passed to another was not in my way of thinking. It wasn't even on my radar.

There had been so much happening that I hadn't even had time to think about Demetri Enterprises. My mind was consumed with the events of the last few days, the events merely mentioned in the Savannah newspaper. Though I wanted to believe I could move on, I suspected—correctly—that those events would forever affect me. I chose to concentrate on myself, focusing on regrouping. I couldn't allow my mind to imagine the far-reaching effects occurring in Savannah or the way my demonstration of loyalty would forever affect the Irishman's *loving* wife or young daughter.

They weren't my concern. I had too many concerns bidding for my attention.

I thought instead about the jewelry stores—three of them—all approved for my purchase. That was where my mind needed to be.

"Thank you, sir."

Standing, I went to the closed door of Carmine's office. As I opened it to leave, I was caught off guard by the ashen complexion on my wife's face. Suddenly, nothing else mattered. Angelina was immediately outside the door, her hand poised as if ready to knock. It wasn't simply her paleness, but her slight trembling that had me instantaneously reaching for her petite frame and pulling her toward me. "What is it?"

"Did he tell you?" Her blue stare was peering beyond my shoulder to her uncle.

I was certain she wasn't talking about the jewelry stores. Angelina didn't care that much about Demetri Enterprises other than that it supported our lifestyle while infringing on her family time. There was no way she knew about the events in California. Out of options, I shook my head and turned back toward Carmine.

For the first time in a while, his lips parted and cheeks rose. It was the largest smile I'd seen on his face since Luisa's party, and at that time it had mostly been extended to the children. Now he was looking at Angelina and me. The adoration in his expression did little to calm my nerves.

"*Zio?*" Angelina said, her voice cracking.

"Here…" He stood. "The two of you need to talk." His large hand landed upon my shoulder. "Son, I know I told you that talking wasn't the way it worked, but this time it is."

*Another Costello riddle.*

This one resulted in another rarity—Angelina and I alone in Carmine's office. I'd never been in his office without him. I wasn't sure anyone had. It was then I turned my concentration to the woman in my grasp.

"*Mio angelo,* are you ill?" No, Carmine wouldn't be happy about that.

"What is it?"

Her head moved from side to side as I directed her to the sofa along the side of the room.

"I said..." she began, "...when Aunt Rose and I spoke... but I didn't mean." Her eyes opened wide. "I don't know. I want to, but then there's Lennox and you, and we never have enough time. But she's so lost." Angelina took a deep breath, her blue eyes filled with tears as she looked my way expectedly...

I knew the look staring directly into my eyes... waiting. I'd seen it before. Yet I had no idea what she was saying or expecting, or of what answer I was supposed to provide.

"Baby, I'm lost."

She stood and paced a small path. "Oren, you never listen."

I couldn't even begin to respond. Nothing would be what she wanted to hear. When I said I was lost, I meant lost as in on a deserted island in the middle of the Pacific—Gilligan's Island kind of lost. I didn't mean that I was in Chinatown and I'd meant to be in Little Italy. This was uncharted. "Please give me a little more."

Her chest rose and fell with a deep breath. "Do you remember the conversation we had a while ago, about Silvia?"

*Silvia...?*

"Yes, the girl who was here."

"She's still here."

"Okay, I haven't seen her. I remember."

Angelina came back to the sofa and sat beside me. "Before she was ever found, one afternoon..." She shrugged. "I don't even remember when... I was with Aunt Rose and Bella. We were talking about Luisa. I mentioned how after they'd stayed with us, when Luisa was little, how you and I talked about a daughter."

I remembered that too. We'd talked about a lot of things during that time. It was after Carmine's shooting and emotions were on overdrive. We both talked about how sweet Luisa was, how unlike the boys, how her energetic and charming presence was the one thing that kept us all from falling into our own worries. Watching her play and interact made it seem as if there really was an inner sense that told the little girl she should love dolls instead of trucks.

However, that was when she was three years old. Now that she's six, I believed one day she'd give her brother a run for his money. She had the Costello spitfire gene for sure. If it wasn't Luca who she'd give a run for his money, it'd some poor man who she'd have wrapped around her little finger and begging for mercy.

We also talked about Carmine, what had happened. His shooting was even more personal than when Gotti killed Paulie. This was more than family business: it was family. It all confirmed our earlier decision that we couldn't—wouldn't—take the chance of having another son. There was no way to guarantee a daughter.

"We did talk about that and we decided not to…" Carmine's words before California came back. He'd mentioned something about a daughter. I'd said I'd need to talk to Angelina about it. We never had.

I let out a deep breath recalling the last few minutes.

Carmine's smile.

His pat on the back.

His words: 'I told you that talking wasn't the way this worked. This time it is.'

"Go on," I finally said, trying not to jump to conclusions.

"We discussed it, and we did agree. Now… she is…" A tear cascaded down Angelina's cheek as her neck straightened. "Let me go back to explain.

"When Aunt Rose asked if we'd want a little girl, Luisa was right there, her sweet curls and big eyes, the way she was trying to mimic her mother. I looked at Bella and said yes. I know we said no more children, and I'm content, but there's a part of me that as a woman would like a daughter." She took a ragged breath. "I've convinced myself that someday that daughter will be Lennox's wife… but maybe…?"

"You want to have another baby?" I couldn't believe that ten years after Lennox's birth we were having this conversation. We were both now in our early forties. Weren't there medical concerns?

And then she's talking about Lennox's wife. In one breath, she was giving us eternal youth; in the next, we were practically grandparents. It was difficult to keep up.

"No," she said. "We both know that we have as good of a chance at a boy as we do a girl. Some articles say better since we already have a son."

She'd been reading about this? Of course she had.

"So you want to marry Lennox off?" I knew that wasn't where she was going, but I was grasping at straws. "I think he's too young."

Her gaze narrowed. "Oren." Swallowing, she wiped the tear from her cheek. "A daughter, not a baby."

*Riddles.*

"Have I ever mentioned how you talk in riddles?"

Her shoulders sagged. "For an intelligent man, you're dense."

"That's helpful. I'll work on that."

"Oren, Silvia. She's fifteen."

"And she's your aunt's domestic help."

"She's a child who has never had what every child needs. Do you know she's been doing this kind of work for nearly four years?"

It was my turn to stand. "You want to hire Silvia." I nodded approvingly. "She's young, but I've been trying to convince you to get help. That house is too big—"

"No," my wife interrupted, standing to meet me. "I wasn't sure I wanted any of this at all. Aunt Rose called while you were out of town. Now... now that I'm talking to you, I am sure. I don't want to hire Silvia. She's fifteen. She shouldn't be working. She should be in school. And besides... the paperwork has already begun."

My vision narrowed as my brow lengthened. "Paperwork?"

"It would be more difficult for Vincent and Bella. Vincent has a criminal record. He's gotten out of most things with just fines, but still there's the issue of felonies and the state of New York would have more problems if they tried to adopt."

My knees gave out as I collapsed back to the sofa. "Paperwork?"

"Uncle Carmine called in a few favors. Her name needs to be Demetri. Do you know what could happen if anyone knows she's a Greco?"

"But... what about your uncle and Rose? They could change her name to Costello."

Angelina shook her head. "They did their part. They raised me."

"But they didn't adopt you."

"They became my legal guardians. My name was already Costello. They never tried to replace my parents..." She sat beside me and reached for my hands. "I know what Silvia is going through." She took a deep breath. "No, I don't. My situation was totally different, but she's fifteen and abandoned by her mother. Her father is dead. Her brother is dead. I don't know what that's like because from the day my parents were killed, I had an adoring family—they were part of my life before. It wasn't easy, but Aunt Rose and Uncle Carmine never made me feel like I didn't belong. Even Vinny. He went from a cousin to a brother overnight."

I leaned back, knowing the decision was already made. It hadn't initially been made by Angelina, but the more she spoke, with each word, each sentence, each comparison and rationalization, her resolve solidified, and the decision went from a possibility to being set in stone.

Finally, I asked, "What about her mother?"

"She'll sign away her rights. She already has."

"Who convinced her to do that?"

"Oren…" It wasn't an answer but more of a warning.

"Vincent," I volunteered.

"All I know is that the woman did it. She'll even appear in front of a judge if necessary."

"So she's still alive."

"For now."

For now, because as I'd learn later, if she were dead at this juncture, Silvia would have become a ward of the state of Illinois, and that wouldn't have worked for Carmine's plans. After the woman signed away her daughter to the family who'd killed her son, her future would be less clear. Her existence would no longer be needed.

"Does Silvia know about any of this? Isn't fifteen old enough to have some say in her future?"

"Yes, it is, and no, she doesn't."

"What does that mean?"

Angelina again reached for my hands. "It means that I want her to want to be with us. I want her to choose us of her own free will. It's not exactly Uncle Carmine's plans, and of course, his plans will progress, but I'd like that for once in her life, Silvia has a say. I didn't want to talk to her until you agreed." Again, her eyes opened wide, filled with the expectancy from before.

I stopped myself from clenching my jaw as I stared back, marveling at the spark, the gleam in her blue orbs that had been absent, that my inattentiveness had dulled.

I never was good at telling her no, at least not when it was something monumental.

"What about Lennox?" I asked. "Does he get any say in this?"

"If I were telling you that I was pregnant, would he get a say?"

"I suppose not. That's a baby. This is… what?"

"A big sister… and I'll talk to him."

"Okay." It wasn't the enthusiasm I had that night long ago when I came home to lasagna to learn I was going to be a father; then again, life would never go back to that night, the simplicity or honesty or blind faith in our future.

Silvia soon-to-be Demetri was now my wife's life's work to pay it forward. Angelina loved and hated with her whole heart. She was generous to a fault with her time and our money. She could afford all the help she needed, and instead she cleaned her own house, cooked our meals, and did the laundry. According to her, doing so was taking care of those she loved, and she refused to allow anyone else to do it.

Carmine had given her the opportunity to have a live-in maid, and instead my angel chose to gain a daughter.

To me, Silvia would be something different. She wasn't our opportunity to share life's bounties with someone in need. This girl would be my wife's reward for *my* service, for my devotion to the Costello family, and for my help in extinguishing a life. Perhaps in a way that helped me—or I hoped it would. I grasped at the straw as a way to justify my actions.

Where Russell had died, with Angelina and me to help, Silvia would be able to live.

"Okay?" Angelina asked, repeating my answer. "Are you sure?"

"No, baby, I'm not. I'm not sure how this will work. I am sure that if you decide it will, then it will. I'm sure that if you're determined to win that little girl over and convince her to want to be part of us, you'll succeed. I'm sure that whatever you set your mind to doing, you'll do."

"We should tell Aunt Rose and Uncle Carmine first. That way Uncle Carmine can keep working on the legalities…"

She continued to talk about what we could do and about what would happen. As we sat in Carmine Costello's office without him, I wondered how many legal adoptions he'd facilitated. Were there others? Was this his first? Were there illegal ones? Why was he so hell-bent on saving this girl when her brother had almost taken his life?

So many questions bombarded my thoughts as Angelina continued to talk, so many that I knew would probably never be answered.

"Do you want to come with me?" Angelina asked.

"With you?"

"Oren? I said I was going to go talk to her, to ask Silvia to come home with us. Please listen."

"I am. No, you talk to her alone. I haven't seen her that much, but I get the feeling she's unsure around me."

"She's unsure around all of us. You, however, frighten her."

"Me?"

"You're a tad intimidating."

"I am?"

"It's not just you. Uncle Carmine and Vincent… and all of the men who grace these halls. I remember what it was like to be a young girl living here. Men in suits. Little girls are afraid of them until we learn the truth."

"What's the truth?"

She leaned closer, her breasts flattening against my chest as she brushed her lips against mine. "That you're all big softies on the inside."

I chuckled, knowing she meant what she said. Nevertheless, my soft side was turning to stone, harder by the day, week, and year, solidifying in the frozen deepfreeze of life's choices. The woman before me was my light, my warmth, my only hope at redemption, and if that meant helping her convince a fifteen-year-old girl to accept us as her family, to show that girl that I was less scary and just simply intense, then I would do it.

It seemed to me that on my list of recent decisions, this was one that was less damning.

# CHAPTER 31

————•○•————

PLAN SILVIA DEMETRI was set in motion and as with many other decisions, I was simply there to agree. After all, this had Carmine's blessing. It had more than his blessing: it was his idea. Usually, when someone adopted a child, there was a delay between 'here's the child' and 'take her home.' During that preparation time, things were done: a bedroom was decorated, clothes were purchased, and family was informed. It even happened when one bought a car, an opportunity for buyer's remorse. That wasn't the case with our situation. None of the preparations happened. This was not a by-the-books adoption. With the legalities in progress, Carmine and Rose were in favor of Silvia making the move immediately.

Angelina agreed with one stipulation. She wanted the girl to be involved. Therefore, after our private talk in Carmine's office and after informing Carmine and Rose we were in favor, my wife went upstairs to talk to Silvia. Convincing her to leave the Costellos and go home with us wasn't overly difficult. After all, moving from one family to the next had been the girl's life for nearly the last four years.

Silvia may have thought that this was like every transition she'd already had, but soon she'd learn it was much different. If things went as

Angelina had planned, she'd never make that transition again, not until she was ready.

I was in the kitchen with Rose when Angelina came down with Silvia. "Aunt Rose," Angelina said, "I've asked Silvia to come home with us. She's worried that you're upset."

I grinned, thinking that in all the years I'd known Angelina's aunt, I'd never seen her angry. I'd seen her face lined with worry for her husband and son. I'd watched as she'd wrung her hands, waiting for a medical miracle or a dismissal from a judge. I supposed those qualified as upset, but an angry Rose Costello—never.

"Come here, girl," Rose said, her unusually stern tone bidding my attention.

Slowly, Silvia approached. With each step her shoes shuffled across the kitchen tile.

Leaning against a wall of cupboards, observing the scene, for the first time I really looked at Silvia. I'd seen her before, but I hadn't looked at her. She was fifteen, and yet she seemed younger. Unlike fifteen-year-olds out and about, she was painfully plain and reserved. Her dull brown hair was pulled back into a ponytail. One sign of her age was her height, tall, almost as tall as Angelina. What struck me was her weight. She was thin, too thin. The lack of nutrients showed in her face and prominent cheekbones. Even her wrists were small and fingers boney. Just visible from the neckline of her top, her collarbone was pronounced, and her clothes hung from her frame. How anyone could live with Rose Costello for even a few weeks and not gain weight was beyond me. Such as the observation I'd made of her brother, she wasn't full-blooded Italian. As I'd been taught, some might consider that not Italian at all; however, that wasn't my wife's way of thinking.

"Mrs. Costello," Silvia said.

Rose's chin went up in the air in a way that I'd never seen. "Tell me, girl. Have we mistreated you?"

"No, ma'am."

"Do you want to go with the Demetris?"

Silvia looked down, her eyes veiled as her hands came together in front of her. "I-I didn't know it was up to me. I thought you sold me."

My chest ached. Her misconception combined with the slight trembling of her hands punched me like no fist could. "We're not buying—"

Angelina shook her head, stopping me from explaining. That may have stopped me, but what kept me silent were the wide brown doe-like eyes turned my way. This girl was terrified of me. It was written on her face as well as in the air. The stench of fear emanated from her every pore. I'd seen that look on men's faces before. I'd witnessed it as Vincent and I would walk into a business or a home. There was something powerful in inciting that kind of reverence. However, this was different. It was coming from a child, and it made me ill.

What had men done to her? What were we getting ourselves into?

Silvia turned her head to Angelina. "Y-you don't want me?"

"We do," Angelina and I said together. Again, my voice snapped her fearful gaze to me. "Maybe if we—" I tried to soften my tone.

"Oren," Angelina interrupted, "please come with me for a minute." Reaching for my hand, she tugged me through the swinging kitchen door, taking me from the room. I turned back, and as the door continued to swing, I witnessed the way Silvia was standing before Rose until the door was shut.

For the first time ever, a part of me worried about leaving the child with Angelina's aunt. I'd never before had that thought, ever.

Nothing was making sense.

Maybe it was my recent inability to sleep.

"What the hell is going on in there?" I said in a stage whisper, my anxiety rumbling through my chest and words.

"This is what she knows."

I shook my head. "Then tell her the truth so that she knows something else. I'll tell her. She's not a commodity. She's not something to sell. Why does Rose sound different?"

Angelina took a deep breath. "Oren, it'll take time. Silvia hasn't known anything different for nearly a third of her life. A life, especially one like she's led, hasn't been a fairy tale. People in her position don't go to sleep a servant—or a slave or whatever Silvia's been trained to believe she is—and wake up a princess."

"This doesn't make sense." Maybe I was too upset about recent events to wrap my brain around the scenario, but I truly didn't understand why we couldn't just ask her if she wanted to be adopted. Maybe she didn't. Then we could move on. If she agreed, then at least she'd know she wasn't any of the things Angelina had mentioned. "Even hearing you say those things is upsetting." I pointed toward the door. "She's a person."

"Yes, and with time—"

Rose's voice came from around the closed door. "Go and tell them..."

We both took a step back. Slowly, the door swung our direction. "Mr. and Mrs. Demetri..." Silvia's eyes were again downcast. "If it's up to me, and Mrs. Costello said it was... if it is... and you still want me to... I'd like to go with you."

*Fuck.*

Angelina looked up at me, her blue eyes brimming with hope before turning back to Silvia. She reached for Silvia's clutched hands. "Yes, Silvia, we would both like that very much. Let's get your things, and then we'll go home."

I shook my head as Angelina took Silvia upstairs to gather her belongings. My mind went to Lennox. He wasn't even with us, but back in Rye at a friend's house. He left this afternoon to go do what ten-year-old boys do, an only child. He'd return tonight to learn he was going to have a sister. Not a baby. No nine months of preparation. He was going to have a girl five years his senior as part of his life forever.

And yet our son's reaction didn't seem as paramount as the scene that had just happened in the kitchen. I was unusually unnerved by Rose's tone and mannerisms. Stepping back through the swinging door, I stared at Angelina's aunt, wondering if I should say what was on my mind.

Like a true Costello, she didn't give me a choice. "Go ahead, Oren, *parlare. Fai una domanda...* Ask about things you know nothing about."

"But yet you seem to understand. Angelina seems to."

Rose nodded. "*Sì.* It's a cruel world. Not everyone has a family like yours or mine."

My family—the one where I'd been raised—was nothing like hers, and yet there was something in her unusually cold demeanor that made me want to understand.

"Yet you are behind this adoption?"

"No."

I tilted my head. "No?"

"*È troppo.* I'm afraid that our Angel has bitten off more than she can chew. Silvia's too old. Her life and behavior is already too engrained. It'll be a difficult transition if one can be made at all. I'm afraid the child's past will darken Angel's future, not the other way around."

"Then why are we doing this?"

Her chin rose again with a snap. "Because my husband believes in redemption—in acts of kindness to offset acts of ill will. A boy was used as a pawn in the game of life. Once Carmine got wind of this child, he sent our son on an errand, telling him not to fail. It took years, but Vincent, he did what he was told. Carmine doesn't believe that any child should pay for her parents' or even her brother's sin." Rose shook her head. "And he knows that if anyone can help Silvia, it's our Angel."

"I agree," I sighed more than said. "Yet I'm still confused. Why are we keeping the buying-and-selling farce in motion?"

"I told the girl that she wasn't sold. When Angel took you from the room, I told her that it was her choice, that Mr. Costello and I are old. We haven't had a sla—worker," she corrected, "in many years. I didn't want one then, and I don't want one now. I told her that she'd be happier with you. There's more for her to do with you and Angel." She lifted her hands. "We're boring."

I hardly thought Carmine Costello was boring, but I wasn't going to debate that issue tonight. Instead, I concentrated on what she'd said earlier. "You…" I had trouble forming the words. "…actually at one time owned a person?"

"We didn't purchase her. She was a gift from Carmine's uncle when we married. I didn't want her, and neither did Carmine." She shrugged. "But it was what it was. Families have, for longer than we've been alive, paid debts with children and women. It's not right, but it happens, and despite other advances, it still happens. Sometimes they're spoils of war.

"Think about that, Oren. Think about your wife. We don't know why she wasn't taken when her parents were killed. I thank God every day that she wasn't. If she had been, she could have ended up like that girl."

"You would have searched for her."

"We would have, but like Silvia, they're shipped away to other cities, to other families. It's easier that way."

My knees grew weak as I eased myself into one of the kitchen chairs. "What happened to her—the gift you were given?"

"Carmine and me… we were young and naive. We released her—gave her freedom."

"And?" It felt like there was more to the story.

"And she was about this girl's age." Rose shook her head. "We were married at nineteen. We weren't in the position you and Angel are in today. We couldn't have adopted someone four years younger than us. And as a new bride, I didn't want a younger woman around my husband day and night even if she was just a scared girl."

I worked to keep my expression from mirroring my thoughts. The story was leaving a sour taste I couldn't swallow away.

"She had no education," Rose went on, "no knowledge other than domestic work. She couldn't support herself after we released her. Her family didn't want her back. She represented something they wanted to pretend didn't exist. Instead of helping her, as we'd intended, we imprisoned her to the only life she was capable of understanding.

"No longer someone else's property, she used the only commodity she'd ever known—herself." Rose turned toward the counter and busied herself with the collection of nonexistent crumbs. "It doesn't work like that in our world, in any world. A woman can't decide that she's in charge of her own body, especially not one who's still a child.

"The world is full of vultures willing to take what isn't theirs. She found her way to a club in another territory, one that capitalized on desperate women and children. Drugs and sex." Rose spun back toward me. "When we heard what had happened, Carmine went to his father. He asked for her back. We knew what we'd done was a mistake. It was too late. When my father-in-law found her, she was dead."

Rose came close and sat across the table from me. "That's why I'm worried for Angel. This will take time. Silvia needs to understand she's more than a body. Thank the dear Lord she hasn't been used in that way. But if my Carmine hadn't been determined to find her, it would have happened. It was only a matter of time."

# CHAPTER 32

———●○●———

ROSE'S STORY RAN through my head as I drove the three of us to Rye. As it replayed, it occurred to me that Angelina's aunt had never used the girl's name—her wedding gift—or the name of the girl's family. Was it her way of coping? Did that help? If I never knew Russell Collins's name or that of his daughter or wife, would his memory cease to haunt me?

I pushed the thought away, instead concentrating on our situation at hand, the one in our backseat. Occasionally, I'd look into the rearview mirror, my gaze catching the large brown eyes staring out at the dark road and surroundings. From my view, I could see the worn pink handle of her backpack being held tightly against her body. All of her worldly possessions, everything the girl owned, were contained in the threadbare *Hello Kitty* backpack.

With each passing mile, I grasped at understanding my newest lesson. Every time I came up with a new question, something I wanted clarified, Angelina's shake of her head would keep the words from my lips. Before we'd left Brooklyn, my wife had asked to keep the ride to Rye as quiet as possible, allowing Silvia to process the transition slowly. As we approached our home, Silvia's expression went from one of fear and curiosity to more wonder with only a side of terror.

Her eyes grew exponentially to the size of the homes beyond our car's windows.

It seemed that each moment through her eyes was monumental. I said a silent prayer that Rose had been wrong, and this wasn't more than Angelina could handle. At the same time, I found hope in Rose's observation that if anyone could change this girl's life, it was my wife.

Silvia's eyes darted from side to side as she entered our house. Her shoes scuffed along the bleached wood floors as she entered, finally coming to a stop within the foyer.

"This is your new home," Angelina said.

"It's so big."

Angelina laughed. "Don't worry about it. It's big, so we have plenty of room. I'll show you your room, and then would you like something to eat?"

Her head moved from side to side. "No, ma'am. I don't need much."

Angelina's gaze shot my way, reminding me to stay quiet. Biting my tongue, I simply exhaled and walked back to my office. When the door shut and I was alone, I realized for the first time since California that life was moving on. I walked to the window and stared out at the pool. The calm water glowed in the tepid darkness with the assistance of underwater illumination.

As the light changed the water from blue to golden, I saw the eyes of the Irishman. Taking his life would always be part of who I was—*he* would always be with me in present tense not past—but maybe helping others would make that reality easier to live with. Maybe Carmine had something. Rose said he believed in acts of kindness to offset ill will. Somehow I'd missed that side of him over the years, but now I knew it was there. The young girl in my house would always be that reminder.

After Angelina got Silvia settled and explained our new family member to Lennox, I found my wife in our bedroom. She was sitting on the edge of our bed. As I shut the door, she sighed and fell backward.

Going to her, I stroked her hair away from her eyes.

"Do you think this can work?" she asked.

I feigned a smile. "If it can, you're the one who can do it."

She propped herself up on her elbows. "She didn't want to stay in the bedroom. I told her where we are and that if she needed anything she can come to us. Oh, Oren, she just kept shaking her head. I showed her the bathroom and towels. I found her a toothbrush. She didn't even have one. And I told her that the attached bathroom is hers, that we all have our own." Angelina's tired eyes peered my way. "Do you know what she said?"

"No."

"She asked how many there were and how often they needed to be cleaned. I'm trying to make her feel at home, and she's making a mental checklist of chores."

"You're the one who said it will take time," I reminded her.

"I kept trying to get her to talk to me. It was like she was afraid to mess the covers on the bed. It's a damn guest room. I want to make it more personal. Maybe then she'll feel better about it. Finally, she told me that it was too nice, that in most houses where she's lived, she didn't have a real room."

"What does that even mean?"

Angelina shook her head. "It sounds like she simply had a space... like a closet or unused pantry off a kitchen. A place for a mat or mattress."

I reached for my wife's hands and pulled her up so that she was sitting again on the edge of our bed. "I spoke a little with Rose. This concept is totally foreign to me. But I'm concerned about you and

Lennox. Do you think that maybe you've bitten off more than you can chew? Since Silvia thinks she's here as help, maybe that would be best."

"No. She thinks that because it would be too much of a change in her life to tell her our plans upfront. She's already frightened and alone. First, we need to make her feel more at ease. If being at ease means she helps me then that's fine. I helped Aunt Rose with housework. Eventually, Silvia will be our daughter, not our maid."

I liked the fact that my wife hadn't used the other labels. I didn't want to add owning another person to my growing list of sins. There were already more than I could count.

"What about school?" I asked.

Angelina's chin fell forward. "Aunt Rose said she hasn't attended school since she was ten, since her father died."

"Ten, so basically Lennox's grade?"

"It's like she's a ten-year-old in a fifteen-year-old body. Or maybe a fifty-year-old in a fifteen-year-old body. She's seen too much and yet not enough."

The next morning much earlier than I normally woke, my eyes opened to the reality of another member of our family. Between that, the Irishman—I decided to not use his name—and my work that had been neglected while I was in California, my mind was a spinning whirlwind of thoughts and mental checklists. With sleep no longer an option, I eased my way out of our bed, showered, and dressed for the office. Though on most days Angelina woke with me, it wasn't usually this early, and well, yesterday had been taxing, to say the least. Therefore, trying to be quiet, I made my way out of our room and down the stairs.

The aroma of coffee and sizzle of bacon beckoned me toward the kitchen.

With her back toward me, Silvia was standing at the stove tending a frying pan of what my nose told me was bacon. "Silvia?"

She spun around, a kitchen utensil clutched against her chest, her brown eyes the size of dinner plates. "Mr. Demetri. I'm sorry breakfast isn't ready." Her words came fast. "I didn't know what time you woke. Mrs. Demetri didn't tell me."

Dark circles hung below her large eyes, and although I wasn't always an overly observant man, I was relatively certain she was wearing the same clothes she'd had on the night before. Now that I thought about it, it may have been the same thing she wore at the First Communion party: jeans and a wrinkled pink and yellow shirt.

This was early summer in New York. The child needed shorts and summer clothes.

I took a step closer, but stilled as she did the same, only moving away from me. "You don't need to cook my breakfast."

Her lip disappeared momentarily behind her teeth. "I-I do. I always do. I have to earn my keep." From the light above the stove, I could tell that her eyes were filling with unshed tears.

Lifting my hand in surrender, I slowly walked the other direction toward the coffee pot. "Thank you for making coffee, but really, you should be asleep. I'm sure you're tired."

Her shoes shuffled across the tile—the sound grating on my nerves—as she inched a little nearer. "D-do you want me to get your coffee?"

I shook my head. "No, I promise I'm capable. I would have gotten some downtown, but this is nice."

My compliment brought a small upturn of her lips. "Do you need cream or sugar?"

"No, just black."

She nodded. "Your breakfast is almost ready, sir."

"Silvia, will you please do something for me?"

"Yes." Her enthusiasm saddened me more than made me happy.

"I appreciate your cooking. However, it's too early. Mrs. Demetri and Lennox won't be awake for at least an hour. Why don't you eat my breakfast while I go into the city? Then once you're finished, go back to bed or read a book. Mrs. Demetri has a whole library down the hall."

Her head fell forward as her shoulders bowed. Sometimes my ability to read people was more of a curse than a blessing. Oftentimes, a simple action didn't make for a pretty story.

"I-I can't... it's your food. If you're worried about my cooking, I've been told it's okay."

I took a deep breath and went to the kitchen table. I had a list a mile long of things I needed to do, and yet I sat. "I'm sure your cooking is delicious. It smells wonderful. Will you please make two eggs?"

She turned back to the stove. "Yes, right away."

As Silvia watched over her eggs and rescued the bacon strips from the grease, I got up and opened the cupboard, retrieving two plates. Again, her doe eyes questioned.

"Silvia, I'll be happy to eat your cooking as long as you eat it too."

Her head shook with increasing ferocity. "I-I can't. Not with you. It's not right."

I smiled. "It's breakfast at the kitchen table. It's not wrong."

"But I shouldn't eat with you. I'll take yours to the dining room. I can eat in here."

"No."

She simply looked at me.

"There are no windows in the dining room." I tried to lighten the mood. "I like to watch the sunrise." I nodded toward the stove. "I think our eggs are about done."

She removed one from the frying pan and placed it on one plate. The second egg wavered on the spatula as she debated. Finally acquiescing, she placed the second egg on the second plate.

"There, that wasn't so hard." I went to the refrigerator. "Would you like some orange juice or milk?"

"I-I can…"

I didn't have time for this. "Orange juice or milk?" I asked again. "Or are you a coffee drinker?"

"Water is fine…" She looked up, seeing me with the two containers. "Milk, please."

Once we were finally seated, she sat with her hands on her lap, looking at the plate.

"Aren't you hungry?"

When she looked up, her eyes were once again moist. "I've never…"

I shook my head, her actions taking away my appetite. "Please, just eat." I took a bite of the bacon. "It's very good. Now eat."

Almost imperceptibly with only her chin moving, she nodded as she tentatively reached for the fork. For the rest of the meal, neither one of us said another word. Nevertheless, within record time, she consumed all of the food on her plate and finished the milk in the glass. Once we were both done, I reached for the plates.

"No."

I opened my eyes wide. "What?"

Hurriedly she stood and reached for the plates. "Please, it's my job."

I didn't let go. "Around here, we all pitch in, even Lennox. Don't let him think otherwise. Now go back to bed or read a book. When Mrs. Demetri wakes, you can ask her what she wants you to do. Until that time, rest. You look tired."

She simply looked at the floor.

"Did you sleep well?" I asked, unsure why I was perpetuating the conversation.

"I was afraid to fall asleep."

Her words stopped me. "Why? This house is safe. I promise."

"The bed."

"Is there something wrong with the bed?"

"No. It's too nice. The room is too nice."

"The room is yours. Mrs. Demetri wants you here. She has plans to make it more personalized. You'll have to help her." I took a deep breath. "Silvia, we both want you here, but we want you to want that too. Just give us a try."

"You want *me* to want to be here?"

"Yes, Silvia, you have a choice."

Her dark eyes swirled with questions. Finally, she simply said, "Thank you."

As she walked toward the stairs, I hoped she would get some more rest. Rinsing the dishes and pans, I placed them in the dishwasher. Granted, it was probably the second time I'd done this chore in all of the years we'd lived here, but I was an intelligent man. I figured it out.

Just as I was about to turn off the lights to leave, the tap of soft footsteps came my way. As I turned toward the sound, a dazzling smile filled my vision as arms encircled my neck. Angelina's cinnamon-flavored kiss was the telltale sign that she'd recently brushed her teeth.

When we pulled apart, I asked, "What was that for?"

"I was watching you."

"You were?"

Angelina nodded. "Silvia spoke to you. You even got her to eat."

"She needs to eat. She's too thin."

"But you did it. I know you. I know the last thing you wanted to do or planned to do early this morning was eat breakfast. Yet you did." She kissed me again. "It's at times like this I remember why I love you."

I kissed her forehead. "I always remember that I love you. If I didn't love you I wouldn't—"

"No, Oren Demetri. You would. Despite what you think about yourself, you're a good man. And each sacrifice or sentence or bite to eat is another step closer to making her comfortable."

"Don't allow Lennox to take advantage of her willingness to help."

Angelina laughed. "Do you think our son would do that?"

"And get out of cleaning his room? In a heartbeat."

"Please come home for dinner. I want her to get used to all of us."

"I'll try."

Angelina nodded, the delight from a moment ago fading from her gaze.

I was doing what she'd told me to do: not making promises I couldn't keep.

# CHAPTER 33

————●○●————

HOW DOES ONE become part of a family?

The daily rituals that become second nature? Attending church and dinners? The taking on of a last name? Perhaps even the occasional laughing and joking with a new younger brother?

I didn't know the answer, but perhaps there wasn't one. Instead, it was the complex combination that occurred over time, combined with an overabundance of patience and understanding. The legalities Carmine had promised progressed with only minor speed bumps along the way. My legal team, the one paid handsomely to keep on top of all things Demetri Enterprises, collaborated with a few very trusted souls who work in conjunction with Carmine's well-compensated attorneys. Together they kept the road to adoption clear and free from unwanted detours.

It didn't hurt that Silvia's biological mother was more than willing to sign away her parental rights. I never asked about any outside motivation. I didn't want to know. Limiting the information we shared with Silvia was for her own good. She already knew her mother 'sold' her as domestic help. There was no need to bog her down with the additional knowledge that an auction had been put into motion, or that now given the opportunity, the woman didn't want her only daughter to return.

It was also important to share only enough with the courts. While it would be beneficial to many children to expose the sales of human beings to the highest bidder, doing so would turn Silvia Greco's adoption into a criminal case and shed light on associates who were better at the time kept in debt with our silence. Another hurdle the attorneys faced was keeping Silvia under our roof and out of the foster-care system.

There were more than a few on-site inspections by the adoption agency to keep the paperwork clean. While the transition from the girl we picked up one early-summer evening to the one who finally took our name nearly a year later was tangled with ebbs and flows, our home was always seen as a suitable environment.

The guest room that was 'too nice' by Silvia's own standards also changed. Many teenage girls were interested in movie stars and singers. Her choices for decor were more juvenile. The child psychologist Angelina hired explained it to us at one of our parental appointments.

Because I didn't have enough on my schedule.

"Mr. and Mrs. Demetri, the items she's interested in, the books and small figurines, they're all a part of childhood, a phase in her life she missed. You could push her to her chronological age, but in doing so you open the door for other difficulties."

I usually let Angelina do most of the talking. She was the hands-on parent.

"We aren't pushing her," Angelina clarified. "I guess I want to know that it's all right to indulge these interests."

"Her world is growing, yet it's still quite limited," the psychologist said.

Though it wasn't a question, we both nodded.

"She's been with you for a few months. When do you plan to expand her world?"

Angelina looked at me before turning back to the doctor. "She's slowly getting comfortable, and I'm afraid if we expose her to too much, she'll slip back or revert to how she was in the beginning."

"Mr. Demetri, have you seen the change in Silvia?"

I leaned forward with my arms on my legs and thought about her question. I should have been at my office doing one of a thousand things, but instead I was discussing Silvia. "I have," I admitted. "It's almost remarkable. She speaks unprompted. I know with many teenagers that's a problem, but with her it was the opposite. She would only talk when questioned or startled..." I recalled the first morning when I found her cooking my breakfast. "...now she volunteers information." I sat taller. "As an example, just last night she brought a book into my office to show me pictures of lighthouses. We took her on a weekend drive a week or so ago. She had never before seen a lighthouse. Now she's obsessed."

When I looked to my wife, she was smiling in a way I didn't often see. I couldn't stop from reaching out and taking her hand in mine.

"I didn't know she showed you that," Angelina said. "We'd gone to the library, and she spent over an hour looking for books."

The doctor leaned back. "I think you're expanding her world more than you realize."

"As Angelina said, we don't want to overwhelm her," I said.

"The world is easier to see from the outside. Mr. and Mrs. Demetri, you're right in the middle of it. I'm looking at the scenes you're showing me," she went on. "The lighthouses, the library... Mrs. Demetri, does she go with you to other places?"

"Yes, the store, small restaurants, and church of course. I tried taking her into the city to the Met—I love museums—but partway there as I talked about some of my favorite exhibits, I had our driver turn around. It was as if I could see her retreat. I'm never sure what to do."

I was surprised to hear that. We'd taken her to Brooklyn, to the Costello home, and she'd seemed to do all right. Of course, that was with Lennox, and often Luca and Luisa were present. Silvia was guarded around Carmine and Rose, but I couldn't blame her for that.

I smiled at Angelina. "Trust *you*," I said. "You're the best mother I've ever known. You won't let her down."

That night Angelina and I dined alone for the first time since Silvia arrived, since... I couldn't remember. At a small restaurant not far from our house, we talked and laughed. Silvia was comfortable at home and Lennox was busy with friends. Without either one of them, we remembered that we were more than parents; we were also husband and wife.

The reprieve was short-lived. We each had too many responsibilities in and out of the home. The months continued to pass. Silvia continued to grow more comfortable. Her world was expanding. One warm autumn afternoon, she sat between Angelina and me as we watched a middle school football game. Baseball was over. I'd meant to get to one of those games, but that hadn't happened. Now I was here, sandwiched between parents and students on metal bleachers.

Lennox's recent obsession was anything to do with his current sport. The party planning that I used to have to do to be Angelina's suburban husband was now necessary to be in my own home. Between current college and professional team statistics, I needed to do homework to carry on a conversation with my own son. I hadn't realized the significance until I saw it, sitting in the stands where I should have been long before. With Lennox on the field, throwing long and short passes, the shouts were not only Angelina's and Silvia's, but also others yelling his name.

"He's good," I whispered to Angelina.

Her blue eyes shone in the fading sunlight as her pursed lips shifted to a grin. "I told you."

Time moved on. The sun showed less, leaves fell, and snow covered the ground. As the cycle continued, it then melted as spring sprung. When the new leaves made their appearance, the time finally arrived.

Nearly a year after bringing Silvia to her new home, she was asked to talk to the judge with regard to the adoption. The young lady who appeared in the private chambers with the family court judge barely resembled the skinny, scrawny child we'd first met. The transformation was more than the way her body had filled out from being healthy and active, nourished and cherished. It was something that food couldn't provide that was noticeable in her newly acquired poise—the way she was beginning to mimic the woman she chose to call Angelina, not Mother.

Sitting there, watching as she stepped into the office, Angelina and I held hands watching the girl that no matter the judge's decision was now our daughter. Though the woman beside me was primarily responsible, I couldn't help feeling a sense of pride, seeing the confidence inside Silvia that was continuing to build.

As time passed it wasn't only in our home or with our family that she exhibited this newfound demeanor. It came out at all times as she held her head high and made eye contact during discussions with each person she encountered. One of my favorite outward signs was the way her feet no longer shuffled as she walked, her steps now assured.

It was difficult to pinpoint the exact moment that it happened, the moment when Silvia realized she deserved to be more than she'd been told she could. And yet it had happened. We'd broken a chain. It wasn't the same one Angelina asked about for Lennox when she was pregnant, but it was an important one nonetheless. Silvia's life was changed. The figurative chains her biological mother had bound her with were gone.

Though I had been there along the way with her, Angelina, and

Lennox, I was also busy. I had an entire life and company and family that occurred beyond our home in Rye. Yet each time I entered that house, and my home was filled with the sounds of a family, I was reminded of the change.

We offered Silvia a home. Angelina gave her more—a family.

Silvia gave us something, too. Encouraging her to interact forced us to do the same. Lennox spent less time in his room playing his games. I made more of an effort to be present even when I had a list of other things to do. It was never as much as my wife would like, but even she admitted it was an improvement.

That didn't mean the year was filled with only roses.

From my perspective, I would have expected for Silvia to be always and forever grateful for what we gave her, and yet as the first year transpired, she hadn't always been. There were ups and downs. Watching my wife negotiate those turns helped me to understand that life didn't always need to be perfect. Lows were as instrumental as highs. It was during those valleys, when Silvia became upset and pushed back, that she was able to see that Angelina wasn't going to give up.

My wife was in this relationship for the long haul. When Silvia threatened to leave, Angelina gave her options. When Silvia decided to sulk and hide in her room, Angelina allowed it with the understanding that eventually she'd need to face her family. Us. None of us would admit defeat. No matter what Silvia did, we weren't getting rid of her. And most importantly, she finally understood that she couldn't be sold.

Not now.

Not in the future.

And it shouldn't have happened in the past.

She knew enough about the people she'd worked for in the past to understand the world in which we lived, where Angelina was born, and

301

who the Costellos were. Perhaps she hadn't been as naïve as we'd suspected, just too scared to talk. In reality, her experiences were her education, and like me, she'd never unlearn what she'd seen. Our hope was that she'd use her knowledge to move beyond. We were committed to that.

Silvia had begun studying. Angelina called it *homeschooling*. Though the parish was more than willing to allow her to attend school, Angelina wanted to get Silvia to a more age-appropriate grade level. Being a fifteen-year-old in a fifth-grade class would not have abetted Silvia's self-esteem.

Once Silvia opened up, we learned that she possessed a love of reading. Of course, Angelina fostered that love. Instead of fifth-grade reading books, my wife nurtured Silvia's interests. Such as the lighthouses, each interest was fostered until it qualified for many necessary educational disciplines. With lighthouses, Silvia learned history and geography. She also studied their different heights and diameters, working on math skills. In the one year since she'd arrived, her reading comprehension had gone from third grade to high school. That growth was evident in her vocabulary as well, constantly surprising us.

Not everything had to be taught to Silvia. She came to us skilled in the culinary arts. While my wife and her aunt were still the best cooks I knew, Silvia was easily the third. It wasn't a chore to her but her hobby, even reward. She enjoyed learning new recipes and perfecting old ones. Together with Angelina, they kept us too well-fed.

The sixteen-year-old young woman who entered the judge's chambers was nervous, yet eloquent and determined. She also went into the conversation to express her choice in life—she wanted to be part of us as much as we wanted her.

The decision wasn't immediate. While we'd expected the approval, it was still joyous when the news finally arrived. The day the adoption was granted and she officially became Silvia Demetri, we celebrated in true Italian-family style. It was while sitting around the table in the private dining room at Giovanni's that the magnitude of the change hit me. Leaning back, I scanned our crowd.

Not large by any means, but plentiful—enough. Carmine was at the head of the table, Rose by his side, Vincent at his left, Luisa between he and Bella with Luca by his mother's side. Lennox was beside his grandaunt with Silvia to his other side and Angelina beside her new daughter. I was on the other end of the table with Angelina to my left.

Costellos and Demetris.

The conversation and laughs continued. No longer scared, Silvia sat beside her new mother, more self-assured than she'd ever been. It was as Carmine raised his wine glass and welcomed Silvia that my cold heart experienced a staggering jolt. The don of the Costello family was toasting the sister of the young man who'd almost taken his life. Of course, that was knowledge only shared with a chosen few. Though the Demetri surname was legally new, we'd used it since she first arrived.

Lorenzo Greco had made a deal with Carl Gioconda in an effort to save his family—a deal with a devil that would have ended our family. Ironically, his goal was achieved. What remained of Lorenzo's family was now safe and surrounded with love and support—save his mother. But that was a story for a later time. Her usefulness was no longer needed.

Even Lennox had become accustomed to our new family member, though he had an interesting perspective. I'd asked him at one time while we were alone how he felt about Silvia living with us. In a typical boy-like way, he'd shrugged and simply replied, "She's not really my sister, even if Mom says she is. Not like Luisa and Luca. We're not related, but that's okay. Mom said she needed a family. We've got one. Problem solved." Maybe it wasn't childlike but a sign that my son was a problem solver.

Silvia needed a family. Angelina offered her ours. No more thought was necessary.

If only life could be as simple as it appeared at eleven or twelve years old, and yet lifting my glass in the midst of the complicated ways of our world, and glancing at the girl who now had my last name and then to the woman at her side… for a moment, I believed in that simplicity.

Blood in. Blood out.

Family was about more than being related. I didn't know if I'd ever truly recognize her as my daughter. I wasn't sure she acknowledged me as much more than Angelina's husband. Whatever the future held, I could accept Silvia as family in the broader sense of the word. Family was comprised of those people who made you who you were, who supported you, and stood beside you when others turned away.

In that respect, Silvia would always and forever fill the bill. If having my last name—our last name—protected her, then it was a small gift. It was a minimal goodwill gesture that may in some way counteract the ill will in my past and future.

"I'm so happy." Angelina's lips moved in her silent declaration as her gaze met mine, just before the glass came to her smiling lips.

With my left hand, I reached for her right one and squeezed. "*Mio angelo*, you're amazing."

She leaned my way for a chaste public kiss. "We did this together."

"Always together."

The family's conversation grew louder as more courses of food appeared. By the time we said our goodbyes, our stomachs were full, but not as full as our hearts. Carmine's hand landed upon my shoulder as we gathered near the back entry, waiting for our cars. "It was the right decision."

"Yes, sir. I wasn't sure, but Angelina can do anything."

"You have a daughter now. Cherish her. My daughter…" His gaze went to Angelina, taking my wife in as she carried on a conversation with Bella. "…when they're in your heart, the blood doesn't matter."

I nodded, my attention going to Silvia. She was standing with Luca and Lennox, the three of them talking. At sixteen, she was at least a head taller than both—boys usually grew later and they were both younger than her. Lennox was used to the height difference; however, Luca wasn't and made me smile. Previously accustomed to holding the cousins beneath him in his court, he fidgeted—his neck elongating as he rolled on the balls of his feet.

Carmine must have followed my line of vision. "One day they'll tower over her."

I laughed. "I don't think Luca is happy that the day hasn't arrived."

In a rare show of pleasure, Angelina's uncle chuckled. "Costello men." He turned to me. "The work on the shipyard, it's impressive. I was looking over the plans you brought by. The work will help the area. And Rose said Angelina is happy with what you're doing."

A lump formed in my throat. "She is. It will be expensive."

Carmine's dark eyes grew sentimental. "Sometimes we change a child's life. Sometimes we create a memorial to fallen parents—I believe Salvatore and Paola would be proud—and in the process, we help many lives. In the end, everything we do matters."

"Oren," Angelina's voice pulled me away from the dark stare. "Testa's here."

I offered Carmine my hand. As we shook, I simply said, "Thank you."

I hadn't discussed my parents with him since before Angelina and I were married, and yet he remembered. Perhaps that conversation wouldn't have been as monumental in my memory as it was had it not been our last.

# CHAPTER 34

HOW DOES ONE become part of a family? It was a question I found myself repeating.

And when exactly does that occur?

It would have been a more fitting story to say that after the dramatic life Carmine Costello had lived when his time came, he went out in a blaze of glory, perhaps gunned down in broad daylight. If that had happened, his name would remain forever in history books for generations to come. There would be movies and documentaries commemorating the life and death of a man who some considered great while others deemed evil.

That wasn't to be.

Instead of glory, the revered boss simply fell asleep.

No fanfare. No flourish.

While lying beside his wife after a typical day and reading the newspaper—the *New York Times*—he closed his eyes. His fingers lost their grip. The dropping newspaper caught Rose's attention. For a moment, she assumed he'd fallen asleep.

Our call came a few minutes later—a few minutes after she realized her misconception—after she said her private goodbye to the only man who ever held her heart. We were the second telephone number on Rose's list.

Despite the late hour of night, we gathered the children and all immediately congregated at her home in Windsor Terrace.

Upon entering the brownstone...the one that I'd feared, admired, and even enjoyed over the last seventeen years, I witnessed a new first. It was the first time I'd seen emotion on Jimmy's face. Even after the ambush and during the assassination attempt, he'd been the model of calm, his expression a mirrored image of what he'd displayed a thousand times before. However, when we arrived at Rose's, the enforcer's eyes were red and puffy; his jaw clenched and unclenched as if he were chewing gum, yet there was none. Jimmy De Niro had pledged his life for and to Carmine Costello. Despite the enforcer's valiant effort even he couldn't keep Carmine earthbound.

Rose was a different story; her demeanor was remarkably calm and equally determined. Her husband was not going to be disrespected by the New York Archdiocese as Paulie had been. Once she received the permission of her son, she was on a mission. Besides Father Mario, she made middle-of-the-night phone calls to every wife of every council member within the parish. Men may appear to have the power, but Rose knew the truth that the rest of us silently accepted. Not one of the women refused Rose Costello's call nor denied her their support.

Vincent was another story.

Sometimes in life grieving must wait.

Families such as the Costello family cannot go without structure. No matter the emotions that he had to be feeling, that structure and guidance began at the top.

When we first arrived at the Costello brownstone, Vincent was holding court in his father's office. Never having been officially made, I couldn't enter, not until later when the capos were gone. That was all right. While I wouldn't have turned down the offer to have my name in the family books—refusing wasn't an option—never yet receiving an offer kept me removed enough that I was still able to sleep at night.

It didn't mean that I didn't have demons.

The Irishman was no longer the only person to breathe his last in my presence or because of me, and yet his was the only name I could recall. Mostly, I tried to forget, and if it were possible to never learn a name, I took that option. I was by no means an enforcer such as Jimmy De Niro, nor was my list of forgettable names the quantity of Vincent's.

I'd simply done what was expected when I was told to do it.

A good soldier, I maintained my place in the family as Angelina's husband.

Through it all, even without the connections, I hadn't become immune. Angelina was still married to a man who experienced remorse. It would be more accurate to say that at each show of loyalty, a little more of my heart died.

To keep it beating and pushing the blood necessary for life and even love, I chose to relegate those actions to the dead part of my heart and instead concentrate my thoughts of family on church services, Sunday dinners, and family celebrations. I remembered to seek acts of redemption to counteract ill deeds. Whether providing a life for Silvia Demetri or spending millions to renovate the shipping harbor, each act worked to make a balance.

Many of the men in the house currently in Carmine's office didn't need that give-and-take. I did.

It wasn't like my hands were spotless when it came to Demetri Enterprises. William Ashley wasn't the only casualty in that wake. Somehow the dirt from those endeavors was easier to wash away.

As the four children—Luca, Lennox, Luisa, and Silvia—gathered in the living room and Vincent and the capos in Carmine's office, I entered the kitchen to find Rose, Angelina, and Bella.

With Rose's phone calls complete, the women were sitting around the kitchen table sharing stories, many of which I'd never heard. With tears in their eyes, they each recalled musings of a man who'd never sent me—or anyone else—to take a life. Who'd never told me to always be prepared and carry my gun, nor one who'd ever benefited from the clean money that became that way after finding its way through parts and avenues within Demetri Enterprises.

The man they remembered was different: kind, generous, and loving.

He was the one who'd welcomed me, Bella, and Silvia into the family. He'd rejoiced at the birth of each child and grandchild and mourned when people he loved died. He loved his wife with all of his heart—despite his infidelities—and would have laid down his life for anyone he deemed worthy.

Listening to Rose, I was honored to be there—to be on his list of people he found worthy. It was fulfilling to know that Carmine had trusted me even when his advisor warned against it. Of all the things that Carmine Costello had given me—his niece, approval, trust, and even the care of a young girl who would never know how much he'd done for her—it was Rose's words that will forever live in my memory.

"He loved you." Her tear-filled gaze moved around the table. "All of you." She reached for my hand, covering it with hers. "And he respected you, never doubt that. There were reasons for all of his decisions."

That was three days ago. Rose's calls had spurred the support of the parish. We were now gathered in the same cathedral where Angelina and I had married. This time it was without a doubt a precipice in each of our lives.

I scanned our pew: Rose, Bella, Silvia, and me—none of us were born Costellos. Silvia, Lennox, and I had a different last name, yet we had our connection: we had Angelina. Her blood ran through our son's veins, just as Vincent's ran through his and Bella's children. No matter what, in that church, in that pew, we were all part of a bigger family, the center of a bigger purpose. Vincent and Luca were the family's future, yet at that moment, we were all its present.

My heart ached for each one in our row: Rose, Vincent and his family, as well as Angelina's and mine. It was never easy to lose a loved one, but when that individual was larger than life, the loss left a gaping hole—an insidious black one. Such as its counterpart in space, what was to be found on the other side was a mystery. It had the potential—and if we allowed it, the power—to suck us inside, leaving our future unknown.

The cathedral grew louder with a respectful din as people murmured and the pews behind us filled to capacity with mourners. While my heart was breaking for us, I couldn't shake the need to be hyperalert. Weddings and funerals were occasions that forced togetherness. This was also a time of transition for the Costello family; having the nine of us together, we could be considered sitting ducks, targets all in one row for those who meant to do our family harm.

We weren't targets.

Vincent was many things, but careless wasn't one of them. Despite the solemn occasion, he had men strategically placed in and out of the church, some more obvious than others. Since the fateful night, whenever I wasn't with Angelina and our children, Testa was. Currently, he sat one row behind us with Jimmy and Dante, Bella's driver. No matter where we were, we were well protected.

Extended family, friends, and associates filled the church, and over the last few days, condolences had come from all the families—New

York's as well as those in other cities.

Carmine Costello may not have been well loved by all, but he was well respected until the end.

As Father Mario spoke the eulogy that Rose ensured her husband would receive, the one he deserved, I knew that because of Carmine Costello, I was a changed man. I was different than the young man who'd entered his office nearly seventeen years ago. I'd changed from the one who'd stood at the altar—the one where now a casket sat—to marry the woman he loved.

I wasn't better, nor was I necessarily worse.

I was different.

Costello 101 thru 400 hadn't been easy. Nothing valuable ever was.

I'd take NYU a hundred times over in the place of the lessons I'd learned from the family, and yet once learned they could never be unlearned.

With Vincent now the boss, Costello life would be different. Like the changes that had occurred in me, that didn't mean better or worse. It simply was different.

No one doubted Vincent's ability. No one challenged his nomination. I hadn't been there; I wasn't qualified. I'd heard what I'd heard from this one and that. The nomination had been made by Morelli and unanimously approved.

The decision was approved by more than the men in Evviva's basement. Vincent had the blessing of every man in the organization. Even those of us unable to vote prayed that the overwhelming support would facilitate a smooth transition. After all, this change in leadership had been in the making since the assassination attempt.

That wasn't accurate. It had been in the making since Vincent was Luca's age. In all probability, the next transition was already being fostered. While Lennox was pitching baseballs in Little League and quarterbacking his middle school football team, Luca was experiencing an entirely different education. I didn't believe he'd made it to Costello 101, but some things didn't need to be taught when one lived the life since taking his first breath.

One time, Vincent had told me that this life was honorable. He asked if I didn't want Lennox to be honorable. His argument was that if Carmine had been a doctor, wouldn't he have wanted the same for Vincent? If he'd been a lawyer? He wasn't those things.

Carmine was a family boss, and like any proud father, he wanted the same for Vincent. He'd gotten his wish. The title was now his son's.

As I peered down the pew, the profile of my son beside his cousin caught my attention. It wasn't that I didn't want the Costello way of life for Lennox, not in the sense of family. Truly there was no better family than those beside him. It was the simplicity of what I'd said to Vincent in California. I wanted Lennox to have choices in life. And now, seeing the young lady beside Angelina, holding hands and comforting her new mother, I also wanted choices for Silvia.

Life was about choices. I'd made mine. They both deserved to make theirs, too.

That didn't lessen the significance of the man in the casket, the one in the front of the church draped in flowers. Carmine had made his choices, too. He'd lived by them, almost died by them, and finally given up the ghost while loving both the consequences of those choices as well as his family. It was more than most men had.

Carmine Costello would always be a part of me. He would forever have my respect.

Later at the brownstone after most of the capos, wives, and friends had left, Vincent called me to Carmine's office. We weren't alone as I'd hoped, but the company was familiar: Jimmy, Dante, Morelli, and Testa.

He didn't waste time, jumping right to the point. "Things are moving fast. I wanted to talk to you directly, hoping you'll understand."

His prologue didn't fully register. My mind was distracted by exhaustion. The last three days had been a string of emotional confrontations connected by uncomfortable obligations. "Okay." It was all my tired mind could think to respond.

Vincent leaned back in Carmine's big chair. Besides his youth, the other difference with the picture before me was the lack of cigar smoke emanating from the ashtray still decorating the stately desk. It was one change I found comforting. I never turned down a cigar when offered, but as a rule, I didn't care for smoking.

"The books have been opened," he said.

This got my attention. Carmine was gone. There was room on the books for another made man. My eyes narrowed as my brain played the trick that clearer vision could improve comprehension. "Have been?"

"Yes."

"They're now closed," I said in confirmation.

"It isn't always about qualifications," Vincent went on. "There was one spot, and many who are qualified."

"It's about trust?" I asked, surprised at my own disappointment.

Vincent shook his head. "No. It's about many things." He leaned forward with his elbows on the desk, reminding me more and more of his father. His fingers came together, creating a steeple. "They'll open again. With everything happening, I had to make a decision. It wasn't easy." He tilted his head toward Morelli and Jimmy. "Pop made some mistakes, but he was usually a good judge of character."

We both knew the mistake was Gioconda, but that subject had been closed by Carmine over five years ago.

"I don't need to lay this out for you, Oren," Vincent went on. "But I am. Pop trusted you. I've trusted you. Never doubt that trust. We're family, and we'll keep things as they are—the way they've been." It was code for money and the use of Demetri Enterprises. His proclamation didn't come as a surprise. I'd never entertained the idea that our system would end. "I'm keeping much of the structure the same. Morelli here and Jimmy..." He motioned their direction. "...they'll retain their positions. Morelli is a smart consigliere. Jimmy, he's devoted." Vincent turned to the couch where Testa and Dante were sitting. "Sometimes when fulfilling what seems like a less spotlighted job, devotion and talent can seem as though it isn't noticed. But that's not true. It was recognized."

I simply swallowed, waiting for the next shoe to drop.

"Dante has been devoted to Bella and the kids. He's a trustworthy man. He'll fulfill that duty for you and Angelina as he did for me. We've already spoken. He's ready for the job."

I turned to Vincent. "Wait. What? Dante is going to be Angelina's new driver? What about Bella and what about Franco?" Franco Testa and I went back to NYU. I didn't want to lose him.

"You know what happened in that alley... the night...?" Vincent didn't finish.

I nodded.

"Jimmy never forgot what Franco did for him, for all of us. The books opened. Franco got the call."

While my heart broke at the loss of Testa's service to our family—Angelina's and mine—my lips turned upward. He deserved this. Being made was an honor. It showed that a man had been weighed and measured and found respected and valued. It told the world that he'd done his part and paid his dues. While I thought I qualified, I knew Franco Testa did. "Congratulations," I said, meaning it.

"Thanks, boss."

"Oren," I said, relieving him of using that title on me.

"Are we good?" Vincent asked.

"Yes, we are. You've got a good man in Franco Testa. You won't be sorry."

"We'll see you Thursday for drinks?"

I smiled. It almost sounded like a question. "Of course." I turned to Dante. "I can drive my family home tonight. Let me talk to Angelina about the change." I nodded at Testa. "You'll be missed."

"Thanks, bo-Oren."

"I'll call you tomorrow," I said to Dante.

"Sure thing, boss."

As I left Carmine's office, my mind went over the changes of the last few days as my soul filled with hope. The Costello family would survive under Vincent's rule. He'd already proven steady under pressure. As I closed the door behind me, I knew he was more than that. He was also fair. I was family—giving me the call wouldn't have been questioned. But calling Testa was better. No one would claim nepotism; Testa deserved the call, having more than proven himself.

My time would come or it wouldn't.

I'd spent the last nearly seventeen years trusting Carmine. Now it was time to trust Vincent.

# CHAPTER 35

———————●O●———————

THE FAMILY—as a whole—flourished. Vincent understood the past and embraced the future. The latter was a trait his father never fully grasped. The families in general were a different breed before Vincent and I were born. Movies and books romanticized the reality, and over time so had old men's memories. Similar to the stories of the Wild West, men in dark suits with machine guns in dark alleyways had its Hollywood flair. The truth wasn't as pretty. There was dirt and grime in the Wild West and Cosa Nostra had that too. Yet through it all, there was a kernel of authenticity that never changed—the devotion, honor, and respect. It may be changing with the times, but the foundation never would.

The RICO trials and feds tried to take away the respectability. Memories dimmed and false news faded away, but some aspects were too steadfast to be easily forgotten.

Oftentimes the dramatized version of our world left out the personal element... the reality that we were family. Each man who met now monthly at Evviva's had two. For very few of us they were one and the same, but even so, the Costello family consisted of a larger portion than just Vincent's and Angelina's families. There were cousins from once-ousted relations that Vincent embraced in a way his father never did.

He believed in unifying where possible—bringing people together. As Carmine aged, his paranoia and difficulty trusting caused division. Vincent made it his mission to build not only bridges, but to fill in fissures and gorges of separation, bringing two and three factions together as one larger, stronger family.

The Rossis—related to the Costellos through Rose's mother—had been on the fringe of the Costello family. With the new reign, Vincent welcomed his cousins into the fold. Another earner, like me, Michael Rossi had shown loyalty when called upon. He too had two families to consider in every decision, the one as a whole and his wife and children. It was a balance, but we all tried to make it work.

For the families—more specifically, for the Costello family—to survive, prosper, and deserve respect, it needed Vincent. Despite our sadness at losing Carmine, the time was overdue. Vincent had told me once that people don't step down from the top position nor that his father could, but sometimes I wondered if he did.

Gioconda's betrayal lingered in Angelina's uncle's mind. It wasn't mentioned, but it resided in the dark shadows of his eyes. The bruised chest may have been his only physical injury, and it may have even healed as the colors faded. Yet the psychological injuries he'd incurred stayed with him forever.

The world had been changing around us, and Carmine Costello had remained steadfast.

Perhaps, I sometimes wondered, if maybe on that spring evening when Carmine ascended from this Earth, he knew it was time to pass the reins and that his reign needed to end so the family could live.

I found myself contemplating those questions and many more.

Perhaps seeing Silvia's adoption through to completion was his final act of redemption. Maybe someday I wouldn't look at her and recall the man I'd taken away from his young daughter. One day she'd perhaps be my daughter in my eyes as well as on paper. In the meantime, I cared for her, not physically, but she mattered to Angelina, so she mattered to me.

Time marched on… the Costellos and Demetris more than survived: they conquered.

The dreaded Y2K came and went, and yet computers had not taken over the world nor had they brought it to its knees. All of the data for Demetri Enterprises that I'd spent millions of dollars to back up and keep safe was still intact.

The world of technology and computer science was growing exponentially by the day—forget that, by the hour. The small handheld console that Lennox had played in the backseat of our car five years ago had more memory than a NASA computer—one that filled a temperature-controlled room—had in the 1960s. The ones he had attached to a television in his room today held more than the first one we'd installed for Demetri Enterprises. The advances were truly revolutionary.

What was new today was old tomorrow. It took continual effort to stay in the forefront. One would think that businesses under my umbrella like laundromats and concrete companies wouldn't be affected by technology. One would be wrong. Everything was at its mercy. I spent endless hours learning and then assuring that each CEO, CFO, president, or vice-president was onboard with moving forward. There was no room for complacency.

When it came to Costello information gathering, no longer were men required to watch from the shadows. The families learned their lessons from the feds' wiretaps twenty years ago. Surveillance could be better accomplished with hidden cameras and microphones. In the last two decades, the size of everything had decreased while their functions had increased. The *Inspector Gadget* fiction of yesteryear was now reality.

Cellular phones were a prime example. No longer simply a mobile telephone, their functionality had increased. Messages could be sent. Data could be accessed. Kids even stored music on them. My first car with an eight-track tape player was as antiquated as a Model T.

I didn't have to be in the office to access Demetri Enterprises' information. I could do it from home or amazingly, from anywhere. With access no longer the issue, now the opposite was a concern—limiting access. In that capacity, Demetri Enterprises employed multiple staffs of people, their primary function protecting our data and keeping it from hackers. Securing information was now the key. My worries included government intrusion as well as competition.

In many ways, that key to success was the same as it had been for Carmine. The saying 'the more things change, the more they stay the same' came to mind. However, instead of securing information by keeping an office door closed and Stefano parked outside, now firewalls needed to be installed and constantly monitored for better security.

While the Costello family progressed, my weekly appearances became a thing of the past. I kept my agreement, cooking books when necessary and cleaning money to allow Vincent his seed money for investments. I'd gotten proficient in a way I'd never expected, and yet I didn't complain. Drinks at Evviva's had gone to once a month. Solidarity could be shown without gathering in one place.

In general, the requests Vincent made were not only less time consuming, but also less messy. It was a pleasant combination that allowed me to concentrate on Demetri Enterprises. I took full advantage. My company's scope and breadth amazed even me. I had vice presidents and CEOs who reported to me. With my fingers in all divisions, I traveled the country, ascertaining the success of each piece constructing the

Demetri Enterprises umbrella. I'd recently taken the company international. I'd been dipping my toe in this investment and that, but with the upswing in the economy, London was the perfect financial mecca, its time zone being one of the biggest assets.

During my Costello 101 training, Vincent had spent a significant amount of time with me, learning about some of the subsidiaries under the Demetri umbrella. As time went on, he had other things to concern himself with than my company, yet he never forgot the lessons he'd learned—just as I hadn't.

He took that knowledge after his father's death and used it to propel the Costello family into the new millennium. The money his father had used in other ways, Vincent invested in legitimate businesses. He used good men and even women to run these legit companies. That wasn't to say that the Costellos were completely out of the illegal spectrum, but even he could account for lawful income. Change began at the top.

Capos, those willing to learn and grow, now had the opportunity to increase their income in justifiable ways.

I'd even begun a few enterprises at Vincent's request. One was brought to me that caught me by surprise. After Vincent's call, we met at Carlisle's, a familiar little restaurant in Little Italy, Jimmy by Vincent's side. The days of seeing my wife's cousin alone were a thing of the past. I didn't question the change. His request for a meeting had come just before I was about to leave the office. Angelina had a dinner or something planned for new neighbors—more people for me to carry on bullshit conversations with. Julie had it written in red on my calendar. Though I'd messaged Angelina that I wouldn't be home, she'd yet to respond.

Besides, it wasn't like I could refuse Vincent. Since his requests came less frequently than Carmine's had, I found that usually my appearance was even more significant. There'd been no more talk of opening the books over the last few years. The state of limbo was working well for me as I became even more proficient at balancing.

Vincent's request, or should I say, entrepreneurial suggestion, was ironically at the inclination of the same man who'd requested the death of the Irishman—old man Montague. While the mention of his name took me back into the world of the Irishman's wife and daughter who I'd unsuccessfully tried to forget, it also brought back my curiosity about their lives.

"Surveillance," Vinny said as we sat near the back of the restaurant, swirling the drink the waitress had brought him upon his arrival. "Talking to the old man got me thinking..."

"You want me to start a surveillance company?"

His head tilted from side to side. "Security... surveillance. The title can be up to you."

*That was big of him.*

Mentally I appraised the amount of time and work that would be before me to complete his task; the project would undoubtedly need to be wedged between my already-set commitments. "I'll need a few months. There's a lot to set up: permits..."

"No more than two. Pop kept the old man as an associate for a reason. I plan to keep Pop's word."

I wanted to correct Vincent and say it would be me, but that didn't seem like a good idea.

As Vincent requested, I'd arranged for the front—the new Demetri Enterprises security company—to get the cameras in place. The old man wanted them in his home and corporate offices, something about keeping an eye on his new son-in-law. As I went to work, I decided that being this man's son-in-law was about as dangerous as being Angelina's husband, just for different reasons.

Once the cameras were up, the rest was up to the old man. My guess was that he had the same issues we all had—trust concerns. While working with the technicians, I caught a glimpse into the life of the wife and girl. While their castle seemed opulent, my general assessment was that it lacked warmth. Perhaps the Irishman had been accurate about his wife—an ice princess living in a frozen world.

Each time the thoughts came to my mind, I moved on.

Another problem that continued to plague the families—not only of New York, but elsewhere too—was illegal drugs. Without a doubt the use and availability of illegal drugs were increasing, not decreasing. Through it all, Vincent stood behind Carmine's policy: the Costello family did not deal in heroin, cocaine, crack, or meth. The list wasn't limited. We also didn't sell prescription narcotics, painkillers, uppers, or downers.

No longer was it simply a family-against-family issue. Each family had its own policy. For example, while the Luchi family had seen its share of transitions at the top, its stance had not wavered. And although the Bonettis in Jersey were still a powerful force, they kept their sales out of our territory. It was a matter of respect. And yet despite our differences, as we moved forward in the new century, there was a new urgency to unite as never before.

The Cosa Nostra was no longer the only broker in town. We needed a united front to keep the Russian, Serbian, and even Japanese underworld factions out of our territories. The people of Brooklyn, Jersey, the Bronx, and more, as well as parts of Manhattan, had paid their dues to the reigning families. They still did. Keeping them safe was as much the family's job as the police's.

Vincent recognized the outside threat and reached out to the other bosses in the commission, making alliances that benefitted not only the Costellos, but others too.

The work on all levels never stopped. I justified it all as it being for my family—not for the Costellos but for Angelina and Lennox and even Silvia.

I'd soon learn that my wife didn't see it that way.

# CHAPTER 36

—●○●—

ANGELINA'S COMPLAINTS ABOUT my absences decreased. No longer was I met by tearstained cheeks or even passive-aggressive comments. Foolishly, I assumed that meant she'd accepted our schedule as part of life. I assumed she'd finally recognized the breadth and scope of my work with Demetri Enterprises as well as my commitment to the Costellos and accepted that I couldn't attend every one, or even many, of Lennox's activities. The way I saw it, a football game went on for an eternity. If I spent the bulk of the game looking down at my Blackberry, I was a bad father. It was simply easier to miss the event and avoid the disappointed glances from my wife.

Besides, in a somewhat justifiable way, I was no longer her priority either. She was always busy with both Lennox and Silvia. Now an adult, the once-skinny, uneducated girl was taking college courses. She had a knack for management, and still she faithfully helped Angelina, refusing to move to a dorm, but instead staying at home to help with the running of the household.

I made an effort to be home more; however, often that meant in my home office. Nevertheless, I saw that as an improvement. One evening while home, I asked Angelina about Silvia's behavior. "Why after all this time does she still act like a maid?"

My wife's eyes narrowed. "Why would you say that?"

"She brings things like a drink or a snack and offers to if I don't ask. I don't know. Lennox doesn't do that."

"I do."

Her answer took me aback. "Yes, I guess, but that's different."

"How?"

*Fuck.*

"It's just that I would think she'd want to live in the dorm. I didn't until my parents died, but it was a good experience."

"She's done enough moving in her life. If she doesn't want to go, I don't agree with forcing her."

"No one said anything about forcing her." I turned back to the spreadsheets I had strewn across the coffee table, glancing first at the movie we were watching.

"You didn't answer my question," Angelina said.

"What question?"

"How is it different if I do those things than if Silvia does?"

This wasn't a conversation I'd win. I should have known by now to keep my thoughts to myself. I guess it was that Angelina was the one person I had always wanted to talk to, to converse with. It was during absences that I forgot how my conversation was easily misinterpreted. "Forget it," I said, turning back to the spreadsheets.

Of course, she didn't forget it. Angelina kept going. "Silvia is simply doing what she's been taught, what she sees. *So is Lennox.*"

The hairs on the back of my neck stood to attention with the way she added the last sentence. "Why do I feel that's about me?"

"Because it is," Angelina said. "Silvia isn't a maid any more than I am. I'm a wife and a mother. I never wanted a maid. I want to take care of the people I love. When she first arrived, it was all she knew. Now, despite what you think you see—on the rare occasions that you actually pay attention—Silvia loves and cares for us. She gets you a drink or a sandwich or cooks meals because it's what she sees me doing, what I saw Aunt Rose doing."

I guess it made sense. I hadn't given it that much thought. "And Lennox?" I asked, soon realizing my question was foolish, and I should have stopped while I was ahead, or at least not too far behind.

Angelina's jaw tightened as her neck straightened. "He imitates someone else."

I took off my reading glasses and tossed them over the large bound books. "Is this another fight?"

"I don't know, Oren, is that what you want?"

"No."

"It is… what it is." She waved one hand. "Silvia sees what I do. Lennox sees what you do."

My stomach twisted. "So he sees a man who works his ass off for his family. Good. One day I hope he'll do the same."

"I don't," Angelina said matter-of-factly, turning from me to the television.

"This is great." I motioned toward the screen. "I came out of my office to sit with you because you wanted to watch this movie. I'm here, and you're still pissed at me. I can't win, Angelina. Ever."

Angelina laughed, the feigned tone doing little to lower the increased temperature of the heated room. "What movie are we watching?" she asked.

I turned my gaze from her back to the television and assessed the movie. I wasn't good with actors' names. I didn't care. Ask me about a CEO of one of my companies or of a competitor. The man on the screen looked familiar. I should know this guy's name. I thought he was a bigger star. "This actor is…" My sentence hung in the air unfinished.

"Russell. Russell Crowe. Does that help?"

It didn't help. *Russell.* It brought back that old familiar ache combined with the new images from the security footage. This guy in the movie had dark hair not red. The new husband was blond. Would a request to get rid of him come next? Angelina's voice pulled me from my thoughts.

"The movie?"

"It's about… well…" I had been sort of watching. "That guy thinks the Russians are after him because he has some secrets. He's either a genius or nut case. I haven't decided."

Angelina sighed. "It's called *A Beautiful Mind.* It's up for many awards. Congratulations, you can minimally multitask."

"Thank you?"

"Oren, you're not watching the movie. You're looking at that." She motioned to the table. "I hope one day Lennox will take the time to be with his family, really be with them. So, no, I hope he doesn't do the same."

I ran my hand over my face, trying to change the subject while at the same time fearful the children were upstairs overhearing our once-again raised-voice discussion. "Where are they? Are they here?"

"They? Lennox and Silvia?"

"Yes."

"No, they're both gone. Silvia's on a date, and Lennox is next door."

I shook my head. "When did Silvia start dating, and why the fuck did I build this house to keep everyone safe if they're never here?"

"She's twenty years old. This young man is in her economics class. I've met him. He came in when he picked her up. You weren't home yet, or maybe you could have done what fathers are supposed to do and assessed if he is safe to have with our daughter. And Lennox is next door because his friend is there. I doubt there's much of a threat at the Millers'. Besides, I'm not going to keep him a prisoner in these walls." She lifted her glass of water. "One prisoner is enough." The last sentence was said softer as she took the glass to her lips and turned back to the television.

"A prisoner? Is that what you think you are?"

Angelina waved me off. "Shh. This is a good part of the movie."

"Un-fucking-believable."

Pushing the pause button on the remote, she turned to me. "Really, Oren. You want to do this?"

"No. I give up."

"You gave up a long time ago."

I didn't even know what she meant. I stood. "When exactly did I give up? When exactly have you gone without?"

She met me word for word as she too stood and met me face-to-face. "I've gone without my husband almost every day since I married him. I've gone without the rest of my family since we moved here." Tears came to her eyes. "I couldn't even get to Aunt Rose…"

I took a step forward, my anger melting away as my wife's shoulders slumped forward. "*Mio angelo*, that wasn't your fault. Dante got you there as soon as Bella called."

Her tear-filled eyes snapped upward. "Bella was able to get there. They moved, but not as far away. She was able to say goodbye. I'll never…"

Rose Costello passed away half a year ago after a sudden massive stroke. It came out of nowhere. She'd called Bella, saying she had a terrible headache and couldn't attend one of Luisa's dance performances. After the performance, Bella and Luisa went to the brownstone. Rose was still alive, but confused. By the time we all made it to the hospital, she was unresponsive. The entire episode lasted three days. Rose was now with Carmine.

"Do you want to move back to Brooklyn?"

She pulled away. "Damn it, Oren. Don't you see? You can't fix everything. I don't want to leave this house, especially now that Aunt Rose and Uncle Carmine aren't in Brooklyn." She turned in a slow circle. "I love this house. It's where we've raised our family, where Lennox knows, where Silvia feels safe. I just want… make that *wanted* more… *I wanted you.*"

"Wanted?" The word was slow to roll from my tongue.

"Yes. I'm tired of wondering when you'll be home and where you are instead. I'm tired of watching Lennox be disappointed, or worse, unsurprised, when you don't show up to his games." She took a deep breath. "I think it's time we face the facts."

I was at a total loss. My mind couldn't churn fast enough. "*Mio angelo,* I don't want to think what I'm thinking that you're saying."

Her eyes closed, forcing a tear to trickle down her cheek. "I want more. I think it's time we admit that this…" She motioned between us. "…is better apart than it is together."

I shook my head. "No, it isn't." I took a step closer, my hands grabbing her shoulders as they had hundreds, if not thousands, of times. "I don't understand. Why are you saying this now? What have I done differently?"

Her head shook. "Nothing, Oren. That's the problem."

Fighting back the anger bubbling below the surface, I admitted to the only truth I could think to say. "You're the only woman I've ever loved."

"I believe you." Her tone was sprinkled with melancholy. "I didn't say that I don't love you. I always will. I'm saying that together all we do is hurt one another. That's not good for Lennox or Silvia. I think I've known this for a long time, but tonight, without them here, I can finally say it."

My hands dropped to my side, and now I turned a small circle. I took in the living room, the fire in the fireplace, the darkened view beyond the windows, and the lights beyond Long Island Sound. "Are you... leaving me?"

"No," she said with a deep inhale and exhale. "I want you to leave."

That anger heated my skin. "You want me to leave the house I built?"

"It's not a house. It's a home. I did that. Are you going to take it away from me?"

My mind swirled, a tornado of thoughts, none of them staying in place long enough to become words. "Is there someone else? Someone from here?" The questions came louder than I wanted, yet I needed to know.

Her neck straightened. "No. I have never cheated on you."

I swallowed, knowing that I couldn't say the same. At one time, she'd said she didn't want a husband who could kill without remorse. The men—many of them—in Rye were a different breed than those who graced her uncle's hallways. These men fit that bill. Had the changes within me over the years, the way my heart had grown cold to the ways of this world, hurt my marriage more than helped it?

"Everything, Angelina, every goddamn thing in my life has been for one reason." My voice grew louder. "One."

"Oren, please. I can't anymore."

"So you'd rather be alone than have me here?"

"I'd rather face the fact that I've been alone for a very long time."

My eyes momentarily closed while I tried to focus. "You have Lennox and Silvia. You're not alone."

"I never dreamt of being only a mother. I dreamt of being a wife and mother. It's time to recognize that I got half that dream. Half is better than none."

I was at a loss. Each sentence out of her mouth was like a bullet, each shot tearing a new hole until my chest was ripped open and my heart no longer pumping. The pain was debilitating. Unlike Carmine, these shots wouldn't leave me bruised, only hollow.

"When?" I managed to ask.

She nodded. "Now would be best."

"Now..." Panic bubbled through me. "But what about Lennox?"

"I'll tell him and Silvia."

*Yeah, Silvia.*

I bent down to gather the spreadsheets. I couldn't comprehend what had just happened. "What if we try counseling?" I asked.

"I can't hold onto straws anymore. I deserve more."

She did.

Less than an hour later, I drove away.

# CHAPTER 37

———— •O• ————

THERE ARE TWO sides to every story—two sides to every argument. Our divorce had more.

"You can take it all," Samuel Romano, my divorce attorney said. "IRS records show you were the only income earner since 1985, since your son was born. She deserves child support. Courts still aren't willing to award fathers sole custody…"

I lifted my hand. "I do not want to take him away from her. I'd never do that."

Romano tilted his head as he set his jaw. "We need to talk about that, but I'd consider child support a given, just until he turns eighteen—twenty-one if he's a student. That's it. You don't owe her anything else. With her lack of employment, I think I can get you out of spousal support."

He was wrong. I owed her everything. "Are you talking the house? I'm not taking the house. It's hers."

"Don't let emotions cost you millions of dollars."

My hand came down hard on the table between us. "Emotions? She's been my wife for nearly twenty years, and you're saying not to have emotions?"

"She's the one who filed. I know who she is. Are you willing to concede because of Mr. Costello?"

The man had balls. I'd been told that before, but to look at me and say that... his were steel. If he thought I was going to bad-talk the family, he was wrong. I laughed. "If you're insinuating that I'm giving Angelina the keys to the house and all the money she deserves because of her cousin, the answer is no."

"No one would blame—"

"I want to talk to her."

"I don't recommend it."

"I don't fucking care what you recommend. I'm going to talk to her. I'll tell her she can have whatever she wants. I'm not contesting anything."

"Sole custody?" Romano said.

"What?"

"I said we needed to talk about it. Will you contest giving her sole custody of your son?"

"Fuck yes! Did she really ask for that?"

"It's been left open. According to her counsel, she hasn't decided."

"Shouldn't it be up to Lennox? He's fifteen." I inhaled, realizing he was the age of Silvia when we got her. She was now an adult. No one would have custody of her. She'd probably go back to calling me Mr. Demetri, something that had only started to waver in the last few years. Once in a while I got an Oren instead. Lennox was fifteen and facing the divorce of his parents. It wasn't a picnic, but it sure as hell wasn't what Silvia could have endured.

"He will have his wishes heard," Romano said.

*Fuck.* I wasn't sure if I wanted that either. Would it be easier to accept that Angelina took him rather than that he didn't want me? "I'm still going to talk to her."

I called her as soon as I left Romano's office. The call went to her answering machine as did the next and the next. It took several phone calls, messages, and a few cancelled dates, but finally, Angelina agreed to allow me to come to Rye and talk in person.

It was a strange sensation, the gates opening to a home that at one time was my fortress, my haven. I had flashbacks of the optimism I'd felt as we moved to this home. As I progressed along the driveway, memories flooded my consciousness, of Lennox and a bicycle along the grass. It was like a surreal out-of-body experience to comprehend that what had been mine was no longer. The trek up the driveway seemed foreign, and yet I'd driven it thousands of times. Leaving the car outside the front door, I slowly got out of the car. As I approached the door, I had questions I wasn't sure I wanted answered.

Would my key still work?

I didn't try; instead, I knocked.

Angelina opened the front door, her expression empty. That was to say, it was neither angry nor elated, neither happy nor sad. If she'd cried over our separation, she wasn't allowing me inside those emotions. Would she allow me in the house?

"No Dante?" I asked.

"No one else is here. I didn't know how this would go, and I didn't want it to be overheard."

My eyes closed and opened, thoughts of being overheard too many to count. "I'm not here to fight."

"Good," she said, motioning inside. "Come in. I'm glad you wanted to talk."

I followed her to the sitting room, careful to keep my distance though I wanted nothing more than to reach for her hand, to feel it in my grasp. To pull her body against mine and relish the warmth she generated. To bring our lips together and taste her sweet kiss.

"Would you like anything to drink?"

I pushed my desires away. "Stop, Angelina. Remember, you said that you take care of people you love. Apparently, I no longer fit that bill."

She took a deep breath. "I told you that you'll always be the man I love."

"Then why are we doing this? My attorney is telling me to take everything. Vincent called. He's not pleased that we're separating, but he said that you asked him to stay out of it. Why?"

"Why would I speak to my cousin? This isn't about him. I don't want him making it about him. And, Oren Demetri, I know you. Despite your shortcomings, you're a good man—you always have been. I don't care what an attorney says, you won't take everything, and if you do—if I've been wrong about the man I married—then I'll face that reality as I have this one."

"I don't want to take it." I looked around the house that had been my home. "This is your house. You designed it. You made it a home. I'm not taking it. I'm also here to tell you that I won't contest an equal division of our assets."

It was her turn to shake her head. "I don't need that much money. I just need enough to maintain the house and our expenses. It would be nice to have a little extra, but not half of everything. You've worked too hard for all of that. It's been your life's goal. You deserve it."

"My goal was to make a life for us. You've worked hard too."

"I haven't—"

"I've made my decision," I said, interrupting. "Talk to me about Lennox. I'm not forgetting Silvia," I added before Angelina made it sound as if I had. "She's twenty and therefore not an issue of the divorce." I consciously held my own hand, realizing that it had begun to tremble. I couldn't recall being this frightened of an answer since staring down her uncle and asking for her hand. It was ironic that this emotion came with the same subject. Now, I supposed, I was in essence giving that hand back. "Lennox..."

"He's young and has his father's..." She smiled a weary grin. "...his parents' temper. He's upset."

"Custody?"

Her lip momentarily disappeared like it did when she knew I wouldn't like her answer.

"Damn it..." I stood. "Angelina, that is the only thing I'll fight."

"What?"

"I'm not giving him up. You can walk away from me. Silvia can too. I can't stop that. You're both adults. He's still a child. I won't force him to stay with me or even fucking talk to me, but I won't give up my rights as his father."

"I can't promise you how he'll respond. My attorney said he gets to talk to the judge."

It was my turn to smile. "I can tell you how he'll respond; he'll be upset. He can even tell the judge he doesn't want me in his life. But, *mio angelo*, he's fifteen. You and I are his parents. We were given that right to make decisions on his behalf." I sat back down and stopped myself from gathering her hands in mine. I took a deep breath. "I may need your help. Please help me retain my rights." I motioned around the room. "The rest is yours: the house and property—all yours. We can divide Demetri Enterprises, or you can simply have half of our stock put in your name. You'll receive the dividends, and I'll still do the work. Or fuck, you can work there. I don't care. I'd like seeing you."

Her eyes narrowed, and the meaning punched me in the gut. "Don't go there," I said. "There's no one there anymore. Believe it or not, it hasn't happened in years." I was talking of women whom I'd slept with. The women she'd faced when she'd come to the corporate office. It wasn't like I introduced them, but she knew. Somehow she knew. Therefore, even now, I knew that her being at the office day after day wasn't something she wanted to do.

Angelina scoffed. "I suppose that should make me happy, but it almost doesn't."

I needed to move to the previous subject. "We have a decent amount of liquid assets. Half can go immediately to an account for you. If you don't use our attorneys and financial planners, please get someone highly recommended. You're a wealthy woman. I'll also continue to pay Silvia's college and Lennox's in the future and keep paying Lennox's tuition at the parish. I just..." I stopped and held my breath. "Please, I won't stop being his father."

"Oren, you already—"

I stood, interrupting. "Don't, Angelina. I never said I was a great father or dad of the year. I've disappointed him more than I've pleased him." Moisture pricked behind my eyes. "I can't lose him completely. I'm already losing you."

My soon-to-be ex-wife stood and walked toward me. Bringing her small hands to my cheeks, she framed my face. "One day he'll see the man you are. He'll know..." She moved one palm to my chest, her fingers splaying. "...that inside there's a heart of gold. He'll know what I knew from the first time I saw you."

When my eyes closed, a fucking tear slid down my cheek. Ignoring it, I said, "Tell me again why we're doing this?"

"Because I'm tired of being disappointed. It would be better if you were the devil Lennox thinks you can be. You're not. It hurts to know what a good man you are... when you're not around. You see, Oren, I've waited for that man to come home to me." Her hand pushed against my chest. "That good man… I can't wait anymore."

When does one cease to belong to a family?

I'd say it was the first night she told me to leave, but then again, it was cemented the night we came to terms over the divorce. And yet like the opposite question—becoming a part of a family—ceasing to be a part of one happened slowly.

It had begun before we were married.

It was the day-to-day erosion of life's expectations. The repeated offenses that individually can be forgiven, yet pile up until they're a wall so great its height could border a country, not simply a heart.

When Angelina and I were first married, I tried to show her that I understood her concerns. I'd bring her daisies or candy. I made an effort. That stopped after California. Before I left, she'd made a comment about gifts. I'd lost a piece of myself on that trip, a piece of my soul that died along with the Irishman on a California highway. Perhaps after that, I decided that acknowledging my shortcomings was too complex—I had too many. Whatever the reason, I stopped bringing her gifts. When I was late or missed dinner, it simply was.

It wasn't until now, driving away from what used to be my home, that I even realized I'd stopped. *Hindsight is 20/20* the saying went. From where I stood, the reflection on my life was foggy at best, clouded in the haze of missed opportunities and poor decisions, the latter necessary or not.

Had I stopped trying to apologize for life's disappointments? In doing so, had I given into the reality and expected Angelina to do the same?

As I drove from Rye back to the city to my new apartment high in the fucking sky, the one with a great view and the furniture Julie had ordered and had delivered, with the empty kitchen cupboards—not only because I hadn't cooked since before my marriage, but mostly because I didn't want to—it was at that precipice that I realized that I was alone.

Alone.

The dictionary defined it as having no one else present; on one's own.

This separation of my marriage was more than a divorce of two people. It was a fault line, deep into the earth, a crevice between the life I'd lived and the one I now had to navigate. It was a fissure so cavernous that I wasn't sure how I'd ever bridge the gap.

Though Angelina had been the one to ask, the one to file, I accepted complete culpability. I never thought I'd feel more isolated, but I should learn not to give life those challenges. It could always get worse; there could always be more.

Yet at this time, I told myself to concentrate on any positive I could grasp.

I still had my son—even if removed. After our discussion, Angelina promised to talk to Lennox. I made promises too, ones I intended to keep. I promised to pick him up next Saturday and talk man-to-man.

While the family I'd known for nearly twenty years was no longer mine, I wasn't sure what that would mean with Vincent. When we spoke, he hadn't mentioned bringing our arrangement to a stop, and yet for not the first time, I longed for Carmine. If he were alive, I had no doubt he'd be upset, but maybe he could come up with a solution. Maybe Angelina would listen to him or to Rose.

That was all speculation. They weren't here to help or even to become angry.

Stopping at a drive-thru restaurant before making my way to my apartment, I picked up a sandwich. Looking into the bag, I surmised that I could survive on this shit, but it wasn't living... not as I'd done.

Once I secured the door of my apartment, I collapsed on the sofa.

It's funny—and yet not—that surrounded by the silence I craved in Rye, I wasn't happy. Now with the freedom to roam, I had no desire. In truth, it had never been a matter of desire. It had been convenient and available. I'd made my share of excuses, but they were all without merit. The only woman I'd ever wanted had told me to leave.

What would Carmine say if he could? What would he have done?

His only directive upon my request had been to keep Angelina happy and safe. She was secure within the walls of the home in Rye. Perhaps without my constant disappointment she may even be happy. "I hope she is," I said aloud to no one and to her uncle. My chest ached as my soul came to terms with my future. "I still love her. I know if you were here, you'd be angry," I scoffed through my tears. No one could see me or hear me. "I wish you were. I wish you were here to yell at me, to stare at me. I'm sorry... I'm so sorry..."

Carmine Costello's ghost wasn't the one who deserved my apology, but in the dark, quiet confines of my new place to sleep, he was who I chose. I could imagine his stare, his seething disappointment. I couldn't think of my own parents. They would have no basis for understanding. The young man they raised and knew no longer existed. His demise had been a slow process as his hardened heart was chiseled away with each decision and choice. "I'm sorry..."

Grieving for the missing pieces, I fell asleep upon the sofa, the lights out and my sandwich still in the paper bag.

# CHAPTER 38

WHEN DOES ONE begin to live again?

I assumed that there were couples who divorced with the intent of completely removing the other spouse from their life, moving on as if the years together never existed. I supposed that was more often the case than not. However, I couldn't comprehend how that was possible, not when there was a child or children. This was about more than Angelina and me.

I couldn't or wouldn't force Lennox to stay with me for a weekend or even a night. Convincing him to go to dinner was difficult enough. His stubbornness was inbred; of that I was certain. Nevertheless, I refused to give up or stop trying, not as long as he was a minor and I had half of the say in making his decisions.

I had power as his father and used it as much as necessary. Knowing one's rights and abilities was inconsequential unless one acted upon them. That knowledge had benefitted me in business endeavors. It was also helpful with my son.

Undoubtedly, it took more than *half* of the say in his decisions to convince him to attend those dinners. Time had moved on. He was now old enough to drive, yet to ensure I didn't end up alone at the table, I insisted on picking him up.

During eighteen years of marriage I missed countless obligations with Angelina and events for Lennox; yet after the divorce, I made every effort to see my son. If it meant cutting a meeting short or rearranging my schedule, I did what I could do.

Yes, I was keenly aware that I should have tried these things earlier.

As I'd sit in the driveway and Lennox would glance back into the house before begrudgingly moving outside and entering my car, I knew the real force, the wonder, the propulsion that made him attend our father-son meetings. Sometimes she'd peer outside and wave. Sometimes she'd simply smile sadly and shut the door. And there were times I never saw her; nevertheless, Angelina was there, encouraging Lennox to see me.

It was at Lennox's high school graduation that I gained newfound appreciation for the woman who had been my wife. Together with Angelina, Silvia, Vincent, Bella, Luca, and Luisa, we sat in the auditorium as one family supporting Lennox. After they announced his name and he walked across the stage to receive his diploma, I realized that Angelina and I were holding hands. I wasn't sure which one of us initiated it; the action was at one time too normal to always take a conscious effort.

"I'm sorry," I said as I loosened my grip.

For the first time in the nearly two years since our divorce was finalized, she smiled—no tears or sadness. Happiness radiated from her being as she squeezed my hand. "Don't be. I'm not." She tilted her head to the stage. "He did it. We, Oren, we did it. Did you see him?"

"I did."

"He's going to NYU in the fall."

"A legacy," I said wistfully, recalling a beautiful girl in my sophomore English class.

"On both sides, second-generation college-educated." She swallowed, her eyes going to Vincent's family, and lowered her voice. "Luca doesn't have plans for school, not yet, Bella said."

I sighed. "His education began a long time ago."

With our hands still intertwined, we both looked down at the way we fit together.

When her blue gaze came back to mine, she said, "Together, we made this happen."

"*Mio angelo*, was it worth it?"

She nodded. "I'd do it again. I'd do it all again. And knowing us, it would turn out the same." Before I could respond, she went on. "We have a wonderful son whom we both can be proud of."

I wasn't sure that was the only do-over she meant, but she was right. I wouldn't do anything differently if it would result in a different outcome for Lennox. I glanced at the poised young lady sitting on the other side of Angelina. Silvia was in that decision process too. "We did good."

Later that night after a celebration in Angelina's home, I was getting ready to leave when she stopped me. "Oren, I need to ask you something."

I looked around, finding us alone. "Yes?"

"I think I know something, but before I ask, I have another question."

My head shook as I grinned. "I never thought it would be possible, but I think I may even miss your riddles."

Angelina smiled. "This isn't a riddle. I wanted to ask you how you'd feel if I were seeing someone."

My breath caught in my chest, and immediately, I recognized the absurdity and injustice. I had recently begun to see someone. If I could, shouldn't Angelina have that right, too? I knew the answer, but that didn't make it easier to say.

Why did it feel so different to think of her with someone else?

My ex-wife laughed softly. "Oh, Oren, I don't know why Vincent and Uncle Carmine think you're such a great negotiator. Your every thought is telegraphed in your eyes and body language."

"That isn't true," I replied, sounding appalled that she'd called me out when at the same time I knew she was right.

"It is."

"Then it's only with you. Only you see the real me."

"Is it?"

"If it weren't, I'd suppose I'd not be here today."

"No," she said. "It *was* only with me. I asked how you'd feel if I saw someone because even though you haven't said anything, I've noticed something different about you lately, just recently. I can see you, Oren Demetri, and for the first time in too long, you seem happy, perhaps lighter. Is it because of Lennox's graduation, or could it be a woman?"

I took a deep breath. I hadn't told anyone about the woman I was seeing. Our relationship was secret and complicated, but then again, my life was a series of complicated secrets. Maybe that was why it felt right. For the first time since the lovely girl in my English class, another woman caught my eye. I tried to fight it, knowing she was married, but the pull was too intense. I'd only experienced that one other time in my life. I couldn't walk away and not try to learn if she felt the same.

"*Mio angelo*, you will always be my first love."

"And you mine. That's not what I asked."

"You asked two things," I said. "You saw my initial reaction, but it was wrong. I love you enough to want you to be happy. It hurts me to think that another man can make you that way, can do for you what I couldn't, but if it's what you want, I support you. Honestly, the question is moot: I gave up my right to an opinion."

"You did, as did I, but I know us. Having the right to an opinion and having an opinion are two different things. We've never had trouble voicing them, so I'll voice mine now. No, I'm not currently seeing anyone. And I don't know if I ever will. If I do, I'll be honest with you..." She allowed her words to hang in the air.

"I am."

"You are honest?"

"I am seeing someone. It just started recently. I wasn't looking. We met at a charity dinner." Technically that was true. I knew who she was, just not how dynamic or lovely or breathtaking. How the first assessment I'd heard of her was totally incorrect. She was the opposite of an ice princess. For the second time in my life, I was rendered tongue-tied. It took a special woman to do that to me. I was looking into the blue eyes of one of those women.

Angelina's petite hand came to my chest. "Thank you for being honest."

I reached up and held that same hand, our fingers intertwining. "I'm sorry."

"Don't be. I want you happy. I want me happy. Maybe one day I'll meet her. For the kids' sake, we need to be honest and open."

"Maybe one day. I'm not sure of the future. It's complicated."

She shook her head. "Our past was complicated. We should make an attempt to make the future easy."

"Oh, if only."

"I saw you and Vinny talking. How was that? How is it going?"

I didn't think she wanted specifics, but despite the lack of information I'd shared over our marriage, my Angelina was intelligent. She knew the way our world worked. "Demetri Enterprises is and will forever be involved with the Costellos. The web is too twisted to break free."

Her blue eyes clouded. "I've had time to think. There was so much I refused to see. It's becoming clearer."

I kissed her forehead. "Be happy, *angelo*."

"You know what, I am. Maybe one day it will involve another man, but right now, I think I need time to get to know me again."

A smile tugged at my lips. "Enjoy the relationship. You're a good person to get to know."

My earlier conversation with Vincent hadn't been about Costello investments or money. Carmine had a rule about business discussions at family gatherings. It was something Vincent honored. His questions were more personal and ones I chose not to bring up to Angelina at this time. Vincent had asked about Lennox.

*"College?" Vincent asked.*

*"Yes, NYU with a business major."*

*Vincent nodded. "There's more to education than sitting in a classroom. The world is a classroom."*

Costello 101.

*My chest ached at the familiar conversation. I spoke low. "Remember me saying that one day it'd be you? Now it is. I hope you remember the entire conversation. Lennox isn't Luca."*

*"No. Luca understands family. He respects family."*

*Standing near the wall of the living room, we both moved our gaze toward our sons. "Angelina and I—"*

*"Can you still use that phrase or that excuse?" Vincent asked, interrupting my comment.*

*"Yes. We may no longer be married, but we're still Lennox's parents. That will never change." I went on before he said more. "And together we wanted him to have choices. NYU will give him that. Demetri Enterprises will need him one day."*

*"That doesn't sound like a choice. It sounds like you've made his decision:*

*Demetri over Costello."*

*I took a drink from the tumbler in my hand, trying to calm my nerves as I constructed an appropriate response. "Why does it have to be that?"*

*"It doesn't," Vincent said. "You managed both."*

*I scoffed. "At the expense of my marriage. Is it wrong to want it easier for my son?"*

*"To want... no. To expect... yes. My work is different than my father's and my grandfather's. We all have had the same title and same responsibilities, yet mine isn't easier than Pop's or harder. It's different. That's what's right for Lennox. Keeping him away from his heritage and sheltering him—pampering him—isn't helping him. He's family, and one day he'll need to respect that.*

*"Luca," Vincent went on, "he's been learning that since he was young. He understands."*

*"I'll talk to Angelina."*

*"His name may be yours, but he has her blood. He can't walk away from blood."*

Blood in. Blood out.

*"I don't want him to walk away. I want him to have choices." That wasn't what I wanted to say. I wanted to say that Angelina and I didn't want him to walk away, but we also didn't want him to be bound as we had been bound. We wanted him to have his freedom.*

*I knew the binding ties brought on by that blood. They wrapped around my life until they controlled every aspect. I willingly accepted that. Perhaps it should be up to Lennox, but the way Angelina and I saw it was that it was our responsibility to break those bindings—break the chain.*

When given the opportunity, I didn't discuss it with Angelina. Not on that night or during other conversations. There wasn't a need, in my mind. From the day that our son was born, we were painfully aware of the dangers associated with Cosa Nostra. Together we'd made mistakes; we'd said things we both regretted. Our decisions for Lennox and even for Silvia didn't fall into those categories. They were made out of love and commitment. Changing Silvia's name from Greco was similar to allowing Lennox to live as a Demetri.

I continued to pray that our sacrifices and good deeds were sufficient penitence for past sins.

The mistake with our way of thinking was in not fully explaining it to our son.

# CHAPTER 39

———●○●———

THE FREQUENCY OF the dinners with my son, or sometimes Silvia, waned as the clock ticked, and the pages of the calendar turned. There came a point in the lives of young people where they felt the need to break free. In retrospect, I don't believe I'd ever had that opportunity. My parents were taken from me at that critical age—the time when as a young person I would have yearned for adulthood yet possessed no idea of what that would entail. My mother was the first to pass, and a short year later, my father followed. I couldn't think about them without experiencing the painful ache that always accompanied the thought of their loss. And yet my son wasn't faced with that same difficulty. His father was present—in the same realm—and he wanted nothing to do with me.

I tried to think as he would. Perhaps as my parents represented a void in my life, Lennox thought of me the same way. I was the devil in his eyes, the one who'd brought his mother sadness, who'd left him alone with Silvia and Angelina. I was the one who rarely supported his extracurricular achievements and had often been quick to reprimand him. I was the one who worked too many hours and had too much happening away from our family. It was a vicious circle, one shortcoming the impetus to another.

Lennox didn't see me as the hardworking father who provided him with countless opportunities or the financial resources for limitless possibilities. He didn't know the sacrifices made on his behalf. And that shortcoming fell on Angelina and me. In sheltering him, we'd limited his scope of vision. At the time, it seemed right until he took it too far.

With organized sports part of my son's past, Lennox Demetri took to a rising sport phenomenon, one with increasing popularity. Prior to his endeavor, I'd heard of mixed martial arts, like a New Yorker heard about polo. It wasn't baseball, basketball, or football, yet it was an activity that some enjoyed. There'd been pictures of fighters on the news and in the newspaper. It was something that others did that had no bearing on me— until it did.

I didn't hear about my son's underground career from him, Silvia, or Angelina. Later, I'd learn that my ex-wife had been unaware. It began while Lennox was living on the campus of NYU. His activities were his— until they meant more.

"Talk to me," Vincent said one evening when he called me to an unscheduled meeting over actual drinks.

With the years lessening our previous familiarity, the spark of fear that I used to experience with his father came back. It was that uncomfortable twist of the gut and acute awareness that only a direct demand from the boss could elicit. "I feel like I should know what you're talking about," I said as my mind did a mental checklist of Demetri-Costello dealings. While I was assessing business connections, Vincent was discussing something much more personal.

His dark stare bore into my gaze. "It needs to stop. The talk is getting louder and, Oren, when it gets to me, it's gone too far."

I nodded. "Everything is in order... everything that I'm aware of."

"Jimmy Bonetti is talking it up. He's making bank and wants everyone to know it's with a Costello."

Jimmy Bonetti was Johnny's son and Benny's grandson, a powerful capo in the Bonetti family by his own right. He'd surpassed his father years ago in rumor and in hits. He also had a big mouth that had begun a fair share of beefs between families and within the Bonetti family.

"Jimmy Bonetti likes to talk."

"I've checked it out. It's real."

I was so confused.

One would think that with time I'd get better at unraveling Costello riddles.

"A Costello?" I tried. "Who is Jimmy talking about?"

Vincent's voice lowered. "We're family, Oren, and I know more about your son than you do?"

My pulse thumped against my veins as the rush of circulation warmed my skin. My dealings with Vincent, with the family in general, had simmered over the last few years—not the boil it had been and not still, but somewhere in between. It had gotten to that place that had become comfortable. The deal I'd originally made with Carmine still worked. The Costellos received a percentage of my income—my tax to the family— with territorial deals. I received a cut from the money laundering. As they said, *it all worked out in the wash.*

However, with the stare pointed my way, something had changed. Something wasn't right. "My son? We've talked about him—"

Vincent interrupted my reminder with a hiss. "This isn't about him. It's about all of us. It makes us all look bad. If you won't teach him respect, I will. Family looks out for family. Sometimes it takes a stronger hand. What do they call that nowadays… tough love?"

"What are the Bonettis saying about Lennox?"

"Do you know he fights?"

I closed my eyes and sighed. "It's a phase. I got wind of it. I tried to talk to him. He's just strutting his stuff." I waved Vincent off. "A rebellious stage."

"No."

"No?"

"Do you know where he fights?"

My mouth went dry as the conversation replayed. I'd been busy with work and deals. The overseas investments were taking more time. Lennox was technically an adult. I'd figured he could make his own mistakes and learn from the consequences. That wasn't what Vincent's expression was saying. "No. I don't," I admitted. "How does Lennox have anything to do with the Bonettis?"

"Does he even understand the territories? The boundaries?"

Frustration grew as I waited for one of my questions to be answered. I lowered my voice. There wasn't anyone close enough to hear. Jimmy had uncharacteristically left us alone, yet as always, he was nearby. "Vinny, I don't know what you're saying."

*Fucking Costello riddles.*

"He fights. Not for the family. Not doing our work. But that isn't the worst of it. He fights in Jersey. People pay to see him. They call him *Nox*."

I took a deep breath. "I'll talk to him."

"You will or I will. It's past time. That boy needs to learn respect for his family."

"He is a *boy*," I tried.

Vincent's chin rose in indignation. "He's a man, nearly twenty years old. Do you know what I was doing for our family at that age? What Luca is doing?"

I had seen Luca's name under arrests in the newspaper. Like his father, nothing stuck. Nevertheless, he was following in familiar footsteps. "Please, Vincent."

His head slowly shook. "This has gone beyond us." He motioned between us. "This is public. Others are laughing at a Costello bringing business to Newark."

"Newark?"

"Oren, be a man and a father to that boy, or I'll take care of it."

With that he stood and without another word walked away, Jimmy once again at his side.

That night I drove to Newark, to a warehouse in the Ironbound District. I knew the location, but I hadn't realized that this was where he fought. There was no signage, but the cars in the dilapidated parking lot let me know I was in the right place. I followed the sound of people and paid for admittance at the door. The stench of sweat and testosterone permeated the stale air until my nostrils flared, begging for something fresh.

As I moved closer to the tall chain-link cage, I heard the chants. Like years ago at a middle school football game, people were calling my son's name, except they weren't saying Lennox. They were chanting *Nox*, that ridiculous made-up stage name.

One by one, opponents entered the ring, lined up to take a chance at knocking down the current champion—my son. As I watched Lennox's technique, I saw something I'd refused to recognize in other settings. There was a side to him that I hadn't seen, a rage that fueled him. I prided myself on my ability to read people, yet I hadn't taken the time to read my own son.

He was quick on his feet, dancing around each opponent. His punches were well timed, fists swinging and connecting with bone and smashing cartilage. The sport was brutal, and yet as young man after young man fell at his feet, Lennox remained relatively unscathed. He was good. Like with baseball or football, my son had talent in areas I'd never pursued.

Oh, I'd taken a swing when necessary. When I did, I never missed and I never lost. However, the fuel behind my actions was never rage. I didn't seek to wreak havoc, but punctuate my point. When I'd been moved to violence, hand-to-hand combat, it had always been for a reason—usually Costello. As in everything, I'd simply done what I needed to do. Watching my son, I saw something different.

He enjoyed the brutality.

The realization hurt as if he'd punched me.

Angelina and I had sacrificed our marriage for his well-being, and yet the reality of his heritage—that he was equally a Costello—couldn't be denied. It reared its head in a desire for destruction that we as his parents never shared.

I left the warehouse that night and a few more times without letting him know I'd watched. Perhaps a part of me wanted to see him defeated. Once that happened, I believed he'd move on to a different interest.

One evening I insisted on taking him to dinner. In his normal demeanor, he spoke in short sentences, huffs, and glares, reacting to my words more than responding.

"Lennox," I said, my tone low but serious, "look at me."

His light blue eyes snapped to my gaze. It hit me hard that they were the color of my eyes, not the vibrant deep color of his mother's. He was still my son.

"This pastime thing, the fighting…"

"Dad, you don't know what you're talking about."

"I do. It's MMA. I've watched you."

He scoffed. "Sure. Just like you watched my games in high school."

I probably deserved his animosity, but now wasn't the time. "About the same." I'd been to three nights of his MMA fighting. I wasn't sure how many football or baseball games I attended. "The point is you have to stop."

"No, I don't. I'm good. If you've been there, you would know that."

"I do know that. Do you realize where you're fighting?"

"In a warehouse…"

"In Newark."

"So?" he said casually.

My gaze narrowed. "Have we really sheltered you that much?"

"If you're talking about Uncle Vincent and territories, that shit is over. It ended years ago. It was all made-up bullshit from the feds and movies. The real deal all ended about the time when I was born."

I consciously stopped myself from shaking my head in disbelief. "It's over? Who told you that?"

"No one told me. I'm not dumb. I know Mom's maiden name. I know Vincent's name. I can read, but all that bullshit is more fiction than real. I've known Vincent all my life and Uncle Carmine too. They aren't what people like to say they are."

This time I shook my head. "Your Uncle Carmine loved you. Vincent loves you. What you're doing… where you're doing it… is disrespectful to him and to Carmine's memory. I don't care what you think you know. You've grown up with blinders on, and your mom and I were the ones who kept them in place."

Lennox's jaw clenched. "Don't talk about Mom."

I exhaled. "It's not about her. It's about you. Stop this. If you have so much extra time, start working at Demetri. It's time to learn the family business." The family business I *wanted* him to learn.

His broad shoulders shrugged. "Just because I'm taking business classes, what makes you think that I ever want to work at Demetri?"

My son was a fighter, and he'd just hit me below the belt. "I don't care if you want to or not. Do it. Gain experience. When you're older, start your own business, one without my name on the letterhead. The choice is yours." Because we've given you a choice. "Right now, working at Demetri would be best."

"Dad, I think you lost the ability to decide what's best for me a long time ago."

My tone hardened. "No more fighting. You're done."

"Sure, whatever."

With my appetite gone, I paid the check and stood. However, before I left, I said, "Come to Demetri after class tomorrow. I'll tell HR where to start you."

"I'm busy tomorrow."

I should have called Angelina. I should have done many things. That was the story of my life. Instead, I did what I had always done and worked. I juggled Costello and Demetri balls while reading reports and avoiding audits. Time passed, but not too much. It was one evening as I was working, one appointment still to go, that I received Vincent's call.

"Respect," Vincent said through the phone. "I told you to teach him... It's time he learned."

"I have. He's young."

"He's had his birthday. He's twenty. That's an old man in our world."

"He's not in *our* world."

"He put himself there," Vincent said.

We spoke for a few more minutes, or should I say Vincent spoke and I did what I'd always done, offering to pay Lennox's price—whatever Vincent had planned—in my son's stead.

"Newark," Vincent replied before the line went dead.

At the mention of the location of the warehouse, my stomach dropped—a free fall from my office high in the sky within the financial district straight down to the street below.

"Hold my calls. Cancel my appointments," I called.

Julie was on a much-deserved vacation. The secretary in her absence was named Michelle. She was competent but didn't hear or understand the urgency in my voice. She told me about a meeting, a man waiting in the outside office.

He was a judge, one who'd helped Demetri in the past, looking for a quid pro quo. He was interested in stopping a trend toward the legalization of marijuana. It was a nickel-and-dime racket compared to the heroin, crack, and other more lucrative substances. But then again, it was a gateway drug, the first step for users on the road to dependence. While the legalization created tax revenue, people like Judge Walters had made their way by scratching backs. Keeping marijuana illegal was his way of helping those who had helped him.

He offered me information on an impending emissions bill in exchange for my assistance. The knowledge alone would save Demetri a fortune. If the bill went through, we'd need to work on our specifications. Knowledge of the impending legislation allowed us to lobby against it. In the long run, despite the money to the lobbyists, we could save millions.

Putting aside the potential, I cut our meeting short, leaving the judge behind as I ironically drove into one of the best-known drug-infested territories. I paid my admission at the door and squeezed my way through the crowd. The scene inside the chain-linked octagon was different than any I'd seen before. When I'd hoped for my son's defeat, my prayers never included having it come at the hands of his cousin.

Perhaps Lennox was a better fighter than Vincent or Luca had predicted. I couldn't fathom what was running through Vincent's head as he sat ringside, watching as our sons continued to fight. While this wasn't boxing, there were rules. It was painfully obvious that the referee slash announcer or whomever the man standing guard was had no intention to call the fight until Vincent gave his signal.

This was Bonetti territory, but the Costello boss was currently in charge.

The boys who'd grown up together, who'd slept side by side in a playpen, and played in tents created from blankets... the childhood best friends were literally beating one another in a fight to the death. If I were to presume the motivation to continue, for Lennox I would assume it was pride. He was the reigning champion and didn't want to be uncrowned. For Luca, I would predict a different motivator. His was more simplistic. He'd been given a task by the boss, and being the good soldier Vincent expected, Luca intended to be victorious.

Both of the boys' faces had begun to swell and turn red and black. With each connection, blood and spit splattered the first few rows of spectators.

Pushing Jimmy out of the way, I sat in my thousand-dollar suit beside Angelina's cousin in the splash zone. "Tell me what you want and make this stop," I pleaded. "They're going to kill each other and then what do we have? We both lose our son. Is that what you want?" I wanted to remind him of the past, how he'd trusted me with Luca, Bella, and Luisa. I wanted to say so much, but fear for my son kept me from overanalyzing. This needed to stop, and it needed to stop now.

My stomach heaved as the crunch of cartilage and bone forced us both to turn toward the ring. This time it was Luca who'd taken the hit. He spat onto the floor, a deep red pool of blood.

During any other fight, the winner would have already been declared.

Despite the carnage, or maybe because of it, the crowd around us was going wild.

"Ten percent on all," Vincent said.

"All?" I asked. I paid the Costellos ten percent of all earnings in New York, but Demetri Enterprises had grown globally. Then again, there was no price too great for Lennox.

"All."

"Fine. Make it stop. You're nearly killing our sons over money?"

"Respect," Vincent said. "I stop this, you pay. Lennox, he's good. He has talent. It's time that he uses it in an honorable way—for the family."

"I'll pay," I confirmed. "Stop this now." Looking up to the ring, both young men teetered on the balls of their bare feet, appearing as though they might fall helplessly to the blood-splattered mat at any moment.

Vincent turned to Jimmy and nodded. Immediately, the man with the power stepped into the ring, and the vise that had been crushing my chest loosened a notch.

Instantaneously, I stood, my new focus on getting to Lennox when Vincent grabbed my arm. "We'll talk."

It wasn't a request but a summons. "Yes, Vincent. We'll talk."

Lennox's left eye was nearly eclipsed by the red and purple swelling as I supported his weight, and he draped an arm over my shoulder. The crowd parted as I helped—carried—Lennox, my over six-foot-tall son, and Vincent and Jimmy did the same for Luca.

"Brooklyn," Vincent said, his way of telling me to take Lennox somewhere else. Luca would be seeking medical treatment in Brooklyn. Both of the boys couldn't be at the same hospital, or it could raise questions.

I nodded and assessed my son. Was he well enough to tolerate the drive to Westchester? "Lennox, do you hear me?"

"H-he... Luca... a hit? It's real?"

"Do you hear me?"

"I'm still alive."

Blood thinned by spit dribbled from his mouth. With each word spoken, it splattered on his wife-beater T-shirt, creating a kaleidoscope of red and pink droplets. He was bruised and battered, but his assessment had been correct. He was alive.

# CHAPTER 40

WITH THE LINE drawn in the proverbial sand, the years of devotion and loyalty hung in the balance as I wracked my brain for alternatives, and Lennox clung on to life. He made it to Rye, though he'd lost consciousness somewhere between. I called from the car, and Angelina met us at the hospital.

I contemplated possibilities. If Lennox survived, I could send him to London. I'd been thinking about moving there. Looking up to see my ex-wife pacing back and forth, I knew she wouldn't be in favor of his move, but with Vincent's alternative, she might agree.

The waiting room around us was empty, save for us and a TV that she'd turned off as soon as we entered. The soles of her shoes over the tile floor created a rhythm, providing a comforting backdrop as my mind refused to believe our son would not be all right. I let my thoughts wander. The windows along one wall reflected the plain interior, turning the night's dark sky into a distorted mirror. Sighing, I sat back on an orange vinyl-covered chair and stretched out my legs. Red droplets upon the top of my leather shoes caught my attention, bringing back the reality. I'd washed Lennox's blood from my hands, but my suit and maybe my shoes were probably ruined.

"Blood don't clean." Testa's words came back to me. The irony that this time it was my son's blood churned my already-twisted gut. This time was different. This time I didn't get sick. Maybe I had grown callous since Carmine's shooting.

"I don't understand," Angelina said, her blue eyes darkening as her comment pulled me from my inner thoughts. "What did you *do*?"

"Me? What did *I* do? I saved our son's life."

"Luca…" She paced back and forth, her head shaking. "This isn't right. We're family, Vincent and I. He wouldn't do this if he didn't have a reason."

"He had a reason. He said he was teaching Lennox respect. He'd warned, but I never imagined…" My words faded away.

Angelina lowered her tone. "Lennox or you? Who did he warn, and why did he call you instead of me?"

I stood and tried to keep my volume low. Twenty-plus years of Costello riddles to my credit, I could answer her last question with the blatant truthfulness that I might have restrained if we'd still been married. "Why'd he call me? Maybe he didn't want his *princess* cousin to show up in the warehouse district and watch her son beaten to death."

Angelina's neck straightened. "You promised something, didn't you?"

I shrugged. "Money. He wants more, a more inclusive cut."

Her lip disappeared between her teeth like it did when she was thinking as her head moved from side to side. "Money doesn't show respect. He wants more." She stood taller, her petite frame radiating authority as she demanded, "Tell me."

The truth pained me, but I didn't know how to help our son. All I could give Angelina was honesty. "He wants Lennox to work for the family."

Her blue eyes widened in panic. "Oh, God, Oren, tell me you didn't

362

agree. Please tell me you said no."

"Fuck, have you ever said no to Vincent?"

"Yes," she said matter-of-factly, "and to Uncle Carmine, too."

"Well, I never wore the crown, so that's never been an option. I didn't answer one way or the other. I purposely left it unanswered."

"Then I will."

I spun like a caged animal, unable to move more than a few feet in any direction, and ran my hand through my hair. "No, you can't. It'll make Lennox appear weak—and me appear weak. It's not a woman's—"

"This isn't about you or how you appear," she interrupted. "It's about Lennox, and I don't care what you think: it's a *mother's* place. If you don't think Bella would fight for Luca, you're wrong. It's a mother's right."

"Do you know how it looks when Lennox's mother is the one who faces down Vincent, fights his battles?"

"It's not his battle yet. He's in the hospital. I'll talk to Vincent before the request gets to Lennox." Her voice grew louder. "I'll tell you how it looks. It looks like we're still a family..." She motioned between the two of us. "...like we still talk, and that we both still care about our son's future. It looks like *the princess* finally decided to take control of her reign."

The door opened as the bottom strip scuffed across the tile floor, drawing our attention.

"Excuse me, Mr. and Mrs. Demetri?" the small woman in light green scrubs asked.

We answered in unison. "Yes."

"You can see your son now."

I reached for Angelina's hand—was it out of habit or because together we were stronger? "I'll talk to Vincent if you want me to. I'd never ask you—"

She squeezed my fingers and smiled. "No. You didn't *ask*. Let me do it. It'll go better. I'm certain. While I've told him no, it's less frequent the other way around."

She was right. It probably would go better.

"The money is his," I confirmed. "I don't give a fuck."

"You do. You care and not just about the money. I guess I always knew that. I was just too hurt and lonely to always see it. We'll do this. Lennox deserves more than what we had. He deserves choices."

Despite the fact that there was someone new in my life, I couldn't take my eyes off of my ex-wife. It was different than it had been. The love was deeper, not superficial or physical, but an adoration that strengthened with time. Sometime during the last twenty years she'd become more, or had it just been since our divorce? *"Mio angelo,"* I began.

She squeezed my hand again. "Oren, stop. This is about our son. We'll make it right."

"I'm just…" I searched for the right word. "…awed."

"Don't be. It's taken time. It took me being me—seeing the world alone—to finally figure it all out. I'm sorry that I couldn't have done it when we were married."

"I wasn't…"

She smiled a sad, knowing smile. "We both did what we know, what we thought was best. We both have regrets. Whether Lennox ever admits it or not, he needs both of us."

Our son's recovery took time. He had broken bones and a concussion. Through it all Lennox managed to keep up with his classes, but doing extra, going above and beyond, was a slow process. When he was finally able, he didn't go back to fighting; instead, he did as I'd told him nearly a year earlier and went to work at Demetri Enterprises. I'm most certain that in his mind simply because his last name was on the company letterhead he deserved… well, anything—everything. He wasn't alone in the entitlement generation. I understood that, knowing we'd done our part in propitiating the attitude.

That was before.

That time was over.

For Lennox to earn the respect he one day would hopefully deserve, he needed to learn to give it.

It wasn't a lesson I felt was best learned in a near-death experience delivered by his cousin, ordered by his other cousin. If I had any say— which since it *was* my name at the top of the letterhead, I did—Lennox would earn it with hard work.

Hard was a relative term. Lennox wouldn't be lifting boxes in a warehouse, but he also wouldn't have a corner office—not yet. Prior to his first day at Demetri Enterprises, I met with human resources. Lennox Demetri was to start his employment in our company as anyone would who came through the doors with an incomplete degree and no experience.

At the bottom, that bottom determined by a customary placement test.

His test assigned him to the accounting department. Apparently, my son was talented in more than sports. He was good with numbers.

I waited for Lennox to talk to me, to complain about his placement or demand more. To his credit, he never did. He did the menial tasks put before him. Did he understand why he'd been placed in that position and the ones that followed? Did he know that I had hopes and dreams for his future? Did he understand that by learning each department, he was setting the groundwork for the future? Did he understand that one day he could be running the entire company?

I didn't know the answers. He didn't share.

I knew my thoughts on the matter. I'd started Demetri Enterprises from the ground up. When it began, I was the accounting department, human resources department, and fucking janitorial staff. Minus one unqualified secretary, I was everything.

It wasn't a Fortune 500 company with hundreds of employees or a budget of millions of dollars. That experience helped me understand the ins and outs of my company. Setting my son up in a corner office would not do that. It would have fostered the attitude that almost had gotten him killed.

I'd made that mistake already. Mistakes served a purpose only if one chose not to repeat them.

Whether Lennox opted to work for Demetri in the future or do something else, the greatest service I could do for him was to teach him what Vincent said he needed. Lennox needed to respect the company and each department as a part of the whole.

Angelina never told me exactly what was said between her and Vincent, only that it was. "Oren," she said, "we're a team when it comes to Lennox and Silvia. Just because we're divorced doesn't mean we can quit the team."

It made me smile. I was never much into sports despite my ex-wife's attempts to make me watch Lennox's games. That didn't mean I didn't understand the concept. It was similar to the lesson Carmine had taught me.

"Family, *mio angelo*. Can't quit family." That was a Vincent quote.

# CHAPTER 41

———●○●———

I GRIPPED THE steering wheel tighter as twenty–three years of memories ran in fast-forward through my mind. They went back even further than that, back to my English class: the giggles, the looks, and my inability to talk. Our dreams were for forever. Though our marriage hadn't lasted, our love still prevailed. It was different now, a respect and adoration, an understanding for each other's accomplishments and sacrifices.

The phone call I'd received earlier played on repeat, becoming the soundtrack to the vision of memories. Like a sad song, its melody was melancholy.

I pushed the damn button on the gate, my car no longer having the ability to open it and access the house in Rye. With each second I waited for a voice, my gut churned with what I would find.

"Hello."

I recognized the voice. "Silvia, it's Oren."

With her finger on the button I could hear the echoes from within. "Why the hell is he here?" Lennox barked.

"Angelina called him, Lennox. Shut up… Come on in," she said the last part to me as the gate moved to the side.

My son was now graduated from NYU and almost done with his

master's degree. He was also taking more of a role at Demetri Enterprises. It seemed that through the years we'd worked out a compartmentalization of sorts.

We could coexist within the walls and confines of Demetri Enterprises. We could discuss deals and any issues that arose. We could even spend hours hashing out contracts and proposals. He was gifted in more than numbers. Lennox had the ability to decipher the fine print.

I probably never told him that, but it was true.

I also never told him that I liked having the second set of eyes. That didn't mean we didn't have arguments. We did. From my perspective, at first, I had difficulty relinquishing even a small part of my control, but now that we'd been doing it, we'd found our system.

That coexistence never had, and obviously didn't now, extend to our personal life. My son was dating someone. I'd met her briefly a time or two. A nice girl from the Midwest, they'd met at NYU. It was nearly impossible for me to think of him as old enough for that kind of relationship, yet he was. Jocelyn seemed smitten yet a little too quiet for my taste. I didn't see the spirit and spitfire of his mother in her. The *forza*—the strength.

It was true that the woman I'd been seeing for nearly five years was also different from Angelina in that regard. However, my current love's story was complicated as was our relationship. Her strength and fire simmered deep inside her, a flame that despite life's expectations and without anyone's assistance she'd managed to keep burning. Over the years I'd watched that flame grow, fascinated by her determination regardless of the hurdles set before her.

Now it was time to think about my first love and the obstacle she was facing. By my son's voice, it was painfully obvious that I was an outsider in his eyes. Yet our division of personal and business didn't apply.

Angelina had called me. I couldn't refuse.

Bringing my car to a stop near the front door, I looked down at my hands and willed my expression to hide the turmoil raging within. No matter our past decisions, the woman inside the house was my family.

We don't quit family.

The front door opened, and Silvia stood just within the archway. Her expression was solemn, yet her dark eyes hinted that I had my own obstacle waiting. "Mr. Demetri."

"Silvia." I'd given up trying to get her to call me Oren again. It was easier to fight battles I could win. I stepped inside. "Where is she?"

"In the kitchen."

Lennox came closer, his presence growing as if he could loom over me and push me back outside. Silvia's hand came to his chest. "Stop. Don't do this in front of Mother."

"I don't understand why you're here," he said, his voice a low rumbling growl.

"Because she called me."

"Maybe if you would have come when she called before—"

"Stop," Silvia commanded again.

Turning, I saw Jocelyn in the sitting room, keeping her distance from the family dramatics. "Hello," I called.

"Hello, Mr. Demetri."

I'd told her to call me Oren too, but right now, I didn't care about anyone except Angelina. Each step through the house that had once been my home, each step toward the kitchen was harder than the last. As if the bleached wood had changed to a murky bog, my footsteps took will and determination. Turning the final corner, I saw Angelina, standing near the stove, waiting on something from the microwave. She appeared tired but beautiful. The epitome of my life's desires and goals embodied in one person.

She turned my way. "Oren, I'm having a cup of coffee. Do you want one?"

"Mom." Lennox pushed past me, being only a step behind. "We can get that for you."

"Nonsense."

"*Mio angelo*," I said in response.

The view beyond the windows sparkled with the sinking evening sun. The Long Island Sound glittered like diamonds as the trees of orange, yellow, and red swayed in the autumn breeze.

"Angelina, I can get you whatever you need," Silvia said.

Everyone with the exception of Jocelyn had followed me into the room. I looked again to the panoramic view, unable to look at Angelina to see her as she was and not see her as she had always been.

"Lennox," Angelina said, "do me a favor?"

"Anything."

"Take Silvia and Jocelyn and go get dinner."

"No," both Lennox and Silvia said together.

"Go. I'm fine. Besides, I want to talk to your father."

Lennox's light-blue glare shifted my way before he turned back to his mother. "We can get you something?"

"Fine, bring me back something you think I'll like."

"I'll stay here," Silvia volunteered. "I'll go somewhere else, so you two can talk. Lennox, pick me up something too."

Angelina's smile caused her cheeks to rise as her nose scrunched. "I want you all to leave. I wasn't really asking."

"Fine." They both agreed begrudgingly as they each offered Angelina a kiss on her cheek and slowly stepped away, leaving us alone.

As Angelina reached for the warm cup of coffee, she turned my way.

"Please," she said as she came closer, placing the cup on the table. "Don't look at me that way."

I couldn't stop the tears as I took her in. Stoically, I squared my shoulders and swallowed the pain. "What way would that be?"

"Like I'm going to die."

I couldn't take it anymore. One step, maybe two, and she was in my arms, her soft body against mine. I can't be sure how long we stood there, but as we did our shoulders shuddered, and we both released the emotion I'd assume she'd been trying to keep from the children. When she finally took a step back, I spoke.

"I'm not looking at you like that."

"Right." She reached for a box of tissues and set it on the table, taking one and dabbing the tears from her cheeks. "Then tell me how you see me."

"It would take a lifetime to tell you that."

She motioned toward the table and we sat, never looking away from one another.

Inflammatory breast cancer, stage four. No signs until there were. Fueled by hormones, it's most common in women entering menopause but can happen at any age. A double mastectomy was an option, but according to what she'd told me on the phone, the cancer had already metastasized. The doctors were doing more tests to find out what could be done—if anything.

I reached for her hand. "Let me tell you." I forced a smile. "I see you as a young student, as a bride, and as a new mother. In your eyes, I see years of happiness and too much sadness. I see all that you have been and all there's yet to do. I see a fighter, someone who will fight and beat this disease."

She'd managed to suppress her sobs, yet tears coated her cheeks.

"Thank you. I needed to do what we just did. I needed to cry, and I didn't want to do it alone."

"The kids…"

She shook her head. "Silvia is determined to get me to eat, ten times a day if she could. And Lennox, he hovers. Poor Jocelyn is unsure what to say or do. I just want normal."

"One day, *angelo*, after you beat this thing. You asked what I see when I look at you. I see *forza*. I see strength within a fierce and worthy fighter. I see a woman who's never backed down. Do you remember telling me that growing up with Carmine and Rose, the men around your home were intimidating?"

She laughed. "Like you."

I shrugged. "I don't feel very intimidating right now. But you said they were. By the time I met you, really got to know you… you were the intimidating one." My cheeks rose. "I believe, Mrs. Demetri, that I even confessed that before our first date."

She laughed. "You did say you were scared of me."

"Terrified was the word I used. By the way, it's one of the things I've always loved about you."

"Can I get you a cup of coffee?" she asked again, standing.

I didn't need coffee, but I saw the truth in her eyes. I remembered her words, *I want to take care of people I love*—maybe I was once again on that list. "I'd love a cup. Then let's go sit on the deck. The sound is spectacular this evening."

Her smile grew as her head tilted. "I have a better idea if you don't mind?"

"I'm confident that no matter what you're thinking, I won't mind."

As the sun sank lower in the evening sky, Angelina and I sat on the balcony outside of what used to be our bedroom. With a bottle of red wine, we reminisced and laughed. We recalled stories I'd forgotten. As was common with memories, we highlighted the good ones, the fun times of our life together and of the children.

"I'll never see my grandchildren," she said as the stars sprinkled the now-darkened sky.

"Don't say that. Lennox and Jocelyn are engaged."

"The wedding is set for next July. Oren, I might not be here."

I squeezed her hand. "We'll spare no expense. Get the best doctors in the country… in the world. Together we'll fight this."

"No. I know you mean well, but that decision is up to me. I will fight, but only until I can't any longer. The oncologist was honest. He said I could do the surgery, chemo, and radiation, and I still might not make it six months. He also said I could do none of that and not make it six months. He said to consider my quality of life.

"I'm sorry," I said, "for everything."

"Never be sorry. We have a love—have, not had—a love that most people never find. I'm not sorry for anything. I've known the fulfillment of marrying the man of my dreams. I've brought a baby into this world. I've done what I could for him. I was blessed with a daughter, one who I've watched become a remarkable woman. I had a husband who sacrificed his soul for me." She turned my way. "Don't think I don't know that. I've also known the love of parents, and of an aunt and uncle, and a cousin who became a brother. I have no regrets."

I did.

Now wasn't the time to voice them.

"Fight, *mio angelo*. Please fight."

She didn't respond as we both sat, our fingers intertwined, listening to the once-familiar noises of the darkened Long Island Sound, the soft waves and the rustling of the trees. In the soft din of nature, I recalled a time before the house was fully built when she'd brought me up to this balcony and explained what it would be. Everything she promised had come to pass. Her sketches became our home. As we stared into the darkness and she settled her head against my shoulder, I had too many regrets, and yet my love for the woman beside me was not one of them.

That love had propelled a life full of decisions that I'd willingly chosen while at the same time gave me more than I ever imagined.

Her breathing steadied, and I knew that she was asleep. Slowly, I continued to rock the glider we were sitting on back and forth, allowing her to rest. During our talk, she'd said that sleep had been spotty at best; each time she closed her eyes, she would wake with a jolt, her mind filled with the milestones she'd never see.

If I could, I'd spend every dime I'd ever made. I'd sell what was left of my soul to the devil himself. I'd do anything to take this disease away, to make her body healthy. Unfortunately, some wishes don't come with a price because they're not meant to be.

# CHAPTER 42

———•○•———

SITTING AT A small table at Carlisle's, I waited for Vincent to arrive. I hadn't spoken to him in months; our relationship wasn't as close as it had been at one time. I paid my dues and continued to uphold my end of our agreement, but with technology it wasn't the envelopes of cash Carmine had seen in his younger days. Today there were electronic transfers and untraceable bank accounts in foreign countries. It was a complicated system and yet much easier and cleaner than it had been in the old days.

While my ex-wife came closer to life's end, my over-five-year relationship also had come to an end. The two weren't related, and yet I was helpless to stop either one.

I'd been honest with my second love. I'd shared my dark secrets and my heartaches. She'd shared her own. Though her situation wasn't the same as Angelina's, I wanted to save her too. I supposed it was a man-thing, wanting to ride in on a white horse and save the day. I wasn't capable of that with Angelina, and with Adelaide, she wouldn't allow it.

She told me goodbye, saying that she was setting me free to find another Angelina. She said she didn't deserve me, but she couldn't have been further from the truth. I didn't deserve either of the women who held my heart. They were both too good for the likes of me. Yet even in their absence, I would be a prisoner to their love.

A man like me rarely shared his heart, but when he did, it was forever.

My saving grace was my company. I still had Demetri Enterprises. The company had ridden the economic wave and was prospering internationally as well as domestically. Our legitimate holdings far outweighed any questionable alliances. We were now a reckoning force in all things, including the political structure as laws and regulations affected our investments. We had our hand in lobbying as well as greasing a hand here and there.

Lennox had taken a stronger role. Despite what Angelina had hoped for in our son—the opposite of me—I saw the determined work ethic in him. Our son was no longer the entitled child who'd failed to show respect to his family. He was dedicated and hardworking. Understandably, he was currently spending more time in Rye with his mother. Her days were numbered. Angelina and Lennox weren't alone; they had Silvia and Jocelyn, too.

I still visited but made a point of visiting when Lennox wasn't there. Our separation of business and personal was at an all-time high.

Silvia seemed to understand my presence better. She knew that despite the divorce, Angelina and I had an enduring connection. The last time I saw my ex-wife, she was a fraction of the woman I married.

"Don't look at me like that," she'd said, her voice weak as I entered her bedroom. Sitting up in a chair with a blanket over her lap, her cheekbones were too prominent and her hair thinned.

"Like what?" I said with as much amusement as I could muster. Instead of letting her answer, I did it for her. "Like I'm seeing the most beautiful woman in the world, the one who stole my heart?"

"Oren."

Our visit was short. While her skin was too pale, even the terrible disease couldn't take away the spark in her eyes. They twinkled as she spoke about the impending wedding.

"Oren," Vincent's deep voice brought me back to the restaurant.

There'd been a time in my life when no one would have caught me unawares, but apparently, I was no longer there. I'd been lost in memories and regrets as the Costello boss approached my table.

"Vincent," I said, standing. Nodding, I added, "Jimmy."

The three of us sat with our backs toward the wall. Old habits were hard to break.

"I'm not a man to mince words," Vincent said.

I agreed, but remained silent.

"I wanted to talk to you about Lennox."

My neck straightened. "What about him?"

"I've been watching. He's doing good."

"He is."

"He's getting married to that girl?" Vincent said, partially in question and also in declaration.

"Yes. Soon, I hope while Angelina…" I didn't finish my sentence.

"Yes. We received our invitation. I wanted to tell you what I told Angelina years ago, but now…" His dark eyes clouded. "It's not right that we lose her."

"I couldn't agree more."

"I don't agree with the decisions you and my cousin made for Lennox, but I respect them. I respect you—both of you. You've worked hard for Demetri. You've helped Costello. We'll keep our business between the two of us. For Angelina, it's better to keep your son out of it."

An invisible load lifted from my shoulders. "Thank you, Vincent. You know I'll do whatever you ask."

"I've been giving that some thought. I'll be calling."

My relief evaporated as he stood and walked away.

*I'll be calling…* It had too many meanings.

*Costello riddles.*

Though I didn't know what he'd meant, I decided to take comfort in knowing that Lennox's freedom from family obligations had been proclaimed by the boss himself. No one could argue as long as Vincent was in charge.

LENNOX AND JOCELYN'S wedding was small in comparison to other Costello events. They were married on the lawn between the house and the Long Island Sound on a sunny summer afternoon. The date had thankfully been moved up to accommodate Angelina.

Jocelyn was beautiful in her dress and Lennox handsome in a custom suit. The parish priest agreed to marry them outside the walls of the church due to the circumstances. He performed the mass and ceremony beautifully.

Angelina was stunning in a long dress that hung from her too thin body. Unable to walk the length of the yard, she sat beside me in a wheelchair and watched our son say his vows.

A week later, we were once again listening to the priest's words as we all said goodbye to Angelina. In her own angelic way, she glowed, lying peacefully surrounded by white satin, her hands folded one over the other and the ring I'd given her on her finger. As I stood before the casket, I longed for her eyes to once again open—one more time—so I could see the spark.

But I knew once would never be enough. I'd always want more.

It was another wish that would never be fulfilled.

Later that evening, Vincent asked to speak to me alone in what used to be my office. I supposed now it was Lennox's, but I was too sullen to stand on formalities.

As his father had done before him, Vincent went to the desk and sat on the business side. I took a seat facing him.

"I'm making the call," Vincent said. "Morelli was a good man. Like Angelina, the cancer took him fast."

Morelli had fallen to lung cancer, not a complete shock when I recalled the smoke-filled rooms, yet heartbreaking nonetheless. He left behind a wife and two grown children.

And then his words resonated: he's making *the call*.

I swallowed, my mouth suddenly dry. We were just returning from my ex-wife's wake, and Vincent was talking business. This went against Carmine's rules, yet I wasn't the one to call him out.

Not long ago he'd given my son the freedom I'd asked for, that Angelina had asked for, and now it was my turn to pay. No one rejected the call from the boss. It wasn't done.

In seconds, I completed a comprehensive assessment of my life. From the beginning of my education with my father on the docks to the first night on the street with Vincent, and on to the introductory class in Costello 101 and 400 level, receiving *the call* had always been a possibility. I'd made the necessary sacrifices. I'd paid my dues. I was on the track, and yet with the opportunity before me, I knew what I couldn't say: I didn't want it.

Instead, I sat taller. "The call."

"The books are open, Oren."

"It's an honor," I said, believing in my heart that the words were true.

Vincent nodded. "It is. I believe that. Only a man of respect can be considered."

I wasn't sure what to say.

"Pop respected you," Vincent went on. A small upturn of his lips brought a smile to his cheeks. "From the first time you had the balls to ask for Angelina's hand."

I grinned in response. "I was scared to death."

"As you should have been."

We both laughed.

"It seems like a million years ago," I said.

"It was. I wanted to tell you about the books because like Pop, I respect you, Oren. You've earned it." He nodded toward the closed door. "Not many men would stand up to me about their son. I don't agree, but I respect your and Angel's decision. Lennox has choices—you earned those for him. He also has a family. I hope that Angel's passing won't cause him or you to forget that. We're your family too. Divorce or death can't stop that."

I was suddenly confused. If I were about to be asked to be made, how could I forget the Costellos? "Of course not. One doesn't quit family."

Vincent nodded. "No, not quit, but one can be released."

It was like a movie where the filmstrip had been severed and the reel continued to turn. I couldn't keep up. There was nothing on the screen to tell me which way to go. "I'm not sure I understand."

"We're family, Oren. You helped me, Pop, and our family. We helped you. Not because of what the other did, but because we are family. That isn't changing. We're still Lennox's family, yours, and even Silvia's. I'm here. You have my number."

"The books?" I asked.

Vincent nodded and leaned back. "He's young, but I was young. He qualifies, and one day, he'll be in my position."

"Luca?"

"Oren, having your name written in the books is a gift. I hope one day you'll see that by not writing your name in the books, I'm also giving you a gift. You want Lennox to be free because despite all you've done, it's what you think is right. That doesn't mean fulfilling a role in the family is wrong. It just is. You'd do it. I know you would. I could trust you. I always have. But more than freeing Lennox... I've given it a lot of thought, and I'm freeing you too."

I didn't have words. I wasn't sure what to say. Did one thank someone else for his freedom, or was I perhaps sad that it came with the death of my ex-wife?

"Vincent?"

"Yes?" he said as he stood.

"Thank you."

"We're still here, Oren. Don't forget that."

"Our agreement?" I asked. When we'd met at the restaurant, he'd said it was to be only between us, not Lennox. I didn't know what the future held.

"Like it was, New York only, quarterly payments. With time, perhaps less. Let's see what happens."

I reached out to shake his hand. Vincent reached for mine and pulled me toward him. He'd grown wider over the years, much like his father. For a moment, I was surrounded by his embrace. "Family." His free hand patted my back.

"Family."

---

*Angelina Marie Theresa Demetri, of Rye, New York, passed away after a well-fought illness on June 30, 2008. Angelina is predeceased by her parents, Angelo and Gina Costello, and by her uncle and aunt, Carmine and Rose Costello. She is survived by her loving children, Lennox Demetri and his wife, Jocelyn, and Silvia Demetri, as well as by her cousin, Vincent Costello and his wife, Bella, and many more family members. Angelina will be lovingly remembered by all who knew her for her love and devotion to family and friends. Services were private. Contributions may be made in Angelina's name to the Metropolitan Museum of Art in New York City.*

Staring at the worn newspaper clipping in my hand, I looked up at the television. It had been nearly six months since Angelina's funeral. The world had moved on and the TV stations were now filled with a current story: the financial collapse of our country. Beginning midyear and growing in strength following the election, the stock market plummeted, taking a historic plunge. On paper, the losses to Demetri Enterprises were staggering. In reality, they were worse.

Everything I'd worked for... all the reasons behind my choices... it was all disappearing.

Standing at this new precipice of my life, I was again alone. Lennox would and could handle Demetri Enterprises with me out of the country. My location was insignificant as he was content with his new wife. Together they lived in Rye where even Silvia seemed satisfied.

As I packed my belongings and planned for my departure, I didn't know what the future would hold. I only knew that I'd made my deals, sold my soul, and now I was again as I'd been when my parents died— alone.

My beliefs wouldn't allow me to take my own life—though I understood why many businessmen chose that route during the collapse of 1929. I didn't need to take it because all that I'd worked for was gone. My life as I'd known it was gone. All I could do was pick up the pieces and move forward.

That was who I was. I was a worker, a protector, and too often a loner. Maybe in time that would change, but for now, I needed to move away—move forward.

I'd decided upon London.

It was my equivalent to disappearing. The unhappiness in my son's eyes when he looked at me hurt as much as knowing that his mother was gone.

On my way out of town, I made one last stop.

The November air was crisp, the ground dry.

I knelt before her tombstone.

### *Angelina Marie Theresa Demetri*
### *Loving mother*
### *1955 – 2008*

"*Mio angelo*, I wanted to tell you I was leaving. I know how upset you got when I didn't tell you where I was going." I held back the tears. "Our son will be fine. He has Silvia and Jocelyn. He doesn't need me. We raised him well. You did." I couldn't hold back any longer as sobs resonated from my chest. "I think I wanted to tell you, in case you ever wondered, you mentioned my selling my soul… I don't regret a thing. I would do it all again to be your husband and Lennox's father. I loved your family—I still do. I became a different man because of them, but I don't regret any of it. Nothing. Even the things I could never tell you. They'll always be a part of me, and yet over the years, I learned so much. I couldn't have done it alone.

"That's why I'm glad I had you beside me."

The wind picked up as leaves swirled in small cyclones around the cemetery.

"I know that right now it seems that I'm leaving without much, but that it isn't true. Demetri Enterprises will weather this storm. I'll see to it.

I'll see to it from London, and I'll never fully walk away from our son. You can count on that. He has people around him who will help.

"Your cousin spoke to me after you… after you left us. Loving you and having you in my life taught me something I may never have known without you. I learned the most valuable lesson. I learned respect.

"Thank you, *mio angelo*. I will always respect and love you."

**The End**

**Oren Demetri's story, the making of a man.**

To learn more about Oren and Lennox as well as other characters mentioned in RESPECT, you can read the Infidelity series (not about cheating). For more on the Bonetti family and how two families intersected, stay tuned for Aleatha's next series.

# WHAT TO DO NOW...

LEND IT: Did you enjoy *RESPECT*? Do you have a friend who'd enjoy *RESPECT*?

RECOMMEND IT: Do you have multiple friends who'd enjoy this Infidelity novel or the Infidelity series? Tell them about it! Call, text, post, tweet... your recommendation is the nicest gift you can give to an author!

REVIEW IT: Tell the world. Please go to the retailer where you purchased this book, as well as Goodreads, and write a review.

# STAY CONNECTED WITH ALEATHA

———●—○—●———

Do you love Aleatha's writing? Do you want to know be kept up to date about Infidelity, Consequences, Tales From the Dark Side, Light series, and what's coming next?

Do you like EXCLUSIVE content (never-released scenes, never-released excerpts, and more)? Would you like the monthly chance to win prizes (signed books and gift cards)? Then sign up today for Aleatha's monthly newsletter and stay informed on all things Aleatha Romig.

Sign up for Aleatha's NEWSLETTER: http://bit.ly/1PYLjZW
(recipients receive exclusive material and offers)

Join Aleatha's Facebook group for updates, trailers, teasers, and events.
http://bit.ly/2c4bYYr

**You can also find Aleatha@**

Her website: http://aleatharomig.wix.com/aleatha
Facebook: https://www.facebook.com/AleathaRomig
Twitter: https://twitter.com/AleathaRomig
Goodreads: www.goodreads.com/author/show/5131072.Aleatha_Romig
Instagram: http://instagram.com/aleatharomig
Email Aleatha: aleatharomig@gmail.com

You may also listen Aleatha Romig's books on Audible.

# BOOKS BY NEW YORK TIMES BESTSELLING AUTHOR ALEATHA ROMIG

## INFIDELITY SERIES:

**BETRAYAL**

Book #1

(October 2015)

**CUNNING**

Book #2

(January 2016)

**DECEPTION**

Book #3

(May 2016)

**ENTRAPMENT**

Book #4

(September 2016)

**FIDELITY**

Book #5

(January 2017)

**RESPECT**

A standalone Infidelity Novel

(January 2018)

# THE CONSEQUENCES SERIES:

## CONSEQUENCES
(Book #1)
Released August 2011

## TRUTH
(Book #2)
Released October 2012

## CONVICTED
(Book #3)
Released October 2013

## REVEALED
(Book #4)
Previously titled: Behind His Eyes Convicted: The Missing Years
Re-released June 2014

## BEYOND THE CONSEQUENCES
(Book #5)
Released January 2015

## RIPPLES
A Consequences stand-alone novel
Released October 2017

## COMPANION READS:

## BEHIND HIS EYES—CONSEQUENCES
(Companion One of the bestselling Consequences Series)
Released January 2014

# BEHIND HIS EYES—TRUTH

(Companion Two of the bestselling Consequences Series)

Released March 2014

## ALEATHA'S LIGHTER ONES:

Stand-alone "lighter" romances

### PLUS ONE

### ONE NIGHT

## TALES FROM THE DARK SIDE SERIES:

(All books in this series are stand-alone erotic thrillers)

### INSIDIOUS

(October 2014)

### DUPLICITY

(Completely unrelated to book #1)

Release TBA

## THE LIGHT SERIES:

Published through Thomas and Mercer

### INTO THE LIGHT

(June 14, 2016)

### AWAY FROM THE DARK

(October 2016)

# ALEATHA ROMIG

Aleatha Romig is a *New York Times*, *Wall Street Journal*, and *USA Today* bestselling author who lives in Indiana, USA. She grew up in Mishawaka, graduated from Indiana University, and is currently living south of Indianapolis. Aleatha has raised three children with her high school sweetheart and husband of over thirty years. Before she became a full-time author, she worked days as a dental hygienist and spent her nights writing. Now, when she's not imagining mind-blowing twists and turns, she likes to spend her time a with her family and friends. Her other pastimes include reading and creating heroes/anti-heroes who haunt your dreams!

Aleatha released her first novel, CONSEQUENCES, in August of 2011. CONSEQUENCES became a bestselling series with five novels and two companions released from 2011 through 2015. The compelling and epic story of Anthony and Claire Rawlings has graced more than half a million e-readers. Aleatha released the first of her series TALES FROM THE DARK SIDE, INSIDIOUS, in the fall of 2014. These stand-alone thrillers continue Aleatha's twisted style with an increase in heat.

In the fall of 2015, Aleatha moved headfirst into the world of dark romantic suspense saga with the release of BETRAYAL, the first of her five-novel INFIDELITY series that has taken the reading world by storm. She also began her traditional publishing career with Thomas and Mercer. Her books INTO THE LIGHT and AWAY FROM THE DARK were published through this mystery/thriller publisher in 2016.

In the spring of 2017, Aleatha released her first stand-alone, fun, and sexy romantic comedy with PLUS ONE, followed by ONE NIGHT.

Aleatha is a "Published Author's Network" member of the Romance Writers of America and PEN America. She is represented by Kevan Lyon of Marsal Lyon Literary Agency.

81343983R00240